FORENOTE

The planet Erth, the base from which St. Cyr operates (but whereupon she does not stay), is so nearly like our Earth that name-correspondences are frequent. Pray feel at home on Erth, vintage 2494-95: it is our point of spacetime departure.

Except in true-name allusions to a few historically famous persons (none of whom is an active character in this novel), all characters are entirely fictitious and all names are invented.

Of the numerous works in cosmological science which have served as background for the technical aspects of the story, I would cite particularly *Black Holes, Quasars, & The Universe*, by Harry L. Shipman (Houghton Mifflin, 1976). Dr. Shipman, who expresses himself with clarity remarkable for a scientist, is innocent with respect to my creative modifications.

IAN WALLACE

HELLER'S LEAP

Ian Wallace

DAW BOOKS, INC.

DONALD A. WOLLHEIM, PUBLISHER

1301 Avenue of the Americas
New York, N. Y.   10019

PUBLISHED BY
THE NEW AMERICAN LIBRARY
OF CANADA LIMITED

DEDICATION

Conjointly, to
ST. CYR and CROYD

FIRST PRINTING, JULY 1979

1 2 3 4 5 6 7 8 9

DAW TRADEMARK REGISTERED
U.S. PAT. OFF. MARCA
REGISTRADA. HECHO EN U.S.A.

PRINTED IN CANADA
COVER PRINTED IN U.S.A.

THE PARTS OF THE STORY

HELLER'S
LEAP

Prolog: # A CRYSTAL OF STARS

In 2495, a galactic detective named St. Cyr and a galactic agent-statesman named Croyd were drawn into human events deriving from cosmic action billions of years earlier and a thousand light-years from their home planet Erth.

These events centered on an interstellar distress call and a trio of terrestrial killings. And as matters developed, neither St. Cyr nor Croyd, but instead the prime victim, Klaus Heller, starred in the action.

In an infinite cosmos, most conceivable events are possible. Even within a finite galaxy, there is an enormous range of potentials.

Once upon a time—nearly a thousand light-years from Erth, toward galactic center—six mighty stars were born almost simultaneously. Each of these stars was an inferno having the mass of more than fifteen Erth-suns and burning fierce blue-white. As a society of angry sisters, they formed an octahedron with a star at each of the six points, all arranged in a near approach to crystal-regularity, the distance between any two stars averaging slightly more than two hundred astronomical units. It was a restless constellation, with each star tugged and pushed by her sisters, tormented by the interconflicting forces of gravity and radiant thrust.

So hotly burned the six stars that in a few million years their energies declined from blue-white to yellow-white. Meanwhile, by some species of cosmic multi-parthenogenesis, they had conjointly spawned within their cluster a seventh star, crudely at the center of the octahedron. As time decayed, cooling particles of gas dust from the six sisters coalesced into small gas clouds which eventually would become planets and satellites of planets, all revolving around the central daughter star, but experiencing orbital perturbations from the six sisters.

The daughter star, the sun of the planets, which came to be locally named Klarta, was smaller and calmer than her

9

mothers, although not calm or small on a cosmic scaling of stars. Her mothers were now undergoing swift senescence, but Klarta accepted with relative tranquility the possessively competitive yankings about by her mothers and went on with the business of taming her own planetary brood.

Abruptly then, after no more than half a billion years of life, each of the mother stars collapsed inward upon herself; her iron core deflated, having burnt out the energy which had kept it expanded, and most of the star followed inward. In the process their masses decreased, so that each of the six now-lightless star-masses pondered only eight to twelve Erth-suns; but each of these horrendous masses was packed into a sky-tiny sphere of density with an average diameter of about sixty kilometers, approximately the breadth of a very large twentieth-century city. So totally did each star invert upon herself that now even light could not escape from her; and much surrounding light was sucked into her, never to depart. The octahedron of giant blue-white stars had become an octahedron of *black holes* whose colossal gravities continued to pull on each other (but countered by intervening forces of their own spawning) and on their daughter-sun Klarta and her planets, interweaving among the six black holes a perpetual field of spatial turbulence that screened Klarta from all the rest of the cosmos.

Perished stars? Fossilized, rather. Each of the six had achieved a sort of relative immortality; she would remain virtually unchanged for untellable aeons, her perfect inward secretiveness absolutely hidden from every outsider, her very existence detectable only by noticing nearby perturbations and inferring an unseeable gravity center.

As for their daughter Klarta, her relative serenity preserved her alive and merry with a life-expectation of a good nine billion years. During the furious aging and perishing of her mothers, Klarta had merely passed through most of her early youth, emerging as a sprightly yellow star about double the size of the Erth-sun.

Her maturing brood was six planets having four small satellites among them, orbiting their variously settled or erratic ways around Klarta. The inner three—eventually named Callas, Zanzodon, and Zinza—stayed protectively close to Mother Klarta, and their orbits were regular ellipses; but even Zinza, more than two hundred million kilometers from

Klarta, experienced far too much sun-heat to support life. Erth-size Iola (Klarta IV), three hundred forty million kilometers out, did support life, having a favorable atmosphere and a benign-to-steamy climate at the epoch when its life-evolution reached amphibian stage; but Iola did run a delicately perturbed orbit, diverging slightly outward toward one or another of the four black holes on the plane of the planetary system, and then each time easing back into comfortable Klarta-distance. The fifth, Corla, was only half the size of Iola: no appreciable atmosphere, relatively cold, never any macroscopic life.

As for the outermost planet, Godzha, slightly larger than Iola, it did collect an atmosphere. But Godzha's million-kilometer distance from Klarta left its mean temperature far below zero Celsius, and this temperature fell drastically four times a year during Godzha's wild yawings outward toward black holes. Again, no macroscopic life evolved on Godzha —although intelligent life eventually would appear there.

And as for the component of each perishing star which had *not* collapsed into a black hole, this vast remnant was anti-mass, the stuff of which flames are made, violently departing mass rather than clinging to mass. Antipathetically fleeing the neutron-blobs which the stars had become, antipathetically repelling even each other, the anti-mass particles ranged outward until they met and fought with each other at polar centers between black holes. Doing so, they naturally arrayed themselves in a diaphragm-web between holes; for lurking at the core of each sub-atom of antipathy was a core of sympathy, so that their nature was to flee each other but also to stay associated in combat; and thus the ones with the most sympathy relative to their antipathy were hole-haunters.

The outcome of these mechanics was an elastic and irrascibly incandescent cocooning for Klarta and her planetary system, an octagonal indwelling that was virtually impermeable —except by I-rays—from without or from within.

Into one of the black holes around Klarta, late in 2494 AD when Klarta was four billion years old, suicidally leaped an astronaut named Klaus Heller. His purpose was to intervene in an interplanetary war.

As expected, his body experienced hideous elongation during his fall; and ultimately, at the surface of the hole thirty kilometers out from center, Heller's paradoxically decelerating fall was observed to be arrested. Theory said that he could neither fall farther nor escape outward; a black hole is absolutely inescapable. There at the invisible surface he would float unchanged forever. . . .

Part One

HELLER'S LEAP:
HELLER'S DEATH

Interstellar Space, 24-25 November 2494,

interlaced with

Westchester and Manhattan, 1-2 July 2495

1. HELLER'S LEAP: HELLER'S DEATH

In the spacelock room of a spheroid starship named *Lucifer*, diving on Black Hole Three of the weird system Erth-known as Vassili, enthusiastic anticipatory fear had set Klaus Heller fidgeting in his vast overstuffed space-suit several times his own size. Because of the suit's monstrous bulk, and the ship's artigrav, he couldn't pace. He couldn't even thrust his own arms and legs into *its* arms and legs. His own limbs rested in sleeves and boots inside the suit-body to work suit-limbs with servo-mechanisms.

Two others taut-watched him: his good friend and crew astronomer Duke (nobody aboard except Klaus knew Duke's full name) and their yeoman and space-walker Zenia Zalenia who was a reserved young golden woman from Ligeria (Altair III).

Heller was enormously conscious that his friends were here, and they of his probably fatal purpose. They might never see him again after this, although Heller *intended* to see them again, but there was nothing they could now do to help his intention along. So now, bless them, they were merely being cooperative, and friendly, and tense.

He was exploring for a semi-final time, by touch only, the inside-suit controls which he and his expedition-commissioner had designed, testing his instant ability to stab accurately at any of them. Air mix. Repulsor drive-and-orientation. Metabolic acceleration. Altimeter zero-set. Iradio transmitter-receiver. Videosurrogate. Thermal shield—no point in wasting power to activate this until in-suit temperature would become intolerable. The inertial shield would activate itself, rising with velocity changes to hold felt acceleration at or below

15

one G until maximum shielding of fifty-to-one would be attained and maintained; but he could override that, too.

Intercom voice of Captain Diekoff from the bridge: "I am in orbit at thirty thousand kilometers according to plan. Are you ready for gravity-gradient readings to zero your altimeter?"

Heller: "Acknowledged. Ready. Proceed."

Diekoff read a series of altitude/gravity measurements at ten million kilometer intervals from their prior orbit at one hundred million kilometers (just under one astronomical unit) down to ten million; then at one million kilometer intervals down to one million; then at hundred thousand intervals down to one hundred thousand; then at ten thousand intervals down to forty thousand; finally at one thousand kilometer intervals down to their present thirty thousand—a total of forty-four sets of numbers. As Diekoff read, Zenia, with Duke looking over her shoulder, checked his numbers against the computer read-out (complete with curve and formula and small error-margin) already generated by the printer in the spacelock room. "Correct," Duke reported; and Zenia, going to another calculator, punched-in the numbers and generated a new formula for independent comparison with the other two. "Identical formulae," said Zenia.

"Agree identical," responded Duke. Going to Klaus, Duke opened a panel in the back of the suit, made appropriate settings while Zenia monitored, then handed the printout papers to Klaus who used a two-mirror system for checking his suit settings against the formula.

"All correct," Klaus Heller confirmed. "Let's go immediately into launch procedure."

The power and inexhaustible space-fuel supply of a repulsor-driven ship like the *Lucifer* enabled it to orbit a black hole very tight in, much tighter than thirty thousand kilometers. By contrast, the old ships having self-contained fuel would have been in trouble from the hole's horrible ten-sun gravity, all emanating from a tiny sphere of only eighty-five thousand kilometers, if they had approached much closer than a full astronomical unit. From one A.U. out, the jump for Klaus would have required a ludicrously painful-slow eight and a half days; whereas from only a thousand kilometers out, Klaus would have plummeted to hole-surface in a second-fraction. But the real time of transit, and also the apparent time for Klaus, needed to be appreciable. Therefore a

compromise drop-orbit had been chosen. By ship-diving
from one A.U. down to thirty thousand kilometers, they
reduced the eight-day fall to a few hours of power-plunge;
and once Klaus would jump from this altitude, he would be
falling in a comparatively languid way which would require
an entire two seconds, gravity-accelerated from zero velocity
to a terminal light-speed of 300,000 kilometers per second.

However, progressive use of the metabolic accelerator
would stretch Heller's subjective perception of this two-second drop as something more than one hour, so he would be
able to maneuver. The three observers aboard ship—Captain
Diekoff, Dr. Duke, and Yeoman Zalenia—would hook themselves up to similar metabolic accelerators immediately after
jump-launch, so that their subjective perceptions of the Heller
fall would be equally in slo-mo. (It would also render them
all invisible to a normal eye; but since they would all be accelerated, none of them would notice this.)

Heller told them, carefully keeping his voice at its maximum basso: "Now is when I do it. Zenia, please—my helmet."

It was ridiculously tiny compared with the suit, and light
enough for Zenia alone to handle, but strong enough to resist
mighty battering. She adjusted it to his head, secured the rekamatic seal with untrembling fingers, stood back with grave
face to inspect Heller while he tested it from inside: how
blond-handsome he was, how strong-marvelous, after five decades of energetic life! Duke, holding outwardly calm with
his habitual fixed lip-closed smile, but inwardly frenetic, applied the last test: he shone a powerful flash-beam directly
into the transparent face-plate, and it responded like a pet
spaniel by instantly polarizing to temper the glare.

Heller bobbed his head at both of them, managing to
smile, although it was grim that he felt, and he knew it. He
was about to jump and fall into a death situation of the sort
that post-medieval Winston Churchill had called a mystery
wrapped in an enigma; and if relativistic theories were subjectively as well as objectively right, then within seconds after
his jump, time would stop for Klaus, he would be suspended
far from hole-center gravity-glued in one place forever.

But the chips were much higher than mere death-risk-ad-
venture. His purpose was to act as point for the saving of a
star-system.

He said: "Ready, activate." "Drop dead," snapped Zenia in

the old actors' cliché which means "Win!" and Duke smilingly burbled, "Cheers!"

Gravity in the room dropped to 1/100th G, allowing Klaus of his own strength, using his servo-mechanistic legs while waving servo-mechanistic arms for balance, to hoist the tonnage of his suit erect and stagger into the airlock.

Captain Diekoff rotated the ship to present the outer hatch toward the hole whose hungry pull made it the one clamant reference-point for *down*.

The hatch opened. Heller drifted downward-out.

On his success or failure might hinge the life or death of a planet.

His course-trend was to be carried along in the inertia of the ship's orbit which was swift enough to keep him up here indefinitely. But as pre-planned, once he had drifted clear of the ship, immediately he activated his repulsor-drive so that it would brutally brake him. This braking counteracted his orbital velocity so abruptly that the decelerative forces acting upon him rose to a raw-man-intolerable G-level; but simultaneously his inertial shielding rose to maximum while his metabolic acceleration came into play, so that he felt only a stiff jerk. And as his orbital velocity decreased below the threshold for holding orbit, he began to fall toward the black hole in a trajectory like that of a primitive cannonball fired from the top of a high cliff.

The metabolic accelerator was behaving with precision in terms of pre-programming geared to the altimeter settings on the swiftly steepening gravity gradient. The fall from thirty thousand kilometers to three hundred kilometers was objectively a two-second happening; for metabolically accelerated Klaus (who was invisible, though it didn't matter), the duration seemed a full hour—during which there was unexpected action.

Naturally seeing nothing below (since no light could emanate from the black hole), he looked back upward for star-comfort. Shock: another astronaut, fall-following him!

By iradio he'd been reporting to the ship his subjective impressions; the crew could understand his rapid gabble, like that of a tape being swift-searched, since they too were metabolically juiced up. Now he used the iradio to demand of his follower: "Hey, you trailing me—who are you, and what the hell?"

"Simmer down, Klaus," Duke's voice urged. "I'm wearing the spare suit. You didn't think an astronomer could stay out of this?"

"But how the devil could you—"

"Had tried and tested the spare suit, knew my way; once we shoved you off, I hopped into it, fed-in the altimeter readings, waddled out, followed your orbital braking program—then accelerated the fall to catch up with you."

"But it's been less than two seconds since I was—"

"Piece of cake, Klaus. I hit the metabolic accelerator, got into the suit in maybe a half-second, checked-out in maybe a quarter-second, got launched in another quarter-second, caught up with you in another quarter-second. *All* of us are accelerated, remember?"

"Good thinking, good Duke, situationally stupid Duke! Your specific orders were to stay aboard ship, you knew this from the beginning. Look, what the hell good will my suicide do you or anybody else if you don't get back to Nereid, as now you probably won't?"

"You'll make it back, Klaus. I'll follow you, so I'll make it—and go back with better information, first hand."

"Well, my God, Duke, it's too late now, you've done it, but—Christ, you've just blown the whole scientific point of this! I needed your skill for observation, you were supposed to notice and clock my apparent progress and fall velocities and times from the ship so if I should return we could compare objective-subjective similarities and differences—"

"No sweat. I've been training Zenia and the captain, they're both in on it, their data will be as good as mine would be—and thank God I'm incognito, because I wouldn't want VASA to know I'm doing this."

"And if we don't come back, how will the captain account for *you*?"

"Was hull-walking, swept-off in a gas cloud, unrecoverable."

"Now how did you arrange *that* story?"

"Persuaded them that you need my expert guarding. Along with passing them a little of my booze-tot."

Heller beat down his chuckle with cursing, meanwhile noticing in his rate of fall a sharp acceleration that was blurred by the metabolics. He told Duke, "Okay, we're getting into the thick of it now, be alert, I hope you know how to adjust to predicted and unpredicted trouble. Hey, you bastards

aboard ship, don't forget to edit Duke out of the flakes of
this! Particularly you, Captain Diekoff: did you reflect that
you were obligating yourself to falsify your log? Well, you
are so obligated, and you will do so—that's an order from
your expedition commander. Acknowledge, Captain."

Static. Then Diekoff: "Acknowledged, Dr. Heller. Reluctant assent."

"The best way, Captain, might be merely to omit mention
of Dr. Duke during his absence—which will make its own
problems for you later, but that I leave to you. Cheers to you
all; I don't know how long my signals will be reaching you
after now—"

Downward acceleration increased. Klaus grated at Duke:
"Taut now, astronomer, we'll soon be feeling the tide."

Taut answer: "I know about the tide."

Kyria Heller sat nightly with her much-older brother Klaus
Heller over chess in his Westchester mansion. Typically, as
tonight (1 July 2495), they were in lounging clothes, she
wearing virginal gray lounging pajamas, he in bed pajamas
with an ornate brocaded dressing gown; and there was
brandy in large inhalers. Appraising the board, he puffed on
a mighty Havana, she on a little rhinestoned briar pipe. For
both of them, it was always good to be together—but it was a
good made poignant by a lost home for Kyria and a lost love
for Klaus.

He moved a knight, taking one of her pawns; and she
studied the consequences. After perhaps three minutes, she
moved a castle, taking his knight. It was growing tight, it
could go either way. He examined the board. She studied his
wonderful character-face.

He looked up beyond her: his face went taut, almost terro-
rized, then relaxed into beaming serenity. Meanwhile his
chest was opening up. The dressing gown peeled back like
synthetic fabric ignited by a cigar, only there was no smoke
or char; and the pajamas under it peeled back, and the bones
peeled back, and there in his chest was a hole the size of a
Frisbee revealing the heart and major arteries which were
peeling back, and Heller, gasping, fell sidewise off his chair.

Instantly Kyria was kneeling over him, raising eyelids,
checking pulse—until she comprehended the silliness of all
this: he was dead. Self-contained but heart-shocked, understanding the event but soul-empty, she went to the phone and

called the police. What she knew made police involvement superfluous; but the nature of the death would bring them in anyway.

Three hundred kilometers above black-hole surface; fall velocity 100,000 kilometers per second, one-third of light speed, fast enough to fall from Moon to Erth in less than three seconds. From here to hole periphery, otherwise known as the *event horizon* because no light and therefore no event-observation could emerge from inside to outside that level, the estimated fall time was .002033 seconds—which to metabolically accelerated Klaus would seem like thirty-three minutes.

His body had long been feeling a sense of shoulder-compression and leg-elongation. To those in the 'ship above, watching his fall and Duke's, using various distance-instruments with the aid of the green light emitted by the spacesuits (a green which was beginning to exhibit a pronounced red-shift), the Heller legs seemed fathoms long now, while the meter-wide shoulders of his suit appeared no more than half a meter apart. A raw astronaut in a conventional spacesuit would now be feeling the stretched-on-the-wheel agony of bone disjointment. Klaus felt the real distortions only because the legs and shoulders of his suit were equipped with sensors which conveyed non-pain kinesthetic sensations to his brain. The suit legs were stretched, yes; the suit shoulders were squeezed, yes; but *his* legs and shoulders were not stretched or squeezed, the suit arrangement had evaded the tidal torture of the grim gravity, and yet his feet and particularly his toes were experiencing a possibly phantom effect of implacable down-draw.

Presently the sensations had grown so clamant that Heller knew he would soon reach hole-surface, the event horizon described by the Schwarzschild radius, thirty kilometers from hole-center; and he was roaring downward. The internal signals of his suit were undistorted and true; but ship's observations of his chronometer would be distorted by apparent slowing, just as the velocity of his own down-progress would be slowed from the ship's viewpoint. (The *Lucifer* had departed orbit and hurled itself into a spiraling path which allowed it to stay approximately above Heller at all times.)

Prevailing theory held that at a shade more than thirty kilometers from hole-center—almost at hole-surface—a tenth-second subjective chronometer time would be ship-observed as an hour; and that at exactly thirty kilometers out from center, the chronometer from ship's viewpoint would stop, and so would the fall of the Heller body: suspension there in black-hole space forever.

The naturalistic explanation of this theory was, that as proximity to the hole increased, light emanating from near the hole would find its normally straight-line path deformed more and more by the gargantuan gravity, and (its intrinsic one-C velocity unsolved) would require a wider and wider orbit to get clear of the hole, eventually having to orbit the hole several times before getting free. And this meant that the green light from the Heller suit ultimately would take an inordinate length of time to reach the ship. Technically, the result was a red shift; in plain talk the effect for the ship-observers was tantamount to speeding up a camera and therefore slowing down the apparent speed of what was observed. At the event horizon—at hole-edge—light from Heller's suit would take practically forever to reach the ship; whereafter, no light for the ship would struggle free from the hole at all; and therefore, to the ship, the image of Klaus Heller perpetually space-frozen thirty miles from hole-center would seem to be a forever thing.

But Klaus himself would keep on falling in—unless the mercury-density of the hole should cause him to *crash* the surface and *actually* float forever death-deformed there.

And the facts about this were not known. And Heller—who had necessarily forgotten about his follower Duke in the intensity of his self-survival concern—was now a hundred kilometers from hole-surface and had about six ten-thousandths of a second to find out.

Maybe—just maybe—the metabolically accelerated perceptions of Klaus, allowing him to experience this ultra-split second as nearly fifty-seven seconds, would permit adjustments to escape death-mangling.

Homicide, Manhattan Police, crossed governmental lines to ask for expert assistance from Dr. St. Cyr because of the peculiar psychological involvements in the Klaus Heller case. St. Cyr was Galactic Police, but she'd published papers on post-mortem dream analysis. Galactic Detective Superintendent Wong said okay.

Claudine St. Cyr and her aide Lieutenant U. Tuli arrived aerially by solichopper on the morning of 2 July 2495. They drifted down to the pad on the roof of Tel Aviv Hospital, dropped in a downdraft to Floor Four, surfboarded on the conveyor to Room 4-297, entered. The bed was veiled by white uniforms insulted by a sprinkling of detective mufti; they parted as St. Cyr arrived with Tuli, making bedside room for the two women.

The patient, Klaus Heller, was about as dead as they come. No effort had been made to conceal the gaping hole in his chest—an orifice which didn't give stomach trouble either to St. Cyr or to Tuli, although Claudine felt a wee way-back guilt because she *wasn't* queased. Admiring now the well-known Heller face—fiftyish, aquiline-handsome, career-lined—she puzzled over his death-expression: not shock or horror, but a sort of ultimate serenity.

Criminologically the chest hole had been and was going to be a point of concern. But Claudine had been prepped on her purely psychological function, so she ignored the chest hole for now and paid attention to the well-known apparatus enveloping the patient's cranium.

"He is medically dead," unnecessarily explained the grave lean gray-lipped senior doctor; "but at the request of Captain Higbee, here, we've supported life process while the brain impulses are being scanned, and we are continuously immunizing the body against decay bacteria. As for the brain, its memory centers are doing quite well, but little else. Any questions, Dr. St. Cyr?"

"Thank you, Dr. Thorensen, not yet. What happened, Higbee?"

The burly detective-captain was frowning a frown made all the heavier by his massive post-orbital ridges. "We're hung, St. Cyr. You know that this is Klaus Heller?"

Of course she knew it; she'd met and liked this man who had dominated space. "I know. So what happened?"

Said Higbee: "Captain St. Cyr, excuse me, you were brought here as an expert psychologist-consultant. I must ask you to take your lines from me."

"Well, yes, but—"

"Please listen to Dr. Thorensen, Captain." It was an order.

Thorensen cleared throat and asserted: "Mr. Heller's brain has been experiencing a recurrent dream in a sort of reverberating circuit. Captain Higbee and I agreed that psychological analysis of the dream coupled with police expertise might yield—" He stopped, waved a hand feebly, subsided.

She nodded. "Thank you, Doctor. Please call me Inspector, I want to get used to my new title. Pray insert my lieutenant and me into the observation helmets."

Head-swaddled in complex caricatures of twentieth-century beauty-parlor hair dryers, hooked up to a ganglial tangle of wires from the patient's dead head, Tuli and Claudine each experienced the tri-d full-color all-sense dreaming as though she *were* a vigorous fiftyish Heller:

> In his scuddercar he invades the city named 87314, shuttle-threading the city street by street and block by block, only seeing it in small scale from high above as a city map with himself in it; and in the shuttle-threading there is the exultation of returning home and gradually closing in on the point of highest desire. And presently he confronts the point, leaves the car, stands looking up at the desideratum: a many-tiered grandstand of executives looking down upon him with admiring affection, applauding him. Drawn by the reverberating handbeat, he ascends a stepped aisle, touches flesh with the many aisle-side hands extended to him, and takes his place on the highest-tier throne. They are all standing now, turning to him, looking up at him while they applaud with a heavy rhythmic beat.
>
> In his scuddercar he invades the city named 87314, shuttle-threading the city. . . .

The dream repeated and repeated. Having experienced it three times through, Claudine removed her helmet and looked at Tuli; the lieutenant, bored and watching her chief, immediately unbonneted.

Claudine queried: "Tuli?"

The lieutenant meditated. She said, "The men looked funny. And why were they all men?"

St. Cyr, dusk-dark and petite-shapely, appraised her lanky-tall brunette lieutenant. Valuing Tuli's impressions, Claudine didn't make much out of that one.

Higbee demanded, "Captain St. Cyr?" He coughed and managed a correction: "Inspector?"

Claudine stood. "Captain, these dreamings are deep and devious, compounded of memory and imagination and extraneous random detail—"

"Means what?"

"That I'll have to study it out." But she had a distinct feeling that Heller, having recently and prematurely retired from a top-power job and feeling increasingly useless, was dreaming a wishful think: he was returning to his directors and his old executive group in the dream, they were applauding him and his return, they accorded him once again the top seat of power. . . .

Higbee pressed: "No murder clues?"

"Now why," inquired Claudine, staring at the chest-hole, "would you suspect murder?"

"The chest-hole is a medical anomaly, Inspector," interposed the doctor. "You notice that it is an approximate circle, slightly over seventeen centimeters diameter in a chest more than thirty-two centimeters wide, with burned flesh around the periphery as though there had been a cautery. The heart has vanished almost entirely, the shot neatly embraced the maximum heart-width which must have been about eleven centimeters; and the major cardiac arteries and veins are sealed off as though they had been cauterized. I have no idea what sort of device could have done it."

"Might the weapon have been a raygun?"

"What other kind is there, Inspector?"

"I see what you mean, Doctor, although some obsolescent bullet-types do exist. Well, could it be that?"

"Only if you know of a laser gun that will fire in a wide-angle/inverted cone with the apex in the victim. In this particular trauma, the pattern from chest wound to heart-cautery narrows. The angle of convergence is wide, around seventy-five degrees, give or take two or three. And there are no burns on the peritoneal tissues behind the heart."

And that seemed to eliminate the possibility of a gun—but of course it did not eliminate the sister of the victim, Kyria Heller. Claudine arose: "Thank you, Doctor, for now. I'm needing help—you *will* tell me about any ideas you get, no matter how wild they may seem?"

She took a last look at Heller's tranquil face. And something deep within her urged: *Inspector St. Cyr: please, you take this case. Please.*

The inward urge had been so peremptory that it had seemed like an alien voice. A woman-voice. . . .

In six ten-thousandths of a second, Heller fell seventy kilometers. He was now two hundred kilometers above hole-surface. At this height above Erth, the ten-thousand kilometer planet-disk would totally eclipse its sun; but the sixty-kilometer hole-speck was still glared out by the star called Vassili beyond or below. However, the hole-speck became noticeable a hundred kilometers and nine ten-thousandths of a second later: a rapidly growing blackness. In what seemed seconds, this blackness became environmentally total; even his video-surrogate was without light.

His repulsors had long since been deactivated: raw space itself was being sucked into this hole, he was falling into almost as near a thing to perfect vacuum as God could have achieved. In another apparent nineteen seconds (actually two ten-thousandths), he was only sixty kilometers from surface; and now he had to tap his self-contained power-pack to activate leg-rigidity, converting himself into an arrow being gravity-shot-or-pulled into a little ball as dense as mercury. Another 15.8 seconds apparent (.000158 actual): thirty kilometers out; he would hit the event-horizon surface in twelve seconds apparent (.000121 actual), traveling at nine-tenths the velocity of light.

He must *not* crash on the surface. He *had* to penetrate. Only: how deep, before he would be brought to stop? It was never the long fall, it was always merely the sudden stop that murderously mash-mangled.

The velocity of a steel-jacketed rifle bullet could penetrate primitive tank-armor. The velocity of a post-medieval propellor-pulled biplane had penetrated the Empire State Building. The velocity of a photon, having no momentum-mass worth mentioning, can penetrate an ocean profoundly. Suited Heller, having momentum equal to nearly the velocity of light multiplied by the mass of his ponderous casing, drove toward a compact body whose density was five times that of fluid iron.

At the terminus of a thirty-thousand kilometer fall during 2.004 seconds, he hit.

And penetrated—and the slowing jolt was viscous-vicious.

By the book, the ship would now be seeing him as forever stranded on the event horizon.

Equally by the book, he would now hurtle on down to reach hole-center in .000067 seconds. However, the book assumed fall through a vacuum at continually increasing velocity. Instead, he was sludging inward through fluid whose density tore at his suit, retarding his fall.

Jerkily he felt himself beginning to move sidewise, and velocity increased angularly as he was caught in the internal fluid-spin of the hole. By now he was deeply in, his altimeter registered only twenty-three kilometers from center; but he was maelstrom-spun, orbiting the guts of the hole, crowded by sluggish substance whose pressure compressed not only his suit but him within it as though he were a child squeezed in mob panic. Pressure-heat was mounting: patterns of pale pink were beginning to show on his videosurrogate whose little visiscreen registered radiation frequencies far down into the infra-red.

Duke Murchison had accurately predicted such a spin, along with several other complications which were beginning to materialize. For instance, now that he had penetrated one-third of the distance to hole-center, the radial gravity was vastly diminished, being diffused into the interpulling of mass on mass below and around and above him. Again, as he spun downward, and as fluid density mounted precisely because the gravitational noose was compressing mass inward, his increments of downward progress from fall momentum were slowing: very soon they would cease because of his black hole *buoyancy*, and probably he would even be cork-thrust upward—though not upward enough for escape.

His mission, though, was to reach center if he could, and to escape from there if he could. Activating his nuclear drive-pack, he plunged into deepening pressures many times exceeding the submarine-crushing squeeze of profoundest ocean.

"I want the case," Claudine told Superintendent Wong. "No Higbee. No nobody else. Just Tuli and me."

"Since Manhattan Homicide has jurisdiction and has assigned Higbee," drawled sleepy-eyed Wong, "it would be nice if you would give me a good reason why Galactic Police should preempt."

"Look, Wong, if Higbee stays on it, he needs me; but I don't like his jowls, and that will turn off my woman's intuition."

"Lousy reasoning. Manhattan Police will want something better."

"Klaus Heller's interests are interplanetary. How about that?"

"Better—"

"Also, I liked Heller, it's partly personal."

"You wouldn't then feel prejudice?"

"No reason for prejudice—but incentive I *would* feel."

"Then what does Manhattan Police do with Higbee instead?"

"How about the porno murders?"

"Higbee will say that's more in *your* line."

"Not if I know Higbee."

"Go to Hell, St. Cyr. Higbee will be reassigned."

Despite the protective night of his space-suit with its elaborate apparatus for relieving internal air pressure, the hole-diver was experiencing several atmospheres of crush; his ears roared, and he felt a trickle of nose-blood. Would his blood-bubble medication surely prevent bends? One more kilometer to center. The fluid mass that he was drilling through, here at core, was several times as dense as mercury; the gravity below him was now almost canceled by the gravitational mass above him, so that for practical purposes he was getting no gravitational pull-help. He had shut off his metabolic acceleration to extend his safe time for its use: his inertial shield alone was handling the effective downward gravity increment well enough for relative comfort from that viewpoint if not from others.

He consulted his nuclear drive gauge: fuel only one-quarter exhausted, but that was close to the critical mark because of the fantastic acceleration that he must generate going upward-out. Perhaps he should abort the mission. Only, while he debated this, he was continuing to drive inward. . . .

Astonishingly, a gauge warned him that he was approaching a rigid solid object. He reduced drive until it just balanced the upward thrust of his buoyancy and devoted several tenths of a second to consideration of that. If hole-center was rigid-solid, this would seriously disrupt the Murchison equations.

Moving cautiously downward-inward another half-kilometer, he bumped against a solid that felt like metal. He consulted his videosurrogate: it was metal. He felt along it for a distance, getting a distinct impression of shallow-arc curvature and of metal plates with welds. He sent out distance sensors: the solid was apparently a sphere having a diameter of about one kilometer.

It was not *the* natural center of the black hole. Instead, it was a *thing*—a colossal artifact, dropped or shot into the hole and squeezed inward by hole-gravity until at center all gravity drags upon it cancelled each other out and the thing stayed there in permanent freefall.

Again he checked his nuclear drive gauge: fuel thirty percent gone. No time for more investigation—get out now!

He slammed his nuclear drive into full power, orienting his escape upward; in view of the spin, there was no telling where or in what direction he would emerge, if he would emerge at all. His metabolic boost, with a separate power drive, he pushed up to the full 100,000:1, giving him total inertial shielding of 250,000:1. With nearly three seconds already gone from his eight-second safety margin, he felt that he must get out in one second flat to allow for contingencies. This called for sustained hell-thrust of nearly five million Erth-gravities; and while this was only 1.9 apparent G inside his suit, to his worn physiology it felt like his natural limit of seven.

His nuclear jet was churning-flaring, but it was succeeding only in crowding him down against the bottom of his suit, while his helmet was being jammed down by the substance above that he was driving against; as though, interred in a mine-deep Erth-grave, he sought to head-butt through kilometers of overhead bedrock.

Still he was feeling no upward motion—but his altimeter was now reading 0.7 kilometers out from center, whereas his deepest penetration had been 0.5: beginning action was implied. He was profoundly oppressed and confused by mighty and conflicting radial and angular G-forces which penetrated his metabolic and inertial shielding in a vectoral corkscrew. He kept his eyes tight on the altimeter: after the initial gravity-overcoming burn, with luck he might break loose in a hurry. . . .

He broke! His accelerated vision could see the altimeter crawl upward when actually it was beginning to race. Daring the limits of his pack-fuel, his drive-blast was wide open: this was the total last-chance try. To escape, he had to vault from zero to half again the velocity of light in 29.5 kilometers upward through density against ten-sun gravity.

Heller was now rising at half the velocity of his downward plunge, accelerating all the way. In 0.7 seconds which his consciousness stretched to more than nineteen minutes, he had ascended 27.5 kilometers; the next two must fall beneath him in 0.3 if escape was to happen.

One more kilometer: 0.2 more seconds. Theoretical escape velocity attained. . . .

Power died; nuclear pack exhausted.

Agony: would inertia carry him out? All his mind was on two dials: altimeter and chronometer.

Another half-kilometer in 0.12 seconds. Sweat bath: he was slowing. . . .

Another quarter-kilometer in 0.08 seconds. God, God, he was in maximum surface-gravity now. . . .

Another eighth-kilometer in 0.07. The altimeter now read 29.7 kilometers from center. His head was far inside the suit, not in the helmet; he threw back his head and roared laughter-of-despair, remembering Zeno's paradox about trying to walk to a door by clearing only half the remaining distance with each step.

Another tenth-kilometer in 0.1. It was all done, now. Still two-tenths kilometer beneath hole-surface, short of the event horizon—and slowed to less than the velocity of light which cannot escape from a black hole. It had been a noble try, he could take comfort in that: almost it had worked. *Bless you, Clara. Bless you, Duke, wherever you are: if I couldn't do it, I doubt that you will. Sorry, Croyd, no report, you'll have to go in blind.*

In the next ten-thousandth of a second, the altimeter rose to 29.81, then dropped back to 29.79. So he was beginning to fall inward again. No more power. Maybe he should simply cut the metabolic accelerator and inertial shield now, so that the death-agony would swiftly terminate. He would not pray now for a miracle; he had done his praying before his jump, and whatever God might be, the god would be needing no reminder; but on this decision whether to hasten his own death or accept prolonged agony, he sorely needed mind-clarification.

To which of the faces of God in the New Serapis pantheon should he most appropriately address himself asking guidance? Whimsically, the name Mercury came through, an obvious association with the hole's fluid density. Well, Mercury was a specialized version of Hermes, and he in turn a specialized version of Thoth, and all three were antecedent to the clarity aspects of the Jesus-persona; and all of them, whatever else they meant, did signify humane intelligence.

Eh, well, no explicit petition was needed any longer, he

had his decision: it was to hold full power and to hope, but without *expecting* supernatural intervention. . . .

On the instant of his decision-commitment, a mighty invisible fist clutched him and yanked him free of the hole and hurled him across the high space of the central star.

(For the planet Iola, it was Destruction Day minus five.)

Part Two

QUEST FOR
MURDER–MEANINGS

Manhattan, Long Island, Houston, and Nereid
3-5 July 2495

2. KYRIA

What St. Cyr knew about Klaus Heller, from him when they had met and from assorted sources later, amounted to this:

Already a doctor of science in astrophysics with two major theoretical innovations to his credit, Heller was called in 2467 from a Brunildic university to the Vespuccia-based corporation called Aerospace Dynamics at the age of twenty-three. There he was installed as a research scientist in a small department whose work significantly affected the fortunes of the corporation. He was a handsome blond Brunildic with close-cropped hair; his face and nose and jaw and body were long and straight; yet he was casual and facile, good at light friendships (but not at deep ones), and equipped with elegant knowledge of the Anglian and Gallic tongues.

Within two months, he spoke the Vespuccian adaptation of Anglian virtually without accent, occasionally inserting current slang with satisfying felicity. Now he was *in* the firm and *in* his coterie and *in* the country, and his progressive advancement in business and applied science and society were assured. Politics he could manage without. His religious affiliation was The New Serapis which was tolerant of any not-brutal god or goddess as ego-image: Heller liked Enki, Thoth, Hermes, Apollo, Socrates, Jesus, and Low Artemis.

His career-ascent in Aerospace Dynamics experienced swift soarings followed by long plateaus, the former attributable to his intelligence (not exactly genius, but high, high) and helpfulness and corporation loyalty, the latter to his disinterest in corporation politics. Rather unexpectedly, though—after fourteen years as director of his department—he became a vice-president in 2489 and president in 2491, to which he added the board chairmanship in the same year, now having accumulated personal ownership of twenty-nine percent of

the stock along with loyalties and dependencies which nailed
down another twenty-seven.

He was a gentle yet firm and convincing man who by now
was admired for having annexed fluency in another five languages, one of them abstrusely extra-planetary. His driving
youth-fire had continued under carefully honed temper reinforced by amazing patience; he was persuasive while being
definite; and from 2489 on, increasingly he led Aerospace
Dynamics out of time-marking conservatism into adventurous
conservatism. Whenever he proposed an adventure, his board
and executives were conscious that Heller had personally par-
ticipated in a significant number of upleading adventures,
several times at foreseen and realized risk to his life.

After a final space expedition late in 2494 (no data about
this in the Galactic Police library), he surprised many worlds
by retiring in May 2495. Until his death last night, he had
resided in Westchester with his recently acquired immigrant
sister.

Departing the library, Claudine had already a list of things
to do; but before visiting Kyria Heller, she checked in on
Tuli who was sitting dream duty. It would have been possible
to review dream videoflakes, and this would be done for un-
monitored periods; but Claudine valued Tuli's on-the-spot
reactions.

Tuli, in a headset, looked up as her boss entered. "New
dream," she reported. "It just started." Claudine glanced at
the dead man's chest: it was sheet-covered now, she'd re-
check it later; just now, catch the new dream in midpas-
sage . . .

> . . . is at his desk being lectured by a portly man stand-
> ing over him; a sense that this is the President of Aerospace
> Dynamics before Heller replaced him in power. Now cold-
> angry Heller slowly arises and faces the president: "J. G.,
> I've been telling you about an abuse—are you going to
> listen to me, or aren't you?" The president blanches,
> shuffles, begins to temporize, stops, and suddenly thrusts
> out a hand, heartily asserting: "Klaus, you're the only
> departmental director who ever stood up to me. You'll
> benefit from this—and I *have* been listening." Heller takes
> the president's hand, meeting his eyes coldly. The president
> nods once, drops Heller's hand, wheels, departs.
> *Scene shift*: A committee meeting, big shots evidently,

many faces faintly familiar from the prior dream of
grandstand-applause; seen subjectively, so that I am Heller.
At table-head, the president warmly faces me as he an-
nounces: "We have learned that Director Klaus Heller
will retire next month, and we deeply regret this. To
honor his achievements and his unflinching honesty, I am
recommending to the Board his terminal promotion to the
rank of vice-president. Klaus, if you choose to reconsider,
the recommendation stands." Strong sense of Heller-inclina-
tion to reconsider on those terms . . .

Break to exterior of committee room: the closed door is
labeled 87314. Fade-out. Blackout. Dream re-com-
mences . . .

So the dream cycled: on and on, without variation,
through three St. Cyr reviewings.

Urgent inner voice: *Only biography, Inspector! relevant
only in its detail-contaminations. . . .*

She discarded the headset, arose, went to dead Heller, drew
back his sheet, studied the wound. As the doctor had said: internal injuries of smaller diameter than chest-hole, no evidence of burning on the back-up tissue. She covered the
chest, bowed her head, meditated. Again that woman-type
mind-voice: probably no more than her own intuition, which
might be wrong, but her intuition didn't usually sub-vocalize.

She turned to Tuli: "Same dream going on?" Tuli nodded.
"Any special impressions?"

"Nothing special—except that the people still look funny.
What do you think, Inspector?"

Claudine spread hands. "Who knows? Earlier days in his
firm, perhaps. Maybe he was going to retire as a director, but
when they promoted him, he changed his mind and went on
to become the big boss. Or else it could be wishful thinking
again; maybe in that kind of situation he did *not* stand up to
the big boss, and later wished he had. Just fragmentary
dreams, kid; not much to go on."

"So shall I give up?"

"No, hold the duty; can you take it?"

"Ha!"

"Okay, sorry. What did you mean, they looked funny?"

"Didn't they look funny to you?"

"All corporation types look funny to me. Except a few
guys like Heller."

Tuli ineffectually waved a large hand. "Me too, I guess.

The same dream is still going, we can keep talking if you like."

"That's twice you said they looked funny. Did you notice something else funny in both dreams?"

Tuli gave it thought. "Not really."

Claudine hinted: "A number."

Tuli pondered. Then: "Oh—oh yeah. The number was— 87314."

"Exactly. The city name in the first dream, and a door number in this one. Watch for it in later dreams."

"I'll watch."

"I'm off. Try to figure out why they look funny."

Kyria Heller had been admitted to the hospital for rest, and Claudine had obtained the room number. Entering the one-bed room, Claudine found the bed occupied by a large sitting-up fortyish man whose face flagged robust physical health. "Beg pardon," said Claudine; "wrong room, evidently." "No!" he insisted, leaning toward her. "*Right* room! *Right* room, f'gossakes, don't go way, I need beautiful female help!"

Naturally pleased, she responded soothingly, "Well then, of *course* I'll help you! Just let me have a quick look at your chart." Moving to his bed-foot, she scanned the data, glancing at him: he'd pushed the covers back, one hairy bare leg was out. "Well!" she exclaimed. "Acute satyriasis! Poor beast, I'll go get you a nurse—" She heard one of his bare feet hit the floor as she closed his door behind her.

Miss Heller had recovered overnight, had been discharged on her own request with doctor's approval that morning: so the supervisor. "Thank you," Claudine responded; "how about that poor fellow in her room now?" The supervisor sniffed: "Has a soft doctor, diagnosed hypertension, horse buns: likes hospitals, chronic nurse-chaser."

"Get him a male nurse," Claudine counseled, "and tell the nurse to watch out."

Having first phoned Miss Heller at her home, Claudine skimmered to Westchester. (Her skimmer, a brand new compact Buick, was a real luxury after Chevvies, mostly second-hand, while she was in the lower ranks.)

The Heller house was an old-fashioned twenty-third-century mansion designed in the period-mode of the nineteen-

twenties and well set back in a small park with a high metal
picket fence, probably electrified; but no fence had ever kept
out an intelligent murderer. A few seconds after she announced her name into a notifier, the driveway gates, activated from within the house, swung open. She drove up the
curving drive to the front porch; her car door was opened by
a uniformed male-type robot; she was admitted by a human
maid who conducted her into a small sitting room where
Miss Heller was brooding. The maid departed, closing the
door.

Kyria Heller, apparently in her mid-twenties, was tall-slen-
der; her blonde hair was tastefully-conservatively coifed so
that it hid her ears, and no earrings showed. Her face,
brownish as though tanned under a southern sun, was pretty
in a bizarre way, having wide-apart eyes whose color was a
blonde-remarkable hazel, and an unusually wide mouth which
just now was dejected. This face was distress-worn, and it did
not in any way resemble the face of Klaus. Wearing virginal
gray lounging pajamas, she sat in a rocker gazing out a broad
front window with an arched top. As the maid closed the
door, Kyria turned wearily to Caludine and motioned her to
a nearby easy chair, observing without tone: "I'm glad you
came, Inspector. Ask me any questions." There was a faint
accent which Claudine couldn't quite identify as Brunildic.

The interesting aspect of the situation was that so far Kyria was the obvious and only suspect, other than the maid
and the door-robot. If Kyria had done it, her appearance of
cooperation would be expected; and yet her self-control was
admirable.

Claudine opened: "Since you asked for release from the
hospital, you must be feeling better, and I'm glad."

Kyria, vision beyond the window, responded: "One has to
cope."

Claudine sorted questions, weave-ins. Tentatively she tried:
"Excuse me for saying so, but you seem a great deal younger
than your brother."

A fleeting smile further widened Kyria's mouth. "One
could explain that by saying that I am really only his half-sis-
ter by his father's second wife."

St. Cyr noticed the obliquity— "One could explain that by
saying—" but she let it pass, querying: "You lived with
him?"

"Yes."

"You seem very young for that sort of life."

Kyria stiffened. "I loved Klaus. I had no thought of marrying." She softened a little: "Besides, I haven't been in your country very long, I know scarcely anybody."

"You and your brother had no social life?"

Again she stiffened. "I was content with things as they were. Excuse me, Inspector, but I'd rather you'd get immediately to questions about his death." She arose. "Would you like for me to take you to the place where it happened?"

Assenting, Claudine followed Kyria through the entry door to the sitting room into the corridor. They bypassed large open double doors to a spacious salon and entered a much smaller room, no more than six meters square, having a big stone fireplace at the far end. There was a little centered table with two chairs and a chessboard whose chessmen disposition indicated a game well on its way to completion.

Kyria turned to Claudine: "Pray excuse my irritability, Inspector. I realize that your questions were pertinent. Perhaps you would wish to sit there where Klaus was sitting, with your back to the fireplace, while I sit where I was sitting." And Kyria went to the chair on the hither side of the table, and sat facing the fireplace with her back to the door.

From behind her, Claudine said, "Please stay seated there, Miss Heller, forgive me if I don't join you immediately. The shot that killed your brother—did it come from behind you?"

"I heard no shot. I merely watched Klaus die."

"But someone might have shot across your shoulder, through this door?"

"The door was closed. I did not hear it open although it creaks a little. Afterward, it was still closed."

"Could there have been another presence behind you in the room?"

"I have a sixth sense for such things. After Klaus fell, I turned almost immediately: nobody. No, there were only Klaus and I." She turned to look at Claudine: "That sort of seems to make me the one and only suspect, doesn't it?"

Frankness was in point, then. "Yes, it does, but I'm not prepared to settle for that. I won't ask you how the deed was done: either you don't know, or you do know and you will lie. Is there any lead at all that you can give me—even a ghost of a lead?"

Still twisted around facing her inquisitor, Kyria paled:

"A—*ghost* of a lead?" She shook her head in firm negation: "Nothing at all, Inspector. I was alone with him, only I."

"All right, Miss Heller, thank you. Please stay where you are while I take a look at the walls."

Whereupon Claudine devoted the best part of a silent quarter-hour to a minute inspection of walls and door; not merely the back wall, either, because Kyria might be lying about where Heller had sat, but all four walls and the fireplace. No aperture whatsoever, nothing through which an assailant might shoot; and as for the fireplace, the fire was reonic, there was no chimney-opening. Pending a return for more detailed inspection, zilch. Anyhow, the concept of a raygun which could bring off a seventy-five-degree convergent wound at any range beyond point-blank was incredibly far-fetched. Thoughtfully she went back to Kyria—who had been watching her, and who was now smoking a little rhinestoned pipe.

Decisively Claudine sat in the death seat; from here she inspected the wall and door behind Kyria. Still nothing. Kyria was staring at her with eyes exceptionally wide.

Claudine demanded: "When your brother was shot, this was where he sat?"

"Precisely there, Inspector. Across from me, like this."

"Did he have any enemies?"

Her smile was wry and pallid. "Remember, he'd retired. Business grudges don't often survive that."

"Your Anglian is excellent, Miss Heller."

"Thank you. Klaus did it for me, using hypnopedics. For himself, he scorned that technique, he could learn any new language with frightening speed all by himself."

"Are there any kin or fair-weather friends who might have a motive? An heir, perhaps?"

Thinking about that, Kyria leaned her chin on the outstretched fingertips of prayer-joined hands. Curious: there was light webbing between her fingers, down where they joined her hands. . . .

She leaned forward, speaking earnestly. "Inspector, I must apologize, I may have sent you police on, what you call, a chase of wild geese. My brother was killed, yes; I phoned the police, you would have come in anyway. But this was not murder. Inspector, I had a sister—"

Kyria froze, staring past Claudine, her face acutely apprehensive. Claudine whirled: nothing behind her except the fireplace; the room except for the two women was vacant of life. She turned back to Kyria. . . .

The woman's chest was opening up. The lounging pajamas peeled back like synthetic fabric ignited by a cigar, only there was no smoke or char; and the skin peeled back, and the bones peeled back, and there was a hole the size of a small Frisbee revealing the heart and major arteries which were peeling back and the voice was telling Claudine: *This is being done in love.*

"Take me off the case!" Claudine gibbered. "Charge me!" She sat in front of Superintendent Wong's desk, gripping the wooden chair arms, dark knuckles white, lips thin-white.

Wong caressed his own knuckles. "You asked to have the case."

"I'm asking out. Charge me."

"With what?"

"Damn you, Wong—murder!"

"And whom did you murder?"

"I *told* you! Kyria Heller!"

"Did you *know* you were murdering her?"

"Well, no, but—"

"Did you want to? intend to?"

"Naturally not." She was calming, but still she was grim.

Wong spread hands: "Then the worst charge would have to be involuntary manslaughter. What did you slaughter her *with?*"

She had gone cold. "Same thing her brother was slaughtered with."

"Which was what?"

Claudine spread hands.

Wong stood, came around the desk, gripped her shoulders. "You go write your report, then get the hell out of here and crack this case. Now you have a double motive, along with the best possible knowledge about the sort of thing that is happening."

She arose and stood uncertain.

His arm was around her waist. "You're absolutely certain nobody else was in the room?"

"Maybe the invisible man or woman. Nobody else."

"Seems to leave four hypotheses. Want to tell me what they are?"

Claudine, an automaton: "One: it *was* an invisible being.

Two: Kyria inadvertently did it to her brother by something like burning his chest with her eyes, and I did it the same way. Three: he did it to himself, and she did it to herself. What's four?"

"Some real person did it through a wall, maybe electronically activating a burn-out mechanism pre-planted in their chests."

She grinned wan. "Yours, Wong, is too realistic."

"Go check Tuli and the dreaming, or something. Go."

Why wasn't she hearing the voice?

3. THE FROGS

Claudine chose to walk to the hospital on this fair sunny day that was remarkably temperate-crisp for July. The fresh air braced her; in three blocks she was in full self-command and self-realization. That was when her hand-hilt hit her forehead: in her guilty paralysis over the body of Kyria Heller, she had not thought to order decay-retardation and dream-search encephalographics: Kyria would now be permanently cold, and for an indefinite while in a morgue-drawer. And just as Kyria had been on the verge of some revelation. . . . Blow clues, blow clues! What the hell kind of detective-inspector. . . .

All right, let's stay on Klaus Heller's dreaming—which wouldn't continue more than three or four days; and so far it had been classically obvious wish-fulfillment stuff, the dreaming of a recently retired power-man reliving his past and dream-revising it to make himself more glorious. . . .

One verity, though. In the second dream, as a mere departmental director he had stood up to the president and consequently had been promoted—and Heller had indeed been a departmental director when his meteoric rise to preeminence had started.

Besides, when you thought about it: if a man had retired voluntarily at the very pinnacle of renown, why would he have wishful dreams evoking petty office grandeur?

So there might be some kind of real substance lurking beneath the dreamwork-surface of petty nostalgia. . . .

She was now pick-pocking at brisk pace along the dog-littered Manhattan sidewalk (five centuries of legislation-and-enforcement had failed). Let's get to that hospital: what is Tuli witnessing?

She found Tuli standing rigid-white beside Heller's bed, her discarded head-apparatus lying on the floor as though Tuli had thrown it there. Claudine grabbed the lieutenant's cold hands: "What in hell is the matter?"

Tuli grated: "I don't have to watch that kind of dirtiness!"

Repressing a smile: "Tuli, if you saw a male sex-dream, didn't you expect that? All men have those dreams occasionally—"

"—the filthy beasts—"

"—and all women, too. Don't you?"

Tuli went totally taut.

"*Don't* you?"

Tuli's hard-together brows were knitting. "Not very often—and I *hate* it!"

Claudine, clasping Tuli's waist, was looking with interest at the abandoned headset. Releasing the lieutenant, she donned the headset and sat experiencing the new dreaming . . . only, the dream had changed again:

> The spacecraft is a metalloid sphere, it is far out in space, no visible constellation is recognizable.
> *Cut* to interior: three people: Klaus Heller eager-faced in a colossal unhelmeted space suit, and a grim-faced man and woman in ordinary ship-gear.
> *Cut* to exterior shot: all black down-ahead in space, dropping feet first, shrinking below, he is somehow iridescent, you can see him but nothing else in the prevailing blackness. *Cut* to close-up side-shot of Heller, helmet transparent, face terrorized and then agonized; legs lengthening until they are meters long and spider-thin, body compressed until shoulders are no more than twenty centimeters wide and narrowing still. *Cut* to close-up of spacecraft's calendar chronometer: hours, days, weeks. *Cut* to Heller, a speck below, no smaller, motionless, frozen exactly where he had been. *Cut* to chronometer: eight weeks, sixteen weeks, twenty weeks, twenty-four weeks. *Cut* to Heller, undiminished, motionless there forever. Blazoned on his back: 87314. . . .

Twice again Claudine reviewed the recycling dream. Inward voice: *This* is *relevant! Please stay with it, Inspector. . . .*

Wearily removing the headpiece, she offered it to Tuli: "Take it, honey—it's a new dream, pristine pure, no sex."

Tuli whimpered a little.

"Lieutenant, that's an order." Claudine stood and peremptorily extended a finger-point.

Moving in molasses-motion, Tuli took the seat and the headgear; she stared at the latter, licking lips. "Claudine," she ventured, "I have to tell you about the woman in the—the love-dream."

"Go ahead."

"Between her fingers there was *webbing*—and even between her *toes!*"

"Webbing?"

"Like on a *frog's* hands and feet! And her hair was short, and—she didn't have any ears!"

Thinking about Kyria, Claudine was highly alert. "Describe her otherwise."

"Well—it was all clear, hideously clear—slender woman, dark brown hair, very long legs wrapped around—ugh!"

A brunette: not Kyria then. *Inspector, I had a sister*—only, Klaus was brother to Kyria, wasn't he? But then. . . .

"Tuli—were they copulating normally?"

"Inspector! Sometimes you shock me, you're so matter of *fact*—"

"I mean—was she on her back, or was *he* on her back?"

"*No! No!* How can you *say*—"

"All right, you must mean it was normal. She wasn't a frog, then. She was fully humanoid?"

"Except for the webbing and the earlessness—"

"Well, so. I have to go now, Tuli, I have a new thought on this case. You keep monitoring the dreams."

Tuli's anxiety undulated—and then she reached a certainty and calmed and faced her leader. "I just thought of it, Inspector. Why the people in the other dreams were funny. Did you notice their hands?"

"Not especially." But Claudine had a premonition.

"They all had webbed fingers! And now that I think about it, in the sex-dream, her toes had webbing too! And—hey, wait—most of them had their hair styled over their ears, but a couple of guys had short hair—and they didn't have any ears!"

That information sent Claudine pick-pocking to the morgue. A technician silently rolled-open a drawer, drew back the sheet, and let her look at Kyria.

The chest-hole was an approximate duplicate, slightly smal-

ler, of the one in her brother's chest. Flanking it, her breasts
were slight but the nipples were woman-normal. Her groin,
too, was normal—or was the vulva somewhat posterior of
normal? There was normal blonde head-hair; Claudine lifted
it—no ears, only hearing diaphragms. Except on scalp and in
armpits and pubis (the prime sun-protection and sweat-ab-
sorption areas), there was no body-hair. And the webbing between fingers and toes was vestigially frog-evident.

All three dreams returned in detail-sharp clarity. Aided by
Tuli's percept, she confirmed that fingers were webbed and
that a few short-hairs had no ears. And yet in the space-ship
dream, Klaus and both his aides had ears, and the fingers of
the aides were not webbed.

It could follow that the first two dreams, which she had
thought might be corporation-nostalgic, were only corpora-
tion-contaminate: the nostalgia had reference to some other
planet. And Kyria may well have come from that planet: certainly she could be no sister at all to Klaus, who was fully
human.

Kyria here. Legs long relative to torso. Exquisitely shapely
legs, with slender ankles and calves curved smoothly as
though she were standing on high heels; thigh-muscles ath-
lete-impressive. Body slender indeed, shoulders rather narrow—yet pelvis broad, broad. . . .

She drew up the sheet. "Sorry, Kyria. Sir, you can close
the drawer."

Remarked the technician: "This is a weirdo, I'm sort of eager for the autopsy."

"Do me a favor," Claudine urged. "Tell the doctor not to
start cutting until he's done everything he can with x-rays and
such. I think her interior is going to be fascinating."

4. A WOMAN NAMED WILSON

It was a twenty-minute solichopper ride to Aerospace Dynamics which occupied most of the eastern tip of Long Island. The area was walled by enormous hangars and factories and multi-story research buildings, and centered on the administrative and research complex whose apex-building speared two hundred meters upward; the intervening square miles were a labyrinth of skimmer-roads and runways and rocket-pads and blockhouses. This was the heart of what Klaus Heller had controlled: there were three similar but smaller complexes in other geographical areas of Vespuccia, a dozen elsewhere on Erth, and another dozen on ten other planets.

From the beginning, the need for a high-level interview here had been obvious. What had sent her immediately from the morgue to the telephone, and what now brought her here within an hour, was the extraplanetary implication of the froglike people, combined with the dream-image of the faraway-below Heller speck frozen motionless in timelessness.

Her appointment was with the current president, Ms. Clara Wilson, who received Claudine affably and informally in a tower-top office suite as lush as one might expect. Wilson, a slight prim blonde just into her fifties, seated Claudine at one end of a long sofa, personally served coffee in a Wedgwood service on a low table before the sofa, and sat at the other end sipping, listening, responding. She had ears (artificial?) and showed them; had her fingers been unwebbed by surgery?

Claudine began: "It's a pleasure to meet a woman at the head of an organization like this. After all these centuries of trying to beat it, male chauvinism does continue to be a drag, doesn't it?"

Wilson grinned charmingly, spreading her free hand. "Me, I'm a female chauvinist, only I believe in integration. I notice

48

that Ms. St. Cyr has already made the rank of Inspector in the Galactic Police."

Claudine set down her coffee. "I think you've been around here for a while."

"Twenty-seven years."

"That's what I was meaning. Now take Klaus Heller, he was a male, but he was in the organization twenty-four years before he made president. So you did about as well as he."

"That *good* Klaus Heller!" Wilson was frowning down.

"Of course you knew him well?"

"Very well. May I—will it bore you if I reminisce a little?"

Free association was the best sort of testimony, if the testifier was innocent, and sometimes if he was guilty. Claudine leaned toward Wilson: "He fascinates me, I'd *love* that!"

"Well, it's just that I came into his department about five years before he started his final pole-vault into power. He—gosh, how can I tell you? I couldn't be like him in a million years, even with testicles! It was—well, he was friendly with everybody all the time, he laughed easily; if you didn't watch out you'd get tripped into thinking that work in his department was a cinch, you could goof off and get away with it. But it wasn't like that. He. . . . Well, he was a perfectionist for himself, but he was so damn considerate of other people that he couldn't bear to scold them when they didn't perform at maximum, he kept making allowances—but he was so hurt when you were lax, although he tried to hide it, that you died with shame and by God after that you performed because you—well, I guess I have to say, because you knew he liked you and you loved him.

"I remember one time when I did a sneaky thing and he found out about it; it was a case of my own divided loyalties, and I'm sure he had it out with himself agonizingly before he did what he did. He called me in and sat me down, and he discussed what I had done; he recognized that in one sense it was my right to do it, but he pointed out how it interfered with his departmental program in another sense; and he said finally, the words are mind-engraved: 'Clara, I just think you need to have a little conference with yourself about your loyalties.' And I had the self-conference, bitterly, all night for two nights. And I reached my decision. And without apologizing to him or anything, I sort of let him know indirectly by leaving him a little note revealing something that the object of my other loyalty was going to do. I'm sure he got the purport, but he never said anything about it, but after that I worked my ass off for him and for nobody else. By the way, it was on his recommendation that I replaced him as president. Oh, that man—"

Silence. In trouble, Wilson glugged coffee. Claudine waited.

Wilson looked up, straight ahead, not at Claudine. "I feel this so strongly that if you were a news-hen I wouldn't even ask you to keep it off the record. I mourn Klaus, and I want to help you find the assassin if I can—if somehow you can dig something useful out of my subconscious. Please ask some questions."

You played it straight with this sort of person. Claudine ventured: "Do you have any idea how or why he was killed?"

"All that I know is from the newskenners. I thought at first his sister might have done it—but now I learn that she got it the same way. So I guess you're looking for enemies. He never made any before he became president. As the boss of Aerospace Dynamics, of course he had enemies, and at least one was in this organization. But I'm convinced that none of the outside enemies hated Klaus personally, they merely wished he could be eliminated as a dangerous leader of Aerospace Dynamics, and none of them would trail him into retirement on vendetta. And even if somebody would kill *him* on an old grudge, it's insane to imagine the same person extending it to his sister—she was practically a recluse, few people even knew her."

Try another target. "Having recently retired, might Heller have developed an urge to return in power to the scene of his triumphs?"

Voice: *That's a false trail, Inspector. . . .*

Pouring coffee, Wilson asserted, "Any retiree might feel such aspirations, I dread retirement myself. But if you have some evidence that he felt that way, I just can't associate it with anybody's motive to murder him. Be assured that the present president would have yielded to him gladly, lovingly."

Interesting disclaimer: it could be taken at face value, particularly since Wilson was intelligent enough to know that there might be a different interpretation. Heller had kept his corporation stock, he could have challenged Wilson. For that matter, why had he retired so abruptly, and relatively so young? She'd be working her way into both questions.

Meanwhile, thinking about the space-dream and the amphiboid humanoids, she remarked: "I understand that sometimes he rode his own ships into space."

That hit some kind of target: as Wilson handed over Claudine's cup and saucer, the cup rattled in the saucer. Wilson looked down, frowning. Claudine waited.

Wilson said: "Excuse me, I was thinking of something. The general answer is, yes, of course he did, he was a romantic, and besides, he wanted always to know our products intimately in performance. He'd been on a dozen short and long space expeditions before becoming president; after that, we usually managed to persuade him not to go, the best interests of the company were otherwise. I say 'we'—I became a member of his executive committee soon after his presidency began, I was a vice-president at the beginning of the incident which is troubling me—I will call it an incident—I'm sorry, I'm giving longer answers than your questions call for, I never do that in court. You're a skillful lady."

"Only an honestly interested lady, really. Do you want to talk about the incident?"

Inspector, this is on track!

Departing the sofa, Wilson went to a window-wall and peered outward and downward, hands clasped behind her. So facing, presently she inquired: "Are you familiar with the star called Vassili, in Cygnus?"

"Not by name, certainly. It isn't in the Galactic Union."

"Well, Vassili is about a thousand light-years from Erth, in the general direction of galactic center. And now it seems to have a planet inhabited by intelligent beings."

"No!"

"*Seems* to have, I said. We can't observe even the star directly, let alone any planets that it may have: there are intervening black holes and clouds of incandescent gas. Am I boring you, Inspector?"

"I've never yet been bored by an investigation—and this one is more arousing than most."

"All right." Wilson turned to Claudine, and the executive against the brightness of the window was a semi-silhouette with face blurred. "Well, Nereid finally grew interested enough to budget a couple of billion for a spacecraft investigation, and of course they turned to us—"

"Only a couple of billion for *that?*"

"It was worse than you think, because they wanted a craft capable of carrying two scientists along with a three-man crew plus a lot of heavy astronomical equipment plus iradio telemetry, not to mention space-drive capable of traveling five hundred light-years to Natron in a week and then another five hundred light-years to the vicinity of Vassili in another week. That second run would involve a thousand light-years round trip nonstop including an eight-week margin to cruise Vassili, you comprehend? And there would be the added weight of a top-order differential mass and an inertial shield of around five million to one, all plus oxygen-generating equipment and hydroponic rations and the usual crud. And we had to develop two space-suits like small spacecraft, veritable hippopotami, with special equipment sophisticated beyond my nightmares. Well, we had the ship, but developing and building such suits alone would eat up most of the two billion, and equipping the ship would swallow the rest, leaving less than nothing for the expedition itself.

"So Klaus gathered his executive committee, proposed that we take on the project and subsidize the difference above two billion out of company resources, and put it to an advisory vote. Most of us voted no, and I was one. So then Klaus asserted, with an old romantic eye-gleam that I recognized and shuddered at: 'Thank you, ladies, gentlemen. Nevertheless, I am going to take this to the Board with my recommendation to approve. I will report your adverse vote, but I mean to push this through. And apart from a lot of other values, one reason is—I want to go along.'

"When his last five words sank in, there was a lot of dismay and some protest. We all knew that he personally controlled the Board majority; nice guys do sometimes come in first. I held silent, knowing him as I did; but I inveigled him into supper at my place, and urgently I put it to him that the risk involved was a serious hazard to the firm. But he grinned and froze me with his answer: 'No problem for the firm, Clara, because you're the one who will be in interim charge and will probably succeed me if I don't make it back.' It was my first intimation that I was in line for the succession; and I guess I blew the realization, I think I even fell to my knees and pleaded for release from this. But he wouldn't give, he *didn't* give—"

Breaking off, she checked her cutichron. Instantly Claudine

stood: "Ms. Wilson, I'm taking too much of your valuable time; go ahead if you feel other pressures."

"Sit!" Wilson sharply ordered. "I'm this far ahead with you, I want to press on to the end of it!"

"So we computer-played," Wilson continued, "with diversified trip times and requirements, allowing always our standard fifty percent time margin, and came up with the optimum formula along with a couple of tentative designs. It costed-out at just over two billion for design, construction, and testing, with another half-billion for the excursion. Klaus was hot now; his Board had approved a quarter-billion subsidy, and he swung it by shaving the time-safety margin to twenty-five percent, and Nereid bought it, and we went to work.

"I think it was the toughest two months of our lives in terms of work and sweat, with Klaus urging us on in ways that were no different from his old ways—always calm and friendly but working his own ass off and shaming us into sacrificing our own asses too. Or is that arse? And he tried to keep us a happy ship; but in fact, we were a worried crew—we all cared for him, *all* of us, except that one little bastard who was vice-president for experimental research and whom I bounced down to department director this spring as my inaugural act after Klaus retired. But we won, we brought in the spacecraft and the suits for just under two billion leaving about one-third billion for expedition expenses—if you want to call it a win with only a one-quarter safety margin.

"So Klaus and his ship departed Erth in early November 2494—last autumn—and stopped for ship maintenance on Natron III about a week later, keeping us advised all the way by iradio. Late in November they were about one astronomical unit off the Vassili complex. And there—Inspector, do you know what a black hole is?"

Claudine, aroused by the story, had left the sofa and was peering out a different window-wall, watching an experimental ship tooling up for space departure, but listening always. She responded without turning: "Only that a black hole is a burnt-out star which gives off no light and has a hell of a gravitational field."

"That's near enough for now," Wilson affirmed, "except to add that it gives off no light because its gravitational field is too powerful for even light to escape; indeed, it sucks in light

from other sources like some kind of hungry cephalopod
sucking in plankton. Okay, once again I'll try to abbreviate:

"They'd confirmed by reconnaissance that Vassili was
screened by a surrounding complex of black holes which
among them were activating gas-clouds churning themselves
into ship-impassable turbulence. And then—"

Wilson hit a palm with a fist: "Then, dammit, *he* announced that he alone, in one of those awful space-suits, was
going to jump right in to one of the black holes!"

The latest Heller-dream recurred vividly to Claudine, who
spurted: "All *right!* I want to know what you know about
that!"

Wilson ran out of gas. Weakly she worked her way back to
the sofa, sat, stared at nothing. Claudine was the one to pour
coffee.

Semi-refreshed, Wilson reported: "The technical details of
why he thought he might be able to do it and return with information are beyond me. I'll put you in touch with a VASA
astronomer, if you like." VASA was the Vespuccian Aero-
Space Agency.

"I do like—but keep on giving me your own perceptions."

"Ms. St. Cyr, as a corporation president I don't like to
confess confusion, but my perceptions for several months after that are confused. But I'll try.

"So he did jump into this black hole. So the reports back
talked about how he was deformed as he approached it, and
how his approach velocity kept slowing when you'd expect it
to keep accelerating; and how finally, far in, he was poised
stationary and stayed that way. All this they'd predicted from
knowledge of how a black hole deforms time; and extrapo-
lating from those predictions, they had to conclude that
Klaus would remain stationary there for an indefinite period
of time and under no circumstances could get out again. He
must have anticipated this before he jumped, I don't know
why he jumped. The ship couldn't risk diving in for a rescue,
it would only mean certain loss of the ship and its crew. Acting on prior orders from Klaus, they were beginning to think
about returning to Natron base: there was that lousy thin
twenty-five percent time-safety margin.

"But then—this is utterly fey—he came back aboard ship
about ten days after the jump—and yet he continued to be
down there, floating in black-hole space forever!"

"So how did he get out?"

Wilson spread hands. "He wouldn't tell me. I haven't been able to learn. One day in mid-December, I walked into my office—*his* office really, I was only interim president—and there he was, sitting at my desk—*his* desk. He arose as I entered, he looked terribly worn; and he said: 'Clara, I'm back on duty for now, but there's a chance that within a few months I'll have to resign.' Just like that. I demanded to know why—imagine, I'd thought he was dead, now I see my dear friend alive without notice, and all I can think of is to demand why he might have to resign. He came around the desk and took my hands and said: 'Clara, please don't ask questions, I have to do this. One reason is that I have a younger sister, just arrived in Vespuccia. She doesn't speak much Anglian; I must stay home and take care of her.' Inspector, that was the first time I'd ever heard of a sister! I guess I just stood staring, and he added, 'You'll succeed me, there isn't any question. For now—well, take your time about vacating the office, I have a lot to do on Nereid. Bless you.' And he kissed my forehead and went.

"And I guess you know that two months ago he did resign, and I'm it."

Wilson was genuinely desolate, she sat staring into space. Paradoxically, this very grief was grounds for intensive questioning—which, however, it was no time to pursue. Claudine stood: "Thank you, Ms. Wilson, I didn't hope for so much."

The president looked up at her with an expression queerly mingling pathos and humor. "I didn't give you the name of that VASA astronomer."

"True."

Going to her desk and seating herself, Wilson wrote a name on a memo slip, added a phone number from a little reference book, and handed the slip up to Claudine, saying: "Please feel free to mention my name."

"Thank you. By the way—"

"Yes?"

"What was the name of the former vice-president who hated Heller?"

"He was another Brunildic, Werner Voelker, he's been a good boy since I demoted him."

"I don't think you said where Voelker went—"

"We have a ray weapon sideline, they're often needed in planetary exploration, that was one of his bailiwicks as vice-president, now he's director in full-time charge there. I'm not meaning to cast any suspicion on him——"

"I know, but there's a raygun angle to this case. Can you get me entrée to Mr. Voelker?"

"Dr. Voelker. Of course." She scribbled another note and handed it to Claudine. "Anything else——*Dr.* St. Cyr?"

"Where'd you learn *that?*"

"I have carrier pigeons. Anything else?" Wilson stood.

"Only, once again, thank you. I'll be checking back."

They shook hands warmly. As Claudine departed, she heard Wilson saying into her intercom: "I'm free now. Who? Metchnikoff? Tell him to go ahead and activate. Am I too late to pick up that Haley committee meeting?"

The voice was murmuring: *Apart from what she has already told you, Wilson would be a false trail. . . .* But Claudine was beginning to find this new voice of her own old intuition disrupting. Logic had to supplement intuition, structure it, often even displace it. And logic was telling her to stay on the Wilson track.

5. A DREAM OF COSMIC BADMINTON

As a right-now choice between seeing the raygun specialist or talking with the astronomer about black holes in general and that expedition in particular, it was the astronomer who more strongly drew Claudine. She called Dr. Murchison at Houston from the solichopper and had no difficulty raising him and making an appointment for tomorrow; his cheery baritone assured her that he celebrated Vespuccia's Independence Day by working; on disconnect, she had visions of a jovial graybeard.

Whispered the voice: *Good choice; wrong image.* . . .

Voelker would be interviewed later: he might prove a fruitful lead, if you stayed with the obvious hypothesis that murder had been brought off by Erth-natural methods. That hypothesis had to be eliminated before she could pursue the extraplanetary possibility raised by the frog-people. Voelker's alleged hatred of Heller, together with Voelker's raygun connection, might lead to something about an old grudge. The murder wounds were the opposite of characteristic for known rayguns, but who knew what experimental weapons might be hiding in Voelker's lab? There was, of course, an invisibility problem to get around. Or maybe, questioning Voelker might lead to some new thoughts about Clara Wilson: Claudine was sure that Wilson had been closer to Heller than Wilson had admitted, there had been many emotional hints of this; and if perhaps Wilson had regarded Kyria Heller, not as his sister, but as a rival. . . .

But on the other hand, the extraplanetary possibility couldn't be discarded. Heller, less than a year before his death and only half a year before his unexpected retirement, had jumped into one of the black holes which guarded a star having planets one of which might have intelligent life. And there were the froggish people in the Heller-dreams, and the froggish reality of Kyria. . . .

Her dream that night was a wowser; it troubled her when she awakened from it; and it would stay with her, fully circumstantial, intimately personal, deliciously terrorizing. There had even been a little informal prolog, spoken by The Voice:

Inspector, here is a taste of what you are really after. . . .

She was male, she was Klaus Heller, jerked out of his black hole, rushing headlong away from nothing toward nothing, with the yellow-white might of some star called Klarata not a parsec below him, illumining his belly while his back was night. No sign of ship or Duke, no signal from ship or Duke. He sent out iradio inquiries, but there was no response; as for the ship's reception, holes and gas clouds might hopelessly distort the feeble I-rays that his suit could emit; as for Duke, if he was still in the hole, his iradio emissions if any could not get out of it. Forget them, then: *he* was in enigmatic and uncontrollable flight-crisis.

Thoth, when I rang, did I maybe get Hermes? The whimsical rapscallion would *joy* in working out my rescue through some natural phenomenon that I wouldn't know anything about.

His altimeter, as it registered his widening departure from hole-center, rose in its kilometer readings into exponential powers of ten; this continued until 1.496×10^8 k, and then the base shifted to astronomical units which whirled away behind him at a heightening velocity. But when the altimeter read 110 A.U., abruptly the reading dropped to 108 A.U.—which had to mean, that the altimeter's nearest reference point was now *another* black hole located some two hundred eighteen astronomical units from the one he had just invaded and somehow escaped.

Knowing it was ridiculous to do this, he caught himself *looking* for the second black hole.

Distance 84 . . . 42 . . . 31 . . . 19 . . . 11 . . . That was A.U.'s; he was falling into that second hole. Good Christ, not again? But this time it would be hopeless, he had no power. . . . Hell, yes he did, his repulsor unit would work now! Resolutely turning his back on the new hole, he activated full repulsor power, intending gradually to divert himself downward toward the Klarta system.

No change! No change! His repulsor was flaring, but still an implacable *something* was dragging or driving him toward the second hole! Ominously, the altimeter base shifted down to 1.496×10^8 kilometers.

Once more: decision to end it quickly?

Altimeter: 10^2 kilometers. 99. 87. 64. 48. 31. Event horizon: into it! Twenty-eight kilometers from center of second hole; beginning of the fluid spin. Wait it out whimsically, be a Thoth-Hermes; but it was a horrendous whimsy.

Altimeter back up to 29, cessation of spin. 31: out again! 35 . . . 52 . . . 99 . . . 10^3 . . . 10^5 . . . Accelerating backward-upward! He swung his body around, it was better head-first. Once again he tried the repulsor: full flare, but no effect. He began to laugh. Lord Almighty, whichever of the gods or goddesses you are, whatever composite or distillate you are—did *you* invent this cosmic badminton? And he resigned himself to being yanked forward, watching the swiftening altimeter shift to astronomical units, back across the Klarta-star, A.U. numbers ascending then once more diminishing—the first black hole taking over, of course; this time, having penetrated the interior once, he *would* finalize it.

Only, this time the pace of the descending altimeter slowed perceptibly after two A.U. . . . and reversed itself again. . . .

6. AN ASTRONOMER NAMED MURCHISON

She assigned Tuli to Voelker (there had been no new significant Heller dreams). She cleared desk work at her office. She eliminated the maid and robot doorman as suspects or useful witnesses—the maid by a lie-detector test, the doorman by simple interrogation after a factory check for possible malfunction had established that he could not lie.

Then Claudine departed for a 1430 appointment with Dr. Murchison in Houston. That city was a mere 2270 air kilometers from Manhattan: no problem; she hopped a rocket at 1235 and made it.

Murchison, of course, upset her phone impression completely. He was a spare tall blond curly-head, under forty and looking not much more than thirty, with a wide and permanently close-lip-smiling mouth, crinkles around the eyes to reinforce the smile, a dimple-dent chin, and a voice like an Irish politician.

She came to the point immediately. "No monkey business, Doctor, here it is. I am investigating the deaths by possible murder of Klaus and Kyria Heller—you know about them?"

"I read and hear newskenners, Doctor. And I knew them both." His smile did not change; she wondered if any stress would change it.

"Good. Well, I understand that Dr. Heller once had a black-hole connection, and I want you to tell me exactly what is a black hole. Let me start by saying that I know it is an exhausted large-mass star which gives off no light because it absorbs all light in its vicinity. And that is all I know. Can you take it from there?"

"You are a doctor of what, Inspector?"

"Psychology, so that won't help us. But I've had some per-

60

tinent cognates, and I've done some fairly knowledgeable spacing. Give it to me technically, and I'll tell you if it bounces without absorption."

"Excellent," smiled Murchison. "After you phoned yesterday, I dug out my dossier on Heller's Folly. No slur intended, because he made it good. Clara Wilson phoned me to say that she'd given you the ground view of this—"

"Right." Wilson had *phoned* him?

During the next hour, Murchison with great clarity made her extremely knowledgeable about black holes. Beyond what we already know from the account of Heller's leap, a few of his comments are pertinent.

"As you probably understand," he analogized, "jumping into a black hole is about like committing yourself to bottomless quicksand: escape without help is impossible—and it's worse than that, because from a black hole no escape-help is possible.

"Or another analogy. If you're a sky diver, and you jump out of an aircraft at ten thousand meters with chute closed, you can fall free, say, nine thousand meters, building up fall-velocity all the time; but if then you open your chute, your rate of fall will be slowed, and you will hit ground without doing worse than breaking a couple of ankles. At that slowed rate of fall, if you were attached to a line from the aircraft above, the line would arrest your fall completely, and the aircraft could pull you up again. But if you multiply Erth's gravity by more than three million and try the same trick, nothing can arrest your fall, and nothing can pull you back up. And that's a black hole.

"Now, as to the elongation and compression of the falling body. These are effects from the so-called tidal action of black-hole gravity. Because Heller's feet were closer to the gravity source than his head, the feet were subject to much more gravity-drag than his head was, and this acted like a Procrustean bed on his legs; we don't get this effect falling toward Erth because Erth's gravity is weaker by a divisor above three million. At the same time, if you think of gravity as an infinite number of force-lines all converging on hole-center, perhaps you can imagine how they would act as radial vise-jaws to squeeze the shoulders together. Am I clear so far?"

"So clear that you're giving me the illusion of understanding you." Even lecturing, this Murchison was almost boyishly attractive.

"Probably you *are* understanding me," he commented. "Now, as to the decelerating fall and eventual appearance of permanent arrest in space. Consider the final segment of Heller's fall: during that close-in segment, red-shift would cause observers to believe that his fall was slowing, whereas Heller himself would keep feeling more and more acceleration just as you would expect. For instance, as Heller fell from three hundred kilometers above hole-surface down to one hundred eighty kilometers, Heller would clock the time at eleven ten-thousandths of a second, but the observers would clock it as *twelve* ten-thousandths. This difference would keep being augmented as the time and the fall proceeded, until the difference would become extreme and eventually infinite. Do you see why?"

"No, I don't; the differences don't seem to make sense, because light velocity at that short distance is almost instantaneous."

"Well, yes, light's velocity stays unchanged; but to reach the observing ship, light keeps having to travel farther and therefore it takes longer. Here's why. The awesome gravity from the hole is dragging on the green-light impulses emitted by clock and altimeter. It is shifting both to the red—in other words, slowing the frequency, stretching-out the wave-length, and reducing the light's energy. This makes the light-impulses more responsive to gravity. Their outbound pathways are distorted back toward the hole; eventually they even have to orbit the hole one or more times before getting clear out. Now if these impulses are correlated on the ship-flakes with the ship's clock, it turns out that as Heller falls closer and closer in, the light pulses have more and more gravity to fight in order to escape the hole-gravity, and consequently they weary more and more, and turn redder and redder, and are slower and slower about getting out to the ship. So when Heller is actually deep in, the ship is seeing him when he was *not* so deep in."

"All *right*—"

"I've already told you about the slight difference between what falling Heller sees and what the ship sees in terms of his fall-time. And this difference keeps augmenting. So that during the last split-second above hole-surface for falling Heller, about a half hour passes for those aboard ship. And for them, that's the end of the observed fall. No more falling. No more time. No more impulses. Zero. Zilch. A Heller indefinitely suspended in space at the event horizon."

"But that forever-floating Heller is merely a phantom?"

"Exactly. Or, in Kantian terms, merely a phenomenon; not a noumenon."

"But what about Noumenon Heller *to himself?*"

"If the poor bastard has survived all the elongation and compression and three million G freefall, to himself he continues to fall inward. Theoretically he will hit hole-center seven hundredths of a millisecond after penetrating the event horizon. Thirty kilometers in less than a tenth of a millisecond! That works out to a velocity around four hundred fifty thousand kilometeres per second—half again the velocity of light!"

He paused, allowing the stupefying figures to sink in.

Claudine said slowly, sooner than he had anticipated: "Can there be any gravity at hole-center?"

"Obviously no. Maximum gravity is at surface."

"And you say he would hit hole-center at far more than light-velocity, with no gravity there to keep him from roaring on. Could that be how he escaped? Mightn't he have gone roaring out the other side of the hole, just because of sustained inertial velocity?"

"Ingenious, but no dice."

"So tell me why, Murchison."

"Eleventy-seven reasons, St. Cyr, which I will simplify to just a few.

"First, the numbers I mentioned assume that the hole is a vacuum, which it isn't. But even if it were; after he passed hole-center on the way outward, he would be retarded by rapidly growing increments of gravity reaching maximum at the surface-antipodes of the hole. Probably he would be down to light-velocity by the time he reached hole-surface; and he could never break out, any more than light can.

"But second, a black hole is no vacuum, it is not a hole, it is a plenum composed of all the matter in the collapsed star plus a lot more that it has sucked in since. The sun's average density is half again that of water; well, the density of a black hole must be at least fourteen times that of water, which makes it around mercury-density, and that's about three times the mean density of Erth with all rock and metals from crust to core included. Imagine what would happen to you if you plowed into *that!*"

"And yet, Dr. Murchison, think of Heller's high momentum when he hit the surface!"

"Okay, the effect of his momentum could be computed. But admit that even at high contact-momentum, Heller would generate a lot of friction penetrating all that matter, he'd lose momentum in a hurry.

"And I'll mention another difficulty. The matter in a black hole has to be sluggishly spinning. It must be practically fluid. Penetrating the surface, Heller would be caught in the spin; and there is really no telling how long it would take him to reach hole-center, if he ever did."

"May I summarize, Dr. Murchison?"

"Pray do."

"Apart from gravity retardation, and hole density double that of iron, and the way he'd be spun by all this gook, and frictional broiling, and general mangling, there really isn't any serious reason why Heller couldn't go in and come out again."

"True."

"But he did. And I keep reflecting that this black hole has been sucking in all surrounding matter during billions of years, and yet it seems that its mass has not materially increased. So it must be somewhere, somehow, discharging matter; and it may have discharged Heller too. I remember something about worm holes—"

"Forget worm holes. Even theoretically, they're as illogical as a black hole made of vacuum."

"Then does all that matter empty out into another spatial dimension—the past, maybe?"

Murchison's smile seemed a trifle strained, and he spread hands. (No finger-webbing, and his ears showed.)

She grinned. "Forgive this amateur brainstorming."

"We're both pros in our fields. I like to watch another pro in high gear. Want to call me Duke, like the other guys?"

Call him *Duke?* A Duke had been indicated in last night's dream of Klaus badmintoned near a star called Klarta . . . *as for Duke, if he were still in the hole* . . . Aa! Weird coincidence, merely . . . "I'd like that very much, Duke. I'm Claudine."

"Gallic?"

"In part, out of Marseilles. Spawn of about five races from

three planets. Lots of black, that's from Marseilles and another planet. Why would they call you Duke?"

"Nobody dares call me Carmody, and Murch sounds like a social error. But my middle name is Duquesne."

"It is wise parents who name newborn astronomers after universities . . . Jeezt, are we skidding!"

"I like to skid, Claudine, it helps my back burner to cook. And I've just been cooking your remark about another dimension. Not that it's applicable, but it gives me another idea—"

"So may I hear it?"

Tapping teeth with his thumbnails, Duke Murchison reached decision and leaned forward. "Are you game for a little space excursion with me, just us two alone in a VASA scouter?"

She eyed him sidelong. "Not just now, certainly. I have to break this case."

"This might help. It might not, but then it might."

"When and where would we be going?"

"Tonight. To Nereid."

Her eyes widened. All she said, though, was, "Shall I bring a covered dish?"

"I furnish space rations aboard the scouter, Galactic furnishes great food aboard Nereid."

"And what, sir," she inquired demurely, "would we be doing on Nereid?"

"I have an appointment there for some technical discussions and dinner. With a guy named Croyd. I'd like for you two to meet each other."

"Did you say Croyd? *The* Croyd?"

Once in a long while, Claudine felt faint, and this was one time when. Croyd was merely Wong's chief's boss—*her* big boss whom she'd never imagined ever meeting—the number five man in the whole galaxy.

Time was now of the essence; and so aboard the rocket to Manhattan she put through a visiphone call to Detective Superintendent Wong. After some amicable quarreling, he agreed to her excursion, adding: "And don't try to influence Croyd in my favor—he likes to dig out his own men, he doesn't respond well to meddling."

"Worry not, Wong," she assured him. "If he asks me about you, I'll tell him what you really are."

"I know," Wong said bitterly. "An almond-eyed son of a bitch—but deep." Disconnect.

She tried next for Tuli—first at Galactic Police HQ, then at the hospital where Tuli answered. Heller lay in the foreground, looking the same as before—wires and tubes; Claudine had a flash-imaginary of him floating like that in black-hole space. . . . Tuli was out of the headset, and she said rather breathlessly: "Sorry, Claudine, I just came in. My interview with Dr. Voelker was pretty dull."

"Just give me the highlights, Tuli, I have a lot to do personally, I'm off for Nereid tonight."

"Nereid!"

"You shouldn't ask."

"Okay. Well, Voelker. Well, he does know a lot about ray-guns. But he hadn't ever heard of one whose ray narrowed as it penetrated; they all spread, he said, at least a little, it's the nature of the beast."

"Did you ask about the laser-bend possibility?"

"It's been done, he said, but only to shoot around corners at a very wide angle, maybe 120 degrees. A laser wouldn't narrow the ray, it would only channel it."

"Dead end, there, then, unless he's hiding something."

"That was my thought."

"I thought it would be. Did you nose him out about his alleged hatred of Heller?"

"Yes, I was real subtle about it. But the thing finally came to a point, and he averred that he didn't hate Heller at all, in fact he almost loved him."

"Since that was probably a lie, it does sort of revive the question of a gun with converging rays, doesn't it?"

"I thought of that."

"Mm-hm. What did he say about Clara Wilson, if anything?"

"He went on to say that Ms. Wilson was jealous of him and jealous of Heller, that her demotion of Voelker was arbitrary, that now Voelker can't advance because she is holding him down."

"Do you believe that, Tuli?"

"Do you think I should?"

"I think we should both suspend judgment."

"That's what I was going to recommend."

"Tuli, you're a great lieutenant." And permanently a lieutenant, with that sort of yes-business. "What's Heller dreaming?"

"Wait, let me check." Tuli donned the helmet, concentrated briefly, tore-off the helmet with a look of disgusted embarrassment. "Him and that human frog again!"

"In our dreams we can have such wonderful stamina! Or maybe I should say fidelity. I assume you meant the female."

"I guess so, I didn't look very hard."

"And now you feel like a voyeuse."

"What's that?"

"A peeping Thomasina."

"Claudine, you *know* I *wouldn't!*"

"Now you won't have to. Just make sure the stuff is being flaked. Check daily with the doctors to see that all is well, and pick up the flakes and stash them in my safe. Otherwise, you'll have to hang around the office to cover me, but tell Captain Venuto that she's in charge during my absence, keep her informed, take orders from her. I'll give you a ring from Nereid. Got it?"

"Why aren't *I* in interim charge?"

"Because Venuto is a captain."

"That's a good reason, I was going to mention it. Have fun, Inspector."

"I'm Claudine to you privately, remember?"

"Are we private now?"

"Let's make that assumption."

"My idea exactly. Have a ball, Claudine."

That was the St. Cyr send-off into a most twisty adventure.

She met Duke Murchison for early dinner at 1800 hours in the administrative dining room of Aerospace Dynamics; he'd skimmed there from Houston in his VASA two-man scouter which had stubby wings for atmospheric flight but was equipped with space drive. By agreement, they were semiformal, she in saffron with a plunging neckline (the plunge was still well worth it), he in black trousers and white shirt and black bow tie and crimson velvet jacket and royal purple cummerbund: these were the costumes they'd be wearing for dinner with Croyd on the following evening, if this evening they could avoid food-stains; they'd change to flight suits before entering the scouter.

She started out alert, but he was easy-delightful, and over the second cold duck her alert had been dissolved by comfort. Cold vichyssoise followed, and lettuce with blue cheese, and a chateaubriand with a variety of vegetables, along with suitable wines; then baked Alaska and crème de menthe . . .

"I worry," she remarked, glancing down at her gown, "about the crème de menthe."

"Worry not, Croyd and I like green on saffron. Suggestion, though: if you spill, spill not on the gown but rather on the bosom—that I can wash."

"Beast!"

"N'est-ce pas!"

"I'm happy to note that you don't worry about diet."

"There's always jogging. Believe it or not, there are still prairies not far from Houston, some of them as big as three acres. How do *you* eat like that while staying a dreamboat?"

"Bypassing the doubtful assumption," she merely answered, "I am nervous."

"High on adrenalin?"

"High on my perpetual affair with the curiosities of life."

"I think you are not married."

"No. Are you?"

"Yes. Does it matter, Claudine?"

"Not for business purposes. I take it this is business."

"I'd like for it to be more."

"Not this trip, really, Duke—please?"

"But afterward?"

"That would have to develop as it might. As for your marriage, that's your business—so far."

"May I use the oldest line in the world?"

"You mean, your wife doesn't understand you? That's not so old, it's only neolithic."

"But in my case, true. For about three years I've been a free agent, except for some financial obligations."

"Without sympathy, I take that as a mere statement of fact."

"Sympathy would have taken the edge off the whole evening."

What a charming astronomer! *Too* charming—and too young. . . . She demanded: "How long will we be in that scouter together?" Not that she didn't know, from repeated experience—not going to Nereid, but bypassing Neptune the mother-planet of little Nereid.

His reply was straightforward: "Twenty hours, each way. Problem?"

"Not really, unless you make one."

"I won't make one. If a problem should arise, I wouldn't have aggressively made it."

"All right, I can live with that just fine. Business associates?"

"Business associates."

On that, they shook hands gravely across the table.

He queried, "How's your crème de menthe? Or would you like to go stronger?"

"What's on your mind for yourself, Duke?"

"We're coming up on take-off time, I can just manage a quick straight Chivas Regal."

"Same for me, then. In space, are you allowed to drive while drunk?"

"I don't have to drive. I just tell my scouter, 'Take me to Nereid in twenty hours,' and then I can lapse into a stupor."

"From which you look at the moment remote."

"Have another look when I finish the Chivas Regal."

"I will—if I *can* look when I finish *my* Chivas Regal."

The cabin of the two-seat scouter occupied only one-third of the hull. The remaining space was needed for the repulsor engine, which fed on raw space to drive the craft at sustained thrusts up to five hundred gravities (500 G). As for the 1:500 inertial shield, necessary for reducing the apparent thrust felt by pilot and passenger to a comfortable minimum, it was all-around outside, an invisible amnion. A twenty-hour trip of more than four billion kilometers called only for 349.3 G; apparent thrust would be only .7 G which is less than the drag that Erth-people normally feel, in fact very close to freefall.

These were all matters familiar to Claudine from way back. And now she blessed Duke (who seemed cold sober) for his comprehension of her technical background. She'd ask a question about specifics ("What ratio is your inertial shield?") and he'd reply economically ("Five hundred to one"), and would await the next question which probably would be about something else because his answer had satisfied her need.

There wasn't a lot of conversation, because despite her space experience which practically amounted to that of a traveling salesman with airlines, she never wearied of the wonder of watching Erth drop away while stars began to approximate their raw splendor. They lazed off Erth, then rapidly boosted velocity, crossing Moon orbit in about seven minutes, with Moon a brilliant space-filling disk only a thousand kilometers away. An hour later they were well into hard space, with the moon lost among stars; the sun, even through polarized windows, was an unfaceable glare flaring on one side of their craft with white light and hot heat while the other side was deadly cold black night.

When they had thrust past Moon into moon-shadow, and the stars flamed into brilliance, she restudied the constellations—all so familiar here, although (as she well remembered) from many remote planets they were all different. Acceleration continued: velocity would build up to a peak of 123,250 kilometers per second (more than one-third light velocity) after they would cross Saturn orbit, then would reverse into braking deceleration past Uranus into the vicinity of Neptune. The total twenty-hour trip time meant an average velocity of something like 61,625 kilometers per second.

After perhaps a half-hour of star-gazing, she became aware that Murchison had let her alone, saying nothing. He was a nice guy besides being a hell of an astronomer; ignoring him was impolite. Letting out a long sigh, she turned to him smiling brightly: "Thanks for respecting my star-brood. What time is it?"

"It's—a bit after 2100. That's EST, Nereid runs on that too."

"Not GTC?" That meant Galactic Time Convention. She knew the answer but was playfully probing his responses.

He stated professionally: "Galactic is Erthnocentric: GTC is the same as EST."

"For all planets everywhere? Why not a compromise?"

"What would you compromise *on*? No two planets have the same length day or year. On Erth, when international relations grew close, the lingua Franca came to be lingua Anglia, just because Vespuccia which spoke Anglian evolved into the center of international action. By the same token, EST is the tempus francum, using the incognito of GTC."

"All right. What's our ETA—EST and GTC?"

"Estimated time of arrival on Nereid is sixteen hundred hours tomorrow."

"About nineteen hours from now?"

"Approx."

"Maybe I should be sleepy. I suppose I should have asked about the bed arrangements."

"Tight but satisfactory. Touch that button there, your pneumatic chair becomes a horizontal cot and a little pillow inflates. Covers we don't need, we sleep in these nice warm space suits. Mind sleeping right next to me?"

"Do you snore?"

"Sporadically—I am told."

"That's the worst kind, but I can hack it. Be easy about me, if I snore it will be a nice soft steady susurrus. I thought space suits aboard ships had been out for centuries."

"Not aboard these little fellows. Stray meteors, you know. Not much hull protection, and nobody trusts the forcefield screening."

"Now he tells me. No, it's all right, I expected that. Do I dare assume that my suit can be complemented by a helmet from somewhere?"

"Didn't I tell you? That's right, I forgot, I'm drunk. Well, when air pressure drops below a critical level, your suit automatically grows a helmet right around your head. It makes it awkward when a meteor hits while kissing is going on."

"Luckily we won't be testing that. 'Night, Duke."

" 'Night, Claudine." Manipulating a rheostat, he dimmed the cabin lighting to near zero and tilted back his chair. She, doing the same, lay beside him, not a foot from him, gazing at the stars that shone through the cabin ceiling.

Silence.

"Duke—"

"Claudine?"

"What's the deal tomorrow, with Croyd?"

"He's interested in some current research of mine."

"Want to say what about?"

"That black-hole cluster around Vassili. Why would there be a cluster?"

She came up to a half-sitting position. "Tell me."

"That seat-tilt button is adjustable to the posture you want."

She played with it, made it obey her, pressed. "That might be investigation-pertinent. Is that why you wanted me to meet Croyd?"

"That idea came second. First-off, something you said this afternoon brought it home that you and he would enjoy the same kind of conversation."

"What did I say?"

"Something about another dimension."

"I did?"

"Croyd's an amazing guy. He uses one."

Silence. She hit the button and went down—Duke had been horizontal all the time. More silence.

"Duke—"

"Claudine?"

"Am I keeping you from going to sleep?"

"Who else is there?"

"Can you hack it?"

"I'm too drunk to notice."

"Tell me about Croyd."

"Inspector, don't you *know* all about him?"

"I've memorized our dossier and checked newskenners, if that's what you mean. Tell me about him."

"To use a word loosely, he's a phenomenon. He emerged out of nowhere a couple of decades ago and rose on sheer merit as a Galactic agent to become Assistant Internal Security Secretary—which includes external security. He's totally knowledgeable yet totally unassuming. He could break me with his hands."

"I too could break you with my hands. Tell me something special."

"Otherwise you'll break me with your hands? What will I be doing meanwhile, Claudine?"

"How's your karate, Doctor?"

"I can break you with my hands."

"This is beginning to sound like the titles in an old twentieth-century silent movie."

"Do you mean Milton Sills in *The Spoilers*, or Laurel and Hardy in *The Soilers*?"

"Tell me something special about Croyd."

"He can travel at will in space, time, or mind."

"Go *wawn!*"

"Time for beddy-bye, love. 'Night."

Silence. Then: "Duke—"

"Claudine?"

"I'm very sleepy, but—you won't be a creep?"

"If they aren't awake and sober enough to know what's going on, there isn't any challenge."

She smiled, satisfied, richly pleased. " 'Night, good Duke."

There was a thrill-bizarre dream of standing naked atop some sort of lofty platform rising out of ocean, watching a high-above small monster emerging from the black pupil of a skyfilling eye. Down toward her floated the creature, growing larger as it came, her sense being that the monster was drawn by her will. Gut-pleasingly the monstrous weirdity grew as it came, until face-to-face she knew it as . . . Klaus Heller . . . while the inward voice ejaculated: *yes! yes! yes!* . . . and Klaus clutched and shook her.

She awakened in semi-shock to comprehend that Duke was the shoulder-shaking demon, she saw his face confusedly through two panes of glassoid. He was saying firm and hard: "Wake up! Trouble! Red alert!" She sat up, her feet hitting the floor: "I'm awake. What?" "Meteor shower," he crisped; "we have about a thousand punctures, we're depressurized, we may have to abandon ship."

Now she was entirely with it. Touching her face, or trying to, she confirmed that her emergency helmet had materialized around her head. Duke was using some kind of a tool to seal punctures, but she heard no diminution of the multiple hissing which told her that their precious air-mix was being sucked out into space at least as fast as it was being manufactured.

He commanded: "Send a mayday on that iradio, beam it at Nereid, tell them we've had a shotgun blast of meteors and we can't make it for more than five hours on our suit-air. Coordinates:" he ran off three astral coordinate numbers, adding an EST-GTC clock-time which provided the fourth dimension.

The coordinates denoted location in the asteroid belt between Mars and Jupiter. Having flaked the distress call and started it on its Nereid way, she queried: "Why just to Nereid? Why not also to Erth which is closer?"

"You'll know. Just keep it on Nereid."

"Done. Can't we bail out and suit-jet somewhere?"

"You tell me where." He was hard at work, with no noticeable results. She could tell from his helmet-radio voice that he was talking through hard-clenched teeth, and with his permanent smile probably erased: "What I'm doing is a crock of nothing, I can't find and patch all the holes in the five hours of air that our suits provide, but what the hell, I may as well try—"

"You may as well also shut up. Talking uses air."

"Very good. Agreed." Silence.

The iradio kept on sending the flaked mayday. Accidents like this weren't common in scouters, this was just damned unlucky. She discovered how some air needed to be used: "Duke—"

"Mm?"

"Keep working. I just want to say that I like you. This could happen to anybody."

"I like you too. Thanks."

"I hope to be seeing you. Somewhere."

"On Nereid, probably."

"How?"

Pleasant nearby baritone: "Inspector St. Cyr, if you breathe a word about this rescue to anybody, I'll rip-up your job and use it for hull-hole stuffing."

The auburn-haired stranger made them clasp his waist and his wrists while he clasped theirs, and an untimeable period of disorientation followed, and then Claudine found herself in a new apartment with Duke and the stranger. "Make yourself at home here, Inspector," said the stranger. "Duke, let's get out of her boudoir." And the men departed.

Because the stranger had to be Croyd, this had to be Nereid, the seat of Galactic government. Not the fat and sluggish Nereid known to twentieth-century astronomers, but a later-discovered rock-shard no more than two hundred forty kilometers long by sixty-five in diameter, fairly whizzing around Neptune: she fairly demanded the Nereid-name, while the old sluggish one had been rechristened Maia.

Claudine was alone in luxury enhanced by the softened artificial gravity of eight-tenths G. How the rescue had been accomplished was a conundrum whose answer wouldn't appear until Croyd would choose to give it. This wasn't her first time of utter disorientation, but this time it did seem that she might be able to take a while for reorientation; and that was a pleasant change from prior such times when she'd had to make vital-or-lethal decisions in a hell of a hurry.

Hey, there was a bed! She sat upon it: a nice generous double bed, green-satin spreaded, with a semi-hard forcefield mattress. Her emergency helmet no longer head-swathed her, having automatically retracted when normal air had come. She gazed: all was perfectly realistic in a tastefully affluent style. Just above the bed was a squawk-box—good, it was two-way. Kneeling of the bed, she activated the box: "Anybody listening?"

Reply, probably voder: "Yes, Inspector?"

"State where I am."

"You are on Nereid, in the suite assigned to you. We have your two-suiter, you will find it on the luggage rack in your bathroom. Secretary Croyd requests that you finish your sleep here, and we will awaken you in time for you to dress and meet him and Dr. Murchison for cocktails at 1900. May I send up something to eat or drink?"

"Do you have Grandad 86?"

"I am sending a bottle, with a side decanter of distilled water and a thermal jug of chillballs. And two glasses, of course. The dumbwaiter is beside your bed to the right as you lie in it. And, oh, by the way—Secretary Croyd says to tell you, you're a welcome guest: take it easy. Anything else?"

"Not at the moment, thank you."

"Out." Disconnect.

A very slight sound to the right of the bed drew her attention: a little door had slid open, revealing Grandad with the promised trimmings. She chillballed, poured generously, and drank, eschewing water.

The space suit was bugging her: she doffed it laboriously; this left her in two-piece underwear. Pajamas in her bag in the bathroom? Hang up the gown for this evening?

The devil could hang up the gown, and who needs pajamas? Sliding raw under the covers, she gave up.

Part Three

WOMAN–PLANET IN TROUBLE

Iola, 25-26 November 2494

Of all the dreams in Claudine's long and superb dream-ing-experiences, her Nereid dreams were untouchably the most realistic, consecutive, and circumstantial.

The planet was strange to her. At first she seemed to be descending upon it from high aloft, drawn by some power below. It was a fair day, with only a few cirrus clouds drifting above this hemisphere. As she came in near enough so that the disk filled her visual field, almost all that she could see was water, broken most of the way up and down the center by a slender island archipelago that must extend many thousands of kilometers.

After that, while her viewpoint kept shifting and some-times simultaneously embraced several people inwardly and outwardly, the planet often felt as familiar to her as though she had dwelt here all her life and had never set foot on another planet or known another social system. From time to time, though, again it was a strange planet and a bizarre culture, with Erth-experience in the memory-background: not hers, not even female.

Just before the dreaming began, there was a little non-visual voice-prolog: *the* voice. *Inspector, perhaps by now you are ready to begin seeing what really happened, and to take it seriously.*

7.   PULL-DOWN

Attorney Luria Threll, on her weekly hitch at ocean-an-
chored Geek-Watch Three, rayscope-scanning the vicinity of
Black Hole Three which was regularly a Geek threat-point,
spotted an ant-size humanoid figure popping out of Hole
Three and careening through deep space toward Hole Four.
She alerted her station: "Geeks operating, stand by—" She
watched this figure sail at hyper-meteor velocity toward Hole
Four, vanish into Hole Four, than almost immediately pop
out again and head back toward Hole Three.

Intuitive-intellective Luria Threll now comprehended that
the figure was no Geek, that more likely this was an astronaut from unknown outer space being toyed with by
Geeks: they were great at cat-and-mouse games, and this
alien character had been caught in one. Uh-uh, none of *that!*
Her planet couldn't overcome Geek power, but powerless it
was not. She fired a tractor-beam at the hapless astronaut and
dragged the character out of the Geek nack-nock.

Pulling in this creature (who knew how alien?) was a little
tricky, because the planets Callas and Zanzodon were juxta-
posed on their orbits in that sector, and she had to maneuver
the astronaut past both in succession while keeping her away
from the sun. (No question whether the astronaut might not
be female had occurred to Luria.) Luckily inner Zinza and
outer Corla were far out of line. After many minutes of jock-
eying, Luria brought the astronaut to midair rest about seventy lanzas above the tower and checked the creature with
vanzigotics as well as she could through that amazing suit.

Thereby Luria discovered that she was a he; not only that,
but a weird mammal of an order different from the order of
her own human species, some kind of monstrous other-
worldly evolvement. Only, this monster must be intelligent,
because he wore a sophisticated space-suit and had gotten
himself into a black hole. She'd read enough science fiction to

79

be at home with the concept of evolutionary oddities beyond the holes and gas-clouds which guarded the Klarta system, oddities on planets out in the great and virtually unknown cosmos beyond Iola's enshrouded space-reach. She'd better reel in this monster with an open mind.

When he was in and on his back on her tower-floor, awed she surveyed the length and breadth of his suit. She knelt (still holding her gun, of course) and peered into the viewplate of his helmet. His face was much like that of any human male, Flarian or Geek, but—that superwoman body-size! It had to be that this male was from another star-system having a humanoid race. So they too were mammalian, so what? Many philosophers and science novelists tended to believe that all evolutionary lines independently converge on the mammalian humanoid, just because this formula is the best imaginable animal adaptation to any livable set of planetary conditions: erect biped stance for the long view, binocular vision for a fairly true view, eye-coordinated hands for manipulation, big brains for behavior modifiability, internal fertilization and incubation of eggs, milk for the next stage of human feeding, warm blood for fast reactions and survival under a wide range of thermal conditions, and so on . . . Should reptiles somewhere achieve highly intelligent dominance, they would have become warm-blooded humanoids: this Luria Threll tended to believe, discounting its threat to the amphibian and reptile-bypassing origin of her own human species. (Most people found reptiles repulsive; Luria rather liked them.)

Nevertheless, his maleness did upset her preconceptions. Males weren't *ever* so adventurous-competent—except, of course, in the case of the Geeks. And yet, clearly a Geek he wasn't, if only because he was far too big.

Years ago, Luria had thought to become an astronomer, until she found that the leisurely pace of astronomy bored her. Then she had turned to biology, but it had taken her away from space. Ultimately she had settled for law: its pace was swift, its complexity stimulating, and yet it allowed an energetic woman time for hobby-biology and astronomy— even now, when a state of war impelled her to put in one day weekly at Geek Watch while sacrificing endless earning hours doing things for the government. She didn't hate Geeks; she loved her land, and that was enough. But if you'd accused her of patriotism, she'd have laughed and spat in your eye—

then carefully wiped off your eye with a clean handkerchief, and kissed you.

She should remove the monster's helmet; but she saw the possibility that he might not be able to breathe Iola atmosphere. He was breathing now, in there, evidently having a self-contained airpack which might be nearly exhausted. She rechecked the vanzigotics: they showed his suit-air to be equal parts of nitrogen and oxygen; that was oxygen-richer than Iola atmosphere, but the same components. She felt fairly safe, now, in opening his helmet: if Iola-air should choke him, she'd call for an oxygen tank.

The alien helmet-locking devices presented some problems which she solved in minutes. When his head was bare, it seemed reasonably human, but with anomalies. There was a more strongly developed nose than she'd seen among Iola men, and stubbly facial hair. His mouth was narrow, little more than two vinchas wide at rest; even with their much smaller body sizes, Iola-male mouths averaged three vinchas, and Luria was considered an attractive woman with three and a half. She found more anomalies: an unusually pronounced chin, and eyes no more than three vinchas apart from pupil to pupil (hers were four vinchas). And yet, all-in-all, she couldn't call him ugly: some human races on Iola were differently different from Flarians like Luria, yet not unattractive to Flarians, although of course they were inferior.

His breathing in this less-oxygenated atmosphere was slightly faster and slightly deeper and yet not exactly labored, as though he were making the transition easily. She fisted her forehead: of course! in her own space-cruisings, the ship or suit atmosphere was over-oxygenated for fast energy; so with him, probably; Iola atmosphere for him might be just about normal. Then, as she grasped that the change of air was moving him toward consciousness, she shifted her gun to her dominant right hand and stood back a little. Geek or no Geek, alien or no alien, a very large non-docile mammalian male, interested in black holes and not merely in food or sex, and perhaps unacclimated to female mastery, was something unpredictable.

How much different she didn't know yet. But she comprehended the generic difference in facial features, and his huge size for a male—he was even larger than she, how much larger she wouldn't know until he would he extracted from his suit. And his voice, when he tried to initiate conversation by saying something like "Klows" (perhaps his name, or hello, or anything) was deeper than that of any male or female she'd ever known, and as resonant as that of any male crying his lusting cry. It gave her almost an erotic shiver which she quickly quelled by calling for her crew-chief and a doctor.

After briefly examining the recumbent monster, the doctor told Luria, "He seems all right, but I'd recommend hospital for observation. Concur?"

She responded, "Good. Please call Krazia Mujis at Gladowr General—"

"Krazia *Mujis?*"

"Never mind, I'll call her."

Thanking and disconnecting from her high-ranking doctor friend, Luria reported by phone to Geek-Watch Control center, then turned to stare at the monster, reflecting that if one had come, another might come. Her watch-time was nearly over; already her relief was at hand. She code-instructed the scanners to pull in any other humanoid figure who might emerge from Hole Three or Hole Four, and she gave her relief appropriate information.

While she supervised the crane-swinging of the monster aboard the ambulance truck, she was caught once again by his departing smile. The truck rose into air and whirred away.

Stripping, Luria dove off the high tower for a terminal ocean swim, returned for drying and dressing, and boarded a cross-water scudder for town. Her drinks and dinner in a good restaurant were leisurely-thoughtful. An alien entry—at *this* time of terminal planetary peril? There was temptation to go view the alien at the hospital; but it would be well into tomorrow morning before Mujis and her doctors would know much. So Luria tried to pass her evening concentrating on the case of a current client; but the black-hole alien kept distracting her self-discipline.

Suit-stretched in the truck-chopper ferrying him over ocean, Klaus Heller peered through the transparent hull back at the not-yet-distant ocean-spearing tower where that nice young earless humanoid (male? female?) had fish-landed him from on high. He saw a nude brown human figure poise itself on a tower-rail, frog-leap, swan-dive a good twenty meters, cleave ocean with minimal splash, surface a quarter-minute later, and fun-swim in broad circles with seal-velocity.

When the figure was too distant-small to be distinguished from ocean, he twisted his head and saw an island-city speeding toward him.

(It was still the day when he had hit the hole and had been yanked out again. And still for this planet, although Klaus didn't yet know this, it was Destruction Day minus five.)

8. INTERPLANETARY LINGUISTICS

Krazia Korli Mujis, Director of Gladowr General Hospital and also Director-General of World Medical Services, thoroughly comprehended the Iola-Godzha interplanetary confrontation, being a consulting member of the World Council. When she learned from her young friend Luria that an alien monster had been fished in from Black Hole Three, Mujis remembered starkly an almost-forgotten topic: the mayday signals which Iola had been cosmos-broadcasting at random until the iradio equipment had broken down almost thirty ten-day weeks ago. And now, an alien arrives? Delayed response from somewhere? Surely not an enemy, or the alien would not be alone; but if a friend, what could one alien do against Godzha? She alerted Chairwoman Alui of the World Council; and canceling all other obligations, Mujis paced.

When less than an hour later the patient came into her office, de-suited and escorted by two medics, he was ambulatory as hell. That sort of easy lope, on the part of a man just jerked out of black-hole nack-nock, lifted the brood of Krazia Mujis. Smiling, she demanded: "Now why would *you* have to be brought to a hospital?"

> After her awakening, Claudine would recognize
> that she had perfectly comprehended their alien
> language . . .

Heller spread hands, pointed to an ear, pointed to his extended tongue, spread hands, shook head, grinned.

Her smile in turn became a grin. She arose, clasped his hand (an arm-upraised clasp, as in Indian wrestling), and told the aides: "This is a bright one, maybe even an alien ambassador who naturally doesn't know our tongue. Put him in a private room with an easy chair, make it Nurse Lladyr's area; I'll be up directly." But when he had departed, she frowned: this language barrier could take many weeks to crack, and Iola *didn't have* weeks.

She came around 1800 hours to find Heller in hospital gown and bathrobe and slippers in the easy chair, with Nurse Lladyr fussing around him. At the door, Dr. Mujis first consulted with Kyria Lladyr, getting the patient's vital statistics; the trouble was, she didn't yet know what they *ought* to be.

Klaus meanwhile was examining these obviously medical people: a handsome pair of professionals, the younger breast-conspicuously female, the older voice-probably female, although both wore long pants, as had all the people he'd seen so far on this planet. Blonde-haired brown-skinned Kyria, whose hairdo concealed the presence or absence of ears, might be a supervisor. The doctor, possibly the hospital director, was nearly his own height, age apparently mid-fortics (if Erth-standards could apply), brown-skinned again, dark-haired, blue-eyed, round face wearing a habitual expression that seemed firm but not severe and (as he knew) able to smile (if here a smile was a smile), earless like the dark-haired young person who appeared to have rescued him from sky Ping-Pong. All of them had long legs, wide hips, wide shoulders, wide-apart eyes, wide mouths; but whereas the waists of this doctor and of his rescuer were slender, the waist of the nurse was thick: pregnant-thick?

Heller threw his well-honed language-apperception faculty into high gear. He had gone through Black Hell to get here; but before he could even understand their peril, there had to be communication between mutually unknown languages having unknown notations and unknown culture-symbolisms. Luckily these people were high-civilized; and if they had the scientific gadgetry to pull him in from a good three hundred A.U.'s out, then their language was based on a logic that an Erth-human steeped in science could arrive at understanding.

Semi-aware that she was dream-hovering, Claudine watched Heller effortlessly assuming leadership of the hospital director and the supervising nurse in this task-oriented mutual quest for common language. Heller was going for their Flarian, he was not attempting to teach them much Anglian. Engrossed in the process, the detective on Nereid was drawn fully back into the dream-as-reality. . . .

Aided by pencil and paper, within minutes he had their names, and they had his, and he had made a beginning at comprehending the phonetics of their carefully printed name-letters. He had distinguished between their word for *head* and their word for *self, yes,* and *no.* And that was enough foundation, he decided, for establishing something all-important before moving on with language.

Successively he sketched on memo sheets a series of figures. As Dr. Mujis watched the first one develop, she exclaimed to Kyria, "But that's the first mayday message that we broadcast!" and she stood quivering and worked her way behind his easy chair to look over his shoulder while he drew. He ripped off the first page bearing the first three pictures, handed it back to Mujis, and went rapidly on; alternately she studied the first drawings and his new drawings, murmuring "Yes! yes!"

When he had finished the last drawing—the galaxy, with a spot for Vassili or Klarta, a shaded area for the Interplanetary Union, and an arrowed star Sol, followed by the solar system with an arrowed spot for Nereid—Mujis breathed: "Kyria, that is the final message that we *received* from somewhere, just before our breakdown so we never could answer it—" Attentively the women watched for Heller's next move.

It was that he pointed to Erth and to Nereid saying "Klaus Heller. Klaus Heller." He hesitated, thinking, one hand raised signaling Mujis to wait; no, that seemed to suggest that Klaus was the Union boss—how to express *ambassador?* Ripping off the pad sheet and laying it in his lap, he sketched at one edge of a new page a human figure standing erect and pointing outward: this he labeled CROYD, and he several times repeated the name aloud, successively indicating figure and printing; whereafter, on the former drawings, he sweepingly finger-outlined the Interplanetary Union, saying again, "Croyd." Then, on this last piece of paper, he added a figure in a space-suit flying with repulsor drive from his shoulders—both Mujis and Lladyr giggled—directly in front of the pointing Croyd, as though going outward at Croyd's behest; pointing to the flyer, he asserted: "Klaus Heller."

"Yes!" Mujis exclaimed, coming around in front of him

with the other drawings and seating herself while Kyria
Lladyr stood watching. Mujis took the drawing of the galaxy;
she finger-swept the totality saying "galaxy" in Flaric; in
Flaric characters she labeled the Vassili-star KLARTA and
the fourth planet IOLA, saying the names while he repeated
him. Then she labeled the sixth planet GODZHA, saying it;
and she pointed to the picture of humanoid standing on supine humanoid, calling the victor "Godzha," calling the
victim "Iola." She pointed to Kyria and herself: "Iola"; and
she spread hands.

Nurse Lladyr answered an intercom buzz, then summoned
Mujis. Having listened, the doctor spoke rapidly; then she engaged Lladyr in conversation. Since they were standing, Heller stood also, understanding nothing but listening for
sounds. . . . Then Korla Mujis departed, leaving Klaus with
Kyria.

During the next few hours, Lladyr worked with Heller, or
was it rather vice versa? Language master in action! Around
his bed, he learned *bed, pillow, sheet, blanket,* and *bell* (for
the thumb-press signal). In the corridor, looking at the over-
hanging sign showing his room number, he got *number* and
three-four-nine; then, pointing to the number-badge on her
uniform, he read it correctly: "Three-nine."

Along the corridor came the food-cart. He learned *supper;*
then, mounting a chair to point to hours on a wall-clock, he
distinguished *breakfast* and *lunch,* and he generalized *food.*
Leaping down from the chair, he stood looking into his room,
frowning, and brought off his first Flaric sentence: "Klaus eat
supper three-four-nine, yes. Bed, no." He turned to her with
the interrogative hand-spread. She passed him, entered the
room, indicated his chair: "Chair?"

"Chair, yes," he affirmed, following her, seating himself;
"Klaus eat supper food, three-four-nine, bed no, chair yes."
And the aide came in with the tray.

"No!" sternly said Supervisor Lladyr. "Up!" she commanded, hand-drawing him to his feet. Puzzled, he queried:
"No eat? up?"

"Bathroom," she ordered, indicating an open room-corner
door. "Hands!" she pointed to his. "Wash!" and she went
through motions of washing her own hands and toweling
them.

"No!" he asserted.

"No?" she demanded. The food was now on the portatable.

Drawing himself erect, he stated with dignity: "Bathroom, yes. *One:* pssss. *Two:* wash hands." She pulled her head down in a blushing snicker as he marched into the bathroom.

During supper, there were words for dishes; and then, with astonishing dramatics, Heller began to go for relative and demonstrative pronouns and abstractions. As part of it, he established that she was a *glir* or nurse, that she was a *kra* or lady, that Mujis was a *krazia* or doctor; whereupon she learned that he too was a doctor, although (she surmised) not of medicine. Then, in the corridor at the desk, he learned *book*, and *word*, pried a dictionary out of them by specifying "Word book," and went back to bed for laborious word-study. And there were incidental courtesy-word learnings.

It was Sabbath on most of Iola including Gladowr, Sabbath being the last day in each ten-day week of which Iola had a neat forty annually. Luria Threll, off Geek-Watch duty until the day before next Sabbath and practicing law assiduously, found opportunity to drop in at the general hospital around 1000 hours. There she first hit-up Krazia Mujis who happened to be at her desk.

"Korli," exclaimed bursting-in Luria, "I had to come check up on the guy I pulled in yesterday. How is he?"

Mujis, who had slept five hours and would stay weary for another hour, looked up with a wan smile. "Until you see him, Luria, you won't believe."

"Tell me!" Luria urged, pulling up a chair to Korli's desk.

Well, it seemed that Kyria had worked with him on language until maybe 2130, then had left him in bed with a dictionary...

"A *dictionary?*"

He had slept soundly without medication. This morning they had brought him breakfast ot 0600 and had to awaken him for it; he had wolfed it down, full tray, despite what had to be alien food for him; then at 0800 they had taken him below for tests. As a result of notes left by Kyria, who was off duty today, he was being courteously treated and addressed as Krazia Heller...

"*Krazia* Heller?"

"Why not, Luria? He *is* an ambassador from outer space, come here to help us, though Goddess knows how he can."

"Holy *Harmnion*—"

"I haven't been able to raise Chairwoman Alui, but I left a message."

"How about his tests?"

"I think he's a super. . . . I started to say superwoman, but he's male. Well: if a normal woman rates physiologically and psychologically a hundred, and a normal male rates ninety, Heller rates a hundred eighty-eight—and that's only his average."

Brood. Both women knew that Heller's average was higher even than *their* averages.

Said Mujis: "They brought in another one last night."

"Male again?"

"Right. That must be *some* civilization."

"How is the new one?"

"Beat-up—but not all that bad, really."

"Have they met?"

"Not yet. Would you like to introduce them?"

"I'd *love* it, but—"

"Luria, why don't you go see Dr. Heller and get acquainted? You might even want to take him to noon chapel—"

"Is *he* one?"

"I don't know what he is, let's find out. He is talking Flaric rather well—"

"Talking *Flaric?*"

"Starting from nothing last night. We think he likes to be called Klaus. It's Room 349. You're on your own."

> Partial Claudine-rouse. If her series of dreams had meaningful continuity, would "the new one" turn-out to be Duke?
> Would it be *Murchison?*
> Relapse into the fullness of reality-dreaming . . .

Luria found Klaus in his chair working on the dictionary. She said at the door: "Hi, Klaus Heller, I'm Luria Threll." He sprang to his feet, smiling luminously; they squeezed four hands together, he exclaiming: "Hi, Luria Threll! *Again!*" and then he gazed into her face querying "*Kra* Threll?" "Right," she confirmed, "but please call me just Luria." Puzzled, he repeated "Right, but please call me just Luria—" and then his male smile broke open again: "Please call me just Klaus."

Although he didn't know it, the first three women he had

met here happened to be among a very few women on this planet who would meet a man open-mindedly and treat him as a potential equal.

The next thing he did astounded her. He pointed at the ceiling saying "Sky," then made his high-held hand go to-and-fro rhythmically like a ball in a game of nack-nock; after a few swings, he brought his hand down in a fast swoop and smacked it against his other hand at waist-level; then with one hand he pointed to himself while with the other he pointed to Luria, and a deep hearty laugh rippled out of his chest. She went into knee-weakening laughter; but as she came out of it, she saw that he had sobered. Again swinging his hand on high, he demanded: "What?"

She said, "Nack-nock."

He pressed: "Who nack-nock me?"

She said: "Geeks. Godzhalks."

He queried: "Godzalks? Godzha?" Slowly she nodded, marveling. Calling his fist "Godzha" and his other hand-palm "Iola," he slammed fist into palm, then looked his question.

She asked: "You learned all that just from the dictionary?"

He said soberly: "Dictionary help but hard. Have to think hard with dictionary. Learn better from listen talking."

Half an hour later, she said, "Come with me." He allowed her to escort him, her hand on his arm, down the corridor to a lift and up a floor and up another corridor. They entered a private room.

A pallid man lay there sleeping.

Duke Murchison it *was!*

"Good God," murmured Klaus in Anglian. "*Thank God*—"

After he had meditated a few moments over unconscious Duke, Luria inquired softly: "What did that mean?"

"What?"

"What you said." She imitated the sounds closely enough for him to understand the reference.

He frowned thinking. Then he said in Flaric "Good—" and he pointed upward and sank to his knees in a prayer-attitude, saying in Anglian "God." He looked up at her: "Thank—" and returned to prayer: "God."

Luria, an agnostic, nodded in full sympathy: if your agnosticism is human-sincere, you respect every sincere non-selfish belief. She murmured: "Good Mardis. Thank Mardis."

Mardis meant Goddess-of-goddesses; the tiny difference escaped Klaus, but when later he knew, he felt no problem.

Heavily he came to his feet. She invited, laying a hand on his arm: "Come away now. I want to take you to church."

"Church?"

"You will understand, Klaus, when you get there—I think."

As they departed Duke's room, he muttered in Anglian, not troubling to attempt translation: "Duke, my friend, whatever you may encounter here, control your impulses: for the love of God, don't blow my mission."

9. HUEENA

The hospital roof above the sixth floor was a vast garden. It was Heller's first venture out into daylight since his arrival, and this venturing would be many-ways memorable. He would learn that all seasons in this area of the planet were warm: on their scale which was practically identical with Celsius on Erth (logically and independently so, being based on the freezing and boiling points of distilled water), the mean annual Gladowr temperature was 21°, about like that of Houston, and the extreme variation was only six points either way. Today, with the planet's orbit slightly perturbed in the direction of Hole Four, but with Klarta's radiation obligingly flaring farther outbound toward the holes in compensation, the temp was slightly above the mean; and now, nearly at high noon with only a few white cloud-puffs, it was warmglorious.

Luria, who had been wearing a blouse and trousers, shed the blouse and laid it in a niche of the parapet; "Want to?" she asked Klaus, going behind him and taking his bathrobe lapels—she was nearly as tall as he. Obediently he let her shed him, and he took off also his pajama shirt. Many up here were bare to the waist; Luria, like most of these women, had firm delicate breast-suggestions that required no support (and yet, that Kyria had been full-breasted, and some of the women who still wore their upper garments looked fullbreasted).

As seen from this roof, everywhere the vistas teased the mind. Gladowr was a long narrow island, a piece of the long narrow quasi-continental archipelago which divided the seas of Iola almost from pole to pole. The island was maybe thirty kilometers from north to south (of which Gladowr City occupied the southern twenty) and seven from east to west (of which the city occupied all). It was a hog-back city with a central worn-down mountain ridge irregularly running its length; a potpourri of low buildings and high rises, a solid street-threaded mass of people-housing. The hospital stood on the eastern downslope of a very low central hill, edging a broad park and a deep ocean-bay cut into the eastern shore; from the western parapet he could see large segments of distant ocean beyond the ridge and the city, and from the eastern low-wall a full horizon of bay and ocean. Three distant off-archipelago islands were visible, and the tall profiles of two of them suggested sleeping volcanoes.

Freeing his eyes from the landscape and seascape, he leaned against the parapet looking inward at the rooftop scene. The hospital and its roof were long and relatively narrow, perhaps three hundred meters by fifty. Many hundreds of people were up here, a mix of patients and doctors and nurses and aides. The prevailing mood appeared to be *holiday*.

If there was an interplanetary attack-crisis, then precious little crisis feeling had been suggested by anything he had seen here since his initial pull-down. He wanted to ask Luria about that, but as yet he didn't have language for the question; by tomorrow, perhaps he would have it—and nothing about the scene suggested that he couldn't wait for tomorrow. Had it been a false alarm? Had he braved a black hole for a lark?

He began to notice that there were generally two clusters of people, the larger cluster at this end of the roof, the smaller at the far end. Presently a subtle fact came through to him: among those who stood by the far-end parapet, smaller proportions of their bodies rose above it; the parapet was waist-high for him and floating-rib high for Gelia and most of this end's people; whereas at the far end, no more than the heads and shoulders rose above it. Some kind of tall-short class or caste dichotomy? At this end, all the talls about whom he could make a sex-decision were women; then were the shorts men? And if they stayed segregated, what was Klaus doing with the women?

With some difficulty, he elicited from Luria (who had been watching him continually) that in fact their large tall-cluster *was* women while the distant short-cluster *was* men. She helped the explanation by producing a pencil and memo pad, from the pocket of her blouse in the parapet-niche, and sketching two stick figures, tall and short. Beneath the short one she drew what had to be a wiggle-tailed sperm, below the tall one a dot-centered circle which must mean egg; and she spelled it out verbally: "Tall, woman, female, eggs; short, man, male, sperms."

He said: "Yes. Understood now. Luria—you not talk little like that. Talk like you talk always." And when she began to laugh: "What that?" She corrected him, giggling: "What *is* that. That is laughter, Klaus. Because what you said is funny."

He, smiling: "Now I say better, not talk funny. I—*learn*—learn good from talk like *you* talk. What that? what *is* that?" Now he was pointing at a roof-pavilion at this end, a pavilion with a permanent metallic overhead shelter; at the far end was a similar structure near which the men were clustering while the women were gathering around this one.

She explained: "That is a chapel. For praying" (she made a prayer sign). "This one is for women. Down there is another chapel—for men."

Time for a crucial question. "I go down there, then? With the men?"

"No no. You stay here. With us talls."

"Why?"

"Because you are tall, you are a krazia, you are more like us women."

"This I not understand. We is tall, they is short, so what? I is man, I is male, I have sperms."

Luria, smiling most broadly: "Believe me, Klaus, you are more like us women—this way" (holding a hand high) "and up here" (tapping her forehead).

A nearby chime sounded, and far down-roof another. "Chapel time," asserted Luria. The women and men were going to their respective chapels; Klaus was forming a hypothesis. Luria, taking his arm, waited until most of the women had entered, then drew him in after. As a matter of discretion, she stood with him near the back (there were no seats): even if he had been wearing his bathrobe or his shirt, his stature and his ears would have drawn attention; and now, in addition, here was his bare hairy man-chest.

The chapel floor was circularly down-terraced to a circular arena of water, perhaps ten meters in diameter, out of whose center rose a three-meter island daïs, doubtless a chancel; and an open circle in the roof warmed moat and chancel with bright sunlight. Centered on the chancel was a sort of drum-stool; there was no other furniture. Klaus listened to the prevailing silence.

A naked silver-tiara'd blonde-haired brown-bodied priestess, slim-breasted like most of the women here, rose out of the water and swam the circumference of the moat, the liquid grace of her froglike stroke merging with the water. At her entry, all knelt, Luria and Klaus among them. The priestess came out of the water onto the chancel without hand-touching the chancel-floor, as a dolphin might do. Dripping, she stood with upraised arms on the chancel drum stool, and what her melodious contralto emitted seemed not so much an exhortation as a ritual prayer; she paused at intervals, and the communicants took it up with words which clearly were rote—no books were in evidence. (Luria kept her head bowed but did not participate.) Now the priestess frequently broke into chant-song sometimes quite complex; and the communicants came in at intervals while the priestess full-arm conducted their chant; the effect grew insidiously hypnotic. . . .

The priestess cut it off, and went into loud exhortation while Heller strove to distinguish words. As her pleading continued, one woman, then a second, then a third stood and stripped; and with bowed heads they descended to water's edge. "Yahaël!" high-cried the priestess; and all the communicants echoed "Yahaël!" The priestess descended from the drum stool, and at her motion the communicants resumed their feet most eagerly, peering down at the three who had come forward.

Luria whispered, "This is the high point, it is called *hueena*. Watch closely, Klaus, *closely*."

The three women knelt with their knees at the edge of the moat. When the priestess pointed, uttering a ritual command, one of the women went into a crouch and twanged into the air; she twisted in midair, head-arrowed into the moat, dolphin-leaped onto the chancel standing, mounted the drum stool, and held her streaming face upward and her hands and arms outward-upward toward the sunlight. Spontaneously without leadership the worshipers went into a loud litany not routine but highly aroused. Below the woman, facing the woman, the priestess knelt and with folded hands supplicated heaven.

The woman vanished.

Klaus peered at the vacated drum stool: nothing. A magician's mechanical trick? He turned to Luria, who was watching him; gravely she nodded and pointed him back to the chancel.

The woman reappeared as instantaneously as she had disappeared, having been invisible during several minutes. She seemed about to swoon; the priestess assisted her down; she squatted at chancel-edge, recovering, watching the stool. Now *how...*

A second woman stood exultant on the stool. And *she* vanished; he timed her period of evanishment at exactly three minutes. Returned, though, she swooned altogether; the priestess had to catch her as she fell, laying her supine on the chancel floor.

The third woman did best: after the vanishing and unvanishing, she stepped down and with dignity dove into the water, emerged on hither side, went to her place, and knelt nude facing the chancel, to pray and to dry before resuming her trousers.

Priestess and communicants entered into a final climactic chant-chorale, during which kneeling Klaus kept his head bowed in what appeared reverence but was in fact conjectural thinking. Luria whispered toward the end of it: "We'll sneak out now, so you can see the outdoor finale."

She took him to a point halfway between chapel and eastern oceanside parapet, and stopped him as the chanting behind them terminated. Came the joyous priestess-voice: "It is time for the holy swimming! But be realistic about your individual strength, you hospital patients! Those who *can* safely dare the parapet, them the goddess blesses! Those who should descend first to ground-level, or who should be content with paddling in the holy moat, or who should not yet be swimming again at all—them too the goddess equally blesses! All of you are blessed! Go with the goddess!"

Some words he understood; the other sounds he remembered and translated later; but the action-meaning came immediately clear. A crowd-shrieking capped the utterance, and happy squealing screaming women (echoed far downroof by happy squealing screaming men) poured out of the chapel toward oceanside, shedding garments en route, jumping naked to parapet-top, frog-leaping off! Klaus ran to the parapet and peered downward: women were midair-streaming into far-below ocean; from the other roof-end there were men downstreaming.

To Luria beside him, he blurted in Anglian: "My God, it must be a thirty-meter drop!"

She in Flaric: "I beg your pardon?"

"So far down—"

"Klaus cannot do it?"

"I know; Luria *can* do it."

Those who had dived were surfacing and swimming powerfully, their pleasure-cries from far below were calling to him. It was thrillingly alluring, but his loftiest prior dive had been only half as high—except, hadn't he just hurtled thirty thousand kilometers down into mercury-viscosity? But he'd been formidably suit-protected, although the gravity there had been four million times the gravity here . . .

He began to unfasten his pajama pants, but Luria's hand on his hand restrained him: cool she warned, "Don't reveal your sex here where the women can see you, come over there where we'll be alone." Leading him to a midroof point, she shed and bade him shed, remarking: "No women or men swimming below here, and the water-depth is five times your height. I'll go first, and then I will look up: if you're coming, wave a hand; if you decide no, wave both hands."

Springing to parapet-top, she crouched, frog-catapulted twice her own height into air, swan-fell. Halfway down, it came over her that his different species might find such a dive perilous or fatal; concerned, she twisted her head to look upward; he was parapet-standing, one arm waving; she straightened for her own water entry, then surfaced immediately and looked.

He was halfway down, looking good; but just above water he lost balance and his leg-backs whacked the surface going under. Terrified, she dove after him: he was back-floating four meters under; frogging over to him, she clasped him to bring him up; he winked at her, grinning, then brought *her* up.

Surfaced, he made a hideous face. "Oo! Pain!"

She sang-out laughter. "Chase me and forget it!" She boiled away; he poured on freestyle speed, but she was widening the distance. Giving up, he back-floated while she languidly breast-stroked back to him. As she came head-to-head close, gravely he greeted her with a high-arched, accurately face-aimed waterspout.

And then he seized her shoulders and demanded as they trod water: "Luria—*hueena*! how?"

She gazed at him, trying to formulate some kind of reply, distracted by the male grip of his hands.

There came a distant rumbling out seaward. They turned to look: one of the volcanic islands emitted a steam-spume. Then it quieted . . .

Said Luria: "That will be the manner of our death."

Part Four

A PEGASOS NAMED GROYD

Nereid, 6 July 2495

10. NEREID HOSPITALITY

When Claudine proceeded by voder directions through corridors to the rendezvous and entered the reception room of Secretary Croyd's apartment, Duke Murchison was there with the auburn-haired stranger who had somehow pulled them out of interplanetary space. "Claudine!" exclaimed Duke, spreading his arms; she moved smiling toward him, and he met her halfway, and they embraced (although she felt somewhat diffident about the small intimacy, because of doubts irrationally raised by the dream).

They broke quickly, and Duke gestured toward the stranger: "Inspector St. Cyr—Secretary Croyd." This Croyd was as tall as Murchison; he had exceptionally blue eyes in a lean face with high cheekbones; he seemed to be in his mid-thirties; he was smiling now at Claudine, and he quickly took her hand as counter-smiling she extended it. "Thank God you're on time," he commented, "because we're overdue to start drinking. What's yours? Liquor, wine, soda pop——"

Claudine was enchanted! "Your Grandad was great—but right now, how's your Scotch and water? Maybe three and two?"

"Same," said Duke. Croyd went behind a semicircular bar at the side of his salon and mixed three Johnny Walker Blacks with water and lots of chillballs in short glasses. Meanwhile Claudine and Duke moved to the bar so that Croyd wouldn't have to bring the glasses over; across the bar the three touched glasses and sipped reverently. "Not Chivas Regal," Croyd remarked, "but it fits my taste better—how about you, Inspector? I can make you a Chivas Regal instead, and drink your Johnny Walker."

"He never gets drunk," Duke explained. "His system promptly reprocesses alcohol into glucose which he fat-stores before it hits his liver, and then he works off the fat."

"Every Scotch," Claudine declared, "is different from all

101

others, Mr. Secretary. I order Scotch or Bourbon by name to fit my mood at the moment, and this is what this drink is doing now. Gosh, am I comfy—and I thought I'd be scared, with you! How did you pull off that rescue?"

Again Duke helped. "Call it a sort of Tarzan operation. He invades a realm which he calls Antan, which means remote past, and he swings from biofilament to biofilament until he finds ours, and then he runs them forward in time until he comes to us in deep space distress. Holding on to us, he reverses the process. And damn it, Croyd, I haven't *yet* figured out the mathematics—"

That, Claudine reflected, would be a dandy cheating way to solve a murder mystery. But Croyd interjected: "Forget math for now. Inspector, are you maybe the St. Cyr who—" And he referred to several of her most difficult cases. She pleaded guilty, observing however that the most recent he'd mentioned had been fifteen years ago. He demanded: "So what have you done for us lately?" She counterthrust: "Maybe I'm here in the hope of doing something for you lately."

Coming around from behind the bar, Croyd proposed: "Duke, as a crass change of subject, let's give Inspector St. Cyr the grand tour of these apartments. Inspector, please feel comfortable with us two men."

By the time the tour was done, it was Claudine and Duke and Croyd—it seemed that he had no other name. She couldn't imagine a more democratically friendly Galactic minister; and yet he was effectively the fifth most powerful person in the galaxy, and he was known to be vanadium-hard when the situation called for it. And at such a tender age! In his middle thirties? That had to be wrong, because of his twenty-year flitting history as a Galactic agent. He was unintentionally compelling her attention far more than Duke was, and she felt a bit guilty about it; but turning occasionally toward Duke to ameliorate this, she sensed in Duke nothing but amused approval, as though the astronomer liked Croyd and comprehended that this unusual man would always and inevitably draw prime attention. It gave her a new appreciation of Duke.

Their dinner place was in a compact glass bubble higher than most turrets on Nereid. The little asteroid offered horizons so nearby that from this tower they could see stars in every direction including below the horizontal; and the stars

were spaceship-brilliant because Nereid had no atmosphere, it
was a space rock enslaved by but not surrendering to Neptune. Above one horizon a little bit of the Neptune-disk
glowed upon them: other than two little table-candles, its reflected light together with starlight was all the light they had.

Over a profusion of magnificent food, served by garçon-
costumed androids, the dinner conversation ranged the
heights and depths and breadths of galactic culture: from
Michelangelo through Rodin to quasi-African sculpture of the
planet Wambo; from Aristotle through Hobbes and Locke
and Whitehead and Nike Pan to the ultra-modern feudal
scholar Volumina of the planet Keris; from Aristophanes
through Shakespeare and Racine and Shaw and O'Neill and
Kedostris to Glamis and Merganthu of the planets Llana and
Leikpritz.

It ended on a mighty thickness of apple pie with a sugared
crust, accompanied by rat cheese and Alexanders. Claudine,
who had eaten all of everything and wine-washed it generously down, was sure that she should be bloated and stoned;
instead, she was in all ways comfortable.

The men smoked cigars, ignoring her by her own request,
talking intently between themselves over brandy in a star-
washed salon. The brandy was delicately laced with a taste-
less anti-intoxicant. She leaned back in content, sipping,
savoring the good rich cigar smoke, listening.

Murchison was deep into celestial mechanics, occasionally
utilizing a pencil and memo pad thoughtfully provided by
Croyd on a side table; Croyd listened frowning, sometimes in-
terjecting a question or a contribution. This chief among
those who governed the security of the galaxy, she reflected,
was profound in art and literature, able to cope with the
space-math of Murchison, one who somehow commanded
personal access to spacetime, yet easy and unassuming.

While they weren't talking much non-technical Anglian, a
few of the phrases in calculus arrived at suggesting to her the
coordinates of the star called Vassili, and opening eyes she
watched and listened with special acuteness. Presently Croyd
inquired: "But what about that peculiar arrangement of black
holes around M-8731?"

The number hooked her; closing eyes again, she let it
welter in free association, hoping that it would find its own
grounding. In the background of M-8731 was floating an-

other faraway wandering number: 4. Sense of wrong but with a feeling of warmth.

Her eyes came open. The men were looking at her; and Duke queried, "Claudine—something?"

She leaned toward them: "M-8731—would that be the Messier number of Vassili?"

"Right."

"Then could 8731 have a habitable planet—and might it be the fourth planet?"

"Now whence," Croyd demanded, "did you come up with that?"

Her mental state was weird. Because possibly her aperçu could have merely surfaced out of free hintermind association from previously uncovered material: the black holes of Vassili into one of which Heller had leaped, the now-learned Messier number of Vassili, and the appending of the digit 4 in the Heller dreamings. But on the other hand, in last night's dream, Iola was the fourth planet of Klarta. Was it merely that her hintermind process had given form to the dream? Or . . . or what?

She restricted herself to explaining: "I've been monitoring the posthumous dreaming of Klaus Heller. Every dream so far has been tagged with a number: 87314. I'm just realizing that this could mean a planet: Vassili Four."

Long silence: "You have a theory, Claudine. I want to hear it. I knew Klaus well—and Duke knew him even better, he was a member of the Heller black hole expedition."

Good God, *another* dream-confirmation!

She looked reproachfully at Duke; he averted his eyes, looking reproachfully at Croyd—who raised an admonitory finger: "Duke, just among us three, you have to drop the incog. Claudine is Galactic Police—one of *my* people."

Frowning heavily, Duke spread hands.

Now Claudine was beaming upon him. "Duke, you're *involved!* You couldn't bring yourself to confess it to me—but you brought me here for Croyd to confess you to me! Beautiful Freudian dodge, beautiful—" She whirled on Croyd: "So *how* is he involved?"

"Not in any criminal way," Croyd asserted. "I sent him with Klaus to Vassili as crew astronomer, that's all. He insisted on going incognito as Dr. Duke."

Injected Duke, almost surly: "Ship-Captain Diekoff was brother to my estranged wife. He and I hadn't previously met, and I felt—well—"

"Comprehensible, Monsieur," Claudine assured him. "Croyd, please tell me about that adventure."

"Tell me your theory first."

"Adventure first."

"Theory first."

"You must know the old joke about the returning soldier. But admit that I need the adventure to round off my theory."

"Admit that the sporting thing is to state your theory before learning about the adventure."

She smiled: "All right, you're the big boss. But this will be perfectly awful."

Concisely she summarized the evidence thus far adduced: in hard fact, it amounted only to the seventy-five-degree convergence of the wounds in both cases, plus the suggestion that an employee of Aerodynamics was a raygun expert and had hated Heller. But there were the difficulties of the invisibility of the assailant and the impossible wounds. "It was unerthly, really; and the same angle on the two shots suggested a religious involvement. But I had to—*have* to—eliminate first the possibility of *something Erth-natural*."

She went into Erth-natural possibilities. A business enemy, Werner Voelker or another; but the problem of invisibility intruded. A disgruntled inamorata such as Clara Wilson maybe; but again, the invisibility problem. Add to that the seventy-five-degree wounds which no known raygun could inflict. "Incidentally, I combed the premises, and so did another detective, and we found no way for there to have been a planted weapon fired by remote control."

Persistently she was keeping her dreamings out of the discussion. *Hueena* was an invisibility, perhaps naturally induced, and with a religious implication; but her dream had not revealed its method, and *hueena* could easily have been back-mind dreamwork arising out of her criminal preoccupation with invisibility.

Aloud, she followed now with evidence leading in directions other than Erth-natural: Heller's trips into deep space—most recently, to the vicinity of Vassili. The webbed fingers and earlessness of the people in Heller's dreams, along with the verified similarities of dead Kyria Heller (and of course, in her own dream last night, these identities could have been merely reminiscent—*had* to be so, in fact). The Klaus-dream about jumping into a black hole. The weird invisibility, the impossible raygun angle. And now, the dream-label 87314 which accorded with the current conversation about Vassili M-8731.

(When the Kyria-corpse had come into it, why had Duke quietly arisen and gone to the bar where he was now blundering about the business of making a drink?)

"All right," she summarized. "That sets my Erth-*un*natural theory, with all its weirdness." What she was about to assert had been formulated quite apart from last night's dream, hadn't it? "That Heller on this expedition reached the planet Vassili Four, and there he encountered amphibious humanoids, one being Kyria. That somehow he and Kyria incurred the wrath of these humanoids. That he and Kyria fled, and he brought her back to Erth with him, took her into his home as his younger sister, and resigned from his corporation to minimize personal questions and for some other reason unknown. And that at least one envoy from Vassili followed him to Erth, somehow assumed invisibility, and killed both of them with a bizarre raygun."

She spread hands. "Croyd, you can appreciate my confusion when I contemplate putting enough evidence into this sort of theory to satisfy a court." Then, looking at Duke who was returning slowly with a new drink for himself but none for them: "And now, knowing that *he* accompanied the Heller expedition, can you imagine how I yearn for more words from Dr. Murchison?"

Slumping into his chair, Duke drank deeply, then shook his head, staring at the floor. They waited. He said then to the floor: "Mr. Secretary, you have Dr. Heller's report of the expedition and my report of the astronomical aspects. I was not authorized to jump with Dr. Heller, and so I really have nothing to add. I'm—terribly weary now, I've been working hard—"

Croyd suggested gently: "Go get some sleep, Duke."

When Duke had departed, clutching his drink, Croyd beamed upon her: "Are you likewise pooped, Claudine, I hope not?"

"Not too pooped for one beer and a story from you."

"What sort of story?" He was going to the bar.

"You know." She was joining him.

He—amid business of cold plastic bottle opening, pouring, handing, sipping, opposite-side bar-leaning—briefed the background for the expedition and the summons to Heller.

11. HELLER AND CROYD

One of Croyd's early projects for security in 2493 had been to undertake a survey of possibly planet-apparenting stars in the galaxy which were not included in the Interplanetary Union. A rather electrifying system of phenomena was presented by a star named Vassili, M-8731, whose linear distance was close to a thousand light-years from Erth. Vassili seemed to be a large G-type yellow star which might well have a life-supporting planet for all anybody could tell, but whose very stellar nature was obscured from even I-ray observation by more than one black hole and a plethora of seething gas-clouds. Vassili was marked as a prime target for investigation.

Claudine interjected, thinking about a dream: "Might Vassili be called also Klarta?"

"That is correct. Again, how would you know that?"

She shivered. "Go on, and please call it Klarta."

There was a piquant complication: a planet of Klarta had iradio, and this planet appeared to be in distress from some alien source. It was projecting mayday signals randomly into space.

"Randomly?"

Croyd, smiling appreciatively at his detective-subordinate, explained how he knew the signals were broadcast at random. I-rays being directional, Croyd was able to establish the randomness by directing ships in widely dispersed galactic segments to sweep their areas and report back. Any single receiver would catch the signals up to four times, whereafter no more signals there; but then another receiver far distant would make a pickup. Triangulation established the source as probably Vassili—or Klarta; distortion patterns corresponded with interruptive activity in the gas clouds between the black holes around Klarta; and sectors where there was no reception were evidently shadow-zones from the holes.

That they were mayday signals was evident from the pip-pattern. It was arranged as irregular on-off bits in lines demarcated by punctuating buzzes. These, projected on a screen by a scanning neutrino gun, presented a series of three pictures: a humanoid figure standing erect, then a second man-like figure descending upon the first from above, finally the first figure prone while the second stood atop him/her . . .

Rigid Claudine interrupted: "Croyd, can you draw those pictures from memory?"

He obliged, using Duke's memo pad. She studied them; her teeth almost chattered. He watched, sensitively aware of her disturbance.

She looked up. "There will be more pictures—no?"

"Yes. Tell me."

"Not yet. Keep on with the story as you were telling it."

Well, Croyd had found all this important for reasons practical as well as scientific. Every inhabited planet was a potential member of the Interplanetary Union, and one advanced enough to have iradio was a high-potential member—or enemy. He decided to try responding; although in punching a transmission through incandescent gas storms between black holes at such a distance, he would have more difficulty getting in than the distressed planet was having getting out.

In similar iradio signals arrangeable into a single picture, he projected on the left their Picture Two (humanoid descending on humanoid, suggesting attack), and on the right their Picture Three (humanoid standing on humanoid, suggesting completed conquest), and underneath an arrowhead oscillating from one to the other, suggesting a question as to which state of affairs was actual. (Arrowheads are fairly sure to be part of the protohistory of any civilization.) In an immediately following transmission, he tried to establish an interrogative sign for future use: only the oscillating arrowhead showed, and beneath it a large question mark; and then the arrowhead vanished, leaving the question mark.

Next day came a reply from Klarta beamed directly at Nereid: the original Pictures Two and Three, *attack* and *conquest*, with an arrowhead fixed beneath *attack*. (As yet, evidently, no conquest, only threat.) This was followed by. . . .

"Hold," commanded Claudine. "Let me make a few sketches first." She spent a few minutes drawing rapidly;

then, without showing him her pictures, she directed, "Go ahead with the following transmissions."

That next Klarta transmission was a crude image of the Sol Galaxy spiral, with a prominent spot arrow-marked in approximately Klarta's position. Now came another picture: a central six-pointed star, obviously Klarta, surrounded by six orbital rings, with a planet-spot on the fourth ring marked by a heavy bold arrowhead, and with a planet-spot on the sixth or outmost ring from which an arrow pointed inward toward the fourth planet. One inference: the fourth planet was transmitting, and was under attack from the sixth planet. Their last picture consisted of one large question mark, possibly meaning "Can you do anything?" but implying also that the senders understood Erth's interrogative symbol.

Croyd responded immediately with three pictures: (1) the galaxy, showing a spot for Klarta, spots in a shaded area for the stars forming the Interplanetary Union, and an arrow pointing to Sol; (2) a simplified solar system with nine orbits around the central star, a ringed spot on Orbit Three for Erth, and a large spot on Orbit Eight for Neptune with a small neighboring arrowhead spot for Nereid; (3) a question mark—"Your response?"

None had come.

Conquest completed, ending transmission? Apparatus conked out?

Now Croyd inquired of Claudine, "Care to show me your drawings?"

She surrendered them. She had approximately predicted every one of the following transmissions both ways.

Alertly he looked up. "Your comments?"

"None yet," faintly she told him. "Please continue the story."

After the communications cut-off, Croyd took new action. He sent a series of automated probes from Natron which was the Interplanetary Union star nearest to Klarta although some 490 light-years from Klarta. These probes were, of course, designed and built by Heller's Aerospace Dynamics, Natron Division; and by virtue of current space-propulsion and relativity-evasion techniques, they were able to reach the vicinity of Klarta within days and report back by iradio almost instantaneously.

The first probe tried to penetrate gas clouds between two

of the black holes; turbulence swept it into a black hole. The second tried the same approach between another pair of holes; like the first, it was engulfed. Croyd, communicating directly with Heller by invisiradio from Nereid, worked out a broad sketch for a third probe which would deliberately punch itself into a black hole and then would use sophisticated techniques to get itself ejected toward Klarta; this was designed and built in three months cold, and was launched from Natron a month later. It got into a hole, all right—small wonder!—but it never emerged.

That was when Croyd send for Heller.

It was January 2494. Croyd and Heller, on Nereid, analyzed a tri-d animated color film which illustrated the recently published Murchison theory of black holes. Then Croyd showed animations of the third probe, giving closest attention to its wiring and programming as these were related to the Murchison theory. This film ended with a speculative animation showing the conjectured misfortunes of such a probe within a black hole, nothing definite being known since there had been no escape and no communications feedback.

Croyd told Heller: "I believe that with suitable equipment, a suitably trained brained human might well deploy itself within a hole more opportunistically than any automated probe can do—deploy itself so well as to escape from the hole and report. Or, of course, the human might well be trapped in there forever. But reflect that nothing seems able to penetrate that inter-hole membrane. The try tempts me personally, but current events are saying no to me."

Responded Heller, "I have the ship to take a crew there and scout a hole close in, within freefall minutes or even seconds of the event horizon. But I see four major survival problems: radiation including heat, gravity acceleration, internal spin-acceleration, and the probable internal density of a so-called hole. No, excuse me, I also see a fifth: acceleration energy to escape the black hole once the fellow was in."

"Then let's take those five one-by-one. Go ahead, dream aloud."

"I'd like to consider gravity acceleration first," Heller proposed. "As a secondary matter, this is known to create tidal action near the hole which would stretch the astronaut vertically while compressing him laterally; but suitable suit protection might take care of that. However, gravitational force at

the surface of a hole having the mass of ten suns would be of
the order of three or four million Erth-G. This would yank
the astronaut into the hole at light velocity; and if nothing
were to slow him, he would reach hole-center in less than
one-tenth millisecond. One: how could he sustain a fall at
that kind of acceleration, when the best-trained astronaut I
know can handle no more than ten G without blacking out?
And, two, even if that problem be somehow overcome, how
can he make any maneuver-decisions in less than the snap of
a synapse?"

"All points well taken, Klaus. Go on with your thoughts."

"Well. Take resistance to the acceleration. We can't depend
on antigrav, because there isn't any fuel, a black hole isn't
raw space. We could have the suit generate an inertial shield
of something like a hundred to one, but that's about the limit
for any suit that I can imagine short of a scouter. Can't we
use a scouter, Croyd?"

"A man maneuvering a scouter isn't the same as a man
maneuvering himself in a suit. He needs to *feel* that he is *he
alone* in the hole."

"All right, then: a souped-up suit. But even with a hundred
to one inertial shielding, still we have reduced the force by
only a hundred to one; and that leaves an impossible experience of forty thousand Erth-G raw, hitting a man who can
handle only ten. Why can't you try punching into the hole
with a battleship?"

"Candidly, cost—in a lost ship, and more, a lost crew—until we know more."

"Okay, accepted: one man is a cheaper loss. But please notice that the acceleration problem remains impossible, and we
haven't even looked at the problem of perceptual reaction to
an entry started-and-completed in less than a ten-thousandth
of a second."

"What if you were to speed-up the perceptual processes of
all body and brain cells by a factor of, say, a hundred thousand?"

"Can that be done?"

"We've tried it experimentally, Klaus, and with success.
But there's a time limit: that full metabolic acceleration will
burn out the brain if maintained for more than eight seconds
at a time, and eight seconds would age you nine days. However, acceleration can be turned off and on, or diminished, to
stretch-out the limit."

"Well!"

"It would mean, Klaus, that from hole-entry to center, even if the hole were a vacuum which it isn't, the time would *seem* to be a full seven seconds, allowing time for action-decisions. But there's a dandy secondary effect. It appears that a body speeded-up by a factor of a hundred thousand is thereby giving itself an inbuilt 50,000:1 inertial shield. That reduces your four million G gravitation force to eighty G immediately. Now if you factor-in a suit-shield of a hundred to one—"

"It would mean only eight-tenths G apparent gravity, and for a ten-G man it doesn't have to be that easy-low! Croyd, with that kind of speed-up, we could bring the shield down to maybe fifty to one, and a ten-G man could handle the resulting four G without trouble, and it would lighten the suit!"

"Exactly. We'll do it. So that's solved. What was your next problem?"

"Hole density—hitting the surface of a hole having density several times that of iron, and hitting it at three or four hundred kilometers per second. Einstein to the contrary notwithstanding, the jumper's mass would *not* be infinite. Quick squash, Croyd?"

"Except that the Murchison calculations find this density to be mostly molecules in a fluid state, Klaus. A better comparison is: about the density of mercury."

"But that's more than fourteen times the density of water! And you know how it feels when you hit water in a high dive—"

"—at low velocity, Klaus: only about four meters per second. The astronaut would be hitting mercury, nearly fifteen times as dense, at a velocity about three hundred fifty million times greater. He'd penetrate."

"So that's done."

"It seems so, Klaus. Next problem?"

"Radiation including heat: give me Murchison's figures, and I can make the suit. Internal spin-acceleration: that's one which the astronaut's brain will have to meet and cope with. I think we may be clear on all but my fifth problem."

"Which was?"

"Say the astronaut gets into the hole relatively undamaged. Say he cheeses down through the mercury, slowing all the way, until he reaches hole-center. By that time his velocity is enormously reduced by friction, for practical purposes we'll say almost to zero. Now: from that position he has to accelerate enough in thirty kilometers of outgoing hole-radius to be considerably exceeding light-velocity by the time he reaches hole-surface again, otherwise he'll never get away. He would have to reach in thirty kilometers, fighting gravity and mercury-friction all the way, a surface velocity of—say—six hundred thousand kilometers per second, almost double his entrance velocity. And that would require a G-force around sixteen million. With the inertial corrections, the astronaut can handle the six-plus apparent G, with difficulty but he can do it; only—with repulsor-power negated by the hole-mass, how does he *attain* that thrust?"

Croyd said slowly: "Now you know what kind of self-contained power-pack you are going to have to build into that suit."

"And that is going to be *some* suit!"

"Yo."

Klaus inhaled, and exhaled, and asserted: "The way this has worked out, the highest apparent G the astronaut will have to handle is a mere 6.4 while escaping. Well: even at my age, I can handle seven. and *I want this mission!*"

12. CONCERNING VERIDICAL DREAMS AND MURCHISON IMPULSES

"Now," Croyd added to Claudine—they were back in chairs with more beer—"about the aftermath.

"Heller entered the black hole late in November of last year. A bit later, he got through to me by iradio from Klarta Four, which, incidentally, calls itself Iola. He sketched the situation there: war threat stabilized for the moment, but our immediate action would be needed. He gave me some expert advice on negotiating a battleship through the hole, along with a couple of cruisers. He added that they had an experimental means of sending a body by iradiology through space, analogous to our short-distance rekamatic pullmans, and he wanted to get himself and a native away from that star-system immediately by that method. He wondered whether the iradio receiving equipment on the expedition ship *Lucifer*, which presumably was still cruising out there, might be adapted to receive and reconstitute the bodies. As it happened, the ship had the equipment; I'd seen to that, anticipating the possibility of having to iradio parts in emergency; but there was a question of adapting their receiver to the local design of the transmitter on Iola. Despite my urgent warnings—for instance, the gaseous turbulence around Klarta which could easily scramble Klaus or his native en route—he raised his ship engineer and, in a rapid translated conversation with Iola people, arrived at a few modifications which could easily be made. A few hours later, Klaus and his native were aboard his ship."

"The native was Kyria?"

"It's entirely possible; I never saw this native. Klaus paused briefly at Erth before coming to Nereid to report—with Murchison along, of course."

"How about their reporting, Croyd?"

"Klaus confined his report to physical, political, and belligerent facts, along with some first-hand data, superb data, about black hole interior and gravity manipulation."

"And Duke's report?"

"Quite properly, he confined himself to objective data from ship's viewpoint."

"And you let it all go at that?"

"Of course not, there were too many gaps. I tried to get some personal and local color, but Klaus asked that he and Murchison be returned to Erth for a rest before saying any more, and they certainly were exhausted. I respected this, and away they went; and then I learned that Klaus had retired. I've been trying to set up another appointment—"

"But couldn't the Assistant Secretary for Internal Security have . . . Oh. Excuse me."

"Excused. Right. I had no grounds for compelling Klaus. And then somebody killed him—and Kyria."

"Yes."

Brood.

Croyd mused: "You know, I've never been dead sure that Murchison didn't follow Heller to Iola."

Alert: "Tell me why."

"No good reason. But I've read the captain's shipboard log. He mentions Dr. Duke almost every day, in one connection or another. But there is a period of about ten days when Duke is not mentioned at all; and this period coincides exactly with the period between Heller's departure and Heller's return."

"Fascinating! Did you question the captain?"

"By the time I was sure of the discrepancy, Captain Diekoff was away on another prolonged assignment. Since then I've lost track of that detail, which I had been considering a trifle. But then Klaus and Kyria were murdered. So I rather urgently invited Duke here on the pretext of talking about black holes—but he brought you along, and apart from the pleasure of knowing you, I'm not sure what that may have helped or headed off."

The quizzical comment brought her to a difficult decision. She wove in on it. "Believe me, Croyd, it has certainly helped me in many ways, and it may have helped with the aspect of Duke's involvement. Tell me, though—was the attacking planet called Godzha?"

He considered her. He said then: "Yes. And doesn't that bring us right back to the question, how you know a lot of things that you wouldn't be expected to know?"

"Indeed it does," she murmured. "I'm beginning to think I was there."

"On Iola?"

"Precisely."

"When? How?"

"Don't laugh. In a dream, last night. And maybe in a couple of prior dreams."

He stared. "Does your dream-sensitivity to reality explain your success as a detective?"

"I have never before in my life experienced what is technically known as a veridical dream. And I haven't believed in them, because I haven't been able to figure any theory for them. But, damn it, there were things in this dream that you have confirmed, and I couldn't *possibly* have known them independently! The name of the star. The names of the planets Iola and Godzha, and all four of the others. The drawings that were transmitted between you and Iola. Even the fact that the interior of a black hole is about like mercury—no, Duke told me that. Other things in my dream might have been my own free association from independently known or suspected facts; but the items I just mentioned were in my dream and nowhere else for me."

"*Was* Murchison there?"

"In my dream, he was."

"What happened?"

"I don't know, my dream dealt only with the first day or two. Croyd, what *did* finally happen—between Iola and Godzha, I mean?"

Somberly he told her: "Perhaps it is a little late at night for the total story as I know it."

Meditation.

She tossed off her beer and stood wearily. "Bed for me, now, too. Believe me, it has been an indescribably fine evening. By the way, with the scouter wrecked, how do Duke and I get home?"

He was standing. "Faster than coming here. I have current business on Erth, I'm leaving in a frigate tomorrow: ten hours en route, not twenty. Can you be ready to leave about noon?"

Undressing, she heard a door-tap and a low voice: "Duke here; are you decent?" Negligée'd, she let him in. She offered him a chair and brandy; he refused both. She sat, watching him pace distraught, waiting for him to come to some point.

He interrupted his pacing, stood rigidly in front of her, and enunciated his point with taut difficulty. "I think we should bed-down together, with eventual marriage a distinct possibility."

Well, God knew *that* wasn't romantic! Besides, it was so absurd that she wondered what might be behind it—especially since, as of this evening, there was reason to wonder whether Duke was totally uninvolved in the Heller murders. She remarked: "That sort of came out of a clear sky, didn't it?"

"For me, it came out of that clear sky yesterday in my office with you, and it's been growing ever since. I meant it. All of it."

"I like you, Duke—but to equal your own bluntness, I'm not aroused."

"I am, though."

"Then you might at least try pleasantly, not that it would help—"

"I would, but I won't, because first I want you to arrange your thoughts about that marriage thing. I've bitterly learned that marriage is a lot more than arousal, and you'd better have your mind made up for the rest of it before we hit bed."

"You mean: bed, yes, but no bed tonight, no?"

"Not unless tonight you go yes or no on marriage. Which I suspect isn't likely."

"Why marriage, Duke?"

"Because it's a mutual commitment. Anything else is not."

"But either of us could dissolve our marriage on unilateral declaration followed by a ninety-day incubation period. So how is it a commitment?"

"Because it is, to the extent that even making a unilateral declaration would require a positively decided-on counter-commitment."

"Even so—why should *we two* be married?"

"Because I get along with you better than with anybody I've known, and I have this feeling that each of us could become more valuable to the other than anybody else. By the way, with respect to that unilateral divorce action, I filed it a month ago on my present wife. And I don't think she'll raise any obstacle, she has a lover."

Claudine had a sense that this had hurt him deeply, and the sense was succeeded by a wave of Duke-tenderness in her. She fought it down: in a case like this, with no clear solution, just anybody recently associated with Heller was a potential suspect; Duke's association had been close indeed, and he had been most reluctant to admit it. And if in fact he had followed Heller to Iola, quite likely he had known also Kyria.

Unwilling to turn him off sharply, she temporized: "I'm forty-six, Duke. Forget kids."

"I'm thirty-nine, Claudine, and I'm sterile. I *have* forgotten kids."

Turgid silence.

She said presently: "I'm weary tonight, Duke, you wouldn't enjoy me, and I'm in no shape to think straight about marriage with anybody." She arose: "I think you'd better go now—"

He embraced her, kissing her mouth.

She pushed him away. "Duke, my good Duke—scat!"

He blundered out of there.

She poured a short brandy nightcap and sat to think about it. Presently she blurped a chuckle. Had Duke remembered that a wife couldn't testify in court against her husband?

Part Five

THE MASTERS OF GRAVITY

Iola, 27 November 2494

Human (def.)—Having sufficient neural complexity to use symbolic language in order to sublimate survival and reproductive interests in more complex levels of aesthetic development, individual or social (but without necessarily denying the more fundamental levels of living).
                    —Code of the Interplanetary System
                        (from *Dr. Orpheus*)

13. GODZHA MENACE

From over the sea at high noon she came in on a building which long-gracefully undulated atop the ridge and then, several stories up, narrowed and lofted into a twelve-story tower. She drifted into an open-to-the-breeze top-floor dining room, floor-tiled in light pastel colors, with alternating rectangular and elliptical tables covered by white linen (how dis she know that the linen was synthetic, lending itself to doodling, cleansable in one quick pass through the minilaundry?). About half the tables were occupied; and among them silently scudded roboservers having nice clipped contralto voices. All the occupants were women, except at one terrace-table where Klaus and Duke were lunching with Luria and Kyria.

This was not the hospital. The sense was that the Erth-men had been released this morning in the care of these women, that they had been given lodging in this woman-residence because Dr. Mujis hadn't dared lodge them with Iola-men.

Klaus and Duke, dressed in the clothing they'd worn under their spacesuits (and freshly fabric-laundered at the hospital) actually weren't all that conspicuous: most of the women were similarly dressed in blouses and pants, although more decoratively, and were almost as tall, a few equally tall. Indeed, Luria had been able to scrounge the men a few clothing changes, and the fit wasn't bad. Nevertheless, the other women knew that these were alien men, and furtively they glanced and turned quickly back to their own table-concerns.

Klaus, catching all this, thought about a couple of turkey-type novels and cinemas themed on a classic male fantasy involving a man who finds himself the sole male on a planet of women. For some non-reason, the assumption always was that the women would fall all over the man; in fact, he reflected, what you'd expect would be transient interest, an ex-

perimental hay-rolling or two, and otherwise a large sexual
ignoring of the men while the women returned to their own
lesbian and parthenogenetic concerns. It wasn't a perfect parallel, because this planet did have males and he had seen no
evidence of lesbianism; but anyhow it was all beside the
point, because he and Duke were here on strictly asexual human business.

They were drinking habituras, which were almost like dry
martinis, and Kyria was explaining something to the men,
putting it in good basic Flaric. "This place is called a warren.
Its name is Warren Heldo. It is one of many warrens where
women live. There are warrens for men, too, of course, but
naturally most of ours are better than any of theirs."

Luria cleared throat. Klaus dryly remarked: "Apart from
the sexocentrism, your diction is a bit too primitive for me to
follow." Sexocentrism was his off-the-cuff Flaric coinage.
Luria stifled a giggle.

Kyria, most dignified, pressed on: "Sorry, I'll try to talk
more naturally; only, it will be harder for Duke—"

"Duke doesn't get much of it anyway; he's a scientist, not
a linguist. Finish your thought, I'll translate."

Kyria bent upon Duke a look of kindly pity; he countered
with a look of brooding amour (oh-oh); Klaus glanced at
Luria, and two left eyebrows twitched.

Said Kyria then: "I was going to tell you that our Warren
Heldo is one of the two best warrens. During these hard
times with Geeks, we are all—fighters?"

"Soldiers," suggested Klaus.

"Soldiers, yes. And of course the officers live in the best
warrens. Luria and I have very decent ranks: one is the
highest, Luria is a seven, I'm an eight." Claudine was noticing, for the first time, a little silver 7 on Luria's left shoulder,
and an 8 on Kyria's; but how could Claudine recognize the
Flaric numbers? "Warren Heldo," Kryia was saying, "is for
eights, sevens, and sixes. There is only one better warren in
Gladowr, and that is for fives, fours, and threes. The Two of
Gladowr and the One of the World have houses of their
own—"

"Excuse me, Kyria. What is Dr. Mujis?"

"She is a very important three, a member of the Gladowr
Council and a consultant to the World Council."

"And how are these members and consultants chosen?"

"Threes are automatically members of the Gladowr Council, or in other city-states of their local councils. Twos are automatically members of the World Council."

"Well, then—how are ranks assigned?"

"The local councils designate all ranks up to three on advice from subordinate officers, and they elect their twos. The World Council designates consultants from among the threes and elects the One."

"By the way, Klaus," Luria interposed, "The One of the World has summoned you before the World Council tomorrow morning. We'll talk about that, but you'll want to prepare your mind for it."

So casually did Dr. Klaus Heller, Ambassador from Erth bringing the possibility of unexpected interplanetary help in a time of mortal war, receive his first intimation that his visit was officially recognized!

"They'll also want to meet Duke," Luria added.

Klaus inclined his head; but he was interested in this tight little circular political system which as an ambassador he was obligated to understand in part. Now he had an opening for a test-question: "Will there be any men on the council?"

Kyria ejaculated: "Men on a council? Ridiculous! Oh, I didn't quite mean that—"

"Never mind, Kyria; excuse me while I translate." Klaus briefed Duke, adding at the end in low Anglian: "Positively you have *got* to learn a *few* more words—"

Duke, grinning small, held up his empty glass, saying something to all of them in Anglian. Klaus translated: "He says Dr. Mujis gave us a little money. He wants to buy a round of drinks."

Laughing delight, Luria held up six fingers. That was the signal for Fista their roboserver: across the room, it flashed a green light to acknowledge, then punched four habituras and wheeled over with them, contralto-murmuring: "Okay? Or do you want a change?" Accepting the drinks, Luria ordered lunch and asked to be served immediately.

While they ate (mainly fish), Klaus asked more questions, frequently prompted by Duke, and in the process learned more Flaric while they picked up a little Anglian. It was fun for Kyria to hear and learn their language; to a considerable extent she had a linguistic talent like that of Klaus, only it had been rarely exercised because on this planet Flaric was so nearly universal. The way Duke spoke Anglian charmed her particularly.

Over dessert, Klaus brought it to the point of his mission. "I confess to be puzzled. You claim to be a planet under attack, to be on a war basis. And yet everyone seems to behave quite calmly, as though you were at peace with the galaxy. Please tell me about this war with Godzha."

Kyria looked at Luria, who transformed herself into attorney-on-business, producing a pen and sketching broadly on the tablecloth:

"Small wonder we look calm! There is nothing we can do, so there is nothing we *can* do but lie back and take it! Bloi! We are fish in a barrel!

"First, you need to know about Iola about women and men. Iola is a long thin chain of islands—like this. Here is Gladowr, midway south of the equator. Gladowr and its nation Flaria constitute the high point of our civilization, although there are other high areas. Translate. . . .

"We women have been dominant everywhere on this planet since before we were human. We have to keep the males down, they are too aggressive and numerous; I can't quite explain their superior numbers, it is something about our eggs, more men survive the tadpole stage. Is this too complicated already? Let it go, then; I'll try to explain later.

"Now. About two centuries ago, there was a male rebellion in which a few of the lower women joined. We decided we had to get rid of the rebels, but we didn't want to kill them. So we space-ferried them to Godzha with their few women, and we gave help to them in setting up a colony on that previously unoccupied planet. It is a most uncomfortable planet, its best climate is colder than our coldest northern and southern regions.

"To shorten it, these males on Godzha, these Godzhalks or Geeks, responded strongly to the challenge of Godzha's rigor. Their first concern was for climate control; we furnished them materials and apparatus and instruction, foolishly and because of our guilt, and they built themselves a system of domed cities. With climate control, they brought their breeding to a higher productivity than ours. They educated their males and kept their women ignorant, using them as slaves and breeding stock.

"They turned then to the heavens—and we on Iola are about to die of that.

"Godzha is the nearest planet to the four black holes on the plane of our solar system—here, here, here, and here. Their planetary orbit is widely perturbed by the gravitation of these holes, and the hole-draw on Klarta is not enough for Klarta-warmth to reach out as far as Godzha for compensation, so they have four vicious winters every year. They have turned this to their own advantage.

"We can manipulate hole-gravity a little. They can manipulate it massively and with precision. Klaus, you and Duke both remember how they pulled you out of that black hole and made nack-nock sport of you.

"Got the picture so far? Good; translate. After-lunch liqueurs?"

Luria ordered while Klaus was translating for Duke. When the men sipped it, they found a resemblance to good cognac; but Luria had no time for drink comparisons now, she was off and running.

"Excuse me if I press on with this, I have an after-lunch appointment. Kyria is going to take you to our Science Institute this afternoon. Well:

"About a hundred years ago, the Geeks had progressed to the point of space travel. They got themselves a hold on Klarta Five or Corla, their neighboring inner planet; Corla is a mother lode of materials for construction and energy but is virtually uninhabitable because it is too small to retain any appreciable atmosphere. Are you following this, Klaus? Holy Harmnion, you *are*? A few questions though, eh? Let's pick 'em up tonight when you'll know twice as many of our words.

"Next, the Godzhalks bypassed us and invested Klarta Three or Zinza. Despite the intense unlivable heat of that planet, they adapted their climate-control devices and colonized even Zinza in a small prospecting way.

"And then, about twenty years ago, they turned their attention to us—partly out of envy, partly because of the old grudge. They determined to return to Iola and take us over as our masters. Eventually—far, far, too late—we became alarmed at their increasingly frequent stratospheric reconnaissance of Iola, and we began to chase their ships away.

"That was when we became alarmed enough to declare a

Yellow Alert. This involved calling out the militia for training. And we undertook our own intensive reconnaissance of
Godzha, not in ships, but with instruments based here on
Gladowr Island—instruments capable, not only of mapping
the Godzha-globe, but of penetrating their control centers to
learn their attack capabilities. And with dismay we learned
what they could do with black-hole gravity. We had been
building a fairly respectable military space fleet to supplement our peaceful space freighters and exploration craft; but
it was beginning to come clear that space fighters might not
be what we needed for defense. And we began discussing a
preventive strike at Godzha's gravity-control installations.

"Early last year, it came clear that none of our leaders had
the heart for an unprovoked first strike. Instead, we put our
fleet into readiness for a crushing counterblow in event that
they should attack first. What, though, if they should strike
first, not with ships, but with their gravity devices? That was
when we began broadcasting mayday by iradio, in the faint
hope of locating somewhere a civilization which might give
us some technical advice and might even send aid. And it appears that we did locate *your* civilization; but our galactic-
range iradio broke down during the initial exchanges, and I
don't know whether it has been reconstituted yet.

"Meanwhile, only eight weeks ago, we had our provoca-
tion: Godzha sent a raiding expedition of twenty-five ships.
The command went out: Chase them home and strike their
planet! We shot down about five of them in our own space,
losing maybe seven of ours; but we outnumbered them two-
to-one, and the other Godzhalks ran for home. We chased
them, but they were faster; we were stupid not to grasp the
fact that they were baiting us, keeping just beyond our range
all the way. Reconnaissance told us that these were their best
ships and eighty percent of their whole fleet; we were counting on backing them into their own space and destroying
them, whereafter any single survivor among our ships had
what it took to pulverize their control centers."

She drained her liqueur, napkined her mouth, and spat:
"Here's the quick finish. When they'd sucked us into their
own space, they scattered while their tractor-beams wrecked
all but three of us and crippled the three survivors. We
limped home. End of our space fleet.

"Four weeks ago, they sent us a warning. You'll hear

about that tomorrow morning at World Council. And now you have come. And, bloi! Of course you can do nothing—"

Luria stood, quivering. "Excuse me for now, I'll see you tonight. Kyria, you sign my name to the check. Bloi! *Hista bloi!*" She stormed out.

14. PLANETARY VULCANISM

Squired now by Kyria only, the men cabbed it to town-center and dismounted; Kyria paid and tipped the cabbie who was a woman with a 15-badge at her shoulder. In the cab and afterward, Duke and Kyria were so deeply engrossed in each other that occasionally Kyria, with a guilt-stab, would turn away from Duke to address Klaus.

Central Gladowr City was ranged on both sides of the very low segment in the hogback, where the hospital roof could peep over. The western slope of the ridge began as downtown tall buildings which tapered into tenements behind. But on the eastern slope, ranging down to the coast, was a broad park-like area; and to this park Kyria directed their attention.

High rises half-ringed this area of perhaps four square kilometers which eased downward to the visible surf. Here and there in the park, children were playing (females, Klaus would bet); but clearly the park had been designed primarily for the widely spaced-out government buildings, including the general hospital to the far left where a bay cut deeply into the mainland. *Klaus diving into and swimming in that bay with Luria. . . .*

A lofty high rise was positioned at park-center. Kyria took Duke's arm and pointed to the skyscraper, speaking to Duke although she knew that only Klaus would understand the sense: "That building houses the government offices—for Gladowr, and for Flaria, and for all the world. Those things sticking up from its roof are astronomical sending and receiving antennae for the Science Institute, placed up there to minimize atmospheric interference; most of what they send or receive is relayed by orbital satellites. The astronomical laboratories are located underground in that low building to your left, the Gladowr Science Institute; we'll be visiting there directly."

Correcting her neglect of Klaus, she turned to him. "Klaus, tomorrow morning you'll be received in the top floor of that central high rise; that is where the World Council sits, and the World Council is the twos of all the nations, chaired by the One of the World. Dr. Mujis will be there, she sits on the World Council as a technical adviser with voice but no vote; and the same is true of Dr. Vlotny the Director of the Science Institute. And you two will be in both places—The Science Institute today and the World Council tomorrow! Good heavens, it is so *intimidating* to be a guide for celebrities—"

The Science Institute took particular pride in its Department of Astronomy; and this was ironical in a planetary system which was contained within itself by black holes and gas clouds, offering to astronomy only brief hazy kamat-ray optical views or static-distorted radio information of the stars beyond. Perhaps it was precisely the challenge of these physical limitations which had stimulated the educated women of Flaria to pour so much money and energy into this research—along with, in recent years, the war-challenge by Godzha which made superb intra-systemic instrumentation a survival need.

Some years earlier, the institute had stumbled on I-rays, here called nedi-rays: these, discovered and tamed in the Erth-neighborhood by Croyd more decades ago than he commonly admitted, were in use throughout the Interplanetary Union beginning in 2475. The special distinction of I-rays or nedi-rays was as follows. When the projector was stimulated by a system of incoming photons from a source no matter how distant, rays were emitted which almost instantaneously traveled back up the standing beam of photons to the source and almost instantaneously returned current information from the source. Result: a star might be thousands of light-years distant, which meant that the photons arriving from it gave information only of events thousands of years in the past; but once these photons had found an I-ray projector, the rays thereafter continuously retrieved information from the source about what was happening at the light source *right now*. Analogously, if the light source had an I-ray receiver, right-now information could be transmitted to it. (Thus one epistemological grounding of the theory that simultaneity is relative was eliminated: through I-rays, if simultaneity existed, it could be *known* as practically absolute.)

It was via these nedi-rays that this same Science Institute had projected the mayday signals which had eventuated in the arrival here of Klaus and (unexpectedly) Duke as Croyd's agents. The signals had been interrupted by a massive breakdown of the apparatus which had been out-thrusting at danger-load in the hope of punching the mayday through the hole-and-gas curtain of the Klarta system.

The nedi-ray apparatus would be functional again within days, assured gray Krazia Vlotny the fussy director of the institute who was honored and excited beyond reason by this extra-stellar visit. (She wore a three, like Mujis.) Vlotny was a bit put out that Dr. Duke wished to spend all his time here in the astrolab; but she had to admit that the entire institute could profit from his concentrated visit here, because Dr. Duke could bring their astronomers long-desired news of the outer stars. She presented the visitors to Dr. Myrna, a slight introverted self-contained woman who held the Department Chair in Astronomy.

Klaus was now in a hole again, because in diplomacy he should spend *his* time elsewhere with Dr. Vlotny—but how would Flaric language idiot Duke get along without Klaus to translate? "Not to sweat," Duke confided. "Astronomy is my alley, I'll learn a lot of their technical words, and geometry can bridge a lot of language gaps." Kyria volunteered to go with Duke for whatever non-Anglian help she might give him; actually she had at least a hundred Anglian words already.

Just before Duke and Kyria departed with Myrna, Vlotny drew Kyria aside and asked in worriment: "These are *men?* On their planet they are *krazia?* But then, what under any sun are their *women* like?"

Mujis had told Klaus that the two mighty space-suits had been sent here for analysis and safe-keeping; so he first inquired about them and was told that they were well, nobody would take them apart without his approval.

He then wanted to know about the directed energies which the Godzhalks had used to play nack-nock with him, and about those with which Luria had pulled him out of it. The latter were, said Vlotny in considerable detail, nedi-ray modi-

fications of conventional tractor beams; and sighing Klaus
had to admit that in all this Iola was far ahead of Erth.

"By the same token," deeply sighed Vlotny, "in all this,
Godzha is far ahead of Iola. I ask myself over and over why
we were so foolish as to give those Geeks the essentials of
our technology for generations until as recently as fifty years
ago. I can only imagine that we had guilt-feelings about having exiled the Geeks on Godzha in the first place . . . Eh,
but that is psychiatry and historical politics, it is not in my
province; pray help me return to my province."

"That's easy enough," said Klaus. "You have been talking
about nedi-rays and tractor-beam adaptations. Are you going
in any other directions with nedi-rays?"

And that sent Vlotny scurrying to the lift, with Klaus following. In a high-story lab, he was shown a device for transmitting matter with I-rays, almost precisely as one might
transmit matter by rekamatics over relatively short distances:
a body was broken down into reonic patterns, transmitted on
a directional I-ray beam, and reconstituted at the receiving
end. A special ultra-high-power adaptation permitted the
transmitter to reconstitute the body at its destination even
though there was no receiver; but this technique exposed the
transmitted body to the danger of static scrambling. In fact,
Erth already had this, and in a more advanced state of development; nevertheless, Diplomat Heller marveled and
praised—and remembered.

At his suggestion, Vlotny now took him on a fast tour of
the entire institute, apologizing all the way about the time-
brevity in each place, repeatedly inviting Doctors Heller and
Duke to return whenever they wished for more intensive ex-
amination of any part or parts. Vlotny was curious as to why
the visiting doctors of ambassadorial rank had been lodged at
Warren Heldo, and not at the prime warren for the top
ranks; she seemed a bit miffed about it. Heller reassured her,
explaining that he had talked this over with Krazia Mujis,
and they had agreed that the lower-level warren would give
them more freedom of action, expecially in view of their al-
ready-established acquaintance with Kyria and Luria. Vlotny
seemed to be mentally receiving and recording this explanation without necessarily accepting it.

The pace of the tour was slowed in a large hall, a public
museum exhibit with a number of studious women visitors

touring it. This was the central feature of their Iology and Io-
losophy Department (the equivalent of geology and geosophy
on Erth). "I want you to see these globes, charts, dioramas,
and cross-sections," Vlotny told her guest, "because they may
help you to understand the mechanics of the threat which we
face from Godzha."

They stood near a gigantic center-hall globe of sea-blue
surfaces and green-to-brown land-mountain wrinkles, rotating
with dignified deliberation in a continuous bath of muted
space-music. Vlotny precised data about the planet (interestingly, the surface was ninety-four percent water). She remarked, "Other than the archipelago, there are many other
little dots of land, small or very small islands, distributed at
random in the prevailing ocean, as here and here for instance. Of course, this distinction between land and sea is a
bit silly, since the ocean is always a relatively shallow puddle
on top of low-lying land: what we call an island is only a
high place, often volcanic in origin, as contrasted with a low
place having water on top of it; iologically it would be truer
to compare *volumes* of non-water with volumes of water, and
then the superior percentage of non-water would be astronomical. On the other hand, from a viewpoint of air-breath-
ing life, and particularly of human life, the distinction *is*
important—not so?"

"So."

"Now look at that floor-to-ceiling wall-plate over there, it
is a circular schematic cross-section of the planet Iola. By the
way, don't you find the luminescence behind the painting on
frosted glass impressive? we have a clever technician, she
dreamed up that light-and-shadow motion behind the amber
colors.

"Look well at the amber: it is a fluid magma flowing
beneath and within the planetary crust. Notice how exten-
sively around the planet this magma is distributed. Almost
any fault almost anywhere can result in a volcano. However,
you see that here, in the general vicinity of Flaria, the prevailing depth of the magma is great enough so that an acci-
dental volcano is extremely unlikely, and in fact there has not
been an eruption in this vicinity during many millennia. In
passing, I may observe that Godzha is known to have similar
volcanic potentials.

"Now check the adjacent plate. It is a schematic blow-up
of one section of crust, comprising about two-tenths degree of

arc, showing a tiny island with ocean all around. Notice how the fluid amber magma is concentrated and turbulent beneath that island? Evidently the island is prey to violent vulcanism; and if you study the island, you will see the cone of a frequently active volcano at its center."

Testing his own comprehension of this Flaric lecture, Klaus asked: "A volcano would be a place where the magma erupts?"

"Exactly; erupts as molten lava. And you can imagine that such an island would also be subject to ioquakes—"

"Shakings of Iola? We call them erthquakes."

"Of course. Anyhow, I could show you how the buildings on Gladowr, the modern ones at least, are constructed to resist seismic disturbances. Ioquakes."

"We do that too in some places."

"This interplanetary comparison is great, isn't it? Well; the point is, that Godzha intends to use our own vulcanism against us. At this position in the Iola orbit we are perturbed in the direction of Black Hole Four and therefore especially vulnerable to Geek manipulation of its gravity. So the special threat is, that the Godzhalks will use hole-gravity to blow up Gladowr with our own vulcanism unless we surrender."

"Your pardon, Dr. Vlotny. Gravity manipulation is hard to believe. But when I invaded your Black Hole Three, I found a spheroid metal artifact imbedded at center. Tell me about this artifact, if you know about it."

"Indeed I know about it," asserted Vlotny, obviously in chagrin. "We put it there a century ago; and among our other aids and comforts to the Godzhalks, we made the grave mistake of telling them about it."

"*Is* it related to gravity manipulation?"

"Directly, Doctor. It constitutes the other pole of the gradient. Activated by impulses from here—or, regrettably, from Godzha—the artifact in black-hole center responds to planetary activation to polarize gravity in some particular direction. We call it a gravity modulator."

"And—*you* put it there?"

"We Flarians, yes."

"But it is the Godzhalks who are using it—against you Flarians?"

"Regrettably, yes."

"But then, is Flaria making no use of her own gravity modulator?"

"Modulators, Doctor—plural. We seeded one into each of the four black holes on our planetary plane. And yes, we have been using these modulators to tap in on the formidable gravity of our black holes for diversified energy purposes. And as a result, most of our energy is furnished by our black holes, and the balance by ocean tides; we abandoned fossil and nuclear fuels and combustion engines long ago.

"But it didn't occur to us to use this power for military purposes. And meanwhile, the Godzhalks have been more creative with this greatest of all favors that we bestowed upon them.

"Dr. Heller, I have learned that you will meet with the World Council tomorrow morning; I will be there to listen, and to comment if this is requested. Well, on that morning, the Geeks propose to demonstrate their power by blowing up one of our islands. In my opinion, Dr. Heller, we are within days of our destruction."

In fact, it was D minus three days.

Seated in Vlotny's office, Heller assured her, "I do want to return here, and I know that Dr. Duke feels the same way. We may not have the time, of course—"

"Of course. Geeks."

"Right. For instance, I would enjoy studying the sociology and anthropology of the female-and-male social arrangements—"

"We have a Dr. Kaldeen who is Chairwoman of Sociology and Gynology, she could help you with that."

"But I hate to leave here today without asking you one question that is major in my mind. Yesterday I attended chapel at the hospital."

"Ah."

"There was a phenomenon—"

"Hueena?"

"We would call it invisibility. How is it done—or is that a religious mystery?"

"I am a religious woman, Dr. Heller—"

"This I respect, Dr. Vlotny. I respect all sincere and humane religions. I do not wish for you to tell me anything I should not know."

"Thank you for saying that. But I was about to go on and inform you that hueena is a religious mystery, and yet it is not. I mean to say, we induce hueena by technological methods; but what happens to the subject in hueena is indeed a religious mystery."

"Then may I inquire about the technology while respecting the privacy of the mystery?"

"Certainly you may, although they are bound up together. We believe that when we die, our subjective essences are sublimated into a very high-frequency wavelength, too high for any of our senses to detect. During a religious service, we use metabolic acceleration to translate earnest and daring volunteers into something approaching that very high frequency. Of course they become invisible to us. Most of those returning from hueena claim to have seen immortals, and some even claim to have communicated with them; of course, these may be delusions, the hueena itself is a trying experience for the mind. I—myself, I'm afraid I am too cowardly to try the hueena."

Well: how was this any different from the invisibility induced by the metabolic accelerators which Klaus and Duke had used?

15. NIGHT ON THE TOWN

In the near-top-floor two-woman VIP Guest Suite where they were quartered, the men had bathed (each in his own bathroom, in a tub sized for conservative swimming), donned fresh clothing (women's, but what the hell, they had pants even if the zippers were wrong), and sat now in their salon sipping kromoweel, a Scotch-like liquor drawn from their small private stock which the warren management had provided, and discussing the Science Institute while they awaited their dinner dates. Duke reported a very good communication experience in the astrolab, remarking: "In college I did great in scientific Tellenic and Brunildic even though I couldn't make beans of the languages generally." And Klaus commented: "Your facility with their astronomical stuff should give you a confident breakthrough into ordinary Flaric."

"I made a start today, with Kyria's help. She'll teach me more tonight. Give me a few weeks here, and maybe I can speak the stuff."

"As it happens, Duke, we are quite likely to have been blown up before then."

"You mean—like nuclear-bombed?"

"In this case, we'll be vulcanized."

"Volcanoes, Klaus?"

"Gravity-induced magma explosions. Black-hole gravity—Godzha can control it."

"Preposterous! there is absolutely no theory for manipulating gravity!"

"Then you'd better invent one, because gravity manipulation exists." He told Duke about the rekamatic gradients with the gravity modulators.

While Duke nursed that along with his kromoweel, Klaus meditated the abject submission by the women of Iola. The threat had sucked out the marrow of their defiance, they were going through military motions but accomplishing nothing.

Granting that their space fleet was destroped, why wouldn't they be bristling with atmospheric and ground defenses against whatever foot-soldiery invasion would have to follow volcanic catastrophe? For that matter, why had their space fleet been so small, and how had it been so innocently sucked into its destruction-trap—*all* of it? After hundreds of years of space cruising, why hadn't they begun to build a fleet a century ago when Godzha began to go on the interplanetary muscle? Why hadn't they been able to mount hundreds of blindingly swift ships, instead of a mere half-hundred relatively slow ships? And yet they were advanced enough to have nedi-rays, and tractor beams that could pull in Klaus and Duke from the best part of a light-year out?

Were they so guilt-laden with their exiling of the rebellious males to Godzha two centuries ago that they were soul-paralyzed? Even then, had they been so guilt-laden with their oppression of males that they couldn't execute the rebels instead of exiling them and then helping them?

Reasons for their oppression of men were clear enough, especially since Luria had remarked that females had been superior to males even before they were human. And yet it operated in a vicious circle. *Since* the women kept the males inferiorized and segregated to avoid male uppitiness and sexual misbehavior, *therefore* the males were all the more sex-haunted sullen—and so on, and so on, and so on.

They couldn't possibly be maintaining all these males on segregated welfare. They *must* be doing something useful with these little men, other than using them as breeding stock: possibly at hard labor in factories or mines or road work, perhaps a superior minority of males in menial store or office work. And if they were doing that, why wouldn't they be making soldiers of these men? It was hindsight, now—but he envisioned that effective education and employment of men at skilled trades might have helped head-off the Godzha crisis.

Unless, of course, the males were actually inferior to all women intellectually as well as physically. But the very threat from male Godzha denied that thought in spades!

It would not be appropriate for Klaus, a stranger from a far quarter of the galaxy, to attempt a moral judgment on brief acquaintance; for that, he would have had to weigh in *their* moral criteria, including those of the males. But then, must not his suspension of judgment be generalized to include

the criteria of Godzha? In a way, the Iola-Godzha confrontation represented a dichotomy of conflicting wrongs in humane terms: on the one hand, Godzha was making aggressive
war, which was humane-wrong; on the other; Iola was
repressing a sex-caste, which was humane-wrong. Klaus was
an ambassador, not to Iola necessarily, but to the whole
Klarta system. How could he arrive at a judgmental recommendation for Croyd?

One instrumental judgment was for sure: an attack-strike
by Godzha would have to be headed off, if anything more
long-range was to be done.

To Duke, his uninvited volunteer colleague, he shot a hard
question. "If I should decide to make a suicidal two-man raid
on Godzha, would you be with me for it?"

"I followed you into a black hole. But I guess you had to
ask."

They dined at Club Streljo which was one of the best night
spots, frequented only by women at or above the Luria-Kyria
class level. Their table was close to the low stage; and since
no entertainers appeared during dinner except for the inevi-
table string ensemble (female of course), the visiting men
took advantage of their location to study groups of people
while they improved their relationships with Luria and Kyria.
As to the latter, a clear pairing had already developed: Klaus
with Luria, Duke with Kyria. As to the former, the women
sitting in twos and threes and fours looked like ordinary
groups of Erth-men together in the absence of female company: talking earnestly or idly, listening, scene-glimming,
eating, drinking, settling business or sports or war probabili-
ties, possibly even discussing survival possibilities after their
deaths. Among Erth-men, while the presence of women conferred a special quality of warmth and piquancy and sometimes high intimacy, purely male confraternity had values of
its own; and so, Klaus estimated, it was for Iola-women. He
still had to learn whether it would be the same among Iola-
men: apart from probably frequent homosexual incidents,
which might be transient-impulsive rather than fixed habit,
might it not be that men on Iola found their own values in
being together as men?

While they were on after-dinner liqueurs, the show began
with a raucously flamboyant mistress of ceremonies. A series
of comedy acts and pop-song acts and juggling acts and danc-

ing acts occupied most of an hour. Toward the end of it, risibilities were highly aroused by a troupe of male comedy entertainers; the loudest laughter came when one of the little men leaped upon the back of another and began squirming and massaging the flanks of his victim who ran about screaming and trying to shake off his assailant; they exited like that, and the applause was enthusiastic.

Red-faced Kyria whispered to her guests: "You have to understand that most of the women here are drinking, some heavily." But Luria interposed: "Holy Harmnion, Kyria, don't apologize: it's just us!" The men studied their drinks— Klaus reflecting that women's laughter at obscene male comedy might be partially defensive, the women having a suppressed awareness of male power over them when they were in season. Kyria's flush deepened as she realized that the male act had stirred her: liquor must be loosening her inhibitions a little, especially at this time of her times—and yet she was nursing her drinks, resolved to stay sober all evening.

But impishly grinning Luria was murmuring to Klaus: "May I count on you next season for my annual male bash?"

"Delicious thought," Klaus responded, "if we still have a world then. Can we maybe act tonight and dream later?"

"Good thought there. Put it off." Her voice went momentarily soft: "Let's quit the play, Klaus, I'm sorry, I did start it. I like you, my friend—very much. I'd rather think of you as a woman."

"And I like you, my friend, very much. And I'd rather think of *you* as a woman."

"Dog! Now, as to the question of what books I've read recently—"

Klaus glanced at Duke and Kyria: they were into some kind of thing, most intently; listening, he grasped that Duke was trying to learn some conversational Flaric from her, and she was trying to help. All right, *that* was under way; they wouldn't be needing him for a while.

He turned to Luria. "My friend, you are an attorney, and I want to absorb some of your sociological knowledge—about women and men here."

"May I claim a fee?"

"What would it be?"

"You at my forthcoming season."

"No sacrifice, believe me: done, Luria—but you can back out."

"I won't; I'll pursue it—*then*. Start your questioning."

"Luria, all day long I've been seeing women behaving much like most men and also like many businesslike women in *our* world. And tonight I've seen men behaving—well, not like our women, but like some of our men who reject their own sex and wish they were women for sexual reasons. You don't have anything much to compare with most of our women, except for some shoppers I saw today, some that Kyria said were the homemakers in permanent woman-pairings; but when I asked her about the sexual motif there, Kyria blushed and said that women didn't often do that but they often paired permanently nevertheless. All right. But on Erth we have all kinds of women; some are like you career women; some others are interested mainly in being sexually attractive to us men or competitive-attractive to other women. And on our world, women run smaller than men, and men tend to be politically and industrially dominant; but there is theoretical equality, and many women occupy commanding positions—"

He paused, drinking-thinking. Luria reflected on his enormous command of Flaric in little more than two days here, starting from nothing. Surely his vocabulary had doubled since lunch! He had refined his syntax, too; his accent wasn't as thick, his emphases were truer; and he was trying adventures in logical derivation, some ridiculous, some coming off quite decently well. An accomplished programmer herself, she surmised that his computer-brain was exceptionally well stacked and wired in the semantic areas and aided by photophonographic memory for word-meaning associations; only, the computer was operated by a creative soul.

But, hey! while she had been admiring his language— hadn't he been telling her that on his planet, men were bigger than women and generally more dominant politically and industrially? But hadn't he added that there was a prevailing theory of sexual equality that was frequently honored in social action? Double blasphemy! Goddess bless him, *double* blasphemy! Inside, her delight was laughing like a new-sprung brooklet. . . .

Now he pressed: "I have to tell you this, and test you on this: it is essential. I know about the seasonal once-annual arousal of Iola women, although I don't know the mechanics.

However: on Erth, men and women who are interested in each other are normally able to enjoy each other sexually any time of the year, although they may choose to refrain. Does that shock you?"

Luria drained her drink, signaled for more, and thought. She said presently, "There is no question in my mind now. Your humans and our humans have evolved differently. Even though we are all mammals, our primeval origins must have been profoundly different."

"I thought as much. Nevertheless, we are equally human. You agree?"

"I do. Knowing you is expanding my concept of humanity."

"This is deeply true for me also. Now please tell me the basis of your sexual customs, before we start talking about how we may have evolved."

Drinks came, and she sipped hers and then told it: "I suppose you know that our year is four seasons of ten weeks or a hundred days each, and the seasons are related to Iola's perturbations toward the four black holes. We women come into sexual season once a year, in one of those four seasons, mostly toward the middle when the perturbation is maximum. This is the season for Kyria, and mine comes in ten weeks. At climax, we are full of eggs and fluid, and our fierce need is to be clasped by a male who will press-out our eggs into our fluid and fertilize them in our fluid. The current scientific view is, that among our proto-ancestors, the males pressed our eggs into outside pond-water and spermed the pond; but we humans appear to have evolved from a mutation series which progressively internalized this process.

"Klaus, you must comprehend that among us women there are many attitudes about this male clasping. Most women, like Kyria, disdain males and suffer the clasping as annual necessity. A few of us get hooked on the male clasping and frequently sneak down into the areas of the male warrens looking for suitable studs; these women experience social contumely—can you understand?"

"I certainly can. It makes me think of diversified attitudes among men and women on Erth."

"All right. I guess aberration is common to all human species, our big brains can override or distort our instincts. And I guess contumely is equally common, with respect to any departure from local sexual customs."

"Luria, would you want to tell me where *you* fit in that range?"

"Maybe another time, Klaus."

"You needn't ever tell me. Now: except at seasonal climax, most women keep men at a distance?"

"Klaus, we oppress them, they are virtually despised slaves; and I am one who happens to think this a great mistake. I know several men who are highly intelligent, and I suspect that most others could be educationally uplifted if we gave them any life-incentive. Anyhow, most of us do keep them away from us, except seasonally when we must choose two for the coupling."

"Two?"

"They fight in the woman's presence, that's customary; and the winner first clasps her to fertilize most of her eggs; and the loser clasps her then, if he is still able after the fight, but his late-coming sperm won't catch many uncaught eggs, it is mainly to consummate her after-need. I think it's probably an ancient eugenics arrangement, perhaps prehistoric or even pre-human, and we have formalized it. So naturally, males in general are damned pugnacious by nature. I admit that the fight is arousing—"

"And the consequences?"

"In the amnion the tads grow and prey on each other for ten weeks; by that time commonly three have devoured or starved-out the others. Then these three emerge: usually one female and two males, not always. I don't exactly know why this ratio: female adults are stronger, but maybe male tads are hungrier. My brood was different: me and Kyria and only one male."

"If you and Kyria had the same mother and father, why different surnames?"

"Why not?"

"So. Well; and where is your brother?"

"Who'd know about a brother? The males are sent to public farms, you lose track if you ever kept track; he and I may even have had each other, we wouldn't know, it doesn't matter, if we produced any weak ones they were eaten inside me by the strong ones. Is that brutal, Klaus?"

"I see it merely as natural survival of the fittest, happening before morality can be taught: in the nature of your species, taking place before they can even begin to start being soul-human. An Erth-man shoots billions of sperms into at least

one woman during his lifetime, but only a few survive and
make—tads. All right. When your tads are born, how fully
human are they?"

"They have four limbs, their tails are gone, they are maybe
yay long, you can tell they are human, they start learning
right away. They drink woman's milk or a substitute for another ten weeks, and then they are strong enough to go to a
nursery school and drink cow's milk."

"Is this talk bothering you, Luria?"

"It's a fascinating process. Keep questioning."

"How many tads have *you* had?"

"I think fourteen. I was late starting, in my early twenties.
It's more like nineteen years old for most women."

"Do you suckle your own children?"

"For about a week, and after that we have a milk-
bank—at our class-level, that is."

"Did you and Kyria *know* your mother?"

"Not really."

"Thanks for candor, friend Luria; I'll hope to learn more
about this later. Well. This leads me to what is different
about your night spot here. Nobody but women at the tables.
All these women behaving like our businessmen when they
are together at night relaxing over drinks without women.
Most times it is different in Erth night spots. Almost every
man has a woman with him, and he and she are *in some
sense* interested in each other sexually."

"Always?"

"Practically always, but there are many degrees of this.
They may be permanent pairs, and then the sex interest may
be just a general background aura, perhaps growing specific
with the evening if they are young. Or casual acquaintances,
in which case the sexual interest is often important, but they
are restraining it until they know each other better. Or
business associates, perhaps sexually uninterested in each
other, but nevertheless each dealing with the other a bit
specially because of the sex-difference. Or they may be highly
aroused with each other, rather like Iola females and males
when the women are just coming into season but aren't quite
there. Do you follow me?"

Luria nodded, really seeing this bizarre thing. She was
nowhere near season but male-interested nevertheless; and
here with her was admirable mellow-aging interesting Klaus
who was able to dive off the hospital roof with her and swim

strongly despite his lack of finger-and-toe webbing. Was Klaus perhaps sexually interested in Luria? This was impossible for her to know from his attitude; clearly he liked her, as she liked him; but if he had any desire to tamper with her, presumably he had this interest under semi-permanent restraint. Luria, a self-contained woman of high intelligence and short on un-useful inhibitions, usually knew what she wanted, and frequently got it, and once in a long while this was the offbeat thrill of smuggling in a highly select male for clandestine sport out of season. Experimentally interesting indeed it would be, if Klaus were to be her male next season—partly for sensual bizarre; partly to learn whether their alien eggs and sperms might by some unlikely chance be mutually viable, this purpose having particular importance for a well-kept Luria-secret which Klaus would be learning about.

"Well," he was continuing, "the night life among male companions without women, on our world, starts-out interesting, and may grow exciting at moments when beautiful women are on the stage—just as these women, even you, seemed aroused to special interest when those males were misbehaving a while ago. But eventually this quality of male-companionate night life grows relatively dull, the other sex at the same table is missed somehow; at a night spot, we male-accompanied men may drink too much in order to overcome this, or we may decide to go to somebody's house and play cards, or we may try to find sex partners, or we may break up and go home and go to sleep. And I think your women here will be generally behaving like Erth-men in a one-sex situation. Am I right?"

She was frowning at her drink; this linguistic genius from an unknown world was getting it all so pat: he *had* to have high human interest, he *had* to. And were he a political leader here—but Holy Harmnion, how discomforting *that* idea was, to imagine a male leader of women! It wasn't the first time that she had raised within herself the concept that maybe the women in her land were dead wrong in oppressing the men. What if Flaria had been a nation in which men and women were mutually accepted and educated on a basis of equal rights, with suitable safeguarding sexual tabus but with extensive sexual freedom by mutual consent? Wouldn't leadership then be determined, allowing for political vagaries, on a basis of *personal* qualities, sex irrespective? And wouldn't women continue to lead half the time and even usually? And if a man like Klaus should appear, wouldn't he quickly be recognized as a leader without any thought of sexual discrimination?

For that matter—maybe, just maybe—wouldn't the present problem with Godzha have been obviated?

Now he jarred her, though, and Kyria too, by blurting to all three of them: "Let's get out of here and visit a night spot for men!"

Shaken Luria and deeply disturbed Kyria conferred swiftly in low whispers. Kyria came to reluctant agreement with Luria's argument that these ambassadors had to see the male side of things, and that the women had to take them. Luria signaled for the roboserver, punched in her number after the total it showed, and pocketed the receipt; she stood, saying, "Lets' go." Klaus commented to Duke as they arose: "Isn't it great here? Nobody to tip!"

Linguistically, Klaus had been noticing that their words for *woman* and *female* were the monosyllabic root-words, that *man* and *male* were bisyllabic derivatives: the opposite of Anglian usage, as might have been expected. But he remembered that the Gallic *homme* and *femme* were fairly noncommittal.

Club Streljo, the high-level female spot where they had dined, was on the periphery of town-center, but not far enough off the park to encourage disagreeable events in its neighborhood. There was no male spot near the park. Kyria wanted to call a cab, but the men preferred to pick up some local night back-street walking-color. "Some of it," Luria warned, "will be pretty seamy"; and when Klaus demanded the meaning of that word, she told him: "Wait and see."

Luria, who knew her way around, had in mind Club Manzi, the very most élite of the male places: it was low enough there, her guests didn't need worse for an introduction. En route, what they saw caused Klaus to murmur: "Now I understand *seamy*." They passed plenty of male nudity shows; male prostitutes were patrolling the streets in the usual pairs, and once in a while a shame-slinking woman would pick up a pair and move away with them. Smitten Kyria felt an urge to rationalize: "Those may be women in season whose class is too low to get any other kind of mating—" Luria sharply interjected: "Kyria, don't be absurd—*all* warrens have season coordinators!" Klaus patted Kyria's arm:

"Don't feel bad—it's like *our* city backstreets, only reverse
the sexes. Reverse them usually—not always."

At Club Manzi, the little ornately dressed maître d' unctu-
ously murmured an effeminate high-tenor welcome—then de-
light-squealed when he comprehended that the two very tall
women must be the unbelievable alien men whose comings
and goings were big news for the kenners. He waltzed them
to the best table in the crowded little cabaret which jangled
with hard sensation-evocative noises—Kyria shuddered to
think that it was called music. This table was in a wall-booth
slightly elevated above the others, where the newcomers could
easily view the dancing and the stage show and could survey
the patrons at their tables. The maître d' signaled for two
little uniformed male-human waiters who agonized over the
drink orders and scurried off to expedite delivery. Klaus inquired: "No roboservers?" Luria expostulated: "In a *men's*
place?"

Of course their VIP treatment had drawn stares from all
patrons, had even slowed the all-male stage show which was
bawdy to an extreme. Kyria didn't know when she had been
so hideously embarrassed. Once in a while she'd slummed
with her woman-buddies here (they wouldn't dare go lower);
but the special point of embarrassment was, that she and her
sister Luria were entertaining these otherworld supermen who
were equal to the best of Iola-women and charming to boot,
yet exhibiting this Club Manzi as the prime example of
Gladowr's *best* men at play. She tried to nurse her drink, but
it went down faster than she had planned; when she ordered
the next round, impulsively she called for narcotic cigarettes,
an almost never-never for her, feeling a need for sedation
and detachment.

Klaus and Duke accepted cigarettes; Luria waived, and
watched the men. They drew, and inhaled, and exhaled lan-
guorously, and studied their cigarettes, and studied the ceiling, and turned to each other with raised eyebrows. Duke
said, actually in Flaric: "You tell her, Klaus." His eyes full
of sympathy, Klaus leaned toward Kyria: "I'm sorry, we really can't smoke these—we want to keep our senses as fully
open as the drinks will allow." Whereupon he stubbed out his
cigarette; and Duke, gazing upon Kyria with deep regret,
stubbed out his. And of course she killed hers; and then, staring down at the table in confusion, she apologized, making
the nature of her disturbance explicit.

Klaus laid a hand on Kyria's hand on the table; Luria thought it an interestingly reassuring female gesture—Kyria would never have let an Iola-man do that. He said: "Cool it, Kyria." Holy Harmnion, he was inventing slang, and the meaning was crystal clear! And when Kyria looked up at Klaus, he squeezed her hand; and when he released it, Duke claimed it.

Impulsively for an instant Luria squeezed Klaus's hand in both her hands, wanting to do the same for Duke but unable to reach across the table to where Duke sat with Kyria. She said to Klaus: "These squealers here, these little fellows who ogle us and flirt with each other and scream their pleasure at the low-grade stage show—these are the *best* of our men: imagine what the mere average is like! These are the characters on whom we women have to depend for our annual reproduction imperative. Look, you two aliens—can you stomach this?"

After thought, Klaus turned to Duke for translation and discussion; but Duke was all wrapped up with Kyria, expanding lessons in Flaric. Klaus took it upon himself to suggest: "If these men combine their genes with yours to produce your female offspring, the genetic quality of these men can't be all that bad."

"That's the sort of answer I was hoping to get."

"Our galaxy is loaded with planets where once-oppressed races, considered inferior, boosted themselves to full equality when they were encouraged by opportunity and equipped with education. For instance, how do you see men in your economy?"

"Hard labor, naturally. Mines, factories. A few superiors, like the men in this club, get office and store assignments—they've learned to control themselves in the presence of women."

"And in your military?"

"Unfit for military service. Can't meet physical standards."

"They are weaklings, these mine workers?"

"Well, no, most of them have a natural strength, they keep fit, they can dive off the hospital roof—they have to keep fit, if they want to win fights for women. Only, for the military, they are too short, and most of them are illiterate."

"Their small size might often be advantageous in military operations, like sniping, or infiltrating lines, or like crawling through an air-duct on a space-ship. Well, never mind, it's

too late to think about that resource in the present showdown
phase of your Godzhalk war. But—you said most are illiterate; then some are literate. *How* literate are some?"

"Damn you, Klaus, you're forcing me into self-revelation."

"Of what sort?"

"Well—here, I just saw somebody, I want you to meet
him."

Kyria and Duke were beginning to listen to the Luria-
Klaus dialog; and Duke was finding to his satisfaction that he
could now catch a number of words and piece together some
sort of meaning-pattern.

Luria, peering around, re-located a nattily dressed little
wandering man, caught his eye, beckoned to him. With his
face pleasure-illuminated, the man hurried to their booth and
bowed low: "Kra Threll, my honor. Kra Lladyr, you are welcome indeed. And—" He paused uncertain, gazing at the
alien men whose head-height stitting was nearly at his head-
height standing; he was slight, strong, brown, early-middle-
aged handsome. It came into Klaus that he should stand for
courtesy, then that perhaps he should not because of his superior stature; he compromised by half-standing with difficulty because of the table, and Duke half-stood also; the
gesture pleased Luria, puzzled Kyria, and rattled the Iola-man.

Luria said: "Dr. Heller, Dr. Duke—I want you to meet
my friend Herder Maxus, he is the proprietor of Club
Manzi."

Klaus and Duke extended their hands, and Maxus hesitantly took them. "Our great pleasure," Klaus asserted; "my
friend Duke shares my pleasure, he speaks little Flaric."

"Thank you, thank you," Maxus effused. "Please to sit,
Doctors."

As they sat, Klaus was aware that much impropriety was
occurring here: Kyria was ashen, and male spectators were
scandalized. Luria remarked with piquant savor: "Maxus is a
remarkable man, he is also the coordinator of Warren Kreczy
which is the élite men's warren. Without much help, he has
picked up an excellent education—haven't you, Herder?"

"Fair, I guess," agreed flustered Maxus.

"I may be helping a little with his finishing-off. Can you
imagine the initiative of the man? Head of the best warren,
proprietor of the best club, and now he is assisting me in my
law practice!"

"Doctors," Maxus protested, "Kra Threll is exaggerating

terribly! All I do in her office is a few errands that she assigns, and sometimes a little reading—"

"Besides all that," Luria exulted, "he is my chief assistant in a private little project that I hope to show you, Klaus. And further, he has never, but *never*, made an uninvited pass at me!"

Maxus mumbled: "Please excuse me now, I have to visit with all these patrons—"

A devil of curiosity drove Klaus into querying: "Maxus, would your warren perhaps have a vacant room with two beds for a couple of visiting alien men?"

The atmosphere froze. Luria placed a warning hand on Klaus's arm, squeezing gently.

The sensitive face of Maxus grew troubled indeed. "Dr. Heller, if you are proposing that you stay in our warren, I am most honored, and we would like nothing better. But in honesty, I have to say that I do not advise it. And—do excuse me, I see an old friend flagging me—" He fled.

Difficult silence. Duke, weltering in lost subtleties, awaited some clarification. Kyria's fingers were nervously tapping her package of narcotic cigarettes; then viciously she threw the package on the floor, crushed it, drained her drink, and looked around for their waiter.

Luria resolutely asserted, "I agree with Herder Maxus: that would be a bad idea."

Klaus responded, "I think I know why. But Duke and I can look after ourselves, at least when we are together."

"Either of you can fight off any two of them—but, say, any five of them?"

"Is that really likely in Warren Kreczy, the *best* male warren, the one that furnishes self-controlled males to work among women in stores and offices?"

"Can't say for sure, friend Klaus; just can't say. A female office is not a male residence. Here, let's put it objectively. The men in Warren Kreczy would know you are men; but because of your sizes and manners, they would be haunted by a feeling that you are women too, illicitly quartered in their own haunts. And so—what do you know about the urgency of compulsive perversity?"

"I see what you mean. But I want to think about it. Shall we change the subject?"

"Let's give it a good shot."

Duke and Kyria were back into their private communion. Klaus balanced his line of questioning, while Luria expectantly waited.

He opened: "We've agreed that the humans on our two worlds evolved differently. All right. From what sort of animals did your race evolve?"

Cautiously Luria suggested: "It would seem that the ancestors of our primates must have been much like the ancestors of your primates——"

"No no, I mean, farther back, much farther back. At one time, the highest animals on Erth were cold-blooded fish——"

"Here too."

"And then, as land pushed itself up out of the ocean, some of our fish used the land increasingly until evolution brought them to where they could breathe either on land or under water, although they still frequented the water. But still they were cold-blooded, and they laid and fertilized their eggs on water and then forgot them, the young had to survive on their own. We call them amphibians, and there still are many."

"All *right*."

"Well, some of our amphibians got to where they liked land and air so much that in the adult stage they could only breathe air. They kept on swimming, often, but they had to come up for air."

"But the tads, Klaus—the larvae—*they* were still water-breathers?"

"Right. But now: out of our amphibians developed an extensive group of land-living animals, air-breathers from the moment they emerged from their eggs. We call them reptiles, and still there are many of those, but they continue to be cold-blooded egg-layers."

Luria was frowning. "Here too—only, we were talking about human evolution, and you seemed to be growing warmer, and now you seem to be growing colder."

"Not for Erth I'm not. Because one or more primordial reptiles developed warm blood and internal procreation, with milk-exuding glands to feed their young; and originally Erth-primates arose from these. The warm-blooded reptiles were primitive mammals; we are more highly developed mammals."

Luria's frown was now creasing her forehead. "I can't tell

you how fascinating this is—because on Iola we went approximately the same route—only, we are sure that our ancestral mammals developed earlier, directly out of amphibians, by-passing reptiles which evolved independently parallel."

"A-ha!"

"Aha what?"

"Female dominance, internally swimming water-breathing tads, lack of external ears, webbed fingers, webbed toes!"

"The last ten are marvellous for swimming. How can *you* swim so well?"

"We just have to work harder. How many chambers in your hearts?"

"Three. What's your count?"

"Four."

"I hope that's good. If we are so completely alien to each other—how can we be friendly so fast?"

"Simple, my Luria. What counts is the mind, the self, the consciousness, the feeling. The nature of the body contributes to that, but it is secondary to that. We call ourselves human, you call yourselves human; we are *all* human, you see?"

"What do you think it means to be human?"

"There's a commonly accepted definition in the Code of our Interplanetary Union. I'm nowhere near able to translate it—but what it comes to is, you are human, and I am human, and a lot of much more bizarre forms in this galaxy are likewise human."

"Since it is part of your Interplanetary Code, as a lawyer I would like some day to hear the definition in full."

"I promise; but right now I want to derive from my summary of it." He gestured at the wild little crowd; in one cluster an enraged five-man fight had developed (Luria was seeing it as a normal male occurrence not interesting except in season).

"This is the way your males have unfolded," said Klaus. "They are what they are. You accept them merely as necessary to species continuance, but in fact they have minds and wills of their own—that little squabble merely illustrates that they have minds and wills. Your men are emotion-dominated, although you are one who admits that education and incentive offered to good male intelligence can produce a Herder Maxus or better.

"You women have instead gone in the direction of controlled intellectual production for the sake of aesthetic pleasure. On Erth, increasingly the men and women are mentally like you women; but some of us, male and female, are emotion-dominated like your men. Duke and I respect the ways of your differences."

She glowed. Decidedly she must show this Klaus her private project with Maxus. . . .

Duke, who had been listening and had caught the gist with Kyria's help, spoke rapidly to Klaus, who nodded and said to both women: "Duke wants me to tell you this. When we jumped into that black hole, we were not trying to kill ourselves, it was a thing we'd prepared for with great care and cost, Luria has seen my space-suit, and Duke wore the same. We wanted to reach your planet if we could, for whatever response we could make to your mayday. But just as much, we wanted to learn about black holes from the inside, so we could take the information back to our chief who would use it to reach your star-system with an intervention squadron. By good luck and with Luria's help, we escaped from the hole with new knowledge and came here; and now we are learning about your planet. But we *have* to go back to Erth with this new knowledge. We aren't pressing you, we aren't in a hurry, it looks as though I'll be able to communicate with Erth via nedi-rays in a day or two—but this does need to be demanded. When and how can we go back to Erth?"

Luria and Kyria, both shaken, stared at the remnants of their drinks. The concept of returning these men to Erth was so ridiculously impossible that neither woman had given it any thought at all.

Dream black-out.

And in the nothingness, The Voice. *End of dream-information, Inspector. What you've experienced is what Klaus would call a mere come-on. It was all real preparation for what eventuated in the deaths of Klaus and Kyria; but if you were to dream the rest, you would doubt its reality—and you must not doubt.*

Instead of dreaming the rest, you will have to go there-then. Croyd can help you do that. Not there-now, Inspector: there-then!

Claudine came awake snickering, as she sometimes did when a dream had been droll. Such exquisitely staged action!

Bombshell: no hope of returning to Erth. Blackout! And The Voice with a little epilog . . .

Her snicker cut itself off, and she sat up in bed, running a hand back through her hair. Every time, that Voice had been the voice of Luria!

Part Six

HOT PURSUIT

Nereid, Manhattan, Long Island, Houston
7-10 July 2495

16.   OF DREAMS AND THE PAST

Dream-weary Claudine was breakfasting in negligée alone in her Nereid suite when a phone call came; she merely activated the phone from where she sat. Information: Secretary Croyd's frigate would depart at 1230; lunch and dinner aboard, Erth touchdown at 2230. Inspector St. Cyr would please be at the pad by 1200 hours; a skimmer would be picking her up.

Ten hours with Murchison, then—and after all *that!* Oh hell, face it: she *needed* time with Duke; she liked him, and his marriage proposal had seemed genuine, he'd tried to be crass about getting the erotics out of the way first, why not? he'd been burned in his first and now-dying marriage! But Claudine had chased him away. They needed to apologize to each other, and shake on it, and be friendly for a while—with honesty about the fact that he was a potential suspect and she would be ruthless—until it would settle in one way or another. She enjoyed amour when it sparkled, but marriage was an entailment that she had never seriously considered, it was a real value but it could ruin a career that she adored; on the other hand, Duke might become a real friend, and they respected each other as different-field pros. . . .

Potential suspect. The stupid part of it was, that if any truth lurked in last night's dreaming—and certain parts of the first night's dreaming had been independently confirmed by Croyd—then a possible case against Duke was gaining plausibility. To Claudine, Duke had admitted knowing both Klaus and Kyria. Meanwhile, in the dreaming, Duke had seemed well on the way toward falling in love with Kyria. But somehow, Klaus had got Kyria—although *he* had seemed highly in-

159

terested in *Luria*. And that switch *could* have engendered in
Duke a jealousy motif. Claudine chuckled dry: she might be
catching Duke on some kind of rebound.

Oh, and wait, now. Hueena. If the dream-explanation
should be true—invisibility induced by metabolic acceleration. And both men, as Croyd had confirmed, had carried
and used metabolic acceleration in their gigantic space-suits.
Now, if those suits, or one of them, had come back with the
men, it was conceivable that Duke had somehow got possession of one of the metabolic accelerators.

Decidedly, she and Croyd would have a lot to talk about,
this trip!

At the pad, she smiled up at Duke, extending a hand:
"Friends, at least?" His responding down-grin was twisted,
but his handshake was warm: "Friends, at least, until we
know each other better. I'm sorry I came on too fast for both
of us." When he put it that way, what did *she* have to apologize for? She clasped his arm: "Let's hit the ship."

Aboard the frigate, though, Duke seemed to interiorize. He
came out with some perfunctory responses at lunch, and after
lunch over coffee in a salon-stellarium, but much of the conversation even in Duke's presence was almost private between
her and Croyd. He was a man she could go for, and she
gathered that she was a woman he could go for, but neither
of them was going to go, and they were finding each other's
minds engrossingly interesting. Much of the time was spent
swapping reminiscences, he about his agent-work before he
became a minister, she about many kinds of interstellar inves-
tigations. "In a way," he exclaimed, "you and I have been
doing the same sort of work!" Several times, it appeared,
without ever knowing each other they had narrowly missed
colliding.

In one of her tales about distant planets, a description of
one man engaged him closely: a man who had learned to
maneuver in the past—or in uptime, as the man had preferred to say. "My term for it exactly," Croyd mused; "I wonder whether he arrived at it on the same theoretical
considerations."

This part of the talking was halfway through the afternoon, on a Croyd-guided tour of the frigate. (Duke had demurred: "I've seen a frigate"; so had Claudine, but she loved
them.) They were studying the tail-guns that bristled around

the stern repulsors; and Claudine regretfully deferred the topic of uptime, because the topic of guns raised the Heller-pertinent question: concerning a raygun which could project a convergent beam at a wide seventy-five-degree angle. "I never heard of that," Croyd observed, "but let's ask the crew chief." The bright young man he summoned—either a Cathayan from Erth or a golden guy from Ligeria—shook his head when questioned: you might bend the rays inward with lasers, but—a seventy-five degree convergence? To bring the rays about that much, the weapon would have to be enormous!

Croyd suggested: "Maybe it was *two* rayguns, Claudine? fired at a wide angle apart, and converging?"

"Good thought. Only, now you present me with a problem of *two* invisible criminals and *two* invisible weapons!" Then, having a weird thought, she eye-fixed the crew chief: he, comprehending that his two cents had been contributed, saluted and wandered away. Now she eye-fixed Croyd: "Might the two criminals have been Murchison and Croyd—metabolically accelerated?"

He said gravely, meeting her eyes: "You are right to give attention to every suspicion, even of your own boss. Don't drop it until you are sure."

"Do you care to deny, sir?"

"For your record, yes, I deny."

She looked down, feeling foolish; she would only be distracted by playing with absurdity. She said: "Sorry. Remote possibility dropped."

He reiterated: "Don't drop it until you are sure."

"Yessir," she assured him, having dropped it. "New hypothesis. Maybe somebody located in uptime and therefore invisible fired the shots into actuality?"

"So it's even *four* dimensions you think in! However, no: a shot fired in uptime could not affect the target living in actuality."

"Croyd, I am going to ask a silly."

"Give tongue."

"Well: you can go into uptime. Can anybody else do it?"

"Didn't you tell me that you had known one? I believe that anybody above some intelligence threshold can learn to do it, the powers involved are essentially human powers. Why?"

"Could you teach *me?*"

"Maybe."

"How long would it take?"

"You're a fast read; in your case, it might not take very long. What did you have in mind?"

"A possible tie-in with the Heller murders. Are you seeing why?"

"Yes, but I'm seeing also a long-range difficulty for you, Inspector."

"Namely, that ability to enter and experience the past of every suspect I ever investigate would make me an omnipotent-omniscient investigator. So investigation would quickly become boring for me, apart from serious questions of legality."

"Precisely, Claudine."

"*You* have that boredom-hazard, Croyd. How do *you* control it?"

"By not availing myself of the power until and unless extraordinarily urgent humane purposes can't be accomplished in any other way."

"Well; and if I had such power, I would never use it until and unless it became evident that a crime couldn't be solved in any other way."

"Still, Inspector, ethically unsatisfactory."

"I think so too. You tell me why."

"In solving a crime, you are identifying a criminal. The criminal meanwhile is trying to avoid being identified. Maybe he is doing this so wittily well that no normal police methods *could* identify him—but he is using only normal wit for this. And there may also be ethical reasons why he *should not* be identified—as in the case of a freedom-undergrounder committing a patriotic crime against a captor-state. But you. . . . You see what I am meaning."

"That I do."

"Your answer?"

"There is no criminal, ethical or non-ethical, who uses Erth-natural methods of committing his crime and who cannot potentially be identified by Erth-natural methods. But it is possible that some criminal may commit a crime by methods unnatural to Erth and which therefore cannot be identified by Erth-natural methods. I say that such a criminal may ethically be sought by Erth-unnatural methods, just as an Erth-unnatural weapon may ethically be countered by another Erth-unnatural weapon."

"Only, Claudine—have you finally established that the

crime of murdering the Hellers was committed by Erth-un-natural methods?"

"No, I have not, although I may be on the verge of that."

"Then you haven't yet exhausted Erth-natural approaches—or Erth-natural suspects?"

"Not quite. Two Erth-natural suspects remain, maybe even three; I don't yet have the foggiest about approaches—unless maybe, invisibility through metabolic acceleration was one. Croyd—*does* the acceleration make one invisible?"

"Without asking how you arrived at that notion, I'll answer, yes."

She tight-clamped her jaw; she'd be *damned* if she'd mention any more dream-revelations!

He saved her by back-tracking the conversation. "I won't ask for the names of your two or three suspects—"

"Thanks—"

"But how can you be sure that there are only two or three?"

"It is possible that more may emerge, but what I know about Heller makes me doubt it, and I wouldn't know how to start looking for more unless they should just pop out of the woodwork. These are special premeditated preplanned crimes requiring motive, high technical intelligence, and access to an unknown sophisticated weapon."

"Then you are convinced that if these three suspects end up exculpated, the crime cannot be solved by Erth-natural methods. And so you would appreciate having an Erth-unnatural investigative technique at your disposal, on a standby basis."

"Oui."

"How would you like to start the lessons after dinner?"

Along about 2000 hours, with post-dinner brandy about gone, Claudine glanced at Croyd, and he nodded, and she turned to Duke, laying a hand on his arm. "Duke, would you mind very much if Croyd and I ran away from you now? We have some official stuff—"

His smile was twisted, but he laid a hand on her hand on his arm. "Go with God, go with Croyd even. Everything I said stays open-valid."

Arising, she laid lips on his forehead, and she whispered: "I have to warn you, Duke. You're a possible suspect now."

164   IAN WALLACE

He back-whispered: "No sweat, do your stuff, I'm not guilty."

Having squeezed a Murchison shoulder, she retired with Croyd to his cabin.

The session was all business, a discussion of theoretical grounding for uptime; no action-practice at all, there was no time, they would be touching down at 2230.

Before learning to maneuver in uptime, or the living representation of the gone past, it was necessary for Claudine to know what she would be maneuvering in. And that entailed thorough understanding of Croyd's well-tested concepts of space, time, matter, and mind.

Spacetime, it seemed, as a four-dimensional continuum was a mere instrumental construct useful for space-mathematics. But in the being of things, all that was actual anywhere now was simultaneously actual now; for any experiencer, there was never any time except the present, shaded by the transience of just-now-vanishing events and by the imminence of what had already become overwhelmingly probable; in any actuality, real past and real future existed only in this thickness of the present. Time-passage was a given, change occurred through it.

Space was not a vacuum, but instead a continuum of submicroscopic thrust-and-lure centers randomly arising and perishing; and they were the stuff that the repulsor drives fed upon.

Matter arose out of space when some of those semi-particles happened to fall into mutual systematic synchronizations of their thrusts and lures. All stars and planets evolved out of these material developments. Life, and eventually the many forms of human life, evolved out of these material developments—possibly, but unprovably, with some kind of artistic-experimental guidance at major turnings of the ways.

Mind, too, was an evolvement—not an evolvement of matter, but an evolvement by matter; and as it matured, mind grew increasingly different from matter, acquired partial independence of matter, eventually might take control of itself and of its mothering matter. A mind was a continuum essentially similar to raw space, which was in fact subjective in each quasi-particle of the raw space continuum. Aided by the brain which was continually extruding it, but increasingly in command of its own brain, a mind gradually built up processes and controls and memories of its own, independent of its brain. You could call a mind a soul, if you wished—if you stipulated that a soul was always more or less intelligent as well as emotive.

This relative independence of mind conjecturally suggested the possibility of mind-survival after body-death, although there was a strong probability that such a mind would have to find a brain-surrogate in order to keep from being dissolved in raw space. But it also suggested another possibility which was *not* any longer conjectural, because Croyd had tested it repeatedly. And that was the possibility of a strong mind temporarily disengaging itself from its body and traveling among uptime-traces.

For it seemed that particles of matter—and Croyd wasn't sure whether the particles that did it were reons or kamatons or complete atoms, but he favored the kamatons which constituted atomic nuclei—were continually extruding their pasts into space. Or perhaps it was that each kamaton lived for an instant and, dying, budded-off a perfect reproduction of itself, which in turn budded as it died, and so on: the life-continuum of a kamaton (if that was the right sort of particle) was in fact a life-continuum of a whole series of parent-daughter kamatons. And the whole cadaver-string of perished kamatons streamed out into space like a filament. The mass of such a filament was greater in relation to its thickness than any mass in actuality, while the thickness of such a filament was smaller than the magnitude of any actual particle. And this combination of virtually infinite mass with virtually zero thickness meant that the filaments were quite undetectable by any material method; indeed, a filament would simply cheese unnoticed through any star or planet or particle which happened to come into contact with it, leaving the cheesed-through particle undamaged.

These filaments had another property. Since they were formed of perished experiences, they preserved unaltered and unalterable the pattern of every material that had ever occurred. Thus these filaments constituted an eternally unperishable quasi-past. They were not the past, they were its perfect record—complete even with mental events, insofar as those mental events had affected the particles of material brains.

These filaments were *uptime*: a complete record of all the past. Each filament was analogous to a recording of sound on

a magnetized wire (a primitive recording method still used
for certain purposes).

And if a mind should learn how to engage itself with these
filaments, to *run* them, that mind could experience the past
subjectively, just as the past had been; the past would rise up
with new life in the mind.

And this was the sort of endeavor that Claudine was proposing to undertake.

Of course the questions by Claudine were numerous, and
their very direction and point satisfied Croyd that she was understanding.

Once she objected: "Why should my mind have to depart
my body for me to do this? Don't *you* do it body and all?
Didn't your body rescue Duke and me from the scouter?"

He replied: "Curious as it may seem, doing it as a disembodied mind entails fewer complications than bringing a body
along. If we can even get you to the point of doing it as a
mind, we'll be lucky."

She meditated that. And then her eyes opened wide indeed as she thought of a dream-entailment.

She probed cautiously. "Last night you said you had a theory about veridical dreams, but we didn't get into it. Is it
related to *this* theory?"

He responded with a quizzical half-smile: "Tell me how."

She phrased it with care. "A sleeping mind might chance
to intercept and run traces of actual events which had happened to somebody else—perhaps a long distance away, perhaps long ago."

The squawk-box announced: "Now hear this. This is the
captain. We are in terminal deceleration. Touch-down in
twenty-nine minutes. That is all."

"Again," said Croyd, "tell me how that could happen."

She worked it through. "Consider somebody sleeping somewhere on Erth—me, for instance. While I am sleeping, my
planet is moving me in at least three ways: it is rotating, it is
revolving around the sun, it is participating in sidereal motion; and there are probably larger motions too. Just by
chance, a system of filamental traces from some past series of
events brushes me, enters me, my sleeping mind engages it—
and reexperiences."

"That is my theory precisely. But I can't prove it."

"But Croyd—suppose I am sleeping on Nereid—or on

Erth, for that matter—and reexperiencing events that occurred only half a year ago but a thousand light-years distant.
How fast do those filaments grow how long?"

He frowned. "If you are talking about your apparently
veridical dream about Heller on Iola, I think you have a
problem."

"*Dreams*, Croyd. Another one last night. Consecutive to
the first—and to prior pre-dreams."

"Eh! I confess I haven't a notion—considering the short
time in the past, the travel-distance for trace-filaments is horrible. On the other hand, looking at those larger sidereal motions that you suggested, all galaxies are in outward motion
from each other at relative rates averaging about two
hundred kilometers per second."

"But that doesn't work out to anything like a thousand
light-years in six months—"

"There's another faintly possible hypothesis. Perhaps—
maybe—the entire metagalaxy is spinning, involving our
galaxy at or near its rotational center. So perhaps in our
galactic or metagalactic motion, or both, we *have* overtaken
filament-traces from Iola six months old. Having virtually infinite mass, the filaments also have virtually infinite inertia:
they stand still while the heavens move past and around and
through them."

"Still, Croyd, why would my brain and my mind keep se-
lecting a consecutive series of events related to just those
people on just that planet?"

"Well—"

"And besides, that doesn't give us any theory about veridical *prophetic* dreams."

"Aha! There I can answer you—"

Standing, sighing, she patted his shoulder. "We're much too
close to disembarkation time. When do I get my next lesson?"

17.   THE INSIDE OF WILSON

Duke said a formal goodbye and departed to find transportation to Houston. Croyd solichopper-squired Claudine from the Aerospace Dynamics spaceport to her apartment roof; having kissed his cheek, she dismounted and waved him away. It was 2310 on the night of July 7.

In her apartment, she found Tuli pacing (Tuli knew her lock-pass code). Whirling, Tuli ran to her, and they embraced. Then tall Tuli stiff-armed her off and demanded: "Why in hell didn't you call me from Nereid?"

"Tuli! Such language! Tchocking!"

"Well, damn it, I mean it, I didn't know whether you were alive or dead!"

Claudine was remorseful. "You do worry, don't you, friend Tuli."

"You just bet I do."

"Well, it was my fault, I was having fun, I forgot. But if you were as worried as all that, you could have called Nereid: my presence there was punched into the operator."

"But that would be long distance!"

"All right, I see your point, I'm here, good. Why don't you join me in a nightcap and stay tonight? I still have your pajamas in my closet."

"If I stay, I may keep you awake all night. Boy, am I loaded!"

"Good again, I'm a long way from sleep myself. Let's go undress, and then you can unload."

Claudine had a guest bedroom adjacent to her own, and with a button-touch she could dissolve the wall between. Tuli, lying in her bed and sipping beer, expatiated while Claudine, in *her* bed, sipped beer and responded.

"Claudine, I have a confession."

"Absolvo te. So confess."

168

"I burgled."

"You—burgled?"

"I just didn't trust that Dr. Werner Voelker. So I burgled. His lab."

"Good God, Tuli, we could be Congressionally investigated!"

Miserably: "Don't I know it!"

"You sound as though you might anticipate some peril."

"I do. I got caught."

Well, that figured: Tuli's intuitions were better than her operations. "All right, tell me who caught you."

"Voelker caught me. And he took me to the president."

"He took you to Clara Wilson?"

"Right."

"What hour of the day or night did you pull off this caper?"

"It was around 0200 hours this morning that he caught me."

"What was Wilson doing that late at night in her office?"

"I got the feeling that she was waiting for Voelker to catch me and bring me in."

Oh-oh! "So what did Wilson say?"

"She wanted to know what I was doing entering one of her laboratories without permission."

"So what was your answer?"

"Really, nothing. I just showed her my search warrant—"

"Tuli! how did you get a warrant?"

"That's almost exactly what Ms. Wilson asked. So I didn't want to tip my game, so I just told her that what I had said to Judge Wertheimer was a matter of court record if she wanted to go into it—"

"So how did you get in to the judge?"

"He's a personal friend of Captain Venuto's, and you told me to check with her on everything and that she was in charge—"

"Okay, okay. Now: what *did* you tell the judge?"

"Not much, really, he was very nice about the warrant—"

"Tuli, I don't care how nice Captain Venuto may be to him, he's a tough judge. What was your reason for the warrant?"

"Look, Claudine, I'm on *your* side. . . . Okay, I'm sorry. Here it is. I told the judge that Voelker was a suspect in the case, that we had reason to suspect the use of a certain kind

of raygun, that I had visited him and he had failed to disclose
such a gun although he is a raygun expert, that on unsworn
testimony by Ms. Wilson we knew that Dr. Voelker had
hated Dr. Heller, and that I felt we should search the lab for
such a gun. So the judge said he didn't see how he could re-
fuse the warrant, since both you and Captain Venuto wanted
it—"

"Oh, my, God."

"Why?"

"Never mind, it's done. Maybe Wertheimer *isn't* such a
tough judge. Didn't he ask you if you had first requested permission for the search from Dr. Voelker or Ms. Wilson?"

"You know, I don't think that crossed his mind at all."

"It should have done. All right: when you showed Ms.
Wilson the warrant, what did she say and do?"

"She just sort of shrugged and let me go."

"Didn't she *say* anything?"

"Well—forgive me, Claudine—something about how she
hadn't thought you were a—I don't think I can say the
word—"

"Bitch?"

"Claudine!"

The inspector, having emitted a long sigh, commented
sweetly: "Tuli, you're a lamb, your thoughts were in the right
place even if you did blow my credit with a dumb course of
action. Sleep well, Tuli: you're my junior partner, I had already absolved you before you confessed."

"Gee, thanks. Don't you want to know what I found?"

"You—*did* find something?"

"I was looking at it when Voelker caught me. It was a raygun with a special adaptation—here, I made a rough
drawing, let me show you."

Tuli sketched props rather well, even suggesting three dimensions. It looked like a normal hand-gun harnessed with
some nifty adaptations held together with thick wires and
welds. Maybe fifteen centimeters dead ahead of the gun
muzzle was a mirror convex to the muzzle; and all around
the muzzle was a wide reflecting collar concave to the convex
mirror. Presumably front mirror and collar mirror were made
of extremely hard ray-resistant stuff, such as irrodium. Claudine mused aloud over it: "The rays emerging from the
muzzle hit the front mirror, are reflected out-backward to the
collar mirror, and again are reflected forward at a wide con-

vergent angle. Well, I'll be damned. And there's a sight adaptation too, the shooter would see his target with the aid of the same mirrors. And it isn't too cumbersome-unbalanced, a guy could hold it easily. Oh, it's beautiful, Tuli—and I bet it doesn't even need any lasers that aren't internal to the gun. Tuli, did you measure the angles of divergence and convergence?"

"I didn't have time before they caught me. But I could make estimates—"

"Don't bother, Tuli: from the drawing it's approx enough, we *are* maybe on a trail. Where can I find that gun?"

"Ms. Wilson promised to keep it impounded for court study."

Prolonged silence.

Tuli, anxious: "Do you think I hit pay-dirt?"

Claudine licked lips. "Go to work in your mind, Tuli. See if you can think out a way for Voelker or somebody to make himself invisible and pass through walls or doors and shoot two victims with this contraption at point-blank range. 'Night, Tuli. Out."

She touched a button to restore the wall between them.

Pulling a new beer out of her bedside fridge, Claudine sipped, studying the sketch; dropping the paper then, she leaned back on her pillows with closed eyes, thinking.

It changed the whole case because of the Wilson angle. Now why had Wilson been there, in late night or early morning, waiting for Voelker to catch Tuli red-handed and bring her before the corporation president? That Voelker might have gone to his lab late at night because of some work-thought that was bugging him, this would be understandable in a specialist; but the presence of *both* of them there at the same time made little sense—unless Tuli's burglary had been anticipated and both Wilson and Voelker were somehow implicated.

Possible pattern: Wilson had fingered Voelker as a red herring for St. Cyr, although in fact Wilson had been in complicity with Voelker on the Heller deaths; somebody, Captain Venuto or Judge Wertheimer or his court clerk, had tipped Wilson or Voelker about the projected warrant-burglary, and the one had alerted the other, and there they were. *Possible* pattern.

It had, of course, the effect of bringing the case back to

Erth, of blasting the Klarta-track into a cocked hat. The Heller posthumous dreaming could have stimulated *all* of that; and even if there had been confirmed veridical elements of Claudine's dreaming, all the rest of the dream-story could have been Claudine-built around them!

And now her mind raced along the Erth-natural tack. Wilson maybe had felt vulnerable to Heller who may have entertained live ambitions of returning to corporation power. Or Wilson may have been his jettisoned mistress jealous of Kyria. Wilson presumably knew that Voelker had an experimental gun with divergent-convergent rays; maybe somewhere else in her complex of laboratories, Wilson had an invisibility mechanism—hey, hadn't her Aerospace Dynamics, under Heller, built the oversize suits with metabolic accelerators?

Yes, it *was* Erth-natural, in this year 2495, that the Hellers might have been killed by a momentarily invisible person with a modified invisible raygun which first diverged backward and then converged forward its rays to make chest-holes and heart-holes without damaged behind-tissues. And as to the obscure relationship between Wilson and Voelker, together with the not-yet-pinpointed motivation of one or the other or both together, that presumably was Erth-abnormal, and get-attable.

What had been the relationships between Heller and Wilson? Maybe Duke could help her with this question, if she could get him to talk. Absolutely the next port of call had to be Duke—the next, that is, after one earlier and most difficult port of call: Wilson.

Meanwhile, she had rendezvous with Croyd tomorrow evening—*this* evening, now—to take more training in the up-time technique. She wasn't yet convinced that she would have to use this technique; she knew only that she wanted to learn it and be ready.

The day was plenty busy, in large part with rigorous catch-up desk work at headquarters. This included rather a stiff interview with Captain Venuto. As did most of St. Cyr's erring subordinates, Venuto departed the office chastened, hating St. Cyr, reluctantly adoring St. Cyr, a self-correcting officer; in due course, Claudine confidently expected to recommend Venuto for promotion.

She brown-bagged lunch alone in her office, meditating.

She phone-talked with the coroner about the Kyria autopsy. Kyria had been fully mammalian; but yes, particularly in the reproductive organization there were frog-like vestiges, although these were hard to nail down because the ovaries had been excised. . . .

"I think you said the ovaries had been excised?"

"That's right, Inspector. And there had also been some internal work within the uterus."

The dreams—the undreamed *sequel* to the dreams. . . . "Doctor, how many chambers did the heart have? I know that it was destroyed—"

"Yes, but judging by the major arteries from and veins to the missing heart—three chambers, Inspector."

Erth-human hearts have four. Erth-frog hearts have three. . . . Luria said three. But I'm sure I know that about frogs, and Tuli and I were thinking frog-people. Mere dream-work?

As to the chest-wound, coroner's measurements: anterior diameter fifteen centimeters, maximum heart-width of 8.4 centimeters neatly clipped by the rays, convergence short of posterior peritoneum at about seventy-five degrees plus or minus two.

So much for dead Kyria. Now, as to dead Heller. During two hours, Claudine endured a wearying review of all the Heller dream-flakes up to this morning. Much was repetitive and much was simply bleh brain-crud, a brain intraspitting randomly without a controlling mind. (Where if anywhere was that mind now?) She sensed that the brain was deteriorating, the dream-potential was about gone, it was nearly time to call quits and atomize him decently. Nothing of pertinent interest there, other than several flash-images of Wilson and of Murchison—and yet, one flash-image haunted her: Wilson and Murchison together, obviously with Heller there although he was the scene's invisible camera because this was subjective.

And that was all.

Well!

Claudine reached for the phone and called Clara Wilson. The secretary regretted, but Ms. Wilson was not available. "I'm so very sorry," Claudine said, "because I'm preparing a newskenner release on the progress of this case, and I was hoping to see Ms. Wilson first; however, if that's how it is—" After some background muttering on an intercom, Ms. Wilson suddenly became available to Inspector St. Cyr at 1645. Bare margin for solichopper! Claudine got out of there.

Clara Wilson received Inspector St. Cyr with unconcealed coldness, not bothering to arise from her desk seat. "Please find a chair, Inspector. You may have no more than two minutes to apologize for that warrant, explaining that your lieutenant and your captain misinterpreted their instructions." She waited.

Having deliberately pulled up a chair facing the desk, Claudine played it equally cold. "Since you've anticipated the structure of my apology, I won't offer it. I was unavoidably called away, and I left no pertinent instructions, and as competent officers having administrative status they acted on their own experienced judgment which I defend. Administrative styles differ, however, as you would be the first to admit. I was toying with the same idea, but my style is different, that is all. I would first have asked Dr. Voelker's permission to search, and in event of his refusal I would have come to you next. But then, failing permission from either of you, I would have requested a warrant, as they did. And now, officially investigating these murders, I will ask you: *would* you have refused permission?"

"The question is now academic—"

"I assure you that it is not."

Wilson's lips reluctantly and satirically widened. "You fence well, Inspector; I often use the same counterthrust ploy. The answer is: yes, I would have refused permission to search a laboratory of this private enterprise on the merest fishing expedition. Presumably you would then have threatened a warrant; and I would have contacted the three judges who might issue such a warrant and requested legal representation ahead of the decision. Had the warrant then been granted, Dr. Voelker and I would have been on hand to be served. But none of this happened, and so it was a thinly legalized burglary; and my attorneys are now preparing a court complaint against the following: you, your two subordinates, your superior Detective Superintendent Wong, the Galactic Police, and Judge Wertheimer. Well, Inspector?"

"Will your attorneys put into their brief an admission that Lieutenant Tuli did find an incriminating weapon in the laboratory?"

"I beg your pardon?"

"In fact, you assured Lieutenant Tuli that the weapon would be impounded for study by court order."

"Oh. *That* weapon, or more properly, that instrument. It is impounded. Klaus ordered Dr. Voelker early last year to dream up such a device. It would be excellent for space crews to use for certain emergency pinpoint destruction requirements. We did not think about it as a weapon, its range is too short, a simple raygun would be better in combat."

"Provisionally I accept that. Nevertheless, I wish to question Dr. Voelker about it, in your presence."

Hesitation; desk-tapping with long pointed gloss-orange fingernails. Then: "In your news release, I would ask that you omit mention of the burglary and of our secret experimental device. The device isn't yet perfected, much less patented, and it hasn't been tied to the crimes. And now that you have done me the rectifying courtesy of consulting me about the release, I am less sure that I will file a complaint about the burglary."

"Trade-off, Ms. Wilson?"

"Bluntly phrased question, Inspector."

"Nevertheless, I did ask it, so phrased."

Wilson grinned openly. "By *God* I can't stay mad at you! All right: no, I am not trying to bribe a police officer. I ask you as a matter of ethics to omit mention of this secret unpatented device until and unless a crime connection has been shown. And whatever your decision about that may be, I will not file a complaint about the burglary."

"Responding to your request, Ms. Wilson, I will omit mention of the device in this particular news release, meanwhile seeking a court order to inspect it. You may notify your attorneys about my intention."

"Bitch!"

"Bluntly phrased epithet, Ms. Wilson."

"I would have expected an academic doctor to know that one epithet is not a phrase."

"I agree, I am bleeding. However, I now have to change my request to a notice of action. I am not asking permission to question Dr. Voelker; I *will* question him. If he evades or refuses to answer, this will open the door for a later news release."

Wilson was now frowningly intent. "You consider it that serious?"

"I do. Particularly since you told me he hated Dr. Heller."

"In court, I would deny having told you such a thing."

"What else might you falsely deny in court, Ms. Wilson?"

Wilson stood, furious; but then instead of ordering Claudine out, she stared, and her taut face lost tension, and she sat again and mused over her visitor. Presently she soft-inquired: "I have forgotten how you like your coffee, Inspector."

"Black and unsweetened, thank you—the way God made it."

"Same here, I gave my secretary His recipe." She spoke into an intercom, then leaned back doing ceiling inspection. Claudine respected her silent thought. The secretary delivered two steaming coffees in grotesque capacious ceramic mugs. Claudine thanked her and sipped. Wilson seamed unaware. The secretary departed.

Wilson then told the molded plaster arabesques on her ceiling: "I am thinking that it would seem bizarre for the President of Aerospace Dynamics to complain about witness-badgering. Your question was apt. In court, I would deny that unguarded remark about Voelker only because I cannot prove it and it would lay me open to a slander charge by Voelker. I don't think I would deny anything else I've said to you so far. But I am toying with the thought that under oath perhaps I would have to make admissions beyond some other things that I have told you."

Claudine waited. Wilson noticed her coffee, and sipped, and thought.

Wilson asked: "Do you have any idea at all what I mean, Inspector?"

"Perhaps if you were asked in court whether your relationships with Heller were entirely platonic—or whether you ever saw him after his retirement—or whether you had doubts about his relationships with Kyria Heller." Claudine was deferring questions about metabolic accelerators: motivation first, technique later.

"You are woman-shrewd. Yes, that is what I was meaning."

Claudine sighed over her good coffee. "By now perhaps you understand me well enough to know that I don't give a personal damn what your relationships were. But professionally, it stays true that sexual relationships jive up emotions and occasionally precipitate crimes."

"Did I kill Klaus, out of pique or otherwise, with Voelker's gadgeted gun or otherwise? the answer is no. Did I hire or incite Voelker or anybody else to do the same thing? the answer is no. I wouldn't have been party to that, not even in the most exaggerated jealousy or ego-bruise. I cared for Klaus, Inspector—he was an unusually nice guy."

"All right, Ms. Wilson; but I think you played along with my court question for a reason beyond mere voluntary confession before it might be extorted."

Wilson was up again, peering out a window, hands behind her fighting with each other. "He and I used to be together often, at my place or at his. We weren't committed to each other, but it was very good. But since his return from the black hole expedition, I've seen him off-duty only half a dozen times, and—"

She paused; the hands worked.

Her voice came again, taut-calm. "My difficulty in expressing this is not personal embarrassment, it is simply very hard to express. It was as though there were another woman, and yet he still cared for me but was afraid of hurting me. For a while I thought that the necessary other woman might be Kyria, but later I was sure she wasn't. I met Kyria twice, we talked a little, she seemed decent but ingoing, I rather liked her. But she wasn't my rival. I couldn't believe she was really his sister, there were physical anomalies—you noticed?—but I became and remain convinced that at least they thought of each other as brother and sister, and that was all. So if there was another woman, it wasn't Kyria.

"I suppose you're wondering why I didn't break it off. You have to understand that we weren't lovers in the passionate sense, although we never saw any reason why we two good friends shouldn't enjoy physical intimacy. What counted was the friendship. And he still needed my friendship; I *knew* that.

"But Klaus—I don't know, he seemed abstracted—as though he were *waiting* for something. And you know, Kyria too, *she* seemed to be waiting for something." Wilson forced a monosyllabic laugh: "That's me reading into both of them, I know. But that was how they both seemed."

"Did he ever say anything revealing?"

Coming back to her desk-chair, Wilson slowly sat, pondering. She brought out: "Once I was crass enough to ask him point-blank whether there was another woman. His answer was, and this is a precise quote: 'No woman in life will ever be your rival.' I could never bring myself to press him on that subtlety. That was quite recently, by the way. Another time, he said something about working with Murchison on a black-hole question, he seemed quite animated—"

"With Murchison? Excuse me, when was that?"

"About two weeks ago."

"Ms. Wilson, excuse me again, but—were you and Murchison ever together? And was Heller ever present at such a meeting?"

Wilson paled. "Why do you ask that?"

"Perhaps only because you know Murchison well enough to have phoned him with a quick notification of my coming visit." She was thinking about the flash-image in Heller's brain.

Disturbed, Wilson drummed her desk. Her fingers quieted, and she told them: "If Murchison denies what I will say, I too will deny it. But I trust you, and I am eager to get to the bottom of the Heller tragedy. After Klaus largely abandoned me, I—needed male diversion. Murchison was at hand, and he is charming. And Klaus would not have minded. It is however superficial, either Duke or I could terminate it without hurting the other." Then, after reflection: "There were two or possibly three earlier meetings when Klaus brought us together to discuss astronomical entailments of the forthcoming expedition. But that was last year. Klaus has not been present with us during the—recent phase of our friendship."

Claudine ruminated. This Duke did get around, didn't he?

Abruptly Claudine checked her cutichron: 1810. Up went her eyebrows: Murchison again? Closing in? Good lord, no. . . . "May I use your phone?" she blurted. On Wilson's desk phone she called her apartment; Croyd was there, she'd given him her lock-pass code. (That made three friends who had it; the other was Wong.) "St. Cyr here," she tersed. "I may be a bit late, but I'm coming. While you wait, can you run over to Houston and do a quick check on Murchison? I mean, see him, give him my best, and come back to tell me how he is." She listened. "Good man. See you around 1900 or so. Out now."

Wilson was on her feet. "Something I said worries you about Murchison?"

Claudine too was standing, forcing a smile. "Nothing special, Ms. Wilson, it's only that anybody recently associated with the Hellers worries me routinely just a little. Please excuse me, I want to be home when my agent returns—"

"Your agent? The man you were just talking with? To Houston and back in fifty minutes?"

"*Boy* is he an agent! Ms. Wilson, thank you so much."

When Claudine had departed, Wilson meditated momentarily, then spoke through intercom. "Jo. Sorry to have held you so long. Be good enough to find Zambi and tell her to put a discreet tail on Inspector St. Cyr. Warn Zambi that St. Cyr will have a nose for tails. Got it? Good. Then please take off, have a good dinner in a good place, take a friend along, charge it to expenses. 'Night, now."

Claudine, listening from the corridor via her portaradio tap, grinned. Smart dame, Wilson. But also, way down deep, nice. Maybe even sincere. . . .

Then she lost the grin, thinking about the ugly possibility of Duke with a big chest-hole; and she hurried home.

18. UPTIME TRAINING

Arriving at her apartment at 1905, Claudine found a note from Croyd: "I'm off at 1820 to check on Duke, and of course I'll have to spend a little time with him; expect me back around 1920, don't start worrying until after 2000. C."

Beautiful! Sixty minutes to go to Houston, shoot a little breeze with Duke, return to Manhattan—with Houston a cool ninety minutes away by fastest rocket! (With rockets, you had to weigh-in slow starts, slow landings, and in-between atmospheric traffic-soup.) Best bet: Croyd's breezing with Duke would take about fifty-nine of the sixty minutes.

But that was, if he found Duke well.

Bothered now about both Duke and Croyd, she undressed, dry-showered, let the nuclear spray stimulate her thinking. Wilson's gratuitous confessions could mean anything; but if they were taken at face value—and Claudine's not-infallible intuition said *do that*—Wilson herself was off the hook. But as for Murchison, if Croyd found him still alive, Duke was deeper in. If he had truly been infatuated with Wilson, and Wilson had expressed to him pique at Heller and Kyria, why then. . . . Or if Kyria had truly been an import from Iola, and Duke had in fact gone to Iola with Heller and fallen in love with Kyria, only Heller had got her. . . Or both.

On the other hand, facing it logically and brushing aside intuition, if it should prove that Wilson had done a number on Claudine, had actually been infuriated by the Heller-Kyria pairing to the point of. . . .

Ah! women! For that matter, ah! men! Or ultimately for that matter, ah! wounded ego!

She was sliding into lounging pajamas when she heard Croyd's voice from her parlor: "I'm here, removing shoes and socks, no jacket or necktie anyway. Where's the liquor?"

She shouted: "How's Duke?"

"Just fine, sends you his love. Where's the liquor?"

180

"In the kitchen cabinet next to the fridge. Make mine a Beefeater double martini on the rocks with two olives and very dry. Where did you find Duke?"

Voice fainter in kitchen-distance: "In his Houston office."

"So what took you so long?"

Glass-clinking, ice-tinkling; then: "I'm getting older. Is that what's taking *you* so long?"

She emerged in bare feet below not very sexy pink lounging pajamas; he came to meet her, holding a martini along with a tall drink that looked like maybe one-to-one bourbon. She took hers; they clinked; she sipped, he glugged, they intergazed. He said then: "The pajamas are nice, but they're not exciting, but the feet are; pardon mine."

"I thought this meeting was mostly a training session."

"I agree, I merely commented. Do you respond decently well to that sort of comment?"

"I'm a female, my friend, but not a flirt. Are you a flirt?"

"Frankly, no; either I'm just friendly or I go for goal. Tonight I'm just friendly; okay?"

"A-okay. When do we start the training session?"

"When do we eat?"

"Is your appetite under delayed control?"

"One of my fascinating abilities is, I can inhibit appetite until I starve to death."

"I'm not quite like that, Croyd, but I train better on an empty stomach. How about dinner at 2300?"

"Sounds fine. Except that I keep thinking about that just-opened bottle of Grandad in your cabinet—"

"Feeling the need for glucose? F'gossakes go sweeten your drink, I'm fine for quite a while. When you come back, I'll be on the sofa; for you, I recommend that easy chair."

He went sober. "Look, Claudine, this is fun, but we're sparring, and for what we're going to do tonight we have to be absolutely comfortable with each other because it's dangerous. Here, look: as far as I'm concerned, I won't make any passes tonight—okay?"

She, equally sober: "Sorry, Croyd, I fall into these things. No sex, fine, I like. Go sweeten your drink and join me—close on the sofa if it's better for the training."

"Claudine, your intentness on this training almost frightens me, it's as though it were definitely for action-real. Are you then so convinced that your mystery has no Erth-natural solution?"

"On the contrary, my logic is telling me that the solution is becoming increasingly Erth-natural; in fact, a net is closing in. But my intuition is a bitch, and it keeps denying all this without giving me any good reason."

"How've you done with your intuition in the past?"

"Pretty damn well, actually. But let's hedge our bets, good Croyd, and get with the training."

He ran her through the theoretical work they'd done on the frigate; she had it cold, perfectly understanding everything even though she didn't perfectly accept some things.

She wondered why one had to restrict oneself to uptime, why one couldn't also move downtime. He responded: "Too risky, I haven't dared try it yet. Uptime is fixed and definite; and you can't get stuck in it, because something about it tends to force you back down to the surface of the present when you have no more will to stay there. But downtime is a mess of developing potentials; some will actualize, some will perish, some will merge with others and then actualize or perish. You can get lost in downtime and never return. Before I try it, I need to develop a lot more theory."

"You like theory, don't you."

"Theory precedes trial, even in naïve human action: you don't strike unless you pre-think you maybe can win. Theory interbreeds with action to spawn better theory and therefore better action. Action-tested theory is meaning."

"Okay. But why is pseudo-past called uptime and pseudo-future downtime? I would have used the opposite terms."

"It's merely a question of different analogies. Mine is that in actuality we move along with a time-stream of events. If we accelerate our movement forward relative to the timeflow, we move downstream or downtime; if we turn around and manage to swim upstream in the timeflow, that is uptime."

"So then, my project is to move uptime."

"Precisely."

"And in uptime, I am to run back the event filaments of Klaus Heller."

"Only in order to get yourself to Iola *then*. Afterward, you'll want to spread out—and that's a complex late step in the training."

"Why can't you transport me in a space-ship to Iola's *now*, and let me backtrack from there?"

"It's tough to get a ship through a black hole. That's why I sent Heller."

"But didn't you say he communicated from Iola and told you how to do it? And I'll bet you *did* do it—"

"All right. But once you got to Iola in its *now*, you wouldn't find Heller to backtrack. He's *here* now."

"But on Iola, couldn't I grab hold of some native and—"

Positively: "It wouldn't work."

"Croyd, I think you're being evasive."

"If I am, your questioning won't change that situation. Shall we get back to the training?"

"Accepted—for now. What's my first step?"

"This training is going to be dangerous as hell, but there's no sense in talking any more until you've had a taste of it. Care to sign a release of my responsibility?"

"Of course—no, wait, I don't."

"Why not?"

"If I should leave behind a release on some screwy operation like this, somebody could do me in and use the release to back a charge that it must have been you."

"Smart girl. Of course I agree, it's a risk we'll both have to take."

"So you can tear up that release, Croyd."

"What release?"

"The one you've already drawn up for my signature, in your hip pocket."

"Anticipating your decision, I didn't draw it up."

"If I'm a smart girl, what are you?"

"Not a smart girl. All right, let's train. Got that scuba gear?"

"In my closet."

"Whip into it. Air molecules in uptime are unbreathable, they're as dead as everything else."

"How do *you* make out?"

"With some body-tricks that you won't have time to learn, they involve self-induced physiological changes."

"Right, swami. Excuse me now, I'll get into my gear."

They stood side-by-side in room-center, he at her left, his right arm around her waist and her left around his, her right hand holding his left in a double wrist-lock in front. "This is a short trial run," he told her. "No more than half an hour. How much air is in your pack?"

"An hour."

"That should be enough reserve."

"If it isn't, we're over mid-ocean and out of gas. Plunk. Understood."

"Don't let the thought make you hyper-ventilate, because in a clutch I can furnish a sort of parachute. Ready, Claudine?"

"Ready."

"Brain check-list. Right frontal lobe? Left frontal? Right parietal? Left parietal? Hippocampus? Diencephalon? Mesencephalon? Medulla oblongata? Autonomics?"

"Check. Check. Check. Check. Check. Check. Check. Check. Check."

"Breathing? Heart?"

"Slow and easy. Slow and easy."

"Set for sixty minutes uptime, same spatial locus. One—two—three—go."

gut-twitch. . . .

They space-floated in twilight amid ethereal three-dimensional harpstrings of silvery filaments emerging from indefinitely above them and extending indefinitely below, if up and down meant much.

Croyd: "Some of the filaments are traces of furniture and other things in your apartment; some of them are traces of you and me nearly an hour ago. I have us stabilized that much above ongoing actuality, we are drifting downtime at the same rate as actuality only nearly an hour behind it. Take your time, you are learning how to orient yourself on these filaments. Can you identify any clusters?"

Claudine, after a bit: "A few clusters, yes, but not clear shapes. How did you say we could talk when there isn't any live air to carry our voices?"

"Direct telepathy. The voice-sounds are mental constructs."

"I didn't know I could do that."

"I can give and take, and that's enough. Well, shapes: don't look for three-dimensional patterns, try to make a mental cut through a cluster and imaginatively construct its horizontal planar shape."

Having studied a cluster: "Could be maybe the top of my dressing table."

"Good start; that's what it is, along with the mirror and drawers and legs and cosmetic jars all schmeared in. You'd have to run the filaments to get the whole picture, but then you'd be *in* the table. Stay out of tables and other non-living crud, you can get stuck. In general, concentrate on brains, and I mean living brains: this trip, you won't be up to playing-around in computers. Now see if you can find one of *us*."

"How would I know?"

"You tell me."

She, after thought: "We move and breathe, so human filament-clusters would be more blurred than furniture-clusters. . . . Hey, yes, I see one of us, right there. *Gawd* does a human have a lot of filaments!"

"You'll get to notice humans and other animals just by the multiple density of filaments in the clusters: all the body-cells and brain-cells and so on, together with the motion-blur. All right: the one you found, is it you or I?"

"In a tangle like that, how could I tell?"

"If you can find the other of us, I can suggest a comparison."

"Not likely, because right beyond this one I see a wide density of unblurred filaments which is probably the wall or door of my bedroom. At that time I probably was still in the bedroom, and you were in my parlor."

"So then, which of us is it?"

"A-*ha*! It's *me*, because it's on the same side of the wall as my dressing table."

"Well deduced, and you are right. So this makes the next step easier for you. I want you to move into that Claudine-cluster and melt subjectively into its life."

"How do I move, here in uptime?"

"Once you get the full hang of it, you can simply walk, or float: just now, I'll take you there and shove you in. Keep hanging on to me. All—right; there you are, in the middle of you, an hour ago. Now this is the tricky part: I have to let go of you."

"Oboy."

"Do you wish you'd signed that release?"

"What release?"

"Okay. If you get into trouble, mindscream and I'll rescue you. When you come into full identity, you'll be you when you were talking through the door to me. Try to keep part of your mind detached; if your mind says something to me here while your body is talking to me there, I'll hear you here."

"Most of your exposition has been distinguished by greater

clarity. I hope you get back to that. All right, we've let go; what do I do now?"

"First of all, keep cool: whether you scream or not, I'll be yanking you back in fifteen seconds."

"Recognized. Now?"

"You're in the part of your brain that makes sense of brain-interpreted experiences—"

"Aha! Right across the Rolandic fissure from the part that commands responses?"

"I knew you'd be good at this, Claudine. Don't try to grab the filaments physically, they are intangible to material bodies. Let your mind float out, now, and start engaging filaments with it. You won't make much of it at first, but remember that it's yourself you re-engage for a second time around. When you've comprehended enough filaments past some threshold, it will all totalize in a rush. Okay, go."

She let her mind float free in the tangle. Her mind—*she*—began to comprehend filaments, just a few at a time; at first it brought a quasi-electrical thrill that made her recoil, but then she glanced at him and shrugged and went back at it. A few she grasped and mind-held; no meaning. A few more. More. More; it was growing easier, but still no meaning.

Little meaning-flashes like semi-dream fragments when one is just dropping into sleep. . . .

All in a rush, subjective wholeness in her bedroom:

> Croyd's voice: "or necktie anyway. Where's the liquor?"
> "How's Duke?"
> "Just fine, sends you his love. Where's the liquor?"
> "In the kitchen cabinet next to the fridge. Make mine a Beefeater double martini."

Croyd snatched her out: their present bodies were in up-time, her prior body was merely filaments there.

She was breathing hard; she quelled it, realizing that she was shortening the time on her airpack.

Croyd queried: "How was it?"

"I've never had a memory-dream so realistic. *No* dream so realistic—except the ones about Iola."

"As to this experience, it was realistic because it was real. As to Iola, who knows—yet? Well, we've used only about half our time; let's try the next step. I'll take you past those wall-filaments, and you can find me and see how I'm different from you."

"Croyd! Get me out of you!"

He snatched her out. "What's the matter?"

"As you, I saw me coming out of my bedroom—and I began to get a little man-interested in myself. I'm not ready for *that!*"

"In ten seconds, you learned a lot about me, didn't you."

"And about me, dammit, at the same time. Croyd, my friend, it's an unfair way to flirt—we aren't supposed to *feel* what each other feels, I'm only supposed to feel me and judge you—"

"Will it help you if I now say something unkind?"

"Pray cut."

"That's just what you would have felt me doing an instant later. I recognized my own beginning arousal, and I cut it. I have been cool-friendly since, as you'd realize if you'd stayed in me."

"I hope this uptime twilight doesn't show a blush on a dark mahogany face. By the way, where's the light coming from, in uptime?"

"I'm working on the question; for some physical reason, it's always here, except when you're in somebody seeing through his eyes in pitch dark."

"Having just been in two bodies seeing through their eyes, I have a magnitude question. You said I was in just a small portion of each brain. How did you stuff all my body into *that* sort of space?"

"I didn't. Your body stayed out here. Just your mind went in."

"You mean I've already done some of that mind-jumping stuff, and I didn't even know I was doing it—much less how?"

"With practice, you'll be able to control it yourself. Not now, though—our safe time is used up."

"I'd be willing to push it a little farther—"

"I'd recommend against that."

"I accept; you're the teacher."

"Dinner time, Croyd." She was out of the scuba suit and still in unsexy lounging pajamas. "What's your order? I'll punch it in."

"My mood is for pizza."

"Me too. What do you want?"

"For me, one large, with beef, hamburger, pepperoni, mushrooms, sausage, bacon, salami, anchovies, black olives, and green peppers."

"No onions?"

"Good; and onions. And—will yours have garlic?"

"And garlic. I'll have a medium with all the same. What's the best wine for this?"

"Two parts Chianti, one part vodka."

"You mix, I'll punch."

"Boy, Croyd, do you stink!"

"So do you." Long liquid belch. "Ain't it great?"

"That sounded comfortable. All I can manage is little ladylike burps."

"I can teach my noises, too."

"I'd better stay with my genteel bloat. Hey, let's make the next one two parts vodka and one part Chianti."

"Claudine, will that make you drunk?"

"I'm weary, I have an urge to get medium blotto."

"The trouble for you is, *I won't* get drunk. If you get drunk and I take advantage, will you be irritated later?"

She pondered. She said then: "Tell you what. Make it half-and-half vodka and Chianti."

"Croyd—"

"Mm?"

"I wish you were drunk."

"Why?"

"Sober, you're too evasive."

"About what?"

"About why I can't start by going to Iola in the body on a ship, and do my uptiming from there. Croyd—tell me what happened finally to Iola."

Long silence.

"Croyd?"

"Claudine, I'll make a deal. After you have done one of two things—gone with the Heller traces to Iola *then*, or finally decided *against* that uptime excursion—*then* I will tell you about the more recent past of Iola. Your part of the deal is—stop asking me now."

"Please give me one good reason."

"You're entitled to a reason. Let's just say that subsequent events on Iola had nothing to do with the Heller murders which you are investigating. Keep your mind concentrated on what you're after."

After meditation: "I guess that's reasonable. Croyd—"

"Mm?"

"It's a cool night for July. I'm just a bit on the chilly side. Mind pulling up the sheet?"

"That's what you get for not leaving it two parts vodka."

"Croyd—"

"Mm?"

"Where do we go from here?"

"Well—"

"Oh hell, that *was* ambiguous, wasn't it? Sorry; I was talking about the uptime training. On the amour, that's just as it may turn out any time, one way or another."

"Okay, great. Well: when can we do more of that—and this?"

"When do you have to get back to Nereid?"

"I'm in touch several times a day, all's well; in an emergency, a guy there could brain-contact me right here."

"I hope not visiphone?"

"Frontal cortex only; no visual images. Although he would be thrilled."

"All forty-six years of me thank you. So then, otherwise, when do you have to go?"

"A week from tonight at the latest."

"Why don't we make a tentative dinner date for tomorrow night, and go on with that—and this?"

"I'm for all three."

"Croyd, is there any way I can give you a late call in emergency and cancel?"

"Just think *Croyd* intensely, and I'll come in."

"Now look, we aren't *that* close—"

"We established the mental intergradient in uptime, we can use it as needed. But I think that talking is usually better."

"So do I. I've thought maybe that's why humans lost their animal telepathic ability—because talking is usually better. But you know, sometimes—"

"I know. But then it ought to be wordless. And humans in love can still do that."

"I wonder if I've ever been in love. I've thought so a couple of times, but later I wasn't so sure."

"I was once, wonderfully, a long time ago. During an incredible fifty years."

Claudine, having cleared her throat, said small: "How old are you?"

Somewhat later, he told her.

19. DUKE'S DESTINY

During the same night, Klaus Heller's brain deteriorated beyond dreaming-coherency. They pronounced him eighty-seven percent dead (sixty was legal death); and, on prior instructions, they arranged atomization for the following morning, July 10, following autopsy this afternoon, July 9. They also notified Heller's attorney, and they sent a message to Inspector St. Cyr via the head night clerk at Galactic Police HQ. Kyria had already been atomized, which was the legal procedure when one died intestate.

Claudine was handed the death-message when she arrived at her office at 0900 on 9 July. She dispatched Tuli to pick up any final dream-flakes. She then phoned Heller's attorney, whom she knew, and whom she had earlier questioned by phone with unrevealing results. This morning he had already been in touch with the surviving heir after Kyria, named in a very recent will; this heir had affirmed agreement to the private atomization, and had asked that the attorney arrange a memorial service for both Hellers at the particular Temple of the New Serapis which Heller had attended sporadically and supported generously.

To the attorney, Claudine remarked: "You know, Jim, you've been awful damn cagey with me about that will. Don't you think you could now twist your own arm and emit for my private ear the name of that heir?"

Long reflective silence. Then: "Why not, Claudine? Confidentially, you understand. The heir is Clara Wilson."

"President of Aerospace Dynamics?"

"She. Your comment?"

"To put it in one-word religious terms: Christ!"

"Good comment, since I know from her chief attorney that you've been nosing around her on these murders. Well, that was only an inter-pro remark, I'm not an interested party except in the matter of administering the will and the estate. Shall we disconnect now?"

"Go with God, Jim. Out."

She meditated. Perhaps she should. . . . And yet, she was faintly reluctant to call Duke in view of his approach to her on Nereid. Better *he* should call *her,* she'd left herself open; and yet, when you thought about it, Murchison was an inward sort of guy, he did a nice job of playing dapper but in the personality clutch he was inward; maybe he thought she wanted Croyd and had decided to leave her alone; maybe the good-girl thing for her to do would be to use the Heller death as a pretext for calling Duke whom she really liked very much—his association with Clara Wilson was merely evidence of his good taste, and of Clara's. On the other hand, there was this damnable possibility that he and Wilson together might somehow be implicated in the murders, in view of their liaison, especially now that Wilson's inheritance revealed a money-motive; true, Wilson was well heeled, but wealth yearns for more wealth, and Heller was probably worth a hundred credits to Wilson's one. Claudine would have to investigate, and she didn't want to use her personal friendship with Duke as a pretext for *that!*

To Claudine, Duke had actually proposed marriage. Was that the old ploy—to marry her so she couldn't testify against him? Such a marriage would be easy to dissolve unilaterally after trial, and the interdiction of double jeopardy would leave him immune to any new testimony she might submit after the divorce. Or was it maybe that by marrying Claudine he would be escaping some clutch that Wilson had upon him? He had told her that he was not guilty; but that was what they all said. Whirling possibilities! Things stayed put so much better when they could be held objective.

And she did settle the phone-call question by latching on to the objectivity. It had been none of her doing that Murchison had become friendly to the point of proposing marriage. She had introduced herself to him objectively for expert information in the course of a criminal investigation, and he had offered to present her to Secretary Croyd; and that was all there was in their relationship other than what he had proposed and she had gently deferred. The thing for her to do was to leave it on that level until this investigation would be resolved.

So, for the moment, she didn't phone Murchison.

What do you do now? You review the final dream-flake.

Most of it was spinach; but one sharp clear continuity-montage, loaded with emotional overtones, arrested her as matter of probable case-significance.

Episode One: Duke, face distorted with terror-horror, staggering disheveled in through a door yelling: "Jesus, Klaus, Luria: help Kyria in there, I've ruined her!"

Scene-switch. . . . Episode Two: A number of small web-fingered folk enter a room and surround Murchison; the grotesque crescendoes until, at dream-finale, Duke is being held down on the floor on his hands and knees with bared rump which a little half-naked fellow is gleefully male-riding.

Blackout. No more dreaming for Klaus Heller, ever, at least in the body.

Duke himself, in past reality? Traumatizing himself by giving trauma to Kyria, then being himself outrageously traumatized?

All right: now she *did* have to get with Duke again, on business; and she was even prepared to put to him the question of this dream. And then—having interviewed Werner Voelker and checked a few new and pertinent questions with Clara Wilson—she would make action-decision about applying Croyd's training.

Forthwith she visiphoned Duke's office in Houston. Male answering voice, hard police-face: "Sergeant Assam, Houston Homicide. May I help you?"

O god. . . . "Inspector St. Cyr, Galactic Police, calling Dr. Murchison from Manhattan."

"Sorry, Inspector; he's dead suddenly. One moment, I'll get you with Captain Arroya."

Background shufflings and mutterings, police sounds. Claudine felt dead too. *I should have warned you, Duke . . . should have ordered protection . . .*

Authoritative contralto, unsmiling broad smooth female Indian face. "Captain Arroya here, Houston Police, Homicide. What can I do for you, Inspector?"

"Captain, this was a business call for Dr. Murchison, he was helping me as an expert witness. Please fill me in."

"Inspector, he was shot dead approximately twenty minutes ago—"

"Wait, Captain, what I am going to request is deadly important for immediate action. Please *instantly* issue orders to keep Murchison's brain alive and monitor his posthumous dreaming."

"I don't—"

"Time is of the essence, Captain, top VASA brass there will know how to arrange it if you don't. Please execute this *now*, and then call me right back; I'll wait here."

"Will do, Inspector. Out." Disconnect.

Claudine by intercom instructed her yeoman clerk: "Stay by the phone, divert all calls for me except any from VASA Headquarters or police headquarters in Houston—for them, interrupt me. I'll be on the phone otherwise."

Then, haunted by a premonition, she raised Clara Wilson. "Ms. Wilson, St. Cyr here. I understand that you are Dr. Heller's only heir. Congrats."

Strangulated answer: "Thanks, I guess." There wasn't any video.

"I have two urgent questions. The first is whether Dr. Voelker is available there for immediate questioning. The second is whether the experimental raygun is still safely impounded."

"I'll have to inquire into both questions—"

"Here is a third question. Who murdered Professor Murchison, and why?"

Silence; then: "I think you'd better say that again."

"Duke Murchison has just been shot dead. In Houston. I don't yet know the method or the killer, but I have strong intuitions about both, and at least indirectly they affect you. Your comment?"

Without video, Wilson's face gone chalky was almost visible. "At this time I can only tell you that I know nothing about it, I am receiving the news first from you. I really shouldn't say more without involving my attorneys; you'll appreciate that."

"Then what time can I see you here with one or more of your attorneys?"

"I will be in touch—"

"Please check immediately on Voelker and the gun, and it would be best to have one of your attorneys witness both checks. Then—" Her intercom beeped. "Excuse me a moment . . . Yes?"

The yeoman: "I have Captain Arroya from Houston on visiphone."

"Hold her a moment, I'll be right with her. . . . Hello,

Ms. Wilson. I was about to say, right now it is 1027. I will wish for you to make those two checks and then be here with your attorneys no later than 1127. If Voelker is reachable, please bring him along."

"My attorneys may not be immediately available—"

"1127, Ms. Wilson; you'll forgive me for being peremptory, this is a rough morning. Out now." Disconnect.

Ehhhh . . .

"Captain Arroya. St. Cyr here."

"Yes, Inspector. They are expediting removal of Dr. Murchison to the VASA Infirmary, they have the equipment there, but they are afraid that too much time may have elapsed already."

"Well, Captain, if it doesn't work, it doesn't work; thank you very much. Please go on and say what you were about to say when I interrupted you with the body-errand."

"Of course. I was going to say that the killer has been apprehended, a VASA employee tackled and tied him. The weapon was a peculiarly adapted raygun."

Intuition One! Then . . . "Captain, do you know the identity of the killer?"

"He was carrying full identity, he is evidently an amateur. His name is Dr. Werner Voelker, and he is Director of Experimental Weapon Studies for Aerospace Dynamics."

Intuition Two! Jackpot? Oh Duke . . . "Rayguns are an intrinsic part of the homicides I'm working on here, and Murchison was a possible suspect or at least a connection, and so was Voelker. Will you cooperate, Captain?"

"As fully as you will cooperate, Inspector."

"Then we will cooperate fully. May I ask a few questions now?"

"Of course."

"If the raygun was adapted the way I think it was, Murchison had a fairly large chest-hole and a smaller heart-hole; am I right?"

"That's how it is, except that the entire heart is burned away."

"All right. Did you measure the diameters of the chest-hole and the heart-absence?"

"The chest-hole is approximately twenty-five centimeters wide, but we didn't think to measure the heart-absence. We are not doctors, Inspector." The last was faintly trenchant.

Claudine smiled wanly. "I know, Captain, we missed that

in a similar case here, the hospital doctors got it—but would you please get in touch with VASA Infirmary and ask them to be sure to get it?"

"Of course."

"And another thing—have them check to see whether there was any damage to the tissue posterior to the heart."

"I can answer you on that one. The ray-convergence destroyed most of the thickness of his backbone, emerged making a five-centimeter hole, and burned-out his chair-back."

Oh-oh. *Different!* "Do you have the weapon?"

"We do. He was carrying it in a sort of hat-box."

"Good. Was it fundamentally a standard hand-weapon, Colt XL-3294, but rigged with a ray-mirror in front of the muzzle and a circular concave reflector around the muzzle, so that it would fire forward at a very wide convergent angle?"

"Exactly so, Inspector."

"Thank you, that's very nice. Voelker did have such a weapon in his lab here, and we're checking to see whether it is still impounded properly. Meanwhile, consider the chance that Murchison had a duplicate in his office, and that Voelker used it—or that entering, Voelker found Murchison dead, and that in panic Voelker seized the gun and ran."

"Good thoughts, Inspector; we will look into them."

"Your police work is superb. I can be in Houston some time this afternoon."

"Let me know your schedule. I'll meet you at the airport."

"Oh, Croyd—where are you?"

"In a drug store. I just wanted to—"

"Croyd, I have to go to Houston. Duke Murchison has been shot dead."

"Oh good God!"

"I'll give you more details after I've seen him and the police. It was substantially the same MO as with the Hellers, but with some significant differences. Anyhow, obviously I can't see you tonight."

"May I go with you to Houston?"

"Why?"

"I want to pay my last respects to my friend Duke."

"Of course. You are one who can go. But I don't know what time I'll be leaving. I have to finish a little related business here."

"It's 1119 now. Suppose I show up at your office about 1230—with hamburgers and shakes?"

"Beautiful. Filthy Joe across the street from here makes great burgers and luscious shakes. Okay?"

"The name allures me. Done."

"Good; then I want three standard burgers with everything, and make my shake thin—and bring a long plastic spoon, even his thin shakes have high viscosity."

Call from Aerospace Dynamics: "Ms. Wilson is en route to see you in your office, she is bringing her chief attorney who is a Mr. Klar Zambesi. Will you wait for them? if not, I can call their solichopper—"

Claudine's cutichron said 1123; they'd be here directly, Croyd wouldn't have to wait long in the outer office. She affirmed, noticing that no mention had been made of Voelker—natch. After disconnect, she called Tuli on intercom, asking her to join them in fifteen minutes.

Seventeen minutes later, Wilson and Zambesi were announced and admitted; Tuli was already there. Clara Wilson was as pallid as her voice had sounded; she was even trembling a little. Portly portentous very black Klar Zambesi looked troubled.

After St. Cyr-Tuli-Zambesi presentations by Wilson and cold handshakes, the visitors found convenient seats on invitation. Claudine remarked: "I suggest mutual flakings." "Not court-admissible," Zambesi stipulated. Claudine affirmed. Zambesi produced a pocket recorder; Claudine activated a desk button, and waited.

Said Wilson unsteadily: "I am a bit distraught about all this, and so I have asked Mr. Zambesi to speak for me. Of course I will respond to direct questioning if he allows it, or fill when he requests it."

"Fiar enough," Claudine responded.

Zambesi's basso was profundo-rich, and measured; he did not however touch fingertips to fingertips, but instead, draped his fat be-ringed hands languidly on the arms of his uncushioned oak chair. Knowing of him with respect, Claudine batlistened.

He said: "Ms. Wilson is deeply disturbed by the death of Dr. Murchison, and doubly disturbed because an associated question has been asked about her employee Dr. Voelker. To short-circuit some questioning, it is admitted that difficulties are created for us by Ms. Wilson's status as Dr. Heller's heir after his sister, along with the deaths of Heller and his sister by apparently identical methods. We further admit that Ms. Wilson had prior knowledge, from Heller, about the substance of his will. Ms. Wilson wishes me to say for her, in an introductory way, that she is innocent of any wrongdoing in any of these matters. Inspector?"

Claudine looked at Wilson, who nodded affirmation. Claudine queried then: "How about Dr. Voelker—and the impounded raygun?"

Wilson looked at Zambesi, who replied in some embarrassment: "It appears that Dr. Voelker has taken several days personal business leave. Of course, an employee is not required to disclose his personal business, and so Dr. Voelker's immediate superior does not know where he is. As for the impounded gun—well, it is not there where it was impounded."

"And where was that?"

Claudine was one who could detect a black blush. "I must say that Ms. Wilson handed the gun to me for impounding. I placed it in my personal safe in the Legal Department. The gun is no longer there. The disappearance is being investigated."

"Cheer up, Mr. Zambesi, I have had worse embarrassments—for instance, right now, because I did not supervise the impoundment myself. However, I must now inform you that Dr. Voelker is in Houston, jailed on a charge of murdering Dr. Murchison with precisely that experimental weapon."

Zambesi cleared throat and responded: "I presume that the police evidence at this point is thinly circumstantial."

"The thin circumstances are that Voelker was caught leaving Murchison's office immediately after the crime, that he was carrying the raygun, and that the capabilities of the gun fit the description of the fatal wounds."

"Has Voelker made a statement?"

"Not yet. I will see him today in Houston."

"Inspector, I request that I be present."

"My schedule is not clear yet, and it would be inappropriate for us to travel together. I can only suggest, Mr. Zambesi, that when you leave this office, you take the next rocket to Houston, go to police headquarters, ask for Captain Arroya, and wait for me, perhaps counseling with Voelker ahead of me."

"I'll do that, thank you. May I assume that you are not yet ready to make any charges against Ms. Wilson?"

"That is correct, sir. Not yet."

Wilson touched Zambesi's wrist, and they whispered below recorder-threshold. Then Zambesi straightened, and stiffly and tonelessly he asserted: "My client and I want you to know everything that we know. This concerns the disappearance of the impounded gun. When Dr. Voelker was a vice-president, the Legal Department was one of his charges. It is reasonable to imagine that he knew the bypass-codes for the office and safe locks, although my predecessor as Director of Legal Affairs said nothing about such a thing to me."

Wilson added sweetly: "At that time, Mr. Zambesi was only deputy director." When Zambesi glared, she dropped eyes and remarked: "But I will take full responsibility for not ordering that the bypass-codes be changed when the vice-presidency changed." The persimmon-look on Zambesi amused Claudine inwardly: assuming that he had become director *after* the vice-presidency changed, why hadn't he ordered new bypass-codes when the directorship changed?

But there was another thing, and she might as well throw it now. "Ms. Wilson—is there any possibility that someone might have obtained the metabolic accelerators that were built into the oversize space-suits used on the Vassili expedition?"

Wilson looked puzzled at Zambesi; he spread hands and nodded. She asserted positively and competently: "I know at first hand that Klaus himself conveyed those metabolic accelerators to Assistant Secretary Croyd. And if you are further wondering whether someone might have reproduced their design and built a new metabolic accelerator, that would have been impossible. There was a key unit that was furnished by Secretary Croyd, it was sealed and its internal composition was secret; the seals had not been broken when Klaus took out the two accelerators to return them to the secretary."

Silence.

The attorney whispered to Wilson, who nodded. They both stood, Wilson saying: "Thank you for your time, Inspector. We will be available."

When they had departed, the yeoman put in her head to say: "Mr. Croyd is waiting to see you. With a package. Shall I have the package searched?"

Claudine grinned. "Not on your life; you get your own hamburgers."

"Lieutenant Tuli, I want you to meet Secretary Croyd."

"Charmed, Lieutenant."

"*Oo!*"

"Tuli, what's the matter? Aren't you going to offer your hand to the secretary?"

"*Oo.*"

"Claudine, the lieutenant may be going into shock, let me revive her." Croyd produced a hot hamburger from the thermal bag and passed it beneath Tuli's nose.

Tuli: "*Ooooo.*"

Croyd: "Lieutenant, I've heard such wonderful things about you. If you will only say one intelligible word to me, you may have the hamburger."

Tuli: "Does it have mustard?"

20. TERMINUS OF ERTH-NATURAL

Aboard the Houston rocket (really a stubby-winged jet fueled by silica reduction), closely Claudine questioned Croyd about the metabolic accelerators. When they arrived at 1527 EST-GTC, she was satisfied that Heller had personally delivered the two accelerators to Croyd with the secret unit still sealed, and that there was no conceivably remaining way for Wilson or Duke or Voelker or anyone else to have obtained that method of achieving invisibility for the Heller murders. The secret units, not being in general production, had been personally fabricated by Croyd the inventor; as yet, he had not shared the secret even with his own scientists. And neither she nor Croyd knew of any other existing method of obtaining invisibility—unless, perhaps, the hueena method on Iola, which would tend to put the finger on Duke, who unhappily was dead. And if Duke, using Voelker as his instrument, had given Voelker at least the manufactured invisibility device from Iola for purposes of killing the Hellers, why hadn't Voelker used the device when he killed Duke by approximately the same method?

Approximately the same; but with differences . . .

Houston arrival-time was 1427 CST. The Galactic Time Convention was great for interplanetary travel and communication; but on any single planet, time zones based on the sun's position tended to persist under any sun. Those who, like Croyd and Wilson and St. Cyr, had frequent business on GTC carried a double-dialed watch or two cutichrons, or (very expensive) one that flipped from local time to GTC and back at a button-touch.

Captain Arroya was on hand at the airport. She was Ameryn (later she said Navajo) with no trace of white

201

blood, her dark straight hair parted in the middle and
brought back on both sides into a single cervical bun, her
eyes wide apart in a broad face, her cheekbones high, her
nose high-bridged, her mouth grave when at rest, her chin
firm. You got a sense of mature sincerity and friendly
reserve, and occasionally a thin smile illuminated her—as it
did when she greeted Claudine with a double handshake.
"You are welcome, Inspector," simply she said; and when
Claudine presented Croyd as Dr. Thoth a weapons expert
(prearranged incognito): "You too are welcome, Doctor."

They couldn't see Duke promptly enough. He lay there as
Klaus Heller had lain, his head forested in wires. They drew
down the sheet, and a doctor quoted the exact measurements
of the wounds: chest, 24.4 centimeters, heart (entirely gone,
along with a considerable periphery of arteries and veins),
about eighteen or nineteen centimeters; posterior peritoneum,
13.8 centimeters, with most of that segment of the spinal
column burned away; exterior back-skin, five centimeters.

The angle of convergence worked out to fifty degrees, in
contrast to the seventy-five-degree convergences of the Klaus
and Kyria ray-shots.

"We are getting some dreams," the doctor added. "One is
in progress now, and we can show you a flake of the prior
ones that we caught."

Claudine studied the dead man's face; at Arroya's request,
this being a police case, they hadn't composed it. Duke exhibited an expression of mixed terror and anguish.

Whereas the post-mortem expressions on the Heller faces
had been serene.

She asked Arroya: "Have you adequately holographed his
face?" The captain affirmed.

Claudine delicately pushed aside some wires and composed
the face as well as she could; the skin of course was flaccid,
and it was hard to mold a decent expression upon it.
Presently she glanced at Arroya: "Please have a skilled mor-
tician improve this." She planted a long kiss on Duke's forehead and withdrew, watching.

Croyd, working his way through wires, bent to kiss the
forehead. And he withdrew.

Claudine said then: "I'll monitor the current dream, if you
please."

They fitted her with the headset. But the dreaming was
garbage.

Removing the headpiece, she arose. "Now, if you don't mind, Dr. Thoth and I will check the flake."

But it too was all garbage.

Except one dreaming . . .

A brilliant yellow star, with a nearby thin label: *M-8731, two solar diameters, six planets, year-age 5 x 10⁹.*

. . . As though the dream-camera were zooming in, closing on the star-glare, bypassing it; beyond, variously full disks or half-disks or crescents in sunlight, six planets orbiting. Zooming dream-eye closes on Planet One and bypasses it; on Two and bypasses; on Three. . . . And on Four, and holds. . . .

Claudine-whisper: "87314. Iola." Croyd-nod.

Planet Four metamorphoses into a woman's face. The woman is Kyria.

The view opens up to include not only Planet Four but also its two satellites. One satellite is Klaus Heller. The other is Duke Murchison. And Duke is the one farther out.

At Arroya's office, the duty lieutenant reported that a man named Zambesi had been impatiently waiting for nearly two hours, claiming to be Voelker's attorney and demanding to see his client; but the lieutenant wanted confirmation by the captain. Claudine interjected: "Zambesi is okay, please let him see Voelker now, it will go better that way." Arroya confirmed to her lieutenant, then turned to Claudine: "If you want to kill a little time usefully, let me raise our impoundment office on holographic visiphone, you can inspect the murder weapon."

On the visiscreen, a sergeant held up the weapon for scrutiny; his hands were gloved. While St. Cyr peered, the sergeant read off specifications: "Overall length of adapted weapon, 35 centimters, including 20-centimeter basic weapon and front convex mirror 15 centimeters in front of muzzle. Overall diameter of concave outside mirror surrounding muzzle, 39 centimeters. Angle of conical convergence from concave peripheral mirror toward target, fifty degrees. Basic weapon, an ordinary Colt XL-3294 raygun. Inspector, we've test-fired it here, the double-reflected ray-refraction is perfect, I never saw anything like it. Oh—no sweat, prints had been taken, photographically and chemically."

"Sergeant, judging from your measurements and tests, how far from the victim's chest was the gun when it was fired?"

"The range must have been point-blank. I mean, the anterior mirror was probably in contact with the victim's chest. Were they friends, or something? Oh, sorry, Inspector."

"Natural question, Sergeant. Would you mind just rotating the weapon so I can see the other side—and bring it into tight video focus on the top area of the hilt just behind the power pack."

There it was: Tuli's tiny T, inconspicuously pin-scratched on the hilt just where Tuli had said she'd scratched it in Voelker's lab.

"Sergeant, I can't thank you enough. That's all for now." Disconnect.

She turned to Arroya and Croyd. "Same weapon, beyond doubt, out of Voelker's lab; he swiped it out of impoundment. Captain, what prints did you find on the weapon?"

"Those of Voelker, of Murchison, and of several others."

"And on the firing button?"

"A blur of several. We think we can untangle both Voelker's and Murchison's, maybe—there are strong indications of both."

"*Both*—Voelker's and Murchison's? on the firing button?"

"We think so, tentatively."

"Well; Zambesi's had enough time alone with Voelker; let's toddle along after him."

Voelker awaited arraignment in a decent solitary cell, with a molded plastic sink-and-toilet unit at the back end; there was a reasonably comfortable armchair under a wall lamp; and the bunk, on which Zambesi uneasily sat, had not only sheets and a blanket but even a pillow in a pillowcase. Voelker, ignoring Zambesi, sat in the chair with the lamp lighted, reading some heavy technical work which they'd brought from the police library at his request; three other books were on a side table. "We still have to presume his innocence," Arroya remarked low; "if he's convicted, that's the end of the easy chair and floor lamp and the overstuffed pillow. We treat convicts decently, but we don't pamper. Unfortunately we can't give him toilet privacy, there have been suicides."

Claudine and Croyd studied Voelker through bars: he was a stocky fiftyish brunette; reading, he seemed unaware of their presence, although Zambesi spotted them and frowned. She glanced at Arroya, who shrugged and gestured. Claudine said: "Dr. Voelker, I'm Inspector St. Cyr of Galactic Police; may we talk with you?"

Voelker stood, laying down the book spread-eagled on its face; the attorney stood also. Voelker, face and eyes bland, said pleasantly: "I know you've been checking on me, Inspector, I met your Lieutenant Tuli. Please feel free to flake this interview—you too, Zambesi. Captain Arroya, do you think you could open my cell for the inspector and—sir?" He looked at Croyd.

While Arroya unlocked, Claudine got her tongue out of her cheek and presented Croyd as Dr. Thoth, a weapons expert. Voelker said courteously: "I've read some of your papers; won't you come in too?" Claudine turned to stare at Croyd; poker-faced, he gestured her in ahead of him. Having activated gate-cloture, Arroya retired to watchful distance; there was also a guard nearby in the cell-block.

Voelker, after motioning Claudine to the chair and Croyd to the bunk, took a spread-legged hands-in-pockets posture with his back to the cell-gate and waited, while Croyd and Zambesi plumped down on the bunk together. It was a neat Voelker-ploy for psychological advantage, as Claudine noted with interest. With a side glance she mentally photographed the four book-titles: *Reflection and Refraction of Hot Rays* (the one he'd been reading) and three other gun-related topics.

She looked up at Voelker: "Why did Clara Wilson send you to kill Murchison?"

"Now just a minute," roared Zambesi, coming to his feet. But smiling Voelker arrested the attorney with a raised hand: "Wait, Mr. Zambesi, you've advised me of my rights and I thank you, but I will speak for myself." To Claudine he replied: "She did not send me. Murchison had learned about my weapon, he phoned me yesterday to express his interest and to ask if I could bring it here for his inspection. I saw my opportunity, I stole it out of the Legal Department safe, I brought it, I deliberately killed him with it."

Zambesi wavered down, while Claudine reflected that this might be an opening gambit in an intricate defense on grounds of insanity—this sort of bland confession was practically unheard-of among sane people. She countered: "*Why* did you kill him?"

"For three reasons. Murchison was a friend of Klaus Heller who was my enemy. He was a friend of Kyria Heller who was sister to my enemy. And he was entirely too friendly with Clara Wilson who was doubly my enemy because she loved Heller and she treated me unfairly. She was next on my death-list, by the way—only they caught me, so what the hell."

After the three seconds that Claudine needed to find her tongue, she urged: "Please tell me the story."

Zambesi cleared throat. "Dr. Voelker, this testimony should properly be reserved for the court—"

"Not at all, Zambesi, not at all! the police work hard, they deserve to know. Well, Inspector; I have a flake of Murchison's phone call yesterday, you will be wanting to verify that he asked to see the gun. But my resolve to kill him is not on the flake, ha! I packed the gun in a special carrying case designed to look like a hat box, you see I think about even such ancillary details, and I came and met our appointment this morning. After a friendly greeting by Murchison, I suggested that he sit at his desk while I would demonstrate the weapon before he would ask questions; and this he did. I withdrew the weapon from the case and laid it on his desk, describing the device in detail; he studied it with evident admiration—Dr. Thoth, have you ever seen such a weapon?"

Croyd declared: "I should say not!"

"There: you see? The invention is mine. So then I lifted the weapon from the desk, checked it, and aimed it at Murchison's chest; this made him nervous, he leaned back against his chair. I drew attention to its lightness, its beautiful balance, how easily I was controlling it. Then I threw open the safety lock, held the anterior ray-mirror against his chest, and told him, I can quote me: 'Dr. Murchison, I'm sorry about this, I respect you, but I can't let you continue to live. Be glad, at least, that you are dying by means of the same weapon that killed Klaus and Kyria Heller.' Then I pressed the firing button, the weapon worked perfectly and almost noiselessly as usual, although already the reflectors are showing signs of fusing after a dozen tests followed by three murders; I have been working on a more resistant alloy. So then I packed my gun and made my escape. Somebody caught me, I don't know why. Any questions, Inspector?"

Claudine turned to ashen Zambesi. "Sir, do you want a copy of my flake?"

He uttered: "No thank you. I too flaked it."

Arising, she took Voelker's arm and urged him back into his easy chair; he sank into it with evident relief; Croyd promptly stood, and Claudine sat on the bunk beside client-defeated Zambesi. To him she whispered: "Read up on delusive paranoid psychosis, Counselor, but don't call me as an expert witness."

She leaned then toward Voelker and spoke softly. "Dr. Voelker, you must realize that I abhor what you have done and will urge prosecution." The prisoner nodded. "Nevertheless, I can't help admiring the expertise with which you have done it all—indeed, veritable scientific artistry." He smiled with reserve. "You invited me to ask question," she continued. "If I heard you correctly, you told Dr. Murchison that you were killing him with the same weapon that had killed the two Hellers. Was that correct, sir?"

"Of course it was correct."

"You realize that, with your prior permission, all this has been and is still being flaked, and the flake includes your statement that Mr. Zambesi has advised you of your rights? You realize this?"

"Of course. This is my confession for the record. I will sign an accurate transcript."

"Conviction would carry a probable death penalty."

"This too I understand. What the hell, now; let Wilson gloat, she was morally the motivator for all this, and let that be part of the confession."

"Very well. Now. Was it you, personally and alone, who killed Klaus Heller—with the same gun that killed Dr. Murchison?"

"I did."

"Why?"

"He had been holding down my influence in Aerospace Dynamics. And his influence over Clara Wilson caused her to demote me."

"Did you alone also kill Kyria Heller with the same gun?"

"I did. Klaus Heller loved her, so I killed her too."

"Would you have killed Kyria if you had known that Clara Wilson would be the surviving heir to Heller's estate?"

"Is she! I'm glad you told me, because I hated killing Kyria, she seemed nice; but if that made Wilson the heir, it justifies me because the inheritance will torture her conscience."

Claudin turned to Croyd—who now leaned toward the

prisoner. "Dr. Voelker, I've seen that weapon; and as one gun-nut to another, this I've been wanting to ask. The fifty-degree convergence-angle on that particular adaptation—am I right that the angle cannot be adjusted?"

Voelker frowned. "For that particular weapon as adapted experimentally, you are right; but weapons could be rigged for adjustment to narrower convergence-angles. I've been trying for the widest possible convergence-angle for use at short range for such delicate space-tasks as burning open a jammed lock or carving an escape hole through a hull—a sort of high-powered can opener. The same angle can be attained with smaller mirror diameters. Well, anyhow, fifty degrees was the widest angle I could obtain with near-perfect reliability; attempts at wider angles produced high unreliability or failure, and even hazard to the user. With intensive basic research, however, over a period of years one could probably attain. . . . Eh, well, Dr. Thoth: call that my bequest to you, sir."

Over cakes and ale at a nice cocktail lounge (Houston Police picked up the tab), Arroya and Claudine and Croyd discussed the case and got to know each other a little.

"As an afterthought detail," Arroya remarked, "evidently Murchison was pressing his back tight against his chair when he was shot. The diameters of the holes in his back and in the chair were about the same."

"That I believe," Claudine responded; "but I am not convinced that he was leaning back because he was surprised, although beyond question he had to be scared. You see, Voelker's testimony was that of a psychotic, and I've tipped Zambesi about that."

"How psychotic?"

"Well, for instance, the blandness of it all was schizoid, and the motivation of it all was paranoid. But there's a little more."

"You mean, that he killed the Hellers? Inspector, is that maybe your current homicide investigation? All I know about that is from newskenners."

"Croyd, you asked Voelker the key technical question. Care to comment?"

Croyd said gravely: "The shots at both Hellers were at seventy-five-degree convergence angles, not fifty. But Voelker assured me that there was no way to adapt his gun to an angle wider than fifty degrees. Yet he crowed that he had also shot the Hellers with the same weapon. This he could not have done."

Arroya: "Yet you think he really believes he did that?"

St. Cyr: "If he does believe it, he is insane. It may however be that he is intentionally claiming false credit in order to martyr himself; but that again would be paranoid. Captain, I made a practically complete statement about the Heller murders to the newskenners, including a meticulous number-by-number cataloging of the wound diameters and the seventy-five-degree angles of both shots. But space-harried time-harried editors edit for the broad public, and most of them merely generalized on those details. I imagine that Voelker didn't know about those shot-angles and felt safe in claiming credit with his gun. And there's one weird angle that I did *not* give to the kenners. Right, Croyd?"

He nodded, knowing she meant the invisibility. Dead Kyria couldn't testify to the death of Klaus; and even the presence of Claudine at the slaying of Kyria hadn't suggested more than the idea of "an elusive killer" or "a slayer-phantom" to any editor except those of a few tabloids which Voelker would not have seen.

Arroya, curiosity at high pique: "Want to tell me the weird angle—or not?"

Claudine, frowning down: "It doesn't affect your Murchison case, so I'd better not, just yet. But I do see an inter-play-aspect for you to notice and think about. If a finding of insanity should impeach Voelker's testimony that he killed the Hellers, how might that affect his claim that he killed Murchison?"

"But what else is possible? Suicide in the presence of Voelker, with Voelker's weapon? What would be the motive—and where is there any evidence?"

Thinking about a damaged Kyria, a possibly male-traumatized Duke, and a Duke-dream of being a Kyria satellite only outside the Heller satellite, Claudine murmured: "There is a chance that I may find a suicide motive, but I don't have it yet. As to evidence—Captain, are you familiar with the lab technique for determining with certainty which of several overlapped fingerprints is the latest if the time-difference exceeds one hour?"

Now Arroya frowned down. "The multiple fingerprints on the firing button. But you understand that Voelker might have pressed the button right there in Murchison's office, with the safety lock on?"

"Of course; and if so, we'd be dead—but you'll try?"

Arroya leaned forward: "Of course. Inspector, if you'll forgive me, I hate to break this up, but my husband and three kids will be waiting for me to get home and punch dinner."

She took them to their hotel in the police car. There she dismounted with them and shyly extended a hand to Claudine and then to Croyd. She said diffidently to Claudine: "Working with you is good. Knowing you is nice. My name is Dolores."

"Mine's Claudine. Thoroughly mutual on both counts, Dolores, and warmly I mean it."

"Dr. Thoth, it has been a pleasure. I'd love to show you and Claudine around our outfit tomorrow—"

"Do call me Croyd."

"Is it Croyd Thoth?"

"That's my species name. Claudine, what about tomorrow?"

"Regrettably, Dolores, I doubt that we can do it tomorrow. If you don't hear from us, you'll have to forget us."

"Never!" exclaimed Arroya.

The Erth-natural hypothesis, as Claudine and Croyd both understood, was now dead for all practical purposes.

If Voelker had killed nothing else, that he had killed.

21. TIME-INVASION

Admitting Croyd to her room at 1900, Claudine was muu-muu'd. "Fix us a couple of bourbons while I finish dressing," she invited; "sorry I have to do it right in this room with you." He urged: "Go dress, and bless; I'll keep my back turned, I do hate a muu-muu."

Dressed but not over-dressed, she sat, sipped, meditated, reached decision. Looking at him across the table, she asserted: "Now there's only one way."

"I was afraid you'd say that. You aren't ready yet. I'm going with you, I can give you in-service training along the way."

"It may take me a lot of time. Can you be spared?"

"Right now, I think so, for several days anyhow; I can time-surface and contact Nereid a couple of times daily. But I may have to leave you alone, out there—"

"The longer you can stay with me, the readier I'll be to cut it alone. Damn you, Croyd, you're not a doll, you're positively an ikon . . . Excuse me, something can't wait. Houston time is 1917 CST—" She button-touched her cutichron: "2017 GTC, same as EST—dumb of me not to know, but I get mixed on my forwards and backwards. Well, he's likely to be home now, I'll try for him there."

Taking her drink to the beside phone, she punched a Manhattan number from memory; there wasn't any video. After a few seconds: "Wong? Claudine. I'm fine, thanks, how's your wife and kids? . . . Well, I'm in Houston . . . Houston: you know, Texas . . . *Texas*: you know, the. . . . Right. Right. Well: a Dr. Murchison has been wasted here, and it ties in with the Heller murders. . . . No, I'm getting nowhere, but listen. . . . Wait, Wong, listen. . . . Hey, f'gossakes you diagonally ocular son of a laundryman, *listen*, I'm trying to *tell* you something. . . . All right, here it is: I'll be away for

some period between a week and umpteen weeks, I'm taking
off on star travel again. . . . On the Heller case; I have a
lead to a distant star. . . . Vassili, M-8731. . . . What do
you mean, it's implausible? Heller ran aerospace, didn't he?
. . . Can't tell you the angles on the phone, I'll send you a
scrambled flake, okay? . . . . Good man, Wong; kiss the
wife for me. Out."

Running her hand back through her hair in a curiously
masculine gesture of perplexity, she returned to her chair and
sat half-facing Croyd.

He drained his drink and stood. "Let's go to dinner. And
afterward, a solid three hours of intensive training, no matter
what it may cost you, before you take off even with me."

She stood too. "Make yourself another glucose and give me
a quarter-hour. I have to dictate and dispatch a flake and
write a short letter. On the way to dinner, I can mail the latter."

"The latter or the letter?"

"The latter letter. You write the Sullivan music."

As the steak and burgundy neared extermination: "Dessert,
Claudine? liqueur?"

"Facing three training-hours, do you recommend either?"

"For me it doesn't matter. You judge for you."

"I'd better play safe. No dessert, no liqueur. Espresso,
black an unsweetened. But please have what you want—"

He raised a finger, seeming to be listening. His expression
went sober-hard. Rapt, she bent toward him: he was receiving some sort of mind-communiqué, or perhaps something
from a sub-auditory cerebral implant, and it wasn't good, it
wasn't good at all. He was lost in it, his occasional involuntary lip movements indicated that he was mind-replying. . . .

He cut it off and said to her: "Please flag the waiter and
get us two espressos, black and unsweetened. Let me get back
to this for a bit—"

She motioned at the remnants of his steak; he flashed a
ghost-smile and shook his head and was lost in that inward-
ness. She had the plates removed. When the espresso came,
absently he picked up his and sipped it, then set it down and
half turned away from her with his lips sporadically moving.

He snapped them shut. He gazed at the ceiling. He turned
back to her and the espresso, not smiling at all. "Sorry, luv,

we have to make fast changes in our personal programs. A
latent war threat between Wambo and Leikpritz has all of a
sudden hotted-up, I have to be aboard ship en route to
Nereid no later than 0300 tomorrow morning."

"Why 0300 especially?"

"The Wambo ultimatum ends at 0330; I have to be in full
operational communication, I can do that from my frigate."

She stiffened. "So I start with no more training, and I go
alone."

Sipping, frowning, he waved a hand. "I can still train you
this evening. It won't be enough, but I know I can't stop
you."

"You'd get no sleep!"

"Enjoy sleep, but don't need it except when overstrained;
it's good then for dream-catharsis. Let's see, it's 2051 here,
that's 2151 Galactic—three hours training brings us to
0051—ninety minutes to Manhattan makes 0221, then twenty
solichopper minutes to the frigate is 0241—but that assumes
perfect connections, you have to assume an hour or more of
time-fritter, and that would arrive me *way* late—oh hell, it's a
double emergency, I can teleport, no sweat; we have *more*
than three hours, actually from this minute about five. Ready
to leave?"

"Why don't you just teleport me to Iola?"

"Now get this, my friend. *Under no circumstances* are you
to remain on Iola later than last December, which was when
Heller departed. Which means, I can't teleport you there
now, even if I could safely shoot you that great distance,
which I doubt. Understand me? you must depart with Heller,
you *must!*"

"Mr. Secretary, sir, is that a direct order?"

Grim: "Flatly, Inspector, that *is* a direct order." He stood:
"Tell you why when you get back with a personal feeling for
the situation. Order accepted, Inspector?"

She spread hands: "Of course, but you'd better scream for
the check. Which of our expense accounts picks up the tab?"

"My turn, I think."

"That's good for the waiter. Galactic Police allows only ten
percent tips."

In her hotel room: "You remember the generalities of the
deal, Claudine. Your mind departs your own brained body

and occupies Heller's brain when he was alive aboard the *Lucifer* late last November; let's say, on 22 November 2494, two days before he made his black hole jump. I'll have time to teleport you to that spacetime position and get back to board the frigate at 0300. That way you'll have a couple of days to accommodate yourself to being Heller, in a sense, without being able to control anything he thinks or does. And during your second day, I'd recommend a few cautious experiments in reaching out into other crew brains and even generalizing yourself among several or all of them, but never losing your base contact with Heller. Got it?"

"I have your meaning; I'll see how it goes."

"In order to think and interpret situations for yourself, you'll be using Heller's brain and the other brains instead of your own. You had some preliminary practice in that last night in *my* brain, and tonight I'll give you more.

"Then you'll go through the black hole in Heller, purely as a means of getting to Iola. When you arrive, as soon as possible, generalize yourself beyond Heller into others, so that you can observe the whole action with the inter-subjectivity which is objectivity. But never, *never* lose touch with Heller completely—because he's your ticket home. Okay?"

"Check."

"I must warn you of certain perils, Claudine—one of which is comical but still dangerous.

"First: in another person's brain, your mind may go insane if you try assiduously to impose your will upon him, because he won't respond—he, and therefore you, will always be doing exactly what he then did. Lie back and enjoy it, you have no choice, it's what you want to do anyway—you are seeking to know past facts, you cannot change the past.

"Second: you must retain your Claudine soul-identity, your personality, even though your mind in another's brain is continually being bombarded by your host's feelings and observations and sensations and thoughts and action-will. These feelings will feel as though they were yours, but they will not be yours, they will be his; insist on keeping your own soul ultimately separate.

"Third: you could get inadvertently separated from *all* your hosts. And unless you acted instantly to anchor onto somebody, that would leave you soul-weltering in uptime space, with no brained body to help you. And you could easily go mad—which means that your mindsoul would disintegrate and be dissolved in uptime space. Tonight I'll be teaching you how to soul-wriggle back into a brain, in such an emergency. But the safest course is: never let go of all brains entirely.

"Fourth: once returned to Erth in Heller's brain, be very sure you are not still in it when he is murdered. If you are dead set on witnessing that death, arrange to be in Kyria then. But get back to yourself in actuality before *she* gets it."

"Very good, Croyd, and I think I know how to do that. But will my brained body be safe? and where will it be?"

"It will be safe, I assure you. Before I leave you, I'll show you where and how."

"You haven't mentioned the comical peril."

"It is that sometimes the maleness and male sexual attitudes or even activities of Klaus or Duke may deeply shock your feminine mind when you find that you *are* Klaus or Duke so feeling and doing."

"No real problem there, Croyd. I've known some men and I've done some things, I've studied normal and abnormal sexual psychology male and female; I can be enormously objective, even clinical."

"Can you be thoroughly objective if as Klaus you find your woman-soul male-performing upon a woman?"

She looked demurely down: "Mainly I look forward to experiencing the enormous feeling of controlled power that a male must feel in front of a urinal. I see what you mean by comical-dangerous."

She looked up: "You have a ship to make. Let's charge into that training."

Her training progressed as far as it might in a few hours—and that was, to her, thrillingly far, a personal penetration into new dimensions.

Unheard-of entailments! Mind-leaps into the living Croyd brain, immediate empathy with his mind, enthralling partial comprehension of that complicated brain and astonishing mind. In his brain, practice at subordinating her will totally to his, while keeping her own soul separate and partially objective. Bedding-in with the sensory-emotive-cognitive inputs of his brain, many of which had a simple or complex quippish quality—he remarked that mind and brain pick up hu-

morous habits from each other. Sharpening herself to utilize
his brain as a surrogate of her own in a process of concep-
tualizing her Croyd-experience into clear memories, while
Croyd by mind-will rendered his own brain passively responsive to her use. Experiments in dividing her mind between his
uptime brain and her own uptime brain, experiencing both at
once, with a queer illusion of floating above both while shar-
ing both.

"My time is short," he told her after all that. "We'll teleport to where I want to stash your body. Please keep everything about these experiences confidential between us." His
trust was heart-pleasing.

After the expected gut-twitch, followed by a split-second of
nothing at all anywhere, she was peering out of a back hall-
way into a spacious old-Montmartre-type café, table-throng-
ing with demimonde and resonant with a half-dressed
chanteuse and heavily fragrant with cognac and marijuana
and musk. "The Cabaret Montreuil in mid-Manhattan," he
told her. She responded with the address; and this he approved, because, "I want you to know where to find your
body if you depart Heller on Erth when I'm not available.
But how would you get here then?"

"I could find my own uptime traces and run them down to
here—"

"Your own traces might not be readily available to you. In
that case, latch on to the first human uptime traces you can
find, follow them down into living actuality being careful not
to fall into a possible prior death or serious injury, sneak up
on the living mind and neutralize it the way I showed you
with mine, then use the brain to navigate the body here. This
can't be done in uptime, but you can do it in actuality. Then
you make your host take you where I am now taking you."

While he hurried her through the back corridor into a dark
garbage-aromatic alley: "That was a good teleport, there,
Croyd. Instead of teleporting to your frigate, why don't you
go straight to Nereid?" He: "That sort of arrival attracts too
much attention; besides, I enjoy spaceships. Watch where we
are, now—"

He swung her into a dark doorway, slid open the door
heavily ("This'll be tough if your host-vehicle has a weak
body"), shut it behind them, rushed her down a long doorless

yellow-lamp-flickering corridor around a corner. "Wait," he
said; "better count paces." Taking her back to the corner, he
turned her loose: "Walk at your normal pace until I stop
you." When she'd strolled twelve steps: "Stop. Face right. See
a door?"

Negative; then: "Wait, there's a small irregular plaster-
crack here—"

"Good, sharp eyes; I know about that defect, but it's hard
to fix without showing new work, I count on oversight by
casuals. Fix your eyes at about your own shoulder-level, and
travel them to the right from the crack three-quarters of a
meter: see an interest-point?"

After brief inspection: "Nothing yet."

"Excellent; if St. Cyr can't see it when I direct her eyes to
the point, it's hidden. That's the door-latch, but it has to be
mind-operated: direct your mind to it, use your will to make
the door open." She did: a door broke open inward, its left
edge along the irregular crack, revealing a glowing cubicle
within. Behind her, he thrust her into it; at his direction, she
willed the door to shut.

"We're in a lift," he told her; "what G-thrust can you
handle?"

She answered: "Five decently well, eight in a pinch; used
to be a ten-girl, dammit!"

"Fine; use will to command six, you may be experiencing
more eventually; tell the lift to stop at Croyd's place."

"Villain!" she gibed, obeying; and the drop thrust her off
the floor nearly to the ceiling of the lift-car before she settled
back—and then the stop thrust her down as she settled back,
but she cushioned the drop by springing her practiced knees.

He said: "We're here; open the door." She willed it open,
and they stepped into Croyd's deep hideaway. He advanced
her across a pillow-thick oriental carpet past heaped-up cor-
ner-cushions and an austere corner laboratory, and down a
corridor to a tiny posterior room along whose far wall was
ranged a glass coffin.

"That's your semi-final resting place," he told her. "Suspended animation, automatically furnished with minimum
atmospheric and nutrient requirements and waste disposal,
human-monitored from Nereid for practically perfect safety;
I use it occasionally myself."

"But Croyd, I'll be absent from my favorite little bod for

weeks, maybe. How long does it take for practically perfect
safety to slip into being just ordinary safety?"

"When the Interplanetary Union perishes, you'll be done
in. Look, are you for this?"

"I'm going. Should I maybe strip?"

"It's advised. For the second time tonight, I'll turn my
back."

"Don't bother; admire and envy." Already she was out of
her skirt, and the rest followed in a hurry; he took the pieces
one by one and laid them on a nearby chair. She studied the
way he'd laid them, sniffed, and turned her face up to him:
"What do I do now—step in and die?"

"Now your mind leaps into my brain; I lay your body
away, and off we go."

"Croyd—"

"Claudine?"

"For my last leap into your brain—"

"Mm?"

"Since we can't bed-in tonight, could I go out kissing you?"

He enfolded her; they clung in a body-close kiss.

She mind-leaped into his brain. Her body slumped in his
arms; she was he with her body warm in his arms, he laying
her in the life-suspension capsule, closing, activating.

Aboard the ship *Lucifer,* among the filaments of uptime . . .

He: *Can you identify Klaus Heller?*

She: *There.*

Ready to board him?

I think so. What time is it?

Closing on ship-time for me.

*Croyd—when I get back—if I get back—I want to credit
you for help on this case.*

Not a chance. Verboten.

Modesty?

Discretion.

Okay, then. Croyd—

Scared, friend?

Yes, but that isn't what I wanted to say.

*I'm reading what you want to say. Can you read my re-
sponse, Claudine?*

Uh-HUH! That's a real good long-range feeling, there.

It works better when we're separate people. I hope we'll be together often. Cheers, St. Cyr. Get out of me now.

She leaped.

She *was* Klaus Heller—for now. But she didn't plan to be Klaus alone forever.

Her scrambled flake went from Houston to Wong in Manhattan by telephone; it was automatically picked up at his headquarters, computer-unscrambled, and placed on his desk in plain Anglian in a sealed envelope marked PERSONAL TO THE SUPERINTENDENT. There was a record in the memory banks, but only Wong or his successor could ever tap into it.

Wong found it when he entered at 0813. Substantially, it briefed the theory that Claudine had laid before Croyd, short-explained why the Erth-natural hypothesis had gone kaput, indicated her where-when destination, and added a few requests about interim office dispositions.

He read it moodily. He read it again. He laid it down, took up his dagger to play with, and swiveled full around to gaze out the window while playing.

Presently he sent for Captain Venuto and Lieutenant Tuli. Having seated them, he queried: "Did Inspector St. Cyr tell either of you where she was going after Houston?" Both negated.

Wong's eyes drooped nearly shut. "Captain Venuto, I want you to put Lieutenant Tuli on the full-time job of covering Dr. Voelker's arraignment and watching for his subsequent activities in prison or out. Can Tuli be released for this?"

"Well, yes sir—"

Tuli interjected: "Sir, what am I looking for?"

"Frankly, I don't know. Keep a log, and report to me on anything that seems funny. And, Venuto, I want you to do the same thing yourself personally with Clara Wilson."

"Full time, sir?"

"That's right."

"But I'm running St. Cyr's department—"

"I'll run it for now, it's my own old bailiwick," Wong favored Venuto with some running advice on the hazards of tailing a smart power like Clara Wilson, and he promised her a sophisticated legal adviser. "Venuto, I can't say what you're looking for, either. Any questions?"

Venuto shook her head: "None for now—but for sure I'll be back."

"Tuli?"

"Only—sir, have *you* heard from Claudine?"

"Nothing since yesterday." True in terms of message-origination.

"Did she—tell *you* where she was going?"

"I can only say to you, Tuli, that *where* is not the complete question."

"Is it—hazardous duty?"

"I would say, yes, unusually hazardous."

Surprisingly, straight-standing Tuli turned on a big grin. "Thank you, sir, that relieves me; she can handle hazards. I was afraid it might be something worse, like monotony."

Clara Wilson received Claudine's letter at her office late in the afternoon. Idly fingering her mail pile while listening to an expostulating vice-president, she spotted the unopened envelope marked PERSONAL TO MS. WILSON and with the St. Cyr name at upper left. Promptly she extracted it, asked her visitor to excuse her, and with some trepidation ripped it open.

Dear Clara Wilson:

Before departing Erth on an errand which will interest you deeply when you learn about it, I feel impelled to express a thing that has been on my back.

Please don't take too much encouragement from this; you aren't yet quite off my hook, and there will continue to be some Galactic Police surveillance. But whether or not you turn out to be involved, as I now personally think you won't, I regret this pressure because I like and respect you.

The experimental raygun which Dr. Voelker apparently used to kill Dr. Murchison could not possibly have killed Klaus or Kyria Heller.

You'll appreciate that it would be indiscreet for me to say more—this much may be indiscreet. But if you are innocent, which probably you are, this information may serve to lighten your soul.

Claudine St. Cyr

Wilson folded the letter, frowned at it, tapped a hand-palm with it. Tossing the letter onto her desk, she gripped her chair arms tightly and rocked far back, slant-gazing at the letter on her desk.

Presently she murmured: "St. Cyr, you're a good girl. Maybe some day you'd consider a vice-presidency. No, you wouldn't. C'est grand dommage—from my viewpoint, not from yours."

Part 5

Part Seven

DUKE IN ANGUISH

Iola, 28-29 November 2494

St. Cyr semi-mastered interbrain bridging aboard the *Lucifer*. As Heller, she bump-suffered through the black hole jump, and she narrowly missed being thrown clear of him during the celestial nack-nock. She stayed with Heller during two further days, occasionally reaching out to brain-contact others.

Continually she gained confidence as she confirmed that the events of her dreaming had been real. And she arrived at a self-limiting ethical decision. Her brain-infestation would be mostly restricted to sight-hearing-smell-taste-touch, augmented by impersonal use of host-forebrains to facilitate her own thinking. As far as possible (although there would be lapses), she would avoid tapping into the emotions of her hosts: for a police investigator, such taps would be unconscionable invasions of privacy.

Possible exception: that Duke . . . But even with him, minimal emotion-touching: only enough to determine whether there had been motivation for murder or for suicide.

By the evening of 27 November 2494, when the two Erth-men and their two Iola-women companions tasted the central town, St. Cyr with aplomb was mind-maneuvering among them and objectively above them—but, as Croyd had urged, never entirely losing touch with Heller. This was her self-deployment when after midnight the four entered the men's apartment in Warren Heldo for a night-cap.

From now until the end of her time in the Klarta system, mostly forget St. Cyr. She was a mere observer, as we are observers; she had almost forgotten herself.

22.   DUKE OVER-REACTS (One)

They sat in the Klaus-Duke salon, Klaus and Luria at two ends of a sofa, Duke and Kyria in comfortable chairs, nosing drinks and discussing the evening—and Duke was quite hyped-up, he was requiring himself to participate harsh-choppily with the words and phrases which he had learned at the astrolab that afternoon and from Kyria this evening (which now had become very early morning). In the two clubs, the Erth-men had been experimenting with native drinks, they'd tried about seven different (relying on the restorative pills in their medicine cabinets), comparing them variously to Erth-cocktails like dry Manhattans and gimlets and Harvey Wallbangers (here called zangs); the women had stayed with zangs. Now in their apartment, the men were finishing off on kromoweel; Luria had fixed herself another zang; Kyria, scorning restoratives, had gone for the kromoweel out of sheer bravado, insisting that she'd learned how to drink on pure grain alcohol with necessarily female internes.

So bland was the kromoweel that Kyria wasn't aware of her own growing garrulity, although she *was* aware of her growing comfort with this marvellous trio and particularly with Duke. (Piquantly backgrounding this awareness were midriff turgidity and pelvic languor.) Luria was her stimulating sister-friend. Klaus could have been her affectionate wise much-older sister (the concept of "father" or "brother" being inappropriate in the context of friend or even acquaintance). With Duke, however, the brother concept urged itself into her foreground with an aura of childhood fantasy: he was her friendly strong slightly-older foster brother, infinitely superior to any real brother she might have had, born far afield so that language had to be new-taught to him, brilliant in his field; wearing a mask of self-confidence but fundamentally shy, yet curious and willing to try things . . .

These were the feelings that she noticed in her hintermind with faintly puzzled comfort, while with her foremind she enjoyed the alien men and her fast-vanishing kromoweel and her own talk-flow with Duke listening to her fondly and over there on the sofa Klaus and Luria staring at her . . .

. . . As for instance, Kyria: "You Erth-men must abandon your lifelong habitudes, the fundamentals of our humanity are different from yours, and certainly our sexual forms and habits and styling are different from yours." How clear it all was to her now! "Of course we are all mammals, but not the same kinds of mammals: we Iola-people started from frogs or maybe salamanders, you started much later from lizards and snakes and that makes you a lot more primitive. How fascinating that nevertheless you could evolve into beings as intelligent as we women! but you are kindly, and I love that in you, but just the same it shows how primitive you are underneath. Well, all right, there it is, I guess: different lines can evolve toward a con—concentri—tricity, eh? Ha! Well, anyhow, let's get it all together. You males on Erth are intelligent and dominant, and I gather that your females are also intelligent but mostly choosing to play supporting roles as in a theater, eh? But your females *could* be intelligent and dominant, and a lot of them *are*, right? Right. Incredible! Whereas—where was I?"

Just as Klaus suggested "Comparative evolution," she noticed that her glass was empty, and she arose quite easily to refill. Duke stood: "You want, I get." "No sweat," she purred, raising an arresting hand; "we Iola women are used to taking care of ourselves, whatever your Erth women may be used to." Moving quite easily to the bottle, she brought it to the men, offering to sweeten theirs first (both were nursing); Klaus demurred; Duke happily accepted a half-ounce amplification. Kyria went back to the drink table, filled her glass with straight kromoweel, added two frigiballs, and returned to her chair, joying in her own self-control.

Her mind, too! Her mind! Perfectly in order: she could back-trace her entire argument skein! Having sipped, savored, and swallowed, she resumed: "Good, Klaus! Comparative evolution! I'm a nurse, I've been trained in these things. All right: you're mammals, we're mammals, but we have some *lee-tle* differences—I don't mean, just between us as women and men, I guess we all know about *those* differences, don't

we, Luria? Ha! What I *really* mean is—well, look. I don't
know where you got those external ear flaps, I don't know
any reptiles with ear flaps, and yet we started earlier than
you, from amphibians, and ears we got not. Look!" Standing,
she flourished-up her hair to reveal the earlessness that Luria
exhibited all the time. "And look at my finger-webbing—what
have *you* got like *this?*" She stretched out spread-fingered
hands, one toward Klaus, one toward Duke. "And look at my
toes—"

When she attempted a perilous bending from the waist
while raising a foot off the floor to remove a shoe, it seemed
no trick at all to her until she began to topple . . . but she
was caught by Duke, he held her in his strong arms and bent
over her face, his face was now all her conscious world, his
face wore no smile, his face was profoundly concerned in the
whirling and his face came down upon hers, his mouth was
laid on her mouth, he clutched her to him, she clung to him
as a drowning woman might cling to a female lifeguard
whose mouth was absurdly on her mouth . . . and went into
a momentary trance haunted by a Walpurgis of marshes and
fens, and her lying supine in stinking scummy water being
tupped and topped and tupped and topped and wanting to be
tupped and being topped and a throbbing bellyache the whole
while, a bellyache whose throbbings translated themselves
into reiterant distant drums or reiterant triumphant male
croakings; one tupper was her father whom she had never
known, and once hideously it was her mother who clammily
weighed her down mingling juices with juices, and once in sa-
tanic triumph she nude-barefoot trod the hurting belly of a
supine male who pleaded for mercy mercy mercy and then rose
up and threw her and gave her hyah-hyah-hyah . . . and
came conscious with Duke mouth-to-mouth clutching her
body, and knew her time had all of a sudden come, *and it
had to be done NOW* . . . and pulled her mouth away from
his (but clutching him) to gasp (knowing the words must be
simple) "Duke, you do it, not them, *not them, you* do it,
now—" and felt herself swung up into his arms and carried
somewhere.

As Duke disappeared with Kyria into his bedroom and slid
the sound-insulated door shut behind him, agitated Klaus
came to his feet and felt Luria's hand on his arm, and heard
her quiet drawl: "Klaus, my friend—sit."

Presently he obeyed, stared at the shut door, pondered, then turned to Luria: "He could hurt her—"

"He is vicious?"

"No, but—"

"Are you worried because he is bigger than our men? But Duke is a kindly man, I think he will be considerate—"

"Duke is drunk, Luria—drunk with liquor and doubly drunk with love. He's in *love* with Kyria—or don't you women here understand that?"

"I understand love with woman-friends, probably it is much like your friendship with Duke. But love as related to male-female copulation urges—no, I don't understand that. Duke feels *that way?*"

"So much so that he would like to live with her all his life."

"This he told you?"

"This I know."

"Then if he loves her like that, won't he be all the more kindly?"

"I suppose so, Luria—"

She slapped a fist into a palm. "Damn! what a novel-beautiful idea! A male kindly to a female because he loves her—"

Klaus brooded, watching the door.

She turned to him, hand-squeezing his arm. "Klaus—do you like me?"

One eyebrow up, he turned to Luria. "I like you very much."

"In friendship, Klaus, do you love me?"

Intently: "Definitely, Luria, in friendship, I love you."

She waited. He said no more, merely looking at her—but what a look! But this was an all-new thing, under the sun called Klarta! Moistening her lips, she sought to frame the next question. . . .

The screaming of Kyria penetrated the sound-insulated door. It was not a scream of ecstasy. As Luria and Klaus came to their feet, the door slammed open and Duke emerged, and he was disheveled-wild, and he grated: "Klaus, Luria, help her. I've ruined her—"

Klaus went for the door, pulling Luria, telling her: "He says he's ruined her." Kyria lay supine, rolling and groaning, bare to the waist and bare above the pelvis which spurted a reddish fluid.

Luria snapped: "Oh bloi, she's had the breach. Don't sweat, Klaus, it's frequent among us, there's first aid in the bathroom; I'll take care of her, you go call the desk and tell them to hurry a breach-crew to your apartment, that's all, just hurry a breach-crew, they'll do all the rest. Go!"

Klaus went. While he phoned (the woman-clerk reassuringly told him, "Understood, we'll be there immediately, we'll phone General Hospital, out"), he glanced around the room but didn't see Duke. My God, was the character hiding in the other bedroom? Disconnecting, he didn't go looking for Duke; if the guy couldn't take the heat and hang around to help, the hell with him.

Klaus returned to Duke's bedroom where Kyria lay more quietly now, her breasts covered by her pulled-up blouse; Luria, seated beside her, was doing final fastenings on a crotch-bandage that looked like baby pants; but the bed was soaked pink. Kyria looked at Klaus as he entered, she seemed quite calm although still in some pain. She said with difficulty: "Klaus, don't blame Duke, it would have happened anyway. Please go tell him—"

He heard the outer door slam open; a moment later, two white-uniformed women appeared, one carrying a folded stretcher, the other a black bag. Standing, Luria told them curtly, "No first aid needed. I took care of it. Was the hosptial called?" An aide affirmed: "Ambulance on the way." While they were lifting Kyria onto the stretcher, Luria said: "Be sure they know that this is Glir Lladyr, a supervisor, and that Krazia Mujis will want to be notified first thing in the morning." She kissed Kyria's lips and patted her shoulder just before they carried her out.

Then Luria turned to Klaus, and inhaled, and exhaled, and said: "Well! what a disgusting turn of events!"

He queried with concern: "What about Kyria?"

Luria smiled, but it was strained; and she advanced to Klaus and patted his shoulder. "From your expression and behavior, my friend, it's clear that on your Erth, this sort of thing would be a woman-catastrophe. With us, it isn't good, but it is frequent, and it is no catastrophe. Our uterine balances at full term are precarious. If there is any flaw in a full amnion it is likely to breach, on the average it happens about one season in ten, it is a reason why our population is no larger."

230

"But will Kyria be all right?" His hands were on Luria's ribs.

Comprehending that his welcome hands meant no more than comforting from a friend, she smiled at him freely. "First the good, then the not-so-good. The good is, that this trauma is, well, not as common as colds, but easier to treat; the procedures in General Hospital will have Kyria on her feet tomorrow and back in limited action the next day. Now the not-so-good. The upset to the reproductive system is general and incurable. Kyria will almost certainly lose her ovaries and become a freemartin—which won't hurt her socially, she has plenty of company, but annually there'll be an emotional crisis. But she will be all right physically, count on that. And—Klaus, believe me—your friend Duke had absolutely no part in the trauma, he was an innocent by-lier!"

Without hesitation, Klaus nodded gravely: "I believe you, Luria. You are one whom I believe." He dropped hands: "I'd better reassure Duke." He departed the bedroom, with Luria following, and went to the other bedroom.

No Duke.

Having comprehended and accepted Duke's absence, quietly asserted Klaus: "He ran away, Luria. I won't condemn him, he had a bad shock. But he's in no shape to be roving the streets alone."

"He may still be in the building. I'll go phone the desk—" She did, and he heard her say: "Alert all duty-women to block Dr. Duke and bring him back to his apartment. If necessary, slug him, but don't hurt him too much."

Coming to Klaus, Luria took his hand and led him to the sofa. She said, "Don't worry too much about him. Probably he's already out of the building. He thinks he did a bad thing, he wants to walk and think about it; that's what I'd want to do if I thought I'd done a bad thing—"

"Luria, would you run away from the person you thought you had physically hurt?"

She managed a massive shoulder-shrug: "Maybe, I dunno—" Then, simply, "No, I wouldn't—and neither would you, Klaus. Are you angry at your friend?"

"Not angry enough to want him to get into trouble, out on the nocturnal town in a tizzy."

"We could alert the police."

"Any ignominy attached to that?"

"I can handle it so there won't be."

On the phone again, she said: "Inspector Vaxo? Hi, Mella, this is Luria Threll. Got a problem tonight, right now. You know about the two visiting ambassadors from outer space? Good. Well, one of them had a bad personal shock tonight, and he's out on the town somewhere. Right." Description. "Well, if somebody spots him, have them pick him up, address him as *Doctor* Duke, assure him that his friend is all right, and bring him back here. No, that's enough to tell him; if he passes for more information, have them say that I'll explain when he gets here. Got it? Mella, a million appreciations."

She returned to Klaus. "How is your liquor-head?"

Dismal, he spread hands. "Good for one more kromoweel. I surely can't sleep."

She went to the liquor table, came back with two drinks, handed him one, sipped hers. Having considered her, he sipped his. Together on the sofa, they moped, sipped, moped.

She said, "Don't forget your appointment this morning with the World Council. Maybe you ought to slug down that one and another, and conk out."

He shook his head. "It won't be the first time I've hit a high-level conference needing sleep. Sometimes it even works better that way, I'm extra-alert. And I want to be awake in case Duke comes back."

She suggested to her drink, "I can stay and see you through tonight, if you like."

"I'd like that very much. I—apart from my worry, I guess I think you could reassure Duke about Kyria better than I could."

"That's a very sweet thought. I never knew a man like you—hell, on Iola there *aren't* any men like you."

Silent sipping.

She told her drink, "I wouldn't scream."

His head turned slowly her way. "I beg your pardon?"

"It would be interesting to experience that kind of kiss—from you, Klaus—and what might follow. I wouldn't breach, it's the wrong season. And I'd switch on my masochism."

He drained his drink. After a moment, she drained hers. They stood, clasped waists, and went thoughtfully into his bedroom.

Klaus came to life all at once, discovered that it was nearly 0830, felt a gripe of fear, left the bed noiselessly to avoid disturbing Luria, donned a bathrobe, prowled into the salon: nobody there, nobody in the kitchenette. He peered into Duke's bedroom. Alarmed indeed, he went back and awakened Luria. "Morning," he announced gravely, "and no Duke."

Now Luria was alarmed. He gave her his bathrobe and crossed the salon to get Duke's for himself, then returned to the salon to find her at the phone saying, "Herder? Threll here. Look, do you remember the Erth-men you met last night?"

"To a hair," answered Herder Maxus. There was no video, but the sound was open to the room.

"Now listen, Herder. Fix your memory on Dr. Duke, the younger one. Late last night, or rather early this morning, in Warren Heldo here, he experienced a shock, and he ran off into the night. We alerted Mella Vaxo, and he should have been back by now, but he isn't. What thoughts do you have?"

"Unhappy thoughts, Kra Threll."

"Exactly. What can you do beyond what Vaxo can do?"

"I know a lot of places and men. I have some very good men at Warren Kreczy—may I ask some of them to go out on the town?"

"Absolutely yes. But be sure to let Vaxo know that you are in on the act. Dr. Heller and I are at his apartment in Warren Heldo, you can report to us here until 1000, then we have to leave for a 1030 meeting with the World Council, no telling how long we'll be out of touch. What then for communication?"

"My men will phone me here at your office at least every hour or as soon as one of them knows something. Call me here when you're through at council."

"Understood and agreed. If you find Dr. Duke, please assure him that Kyria is all right, and bring him back here. Out, Herder—good luck."

She then phoned General Hospital. Report: "Glir Lladyr is doing fine, she is normal after breach, she told us to anticipate your call and sent a message: See her when you can, but don't push it, you have other problems."

Luria turned to Klaus who was pacing. She went to him, gripped his upper arms, queried: "On Erth, in a situation like this between an independent man and an independent woman—who fixes breakfast?"

For the planet Iola—or anyhow, for its capital city of Gladowr, and consequently for all that made civilized sense on Iola—it was Destruction Day minus two.

23.   ULTIMATUM FROM GODZHA

In World Council Headquarters perched atop the central Gladowr tower, Klaus and Luria, arriving a bit early, were welcomed by a secretary who seated them in outer-office easy chairs and intercom-announced their arrival to her boss the executive secretary in council session. Disconnecting, she stood: "Kra Threll, they would like for you to enter first. Please excuse her, Dr. Heller, I don't think it will be long." Throwing Klaus a look of dismay, Luria entered the council chamber. Klaus wry-smiled, estimating that they wanted her pre-report on him, and went into meditation.

No more than five minutes later, at precisely 1030, an austere brunette opened the door from within and asked Dr. Heller to enter. Council was in session, not in the large chamber which seated a hundred in the visitors' gallery, but in a small one for intimate discussions and interviews. He found the situation familiar: a long table of rich massive wood high-waxed to prevent coffee stains; with seventeen luxurious but not soporific chairs, all occupied except one for him; with side desks for selected staff people. The brunette, who proved to be the executive secretary, seated Klaus in the empty beside Luria at table-foot, then took her own place near table-head next to the chairwoman. Luria squeezed his hand and murmured: "All's well with you—and also with Kyria. Mujis gave me the circle-sign."

Good: no distractions to his concentration, then—except Duke, of course; but Duke was a mature strong intelligent man who had simply made his own bed, that was all, so forget him for now. That all those whom he faced were women constituted no distraction; he had argued positions before the Constellation Board of the Norwestian Women's Congress

(Teamsters). The fifteen were: Chairwoman Alui the One of the World, actually the One of Flaria which was practically the world; the twos from Flaria's ten regions including Gladowr; Doctors Mujis and Vlotny and one other as permanently seated expert consultants; and the executive secretary. He was facing all the top powers of Iola; again good: less would not have been enough.

Chairwoman Alui, alone at table-head, was a heavy-set graying brunette whose experience had hardened on her face and body. In a ruined contralto she opened the talking. "Krazia Heller, we know about your status as ambassador from the Interplanetary Union, although our first knowledge that this Union exists is from you through Krazia Mujis here. We know about the heroic passage of yourself and your colleague Dr. Duke through a black hole in order to learn how your Union might help us in our trouble. Welcome to Flaria. You are hereby accepted by us as ambassador for your Union, and Dr. Duke is accepted as your aide. The report of you by Kra Threll, whom we respect, was impressive; she is here as your interpreter-adviser, and she too is welcome. I do not seem to see Dr. Duke—"

Klaus moistened lips. "Kra Chairwoman, Dr. Duke has had to send his regrets, he suffered greatly during the black hole passage and does not feel quite strong enough to come here today."

"Our compliments and best wishes to him. Dr. Heller, you speak our Flaric excellently well; may I inquire where you could possibly have learned it?"

Luria responded for him: "He has learned it all here, Kra Alui, in something under four days. He is a most able ambassador in every way that comes to mind. I am here primarily as legal adviser, he will need little interpretation or he may not need me at all."

"Very good, Luria. Then, Dr. Heller, I will put the following candidly. All of us here are confused about protocol with you, because you are male whereas this society is female. I will ask you the following question: Can we properly treat with you exactly as we would with a female ambassador?"

"Kra Alui, from our Union we might easily have sent a woman ambassador, even if we had imagined that your society was male. It merely happens that Dr. Duke and I have special technical qualifications for the black hole business. Yes, you can properly so treat with us."

Alui seemed relieved, and so did the others; one even sighed. Alui spoke more decisively: "Then it would be best for you to question us, rather than the other way. If a question should be out of line, we would evade, and I think you would understand."

"Good procedure, Kra Chairwoman, members of the Council. Well, since I understand that your peril is tight upon you, let's get directly to the heart of it.

"You are being mortally threatened by the planet Godzha, by their Godzhalks whom you call Geeks in slang. As I understand it, they have threatened to manipulate black-hole gravity in order to convert an atoll into a volcano as a demonstration this very day; and if this does not bring you to their feet, they will probably convert Gladowr itself into a volcano, following this paralyzing blow by invasion and conquest of all Iola."

"Correct," Alui tonelessly responded. "Their scheduled detonation hour for the demonstration volcano comes at 1100—in twenty-three minutes."

"I suppose it is too late for me to witness that?"

"Not at all. We will see it right here in holograph with sound."

"And if they succeed in bringing it off—will you surrender?"

Alui looked at each of the ten twos; each shook her head in negation. Asserted Alui: "Dr. Heller, we will not. And then they *will* destroy Gladowr and take our planet, having already destroyed our space fleet. And they will kill all our female leaders and enslave the remainder; and they will select our best male breeding stock for their own purposes and kill the remainder."

Best breeding stock—as, for instance, Herder Maxus? "Forgive me, Kra Alui, as an ambassador from a power which may send help, I have to inquire into some ancient and recent history."

"Of course."

"I've learned that you planet has practiced a two-sex caste system since prehistory."

"Necessarily so, Doctor. Fundamentally it is traditional, even genetic; but there is also reason behind it. Our males are physically and mentally inferior, and I must add that they are sex fiends." Luria winced.

"Very well. But they are useful for hard labor in heavy industry, despite their physical inferiority?"

"Their numbers make up for their individual inferiority."

"And sometimes they rape your women who are larger and stronger?"

"It often takes two or three of them to hold her down while one rapes."

"Naturally I agree that this is reprehensible; my Interplanetary Union will not countenance rape. Well, then, about two centuries ago, a number of your men banded together in revolution, is that correct?"

"It is."

"And you dealt with these men by exiling them to the inhospitable planet Godzha?"

"This we did. But I hasten to add that we were most humane about this, we sent some female prisoners along with them, we built preliminary life-support domes for them, our space fleet guided and helped supply their self-improvement, and we have traded with them. Their present behavior is hideously ungrateful."

"It is then descendants of your inferior males who are about to enslave you—and you are helpless before these inferior males."

Alui frowned down. Other Council members were restless; Luria's eyes glowed upon Klaus, she wasn't sure whether to warn him or embrace him.

Klaus probed on remorselessly. "It would further appear, that among these physically and mentally retarded males whose genes are helping to produce your greatest leaders, some of the most energetic were able somehow two centuries ago to organize and threaten your superior female domination so fiercely and intelligently that you felt forced to exile them to Godzha in self-defense."

"I am beginning to wonder," drawled angered Alui, "whether perhaps we would not have been better advised to meet with you earlier when your command of Flaric had not progressed so far."

"I will take that as an affirmation. Now, granting that your space fleet has been destroyed, surely you must have inner space and atmospheric defenses against the invasion that would have to follow the initial blow-up?"

"We do indeed, Dr. Heller, including a significant number
of ships to pursue and knock out *their* invading fleet at short
distances like a million kilometers" (she gave the figure in
lanzas). "Unfortunately these defenses are concentrated
around Gladowr; and even if we were to deploy them aloft in
advance of the gravity-attack, most of them would be sucked
into the gravity.

"And I anticipate your next needle: that these Godzhalks,
in their physical and mental inferiority, have been able so to
exceed our own science and technology that they could
destroy our space fleet and control black-hole gravity to murder us. And this is a tearing needle to have to swallow. Perhaps they are mutants—"

A two put in: "Excuse me, Kra Chairwoman. I think Dr.
Mujis will confirm what I say. Dr. Heller must know that
there is a broad distribution of ability levels among all crea-
tures. Even though our males are generally inferior, there are
individuals among them who attain surprisingly high physical
and mental levels. We have to assume that the self-chosen
males who revolted two centuries ago were among our best
males; and these were the ones whom we consigned to
Godzha."

Klaus responded, "Perhaps this is exactly what I am trying
to convey, Kra Two, Kra Alui." He glanced at Mujis. She was
slowly nodding, not at the two, but at Klaus.

He pressed: "Let me brief my whole thought. The Interplanetary Union has responded to your mayday by sending
me to investigate. I recognize your peril, but I do not yet
recognize that your cause is the better of the causes at issue.
If I can possibly communicate with my Union, we are
prepared to send a squadron to stabilize the situation; but our
desire is for harmony among planets, not for victory of one
over another."

Some staff assistant was whispering earnestly to the executive secretary.

Klaus moved in: "As I am now seeing it, Godzha has a
point. We do deplore their destructively aggressive tactics.
But I am not yet ready to assert that negotiations and adjustments are impossible, both between Iola and Godzha, and between Iola's females and males—"

The executive secretary interjected: "Excuse me, Kra
Chairwoman—we are ready to view the atoll detonation."

"Roll it," Grimly ordered Alui.

The room darkened, a wall brightened: it was a pan-
oramic-holographic aerial view of the ocean, with a broad
coral atoll, foliage-rich, in centerview; the white curl of swells
breaking around the atoll deepened the blue of the surrounding sea.

"H-Hour minus fifty-nine seconds," the secretary warned.

Alui commanded: "Give us an under-over profile." The
color-window shifted: in the top quarter-layer, one shore of
the high-treed island submitted serenely to the ageless majes-
tic swish-beat of rolling surf; but beneath it, all the way down
to room-floor, a cut into the submarine and subterranean
depths of Iola-crust was visible, revealing seams of molten
fire flowing upward-inward beneath the atoll, coming to flaring pimple-head precisely beneath it. The susurrus of sur-
face-waves was mood-muffled by the snarl of the magma.

"H minus eighteen." The Council chamber was silent except for the screen-sounds that filled it. The pimple-head
broadened until it was wider than the island, hot-dissolving
cavern rock, melting upward through; ocean waves were distorted and steam-wisps were visible.

"H minus three—two—one—"

The atoll and the entire cut of sea were replaced by an
uprushing curtain of glare amid noise like Hell at war.

The picture terminated: just a wall now.

Silence.

Out of space, a resonant tenor speaking badly accented but
intelligible Flaric: "Are you listening, Kra Alui and members
of the World Council? What we have done with this atoll we
can do as easily with the island of Gladowr—and we *will* do
it in precisely forty-six hours. We urgently suggest that we
have your decision about surrender well ahead of 1100 hours
day after tomorrow; otherwise operations might already be ir-
reversible. You know where and whom to call. Out."

"You have it now, Dr. Heller," Kra Alui commented. "We
will not surrender Iola, we cannot defend except locally and
perhaps not at all, we will not evacuate you or ourselves since
there is no time to evacuate others. I—I confess that I do not
know what we are doing in session here, other than to rejoice
in the fact that two courageous men—*men!*—would come
here in futility for us. Is there anything further that you
would like to say before we adjourn?"

"There is quite a bit," Klaus asserted, "but I assure you that just now I will not further press the issue of your fe-male-male caste division—which we of Erth would call *apartheid*. I will only say this generally: there is evidence that you may have been missing opportunities with your males."

"Heard, Doctor, but not acknowledged. And?"

"And now I have a question for Dr. Vlotny. I want to communicate with my chief at our headquarters which is nearly a thousand light-years distant. May I learn whether the nedi-ray transmitter has been repaired?"

Vlotny nodded. "We completed repairs early this morning. We would welcome that sort of test."

"Thank you, Doctor. Now, Kra Chairwoman: I do request permission to transmit a report to my chief soon after adjournment of this session."

"May we know its general nature?"

"Essentially an outline of your situation with respect to Godzha, a brief of the issues that we have discussed here, and some technical information about your cosmological situation with special reference to the dynamics of black holes. As to the last point, Dr. Duke may be able to join me, and perhaps Dr. Vlotny or Dr. Myrna will wish to add comments."

Alui looked around, drew nods from all present, and remarked to Klaus: "This is not usually a yes-council; but today we are all rather speechless, there is little for practical debate. Your program seems reasonable, particularly since it is likely that you and Dr. Duke will die with the rest of us day after tomorrow. Permission is granted. Now—"

"Pardon me, Kra Alui, but there are two other little questions."

"Go on."

"May I inform my chief, whose name is Croyd, that Iola, or specifically Flaria which controls Iola, is requesting intervention by the Interplanetary Union? Without such a request from you or from Godzha, we cannot intervene."

"How immediately could such intervention arrive here?"

"Assuming at minimum one day for Union leaders to make action decision, and another seven days to outfit a squadron and make certain technical adaptations to the black hole situation, and another three days for a battleship run at top acceleration—say eleven to fourteen days."

"Dr. Heller, the question seems academic, since the

destruction of Gladowr will occur in two days, and the subsequent invasion and conquest will be immediate thereafter."

"But assume that the question is *not* academic—and soon I will tell you why. In that case, do you make the request?"

"Tell us first what the nature of this intervening would be."

Klaus pronounced: "The first action by the arriving squadron would be to neutralize the situation by coercively restraining Godzha. The legate of the Union, who might be myself or another, would then act as mediator to bring the two parties together for negotiations; and I am fairly sure that the Godzhalks would insist on having some Iola-males as party to the matter. Should agreeable solutions be reached, the legate would then extend invitations to both planets to apply for membership in the Interplanetary Union; and in any event, the squadron would remain on duty here long enough to police full settlements. Otherwise, the squadron would have no recourse except to bless you all and depart, leaving you and Godzha to work out your own problems."

The Council was deeply disturbed by this reply. Having studied faces for nearly a minute, Alui said, "My sense is that this Council is undecided. We need more information—"

"That, Kra One, brings me to the second little question, which is the reason why request for intervention may not be academic. If this Council approves, and if Croyd approves, I believe I can act to postpone destruction of Gladowr long enough for our squadron to arrive. May I outline the proposal?"

When his words sank in, they evoked a Council mutterbuzz. Alui tapped for order and leaned forward: "You can well imagine our interest in *that!*"

Klaus outlined a plan for himself with Duke to proceed to Godzha and attack the black-hole gravity control center.

All grew more tautly alert than they had been at any time since the atoll count-down. There were exclamations of incredulity, a few decidedly hostile. At the end of it, he invited: "Kra Chairwoman, perhaps you will wish to open discussion to questions by individuals, including the consultants and the executive secretary."

"To Kra Threll also," Alui amended. Luria inclined her head.

Said a two, "That is a bold plan indeed, and we thank you; but it cannot work. They would pick off your ship exactly as they have already picked off our attacking fleet; and I doubt anyhow that we now have a ship capable of making the trip to Godzha fast enough."

"Kra Two, I do not recall making reference to a ship. Dr. Vlotny has told me that your nedi-ray equipment has experimentally sent male prisoners sub-rekamatically through space and has reconstituted them at a distance without use of special receiving equipment at the end-point. Dr. Duke and I would submit ourselves to a similar experiment at the Godzha-distance even though it is many times greater than that of any prior test."

After a Council-gasp, Klaus added, "Of course it would be necessary for us to be invisible on Godzha."

The Council froze.

Smoothly Klaus elaborated: "Of course I do not mean hueena, that is a religious mystery sacred to Iola. No, I do not at all mean that, I would not presume. But Dr. Duke and I came to Iola with metabolic accelerators built into our over-size suits; and if it is still in working order, our equipment would render us invisible on Godzha. I am proposing that Dr. Vlotny use nedi-ray transport to get us to Godzha in our suits."

Mujis leaned forward. "Dr. Heller, do you *know* that your metabolic accelerators will make you invisible?"

"If they have not been damaged, yes."

"And if they have been damaged?"

"In that case, this Council would face a grave decision: whether to equip us with your hueena devices—or not send us at all."

Agitated inter-member muttering. Another two: "If I may depart that uneasy topic and face another one—how would you go about locating the Godzha installations? Surely they are decentralized; even our own feeble gravity-controls are decentralized."

"That's curious, since your defense fleet is not. However, you have centralized coordination, and Kra Threll has intimated to me that Godzha too has a control center which your fleet tried to attack when she was aboard. I am sure that your Intelligence knows where it is. The central coordination has to be computerized, so probably we could gain time by cutting a single main cable. However, in order to delay an attack on Gladowr by a span of fourteen days, we would have to destroy or seriously cripple the entire control center—even though, regrettably, Godzhalks would be killed. It is my hope that such a strike would be the final act of war between these two worlds."

"But how, Dr. Heller, could you carry enough explosives besides yourselves in two space-suits no matter how large?"

"Explosives would not be needed. Dr. Vlotny has told me that Godzha has vulcanism much like that of Iola. And your people at your own coordination center can explain to Dr. Duke and me the wiring and keyboarding of your own hole-gravity controls. I think we may be able to adapt this learning to the far more elaborate Godzha coordination—and redirect their gravity effect from Gladowr onto themselves.

"But again, be alerted! This can only be done with invisibility: if not by our own metabolic accelerators—then by your hueena."

Agonized silence, during which the One looked from face to face for help in this religiously hideous decision. No help immediately came.

She swallowed and moved in. "Allow me, Dr. Heller, to summarize our predicament. We surrender to Godzha, or we ask for your interplanetary help.

"In order to gain time to receive this help, we have to confer invisibility upon you and Dr. Duke, two aliens, and men at that; and whether this invisibility is achieved by your methods or by our holy hueena, still it is invisibility which to our people means huecna; and if non-believers are allowed to use hueena, the religious shock may destroy our religio-political unity even though it saves our lives. But if we do not do this, the religion will die with us anyway, however it may be with the immortal godesses.

"But say for the argument that we *do* permit you invisibility, that you *do* succeed in your delaying commando mission. Still we get no permanent help without asking for intervention. But your interveners will judge on their own terms between Iola and Godzha, and we may emerge the losers: even before our males, we may lose. Besides, the history of our own planet, which was not always a one-nation planet, proves that benign but powerful interveners have a way of gradually assuming more power than was originally advertised.

"These are the multiple horns of our vachis. Pray don't speak to these matters now, there is no time; it is already 1239, and we must adjourn immediately until 1500 because of a commitment which I have and which we must all attend.

Kra Threll, the commitment deals with this afternoon's apotheosis followed by an execution; please explain these events to Dr. Heller after adjournment as he may find it instructive to attend."

Klaus inserted: "Excuse me, Kra Alui. If this should be approved, we would have to be on Godzha no later than early morning day after tomorrow, and sooner if possible; and the time for preparations between now and then is minimal and perhaps less than minimal. I urge that now, before adjournment, you authorize me to work with Dr. Vlotny's people and others in getting preparations under way immediately, pending your final decision later this afternoon."

Alui looked around: all nodded. "Hearing no objection, I so authorize you. This council seesion is adjourned until 1500 hours this afternoon."

24. APOTHEOSIS AND EXECUTION

Commandeering Vlotny on the way out, Klaus got her to phone Myrna at the astrolab (luckily Myrna was in, brown-bagging it) to authorize confidential crash action on orders from Dr. Heller. Meanwhile Luria on another phone called her office to check on missing Duke.

Vlotny gave the phone to Klaus (it was a confidential hand-instrument) and departed. Said Klaus: "My compliments, Dr. Myrna—and all this is confidential to you and your staff. First: is the long-range nedi-radio operational now for attempted communication at a distance close to a thousand light-years? . . . Excellent; I'll be right over to use it. Now: pending a time when I can come in on these operations personally, here is what I want you to start. The top-secret background is, that I am going to do a commando raid on Godzha with one aide, probably Dr. Duke. All right, now. One: ready the nedi-ray body-transmission equipment to transmit me and my aide in the oversize space-suits which we arrived in, and to reconstitute us at a specified target-point on Godzha. . . . Yes, I know that you haven't tested it at nearly that range; but we have to *try*, otherwise—top-secret again—Gladowr will be demolished in about forty-five hours . . . . No, don't comment, just do it, please. . . . You can't get both of those suits into the transmission cage? All right, build a bigger cage, we *have* to be transmitted simultaneously; your people have forty hours *at maximum* to get it built and operational, sooner would be better, much sooner would be *much* better. . . . What? . . . Look, this is a planetary crisis; *all* staff members of the Science Institute are to work around the twenty-three-hour clock for two days if necessary, orders of

245

Dr. Vlotny and the World Council. . . . All right, excellent,
thank you; sorry if I seemed bluff. Two: get out those big
suits, check their condition minutely, make notes on any obvious damage, but await my own inspection before attempting
disassembly or repairs. Three: work with the office of Dr.
Mujis to check out the invisibility generators for hueena . . .
that's right, hueena, with a view to possibly installing them in
our suits on a removable-portable basis so we can back-pack
them on Godzha. . . . They weigh *that* much? Well, then, in
our suits, with receivers that we can back-pack to give us
hueena at ranges up to two lanzas. . . . No, this has not yet
been authorized, but it is a possibility, and all needs to be in
readiness pending authorization by the Council. . . . Got it?
Fine, Dr. Myrna; thank you. Four: contact Central Intelligence to pinpoint the location on Godzha of the Central
Hole-Gravity Coordination; your transmitters will have to
materialize us not more than a lanza from that point. Five:
contact Flaria's own Central Coordination of Gravity Controls and alert the director that my aide and I will have to be
intricately briefed on their systems including keyboarding and
wiring. . . . Yes, we do have plenty of background experience. Do you have all five now? . . . Splendid. Those are pri-
orities; but if you have the staff, please come close to getting
it all started simultaneously *now*. Dr. Myrna, it is a distinct
professional pleasure to know you. Get going. Out."

He turned to Luria who had finished her call. Her face was
glum as she came to him. "There isn't any news yet on Duke.
Maxus is receiving frequent reports from six scouts, and he is
passing them advice. And Inspector Mella Waxo has the
same sort of nothing to report."

"Then maybe we should go to the hospital and check on
Kyria?"

"Believe me, friend, Kyria will hold. Better you should be
chewing into stuff at the Science Institute."

While sandwich-munching Klaus conferred with Myrna in
Vlotny's office, munching Luria peered out the broad window
at the gathering crowd semi-circled around a platform in cen-
ter-park below. Presently Luria said, not turning: "You
know, Klaus, you really ought to see this."

"See what?"

"The execution followed by the apotheosis. Both are parts

of our culture. The first will be depressing, but I think you can take it; and the second should prove uplifting."

"Go on," Myrna urged; "it will take me an hour to see to all this." She made exit.

Klaus joined Luria, peering downward. Luria touched a button, admitting exterior noise. The crowd was yelling diversely, there were hee-haws and boos and cat-calls and worse. "Hopefully," Luria remarked, "the disrespectful noises are male; this is an occasion when they can mingle with women under careful surveillance."

"Can you guarantee that all the bad noises are male?"

"No, I cannot."

Crossing the march from the Regional Court Building to their left, moving along a lengthy aisle described by ornate purple roping, came a curious and pathetic little procession. Leading, a burgomistress in antique purple costume coifed by a broad floppy hat with a white feather and carrying a long crook. Behind her, the sergeant of execution, simply dressed in a long white robe, her head shaven and piously bowed. Next, the focal center: a scudder carrying two persons, one the lethargic woman-prisoner stripped to the waist, beside her a solicitous red-robed priestess. Walking behind the scudder, the prison warden, hardbitten-stoical in unpretentious uniform, flanked by two plain-uniformed armed guards.

Attaining to the central platform, the scudder rose to its floor level. The priestess assisted the prisoner out of the scudder, onto the platform, and into the easy chair, while burgomistress and execution sergeant and warden mounted platform steps and stationed themselves at the prisoner's flanks but slightly back (though none directly behind). At the foot-corners of the platform, the two guards stood present-arms.

There was no sound, now, no sound at all. The ancillary figures on the platform were motionless, but all were watching prisoner and priestess: the latter, half-kneeling, privately prayed and consulted with the sedated and semi-stuporous prisoner.

"What is her crime?" Klaus inquired.

"A particularly repulsive murder—but listen."

The burgomistress came forward to read in a sonorous contralto: "Be it known that Krandia Gelpo has been tried and found guilty of willfully murdering a young male by

tying him to a chair, confining him to the darkness of a
closet, and refusing to feed or water him or otherwise relieve
him until finally death came to him. Her plea of insanity has
been denied. She has been sentenced to die on this day and at
this hour by the usual method. All should remember that the
justice of Flaria extends to females and males alike. All
should further remember that an execution of death is not
corrective or retributory punishment, but rather the elimination from our society of one who has committed a capital
crime; and this elimination should be comfortable and humane, it would be cruel and pointless to make it punitive. Let
the manner of Krandia Gelpo's death be a sign to the Immortals that we who are mortally alive detest her act; nevertheless, all are enjoined to pray for Krandia Gelpo, and the
Immortals will make their own judgment upon her soul.
Amen." She stepped back and watched the priestess who still
semi-knelt with the prisoner.

Klaus demanded: "If the execution isn't punitive, why the
blood-sensual crowd of spectators?"

Embarrassed Luria cleared throat. "Probably it is an old
hold-over that the public enjoys, and they have won retention
of it on a plea of deterrence-value. My own opinion that it is
barbarous has been published. . . . Wait: here's action."

The priestess turned her head to the burgomistress and
nodded. Burgomistress nodded to warden and warden to executioner. This Woman of High Ultimate Purpose rigidified
and raised her hand high.

Out of the crowd arose with deliberation two slender
metallic masts; rose to a loft of perhaps four meters. These
masts appeared to be located about twenty meters in front of
the platform and about nineteen meters apart; each was
topped with a little skull-knob from which protruded a short
slender muzzle aimed forward-downward at the chest of the
prisoner.

The high-held hand of the executioner dropped.

A wide hole opened in Krandia Gelpo's chest, and she
slumped dead.

The two towers retracted and vanished.

*Recall momentarily the spectator-presence of St. Cyr.
Soul-overfloating, she murmured: Oh-oh.*

The crowd waited silently as the original procession was reversed, removing the cadaver.

"You got it," Luria remarked, "that she was shot by two tower-guns firing rays in complementary semicircular patterns."

"I did." He had an image of parentheses joining to make a circle.

"By using fixed tower-guns and positioning the prisoner just so, we eliminate the occasional regrettable errors that can happen with human sharpshooters, and we assure the correct angle of ray-convergence into the chest of the prisoner."

"And what is this correct angle?"

"The ritual angle for criminal executions is fifty degrees."

Eh, soul-whispered Claudine.

Klaus managed to utter, "Instead of wondering whether the thing I just saw was true, I will inquire what constitutes murder in Flaria."

"Any willful killing."

"Which means?"

"Any killing which was not done inadvertently, or any willful act which might and in fact does eventuate in the victim's death. Such killing we do not tolerate."

"What about killing in self-defense?"

"Not tolerated; it is murder. Even if you kill to prevent your own death or personal abuse, it is murder. Is that good, Klaus, in your eyes?"

"I will only say now that it seems an over-simplification. What about killing an enemy in wartime?"

"That is different. The law says."

"Oh. Now: this woman who killed the man—what if he had raped her before she killed him?"

"Quite likely he had done so, or had tried to. But she should have reported it and left his punishment to the law, her testimony would have been decisive. Male rape of a female is a capital crime."

"What if a male rapes a male?"

"That is only a misdemeanor, Klaus, and seldom prosecuted because the notion of enforcing the law is ridiculous. Males are like that; we tolerate it as long as they keep it among themselves, it is a way of reducing the danger that they will rape women. . . . Oh, here comes the apotheosis!"

"Kra Alui said that I might find it uplifting."

"It is supposed to uplift us. It is uplifting to the woman

who is voluntarily experiencing it. What it may do for you is your concern."

Music interrupted: an extravagantly uniformed fifty-woman band marched in resonantly beating out a martial air, and the crowd cheered madly and endlessly. A procession of little girls, wearing only bikini pants and sandals, followed strutting and grinning, carrying great baskets of flower petals which they strewed along the route. As the band assembled in a semicircle around and behind the platform which had just groaned under a murder-execution, the next contingent entered. Same burgomistress, but flanked by two women whom Klaus recognized as the Two of the Council for Gladowr Region and World Chairwoman Alui; behind them, all the other members of the Council, trailed by the three expert consultants. Behind them marched the sergeant of execution in a new role, wearing a high-towered and bejeweled blonde coiffure. Came then a splendid scudder, flower-bedecked, carrying two standing persons: a new and older priestess richly robed in gold-brocaded sacerdotal garments, and a wizened little old woman robed in splendid white whose gray hair flowed to her shoulders and who ecstatically threw kisses to the exuberant crowd. Behind the scudder marched soldiers in proud pomp.

Attaining to the central platform, again the scudder rose to its floor level. Dismounting, the priestess offered her arm to the little old woman who took it and hobbled to an entirely new and splendid centerfloor throne and seated herself proudly thereon. The burgomistress and Alui and the regional two mounted platform steps, knelt and bowed before the ancient celebrate, arose, exchanged kisses with her, and ranged themselves behind her—Alui *directly* behind.

Forward now came the priestess and raised both arms for silence. All the crowd knelt while she prayed profoundly and gladly to the immortals. She produced a scroll from a flowing sleeve, and unrolling it she resonantly read:

"Goddess, Holy Immortals, People of Flaria, People of Iola: I bid you listen. This is an encomium to the Iola-meaning of Kra Madis Jur. I will spare you a recital of her magnificent life of public service: you all know it; and those of you who do not are commended to the *Compiled Chronicles of Flaria*, latest edition, available in all public libraries.

"Now to *the* deed by which Madis Jur earned apotheosis.

On 17 Lojis 9469, Madis Jur, atop all her prior accomplish-
ments for all of us, faced single-handedly a squad of
Godzhalks who had secretly landed on our planet for purposes of sabotage. They were armed with rayguns. Madis
with unparalleled courage required herself to stand before
them, bare her chest, and cry to them that they must destroy
her before they destroyed anything else on Iola. The force of
her plea, her personality, and her bravery wilted the
Godzhalks, and they went away."

Klaus muttered to Luria: "Then they can't be all bad—"

"For that single act of heroism," the priestess declaimed,
"crowning as it did a lifetime of public honor, the Regional
Council and then the World Council decreed on 28 Vismi
9470 that after the retirement of Madis Jur from public activity, and responsive to her prayer and schedule, she was to
be apotheosized.

"Madis Jur retired only a month ago. As law and sacred
writ require, I have interviewed her exhaustively to make sure
that she wants and feels ready for apotheosis. I have been im-
pressed by the unbounded modesty and piety of Madis Jur,
but finally she has confessed to me that she does feel ready.

"And now, she will be apotheosized. Let us pray."

All heads including that of Madis Jur bowed while the
priestess prayed exultantly. This prayer was addressed to the
Goddess of Goddesses and all higher-dimension-dwelling immortals, and it ended on a high cry: "We who must continue
for this while to live mortally on Iola commend into your dimension and companionship our heroic friend—Madis Jur!"

The crowd stood and cheered frenetically and prolongedly
while Madis Jur arose from her throne and tottered happily
forward, knelt before the priestess, received a laying-on of
hands and a blessing, knee-twisted toward the crowd while
the priestess bared her to the withered waist, spread out both
arms wide wearing on her mouth a four-inch smile.

The priestess nodded to the executioner who raised both
arms high. Out of the crowd arose the anticipated two towers—not bare, but colorfully flower-bedecked so copiously
that even the top-skulls and the muzzle-snouts were concealed. . . . The *same* two towers? Surely not, thought Klaus.
These also were about twenty meters in front of the platform; but their distance apart was more like thirty meters,
whereas he had estimated the space between the prior two
towers at nineteen. . . .

Claudine-soul: A-HA!

At the executioner's arm-drop, a very wide hole opened in the chest of Madis Jur, and she toppled. Cheering crescendoed.

"For apotheosis," Luria pronounced, "seventy-five degrees."

Precisely, reflected St. Cyr, and lost herself then in the action.

They brought the hovering scudder full onto the platform; Alui and the regional two lifted the honored cadaver and laid it on a cushioned platform which the scudder now mounted. The vehicle was surrounded by eager flower-girls; and when they retreated, the corpse was hidden under a heap of petals. The burgomistress and Alui and the regional two, followed by the priestess, descended the steps and waited; the scudder lofted slightly above the platform and readjusted itself behind these four; the band opened up with a rousing anthem; the flower-girls re-formed behind the officials, the band behind the scudder, the executioner behind the band, the soldiers behind the executioner; and the body of Madis Jur was marched out for whatever disposition of her glorified remains might be decreed by the laws of Flaria.

Cheering diminuendoed as the procession diminished across the park, heading in the direction of the mighty central high rise. By ones and twos and threes, the crowd dispersed.

Silence.

Luria, examining Klaus: *"Were* you uplifted?"

Klaus: "In an oddly mixed way. By Madis Jur herself, certainly; by the public recognition of Madis Jur, assuredly, without comment on the method; by the religious implications, profoundly. But it is already 1442; let me touch base with Myrna once more before we return to the Council."

Then, by their deaths, Klaus and Kyria had been honored. But on Erth, by whom, and how?

Whereas, by the angle of his death-wound, Duke Murchison had been dishonored. Was that merely the coincidental happenstance of an experimental raygun's maximum practical angle?

Klaus and Luria were on hand in the anteroom of the Council Chambers promptly at 1500, but they were not admitted for nearly an hour. The time was not entirely wasted:

Klaus kept in phone-touch with Myrna, Luria with Maxus and Vaxo.

At 1554, Luria put down her phone and went to Klaus: "We have a lead on Duke, and I don't like the look of it—"

The executive secretary opened the chamber door: "Dr. Heller, Kra Threll, please enter now."

Chairwoman Alui, the One of the World, barely waited for them to be seated before she came to the point. "Dr. Heller, we have reached difficult but decisive accord on all your proposals. You may say to your chief Croyd that Flaria does request intervention on Interplanetary Union terms and will look with interest at the idea of perhaps joining the Union. We hope that you will fairly represent our case to Croyd. As for your projected commando raid on Godzha, you have our approval and the full support of all Flaria's resources, including our hueena if that becomes necessary; and I will personally visiphone any officials you may designate in order to give this our full strength. And we will pray for your mission.

"May the goddess uplift and speed you, Krazia Heller, *Krad* Heller. Kra Threll, we thank you, we will not forget. Please, on your way now, for *us*, Krad! Both of you are excused."

Outside the chamber, Klaus demanded: "What was that *krad?*"

"I confess I had to think about that," Luria told him. "Believe me, it was an honor. *Kra* is the honorific title for a woman; there is no corresponding title for a man—but if there were, it would be *krad*. Alui has dredged for that coined title and has conferred it upon you."

He dry-commented: "She should have waited until *after* my mission—but I am deeply pleased." He was hurrying her to the lift: "Now we *are* going to see that Kyria!" In the lift: "What were you going to tell me about Duke?"

"One of the men sent out by Herder Maxus picked up Duke's trail. There's an open-all-night diner near the west coast, and the male proprietor thinks it may have been Duke who ate there early this morning. Whoever it was, he was followed—by two males from Warren Matae."

"How bad is that?"

"Well—it's quite a few cuts below Warren Kreczy."

Out of the lift, into the scudder for the hospital. Klaus: "What can we do?"

"Let it play itself out, I guess. After we see Kyria, I'll alert Mella Vaxo. If Duke is gang-raped, what will it do to him?"

"Morally, it may kill him."

He was thinking: *Ah, Duke, Duke! you lousy distractor— and us on D-Day minus two!*

25.   DUKE OVER-REACTS (Two)

It is perfectly possible to be specifically psychotic in the context of being generally sane. After his nocturnal escape from a main-floor service window of Warren Heldo, Duke Murchison, almost mad with love-terror complicated by soul-guilt, fled, fled, fled. He thought of himself as a chance-damned man, an ultimate alienate, whose crime of loving a non-human woman had visited itself upon her and upon himself. But by God he was going to surmount all this as soon as in hiding he could figure out how.

On a side-street, he happened upon an open-all-night art nook, and he had the semi-presence of mind to enter the shop and browse paintings and small sculptures while he tried to get his emotions relatively untattered. But by evil chance, this shop toadied to current fads in art, and in Gladowr the now-thing was depressive abstraction. Almost every piece was a thrillingly groaning symbolic assertion that the world was hopelessness or torture and that the best resort was to get entirely out of it. Faddism is hard to write theory about, and sometimes it responds to the current *weltanschauung*, and sometimes it goes the other way and asserts the lurking power of a dark alternative to the bright optimistic mood current in real society; in this situation, the dark alternative was all the meaning for Duke.

He was a naturally depressive man, ridden with inferiority feelings, who had rejected these feelings resolutely, symbolized his rejection with his fixed smile, and overwhelmed them with the drive of his career in astronomy. But now, with all his defenses down and with hurt and guilt and frustration and fear in his heart, irrevocably and perhaps permanently distant from his native planet, the dark core of him profoundly responded to the sinister art-images. He browsed broodingly, successively possessed by artist after artist, seeing each painting as the tortured soul of the painter speaking to

255

Duke's tortured soul, seeing the torture as universal and true, too innocent of art-as-a-professional-career to grasp that these artists might just possibly be socially accepted and well-adjusted women who were making decent money and earning prestige by the morbid direction of their expressions.

Not all dark-side art is hypocritical artifact, it depends on the individual artist; but Duke, fundamentally a dark-side man, was here being seduced by hypocrisy at precisely the time when he least needed it. In this art-contemplation he achieved what he falsely felt was serenity for constructive thought, whereas it was really a self-generating conquest of his soul by his depressive underlay. When once the shopkeeper asked if she might help, Duke, comprehending that he was being seen only as a large woman who was a potential buyer, turned his smile on the shopkeeper, shook his head avoiding voice, and returned to his brood: respecting it, the shopkeeper went away. Thus Duke was able to linger here, collecting thoughts and making semi-intelligent plans in the context of pervasive depression.

. . . On a small island in a sea that drowned far more than nine-tenths of the planetary surface. How easy it would be to merge with the sea. . . .

This kind of thinking he brushed off without actually driving it away. He was acculturated against suicide: in his habitudes, this a man doesn't do even when it appears to be the best of all possible solutions. Perhaps he had spent too much time with this depressive art: it had served its purpose by calming him for practical planning. Resolutely (but with regret because the art was so wonderful), he pocketed his hands and stalked out, nodding at the inattentive shopkeeper.

Once outside, he walked rapidly to the first cross-street and took it, having no particular direction in mind, but being desolately certain that he wanted to be inconspicuous and that back streets were best for this. Tawdryness and then ramshackle poverty increased proportionately with distance from the elevated central ridge and nearness to the low-rolling western sea. Few women were on the past-midnight streets as he turned this way and that, but a number of little men were loitering; they eyed Duke with curiosity because he was a prosperous-looking woman, unusually tall, out alone by night in hazardous territory; but they let him alone. Once in a while he crossed a street to avoid a brawl or some other affair involving a police scudder; he didn't really care, it was all degenerate and so was he; this world he would be inhabiting forever—or at least, until the Geeks would blow it up.

He loved her, he had physically ruined her, he had run away. . . .

Long after midnight he blundered into moon-sight of the waterfront, and the befouled salt-water stench nauseated him enough to remind him that he should get something into his belly. He looked for an eatery, not sure how to recognize one; but soon he picked up food smells and followed them to a dirty little lunch-hole with counter only, no tables. Perching himself on a stool in a corner isolated from several men who were hunched there nursing probably cheap wine as the minimum price of a place to loaf, he stared at a chalkboard menu: it was meaningless. Mustering his Kyria-taught Flaric, he requested: "Cheap food and milk." The dirty-white-aproned male stared at him but nodded and brought food which turned out to be something like a greasy hot dog on a bun with a perilously hot mustard. The neighboring men stared also, and one muttered to another: "Big dame, deep voice, thick accent—might be one of them aliens?"

Duke forced down the food, ordered another for luck, got half of it down, suppressed a retch, laid down money, received change, departed heading for the waterfront. He was followed.

Around 0500, under waning stars, Duke was sitting on a pier, legs hanging over, watching moored or anchored ships and letting moist ripple-slap against pier spiles dissolve his deep soul-trouble.

He came to sense that there were presences behind him. He let it go, it did not matter.

One of the presences took a seat beside him, then the other sat at Duke's opposite flank. That was all the presences there were. The three watched water.

One of the men said, "You stranger. Speak Flaric?"

"Little," Duke responded, re-evoking Kyria giving him lessons in the night clubs. (Was she dead? He couldn't go back, how could he learn?)

The other inquired, "Got home?"

"No," he answered. Not any more. Not Warren Heldo, not Erth. And soon, when destruction would come, not even Iola.

"We got home. You want?"

It was rather warming. He looked at the little fellow on his right, then at the one on his left. They were midgets, but they were men. It was good, particularly now, to be with men. He told them: "I want."

"We go," said the one on his left, and all three stood. It was manly, this new comradeship, this generosity to a stranger. He was hideously weary.

They wove through back streets for maybe a kilometer and drew up before the dingy door of an ancient five-story painted-brick building. "This Warren Matae," said one. "You come. We give drink, then bed." They entered, creaked up in a long-obsolete mechanical elevator, emerged on the top floor. Duke eased himself into a stuffing-leaky chair in a deserted salon just dirty enough to harmonize with his own feeling of dirtiness. While one man pulled up a chair in front of him, the other fussed at a bar, then brought him a long drink—half bad kromoweel, half water, no ice. Past being picky, Duke quaffed, laid his head back, drowsed, aroused, sipped, brooded.

"You want bed now?"

"Yes."

"We take you. We bring another drink."

They helped him down a flight of stairs and along a ratty corridor, opened a door, brought him into a small room with a sagging double bed. "You take off clothes," said one. "Then you have another drink." He disrobed to his undershorts and climbed into the bed; there weren't any sheets, and the blanket smelled musty, but he plumped-up the two skinny uncased pillows and lay back on them half-reclining. They gave him the remains of his first drink, which he drained; then they gave him the second drink, and he sipped it.

One said, "Bathroom down hall. You want now?" Duke didn't understand. The little fellow pointed to his own crotch and said "Psssst," then pointed to Duke, who nodded. He set down his drink on a broken table and followed one of them to the bathroom; he was allowed in alone. Afterward both his rescuers helped him back into bed, and one handed him his drink.

One said, "I Jinni. That Kandis." Duke said, "I Duke," and sipped the kromoweel which in this drink was almost undiluted.

Jinni said, "We go now, Duke. You sleep. When you wake, push button. You have good long sleep."

Bathrobed Kyria was sitting in an easy chair near her hospital bed. In a dead voice, she told Luria and Klaus, "Thanks for coming, you can sit on my bed. Excuse me for being so messy last night."

Instead of sitting, Klaus and Luria flanked her, bending over her; and Klaus with deep concern inquired, "How are you, Kyria? Honestly, how are you?"

She looked up at Luria and then at Klaus, and one eye teared. "Believe me, both of you, I came through it just fine, Mujis is putting me on limited duty tomorrow. Only—why didn't Duke come to see me?"

Luria snapped, "You handle it, Klaus. I have to phone Mella Vaxo." She vanished.

Sitting on her chair arm, Klaus hugged Kyria to him. "If you're getting along as well as all that, I can tell you the truth. When Duke saw what had happened to you, he thought it was his fault, and he panicked and ran. And now we don't know where he is."

She stared up at Klaus. She pushed him away—with fair strength, he noted. Unbelieving, she demanded: "He thought he had hurt me—and he *ran?*"

"Kyria, dear sister, this is a thing you have to understand about Duke. He is tremendously emotional, I can't tell you how emotional; he hides it with that smile, but underneath he is a volcano. Listen, now, I know how he thinks. It wasn't that he was running away from helping you, he loves you more than you can understand on this world. He knew that Luria and I would take care of you. But—here, think of it this way. Imagine that you loved another woman enough to want to live with her always, and in the course of expressing your love you thought you'd hurt her badly, and you knew that your friends would take care of her, but you were dying with remorse because of what you'd done to her—wouldn't *you* want to run away and *think?*"

She was rigid, staring straight ahead. He knew that his explanation had done nothing for her. She grated: "Maybe I know what you are trying to say. But it won't wash. If I thought I had hurt her, I would stay with her. I just don't know what kind of a person would run away—"

She began to sob. He held her tightly, having no idea what else to say or do.

Presently she calmed enough to say without intonation, "I

guess I thought I loved him the same way. But now he can
go to Hell. I am going to be hung up enough with myself, ad-
justing to the fact that I have no sex any more."

"Kyria, I'm sure he'll come to see you tomorrow, maybe
even tonight—"

"If he comes, Brother Klaus, I will be polite. But also, I
will be very busy."

It was nearly 1600 when Duke awakened, oriented himself,
and bumped the button. Perhaps a quarter-hour later Jinni
appeared with a breakfast tray: hot coffee and unbuttered
toast. Duke, half-dressed, savored the late-afternoon breakfast, sitting on the edge of his bed; Jinni, fully dressed, owl-
ishly watched him eat.

Refreshed, Duke poured the remaining coffee into his cup
and told Jinni: "You men good. Thank."

"You're welcome, Duke."

"I stay?"

"Stay as long as you wish."

After Hell, his blessings were cup-brimming. He sipped
cooling coffee. He could stay here, with the men. Little men,
but men. Something about Klaus-purposes was nudging at his
mind, but he brushed it away, he was beginning a new life.

Jinni, having decided to talk decently well and teach Duke,
suggested: "We have a gymnasium. Do you like exercise?"

That was too much Flaric for Duke, who spread hands.
Jinni concluded not to move quite so fast with Flaric. Arising, he advised: "You get dressed. I come back soon. I
show."

He returned a quarter-hour later, dressed only in shorts
and slippers; Duke was astonished at the muscular build of
this dwarf. Jinni guided Duke along a corridor past the main
gym-door and into a small locker space; here, at Jinni's invitation, Duke shed most of his clothing. Jinni found for him a
clean but very tight jock-strap and a pair of sloppies belong-
ing to a resident derided for his huge feet; dropping shorts,
Duke wriggled into the supporter like a fat woman torturing
herself into a slim girdle, resumed the shorts, and managed to
thrust his feet so deeply into the sloppies that his heels over-
hung no more than two centimeters. And they went out onto
the gym floor.

What Duke mainly saw there was fighting, broadly diversified and all semi-vicious: gloved fist-fighting at numerous lev-

els of skill and slug-strength, including on one large mat a ten-man battle royal; jiujitsu, judo, kung fu, heni po; wrestling, rassling, rough-and-tumble. Some shorts and jocks were tattered or missing, revealing Erth-human male genitals of assorted sizes, some approaching Erth-normal. Some men rested on the side-lines, hard-breathing, quite commonly cut or bruised on faces or abdomens or limbs. Along the wall were assorted kinds of apparatus, mostly familiar in Erth gyms—ladders, ropes, weights, parallel bars, horses, trampolines—with most in vigorous use; but his feeling was that these were mere conditioners for fighting.

Duke, whose respect for these Lilliputians was mounting, hadn't yet comprehended why the emphasis on combat. But he was noticing that their expenditures for gym equipment far exceeded in proportion what they must be spending on the rest of Warren Matae.

Jinni's hand rested restlessly on the small of Duke's back. "You do too," Jinni urged.

They approached a couple of sideline-resting men (one was Kandis who had teamed with Jinni to rescue Duke) and were warmly welcomed. Jinni said "Two," holding up fingers and pointing to the Iola-men, "against one," erecting one finger and pointing to Duke, who zestfully agreed. Moving to a mat, the two littles and one big went at it, wrestling. Using a one-at-a-time approach, Duke threw Kandis rather quickly, but while he tried to pin Kandis, the other came in on the deal; the temporary stalemate was broken when Jinni got into it, and the three littles did pin Duke. "You men good," confessed the Erth-man, grinning. "Now, maybe *really* two to one?" Jinni and Kandis faced him: it took nearly a quarter-hour, but finally he pinned both of them.

A bit after 1700 hours, Klaus at the observatory raised Croyd on iradio without video. "Klaus Heller on Vassili Four," he asserted. "Call Vassili Klarta, call Klarta Four Iola. Over."

Croyd acknowledged: "Croyd on Nereid. Cheers, Klaus."

Klaus: "Not much cheer, but an appeal for aid. I'll make this quick, we may lose contact. Klarta Six, called Godzha, is attacking Iola the planet where I am; and Iola is defenseless. I'd say that between them there are some interbalancing issues, but Godzha is in no mood to negotiate. Iola is requesting intervention by the Interplanetary Union, and Iola un-

derstands from me what this means in terms of judgments
and negotiations. The intervention squadron should arrive in
two weeks max. Can do?"

"Maybe can do. How about the black holes?"

"I entered Black Hole Three." (Murchison's jump must not
be mentioned; he was supposed to have remained aboard
ship.) "I hope to brief you in detail before the week is out,
but just in case I can't, here's the rough-in. The Murchison
theory is confirmed, with some elaboration. Figure the gravity
at ten sols, with a viscous fluid interior about the density of
mercury, and with spin at about the angular velocity of
Duke's calculations. Frigates with heavily armored and
strutted noses could handle the hole by hitting it at 3C and
maintaining top acceleration throughout; but the Godzha
technology is weird, so you'll need a couple of battlewagons
plus a few frigates, all ships armored and reinforced. Do not,
repeat not, plan to shoot through the center of the hole. Dive
radially into the hole; but having penetrated the event horizon and pushed on in about twenty kilometers, deflect immediately about twenty degrees off the radius in any direction,
with maximum radical penetration of twenty-five kilometers,
and keep acceleration greater than four million G. However,
if you should enter with only double the velocity of light, you
will slow initially to below light velocity, but maintenance of
this acceleration should get most of it back in time to escape
into the Klarta system. Got it?"

"Got it. That simple?"

"Really about that simple, for a warship's thrust and shielding. My suit-jump was foolhardy, really: the suit worked
fine, including the metabolic acceleration, but with the suit
alone I couldn't have made it out, except that I was helped
out. Numerous details later. All right, then, you're coming; I
am pleased, Croyd, really pleased. Who will be our media-
tor-legate?"

"How about you, Klaus?"

"I thought you'd never ask. All right, we still have contact,
I'll try a few more details. If we are cut, don't call me, I'll
call you, but not today—and rush preparations anyway."

"Affirmative. Go on."

"Godzha intends to destroy the major commonwealth of
Iola day after tomorrow by manipulating hole-gravity to
create a massive volcano. They can do it, I've seen a test

case. They play rekamatics on a huge gravity modulator at the center of any black hole, I found one.

"Now listen, Croyd. I am requesting your permission to attack Godzha with a small commando team for the purpose of turning their gravity controls upon themselves and aborting the attack on Iola. There will be some loss of life on Godzha. This will not end the war, but it will provide time for arrival of your squadron. Do you give me permission?"

"Klaus, have you prejudged that Godzha is at fault in this war?"

"I have not. But Godzha will hit Iola with a killing attack day after tomorrow, and Iola as I said is defenseless, and this must be aborted to allow mediation. Do you give me permission?"

Klaus had been aware of growing interference; and now he lost contact.

He stepped away from the transmitter. He was going to proceed with the mission.

After a filling dinner of something like boiled turnips and chunk-pork in the top-floor dining room of Warren Matae, the men gathered in the adjacent saloon for drinks and chat. Duke was the center of attention: naturally, he reflected, in view of his size and alien origin, but nevertheless it enhanced the warmth which he had long been feeling for these little guys, *his* kind of guys: no big brains, but honest, tough, cordial, regular. They took pleasure in teaching him more Flaric, laughing boisterously at his mistakes (and he heartily joined); they pantomimed explanations, as when one said he was a miner, and when Duke didn't understand, lay prone, wriggled forward, chopped at imaginary ore with a phantom pickaxe. It was Duke's turn when they asked him what *he* did; and to explain the Anglian word *astronomer*, he arose like a grand ham, pointed to the heavens, hand-swept the ceiling-blocked heavens, then peered at the heavens with one eye through a telescope made of his own two fists.

Most of them had drifted away after the second or third drink. Duke was detained by Jinni, Kandis, and three others all of whom had contended with him in the gym. "One more," Jinni urged. They maneuvered him to a sofa-center where he was closely flanked by Jinni and Kandis, and they passed him his after-dinner fourth (following three before dinner). Sipping, he felt affectionate about them, yet some-how uncomfortable . . .

Maxus men had been quietly gathering outside since mid-afternoon; and late in the afternoon policewomen in two cars parked nearby and engaged one of the men (whom they knew) in discussion of the probability that Dr. Duke was in Warren Matae. The men wanted to enter and search for him, but the policewomen had no search warrant. As a stratagem, one of the men entered the warren and inquired at the desk; the clerk professed ignorance, and the man had to depart. The police took off on other errands, leaving word for the men to keep them informed via short-wave portaradio—they left a transmitter with one of the men; they'd be cruising in the area. (This police-trust of men was unusual, but so were the men of Warren Kreczy.)

The patrolling men grew increasingly uneasy; and an inter-change with Maxus in Luria's office did nothing to alleviate their unease. Finally, at 1914, a different man checked a dif-ferent desk-ckerk; he learned that Duke indeed was there, at dinner. This gave them some relief, but not much: the night was young.

About 2043, the man with the transmitter contacted one of the police scout cars and advised that at this time in the eve-ning, with Dr. Duke in the warren, police presence at Warren Matae was strongly indicated.

The arriving police heard the shouting and scuffling high above, and then glass crashed and a body hurtled from a top-floor window and crumpled in the street. One of the four policewomen out of two scudders bent over the body with one of the Maxus men, while the other three policewomen followed by the other two Maxus men thrust into Warren Matae, hurried up five stair-flights (the elevator being in use), and entered the saloon. They found two men out and bleeding on the floor while berserk Duke was attacking two others.

Officers One and Two pinned Duke's arms while the two Maxus men restrained the two surviving Matae men; Officer Three shouted into Duke's ear, "Dr. Duke, this is an arrest, please come peaceably," but he wrenched an arm free and backhand felled her. Officer Two dropped Duke with a billy-blow, then knelt to check his condition, while Officer One knelt beside fallen Officer Three. Officer Two, satisfied that Duke was alive, left him and went over to question the Matae survivors. Officer Three sat up, shook her head, asked for a situation report, got it in five words: "He's down, how are you?" staggered to her feet with help, looked around, said, "You stay here with Duke while I question the Maxus men."

The fourth officer entered: "The man on the street is dead, naturally. I've put in a call to the coroner, she'll be here directly; don't move any of the bodies; a Maxus man is watching the body on the street, says the name of the corpse is Jinni."

One of the Maxus men asked and got permission to phone Herder Maxus. Then two of the officers took Duke and the two survivors downstairs, loaded them into one car, and drove off with them, leaving the other car for the two officers who remained to guard the three cadavers and greet the coroner.

Police Inspector Mella Vaxo happened to be on night duty. In her office, after Klaus and Luria had arrived and with Duke and the two Matae survivors abjectly present, an arresting officer made an economical report, adding: "We followed your orders, Inspector—we did call him *Dr. Duke*—but also we did have to club him."

Vaxo, who was built like a dray-mare and had a voice like a veteran cigar-smoking bartender, turned to Attorney Threll: "When you first reported that this Erth-man was missing, Luria, you described him as a *peaceable* man, an intellectual patsy. May I learn whether you have now revised these ideas?"

"First, Inspector, I advise Dr. Duke to make no statement until I have conferred with him."

"That's proper enough."

"Then, I request that Dr. Duke be released into the custody of Dr. Heller and myself. From the arresting officer's statement, it appears that Dr. Duke was being gang-raped, and that he apparently went berserk under this personal outrage following prior stress. He is neither a citizen of Flaria nor a criminal alien, but an honored ambassador to Flaria, and there will be a question of diplomatic immunity."

"Your preliminary representation has been recorded, Kra Threll, but what is this question of diplomatic immunity?"

"It will be raised in court, if it comes to that." Luria had just invented it. She added on a new inspiration: "Tomorrow

Dr. Duke will be interviewed by a psychiatrist on the staff of Dr. Mujis."

Vaxo mused over stuporous Duke. "Remove his cuffs," she directed. She told Luria, "Sorry, but I can't risk releasing him. You understand that he is accused of three capital crimes. He'll have to be detained in one of our infirmary cells under medical supervision. You can bring your psychiatrist."

"Inspector, I presume that your decision will be recorded along with my representations?"

"Both are already recorded."

In the police station anteroom, emotionally drained, Klaus and Luria sat on an uncushioned wooden bench, brooding.

Luria groaned, "O Goddess—murder! *Three* murders! And after running away when he thought he'd killed Kyria—"

Klaus demanded: "How can you call it murder? He was defending himself against rape."

"He didn't have to kill them. If he'd clubbed two of them down, the others would have run. Anyhow, rape or no rape, the killings are classified as murders; I told you about that. The penalty is death."

"By the execution method that I saw?"

"By the method you saw."

"Will you defend him, Luria?"

"Of course I will, you heard my preliminaries to Vaxo. But, Klaus, it may be hopeless."

"But you stated three possible defenses: self-defense against gang-rape, psychiatric disturbance, diplomatic immunity—"

Her smile was wan. "Aren't I the creative one! What's diplomatic immunity? We've never had diplomats except from Godzha, and they have no immunity. On Iola, there's no law about that."

"There is on Erth."

"Fine, but not here. Anyhow, does yours let a diplomat commit murder?"

"Well—"

She took his hands and told him, "Dear Klaus, I will defend with all my energy and ingenuity. But on another plane, you must face right now the fact that Duke will *not* be available as your second on the commando raid. He will be in jail."

Klaus frowned painfully. "All right, I'll face that, it diverts my mind, it keeps my sanity afloat. So who, then? I can't do it alone, and the other fellow has to know computers better than I—"

"Then I guess you'll have to take *me* along."

"Luria—why *you?*" And then, as she gazed at him, he slowly nodded. "You were navigator on a space-ship that attacked Godzha, which means computers. And you fished me down out of space, which means computers."

He bent to her, gripping her hands. "If it's like that, my love, let's grab a late bite and get over to the astrolab. You have our raid to prepare for, while at the same time you work on Duke's defense. Tell me, sweet Luria—how are you on energy and alertness after two days of twenty-three-hour duty?"

26. THE SMALLEST LITTLE MEN

Labor-weary Klaus was called to Vlotny's phone at 1639. "Luria here, I'm at my office, just finished briefing Maxus. The psychiatrist saw Duke early this afternoon and will testify that he is mentally ill; nothing more I can do about Duke just now. Are you at a stopping point?"

"I can use a break. What's on your mind?"

"There's a visit I need to pay before we hit Godzha, and I'd like for you to be with me. Don't say anything, just be on the rooftop chopper-pad in fifteen minutes. Okay?"

She had been exhaustively computer-briefed well into last night and had divided her time this morning between computers and the space-suit, with a break for a phone call to Mujis and a preliminary chat with the designated psychiatrist. Then, after quick-snacking with Klaus, she had departed for the jail. Klaus had checked out the suits and found no need for service except to replenish the self-contained drive-pack and the fifty-fifty oxygen-nitrogen mix; the metabolic accelerators did indeed still produce invisibility, and they were dismountable and portable. The enlarged transmission cage was nearly complete. He had again made contact with Croyd and had won approval for the mission that he had intended to carry out anyway. He ran a hand back through his hair: what was left? Never mind, he'd come back here whenever he would get back from wherever Luria was taking him; they had left at most a bit over thirteen hours to finish and act.

Luria had rented and was piloting an old-fashioned chopper—quiet, but silicon-fueled, with no assistance from sunlight. She was contemplative; respecting this, Klaus remained silent. They overflew Gladowr City northward, north even of

Warren Heldo and still on north; the long island below, and its companion islands extending on beyond northern and southern horizons, together were a slender green ribbon threading the low-rolling universal ocean.

She now said, not looking at him, "What I am taking you to see is a well-kept private secret, I am showing it to you because I have faith in you. Only a few others know, and my sister Kyria is not one of them. Unless you warn me otherwise now before we arrive, I pray you to respect totally my secret."

"I tell you that I will respect your secret; if it ever comes out, it will not be from me. I love you, Luria."

"I love you, Klaus. In the blended way that you talked about, I love you."

"I ought to tell you, though, that on Erth there is a woman—"

"Are you committed to her for life, my Klaus?"

"I am not committed at all. But she is my dear friend, and I would not willingly hurt her or lose her friendship."

"Perhaps it is academic, I have this poignant feeling that I will never get to see that Erth of yours. In any case, she and I and you could arrive at a modus operandi. You never told me how it is on your planet."

"Much like here in planetary size and gravity and atmosphere and fauna and flora. A lot more land and a lot less water—but still a lot more water than land. Our sun is nearly the same G-type as your Klarta, but smaller, giving us heat extremes from steamy-hot in equatorial summer to permanently glacier-cold at the poles. In our temperate zones, our sun gives us in summer about the same warmth as in Gladowr year-round; it freezes us in winter as Klarta freezes Godzha, but we have grand winter sports and warm indoor comfort then. And our spring is a riot of inspiring fecundity, and our autumns are sweetly melancholy poetry. No neighboring black holes, no barriers except nearly transparent atmosphere against a million star-jewels. One beautiful moon which is itself a good-sized planet; poets have rhapsodized our moon for at least five thousand years, moonstruck animals have howled forever under the spell of our moon. Deep forests, lofty mountains, broad prairies, blue lakes teeming with fish, frightening stark-handsome deserts. Men and women co-equally lords of all this wonder—"

"I want to see it."

"But let me tell you also the compensating ugliness that you would find. Too many cities that sprawl broad and suck out the purity and beauty, too much alienation of most people while some can rise high, too many people, too much dirty politics, crap, crap—"

Luria grinned: "I want to smell it. Look below, now: we're coming in on my secret."

They circled a spreading farm at the very northern tip of Gladowr Island, where ocean washed three sides and a broad white-sand beach ran the western shore. There were diversified farm animals, and a farm house and barn and small outbuildings, and meadows having many trees. There were also hyper-active human children.

These clustered eagerly around the chopper as it landed, staying a respectful distance back. They were naked, and they were all boys, and there was a lightly clothed adult man with them. Luria, descending from the chopper, was overwhelmed by boys whose ages Klaus estimated as between one year and eight. She loved them, and made over them, and sparred and rolled with them, during a good quarter-hour while he, standing beside the chopper, watched in delight and amazement.

She struggled disheveled to her feet and gasped: "Quiet everybody!" and then, raising her hands high, bawled "QUIET!" She got something like a giggling hush, during which she said to the children, "I want you all to meet my good friend Klaus. He's a very nice man."

He advanced smiling and demanded: "Hi, guys! who wants to rassle?" And they were all into it again, with Klaus happily on the bottom, while Luria stood on the sidelines laughing with the highly amused little adult.

After a while she again called halt, and the combatants disentangled themselves, and Klaus made it to his feet with two gleeful one-year-olds in his arms. Luria called out: "Now listen. I have to go away with Klaus for a few days, I'll see you when I come back. I'm glad you like my friend Klaus, I like him too. Okay?"

"Okay!" shouted all who could talk. And one of the eight-year-olds called, "Have a good trip, Luria and Klaus!"

"You can bet on it!" she promised. "Now you kids go and play, I have to leave right away with Klaus."

They swarmed over her again, then group-hugged the legs of Klaus—and they deserted, heading for the western sea.

She led Klaus to the Iola-man who was a handsome fellow possibly in his early thirties. "Dr. Heller, I want you to meet Landis Garder from Warren Kreczy, he helps me once a week here, he is one of the men who were looking for Duke last night." Klaus held out his hand; Garder took it tentatively—then, reassured, shook it cordially. She turned to Garder: "How is it going, Landis?"

"Excellently well, Kra Threll."

"Who is on duty tomorrow?" She followed on through the week, getting nine other names; Herder Maxus was one. She told Klaus, "All these men are from Warren Kreczy except one who is a promising young man from Warren Matae—and he wasn't involved in last night's action. These ten and you are the only people who know my secret. How much time do we have?"

Klaus required himself to say, "As much as you like."

"No we don't, and you know it, we have to get going. Landis, now listen, don't say anything about this to the children. Where I have to go is dangerous, and I may not come back. If I don't, Herder is in charge, and I hope you men will keep right on with my children."

"Kra Threll," asserted Garder most earnestly, "we *will* keep it going, as long as the Godzhalks let us. But if you should not come back—where would the new children come from?"

"You can handle more of them, Landis?"

"I'd *love* to have more, and so would all of us."

She bent to kiss his cheek, then stood erect looking down at him. "All of you know that so far they all come from me. But equally you know that this farm is the germ of the future for men on Iola, and its importance transcends me or any other woman—or any man. If I don't come back, I want Herder to lead you in working out a strategy for new recruitment, and Herder knows this. Even if I do come back, still we may do this.

"Thank you, Landis Garder—*Krad* Garder. We have to go now."

She fled to the chopper. Klaus, following, mounted after her. She took off swift-steep; but as they did one final circling of the farm, she swooped low over the children who were nearing the beach. Leaning out, she waved down to them; they waved back, cheering her; weeping, Luria ascended and departed.

When she had self-control: "Now, Klaus, I'll tell you about that. These are all my own boys, eight broods of one or two or three each—for some reason, I never have girls. Soon after my boys are born, I bring them to this farm and I treat them like baby girls, I suckle them myself for a season until they are ready to be weaned. Then I turn them over to Maxus and his nine men; I will say that several of these men fathered some of the broods, and they know it, but they play no favorites. I come almost daily to see my boys, and they love me. I want them to grow up with education and self-respect, yet ready to face the hardships of being a man on Iola. There are two extreme possibilities for our men: degradation on Iola, or a minute chance to become arrogant-powerful on Godzha; hopefully these boys of mine will be able to make inroads into a better synthesis—unless Godzha first wipes them all out, in which case there isn't any hope for anybody anyway."

Mutual meditation. Then Klaus: "I love you in every way there is—but very particularly, I love your mindsoul."

"That's good, that's *very* good. Oh, that is *good!* But now listen, my Klaus, time is short. If I return from Godzha and you do not, I will personally press the defense of Duke with all the powers that I may have. If you return and I do not, then Klaus, I would recommend that you yourself handle the courtroom defense with Herder Maxus as your aide. I have coached Herder intensively, he is highly resourceful, he alone could do it at least as well as I, but our courts are many decades from being ready to admit men as counselors, Herder would have a hard time of it; even if they should admit him, he might well lose on his sex."

"And if neither of us returns?"

"I don't know, my friend, I just don't know. If we die succeeding, so that Iola survives, Herder will try to find female counsel, but frankly I doubt that any of my colleagues would touch the case. As a last resort, Herder will seek permission to defend, he has a letter from me; and he will try skillfully and manfully."

"So then, in going to Godzha, we lay Duke's life on the line. But he was ready to go to Godzha and lay it there anyway. But by being in jail instead, he is laying *your* life on the line. My Luria—"

"I know. You needn't say it. We're sort of there, aren't we, we two."

Part Eight

INTERPLANETARY
MISCALCULATION

Klarta System, 30 November 2494

27. COMMANDO RAID ON GODZHA

Gladowr with pinpoint precision re-materialized Klaus and Luria, giant-suited, at 0800 hours in a barren area on Godzha roughed by rock outcroppings, just under a kilometer from Central Gravity-Control Center which the Godzhalks had considerately positioned in a wilderness area distant from their capital city or any other city.

Pinned to the ground by their suit-weight, through fog-wisping, Klaus and Luria spied a nearby rock-hole, a junior-grade cave. To it they slid along the rough ground, painfully slow-propelled by little bursts of their in-suit power packs. Their metabolic accelerators were strapped to their backs inside the suits. Invisibility had been achieved by minor physiological speed-up: a factor of four would have been enough to boost even red light above the violet; for safety, Klaus was using a factor of three, a mild acceleration which increased the eight-second safe maximum to a full day (the curve was exponential) but also made each minute seem like five.

They wriggled out of the suits into the biting cold of Godzha, for which they were dressed in reonically heated clothing having very little bulk. They wore belts with rayguns and with pouches carrying certain small equipment. Their eyes were fitted with half-moon glasses: the lenses at the bottom corrected their visual frequency downward so they could see objects and people on Godzha; looking above the lenses, in their mutual invisibility they could naked-eye see each other.

At a little distance from their cave, they first sighted this cave and its environs for later recognition. Turning then, they used heat-finders to locate a major heat source which was presumably the giant bubble housing the control center. They

established azimuth from cave to center, and set compasses
on their right wrists for reverse azimuth to simplify back-
tracking. And then they set out through fog swirls toward the
heat source.

In the spacious bubble described to them by Flaria Intelligence which had teloptic photograhs, Godzhalks in Central
Control manipulated gravity and other forces. From there
they expected to destroy Gladowr today at 1100 hours, and
that was less than three hours from now. Personally for
Luria, it would mean the destruction of her tads. The instrumentation was in the bubble; the power-piles mined rock
crust for many kilometers around.

Toward this bubble the two commandos prowled, guiding
on their heat-sensors.

They paused, becoming aware of some sort of low-pitched
roaring distantly ahead of them. Hitting dirt, they lens-peered
awkwardly upward through thickening fog at a ghost-caval-
cade of planet-shadowing aircraft or spacecraft locust-swarm-
ing almost at ground level. In death-fear they undercrouched
the bellies of the fleet during fully five minutes which seemed
like twenty-five to their accelerated perceptions; they marveled at the fleet's hideousness, its daring, its ghostly beauty.
One crashed: not far behind them they saw it ground-skating
in fire-flare, incinerating its people.

At last the fleet was all gone behind them. It was moving
out for Iola, crossing the space-gap, in order to invade and
occupy post-volcano Iola-without-Glendowr. Being over-
loaded with troops, the fleet was taking off tangentially to
pick up catapult-thrust from planetary rotation.

Rising, Klaus and Luria worked their way forward through
icy fog.

The bubble was guard-ringed, but they moved in between
two guards easily. Being invisible, they needed no fog-shroud,
indeed the fog hindered them: something about its chemical
composition smogged even their high-frequency vision. Now
their probing moves were acutely cautious, because a destruc-
tive force-field was known to exist somewhere in here.

"Look above your lens," Klaus whispered. "See that shim-
mering?"

"Blessed be Harmnion," she whispered. "That has got to be

the force-field; it is in our invisibility wave-range. Now what?"

"There must be a small entry-break, probably away from the main entrance to the bubble. Let's cruise."

Inside the guard-ring, minutes later they found the break, not quite on the opposite bubble-flank from the major entrance. They penetrated, with Klaus ahead, and moved back to the entrance between the force-field ring and the bubble.

Klaus confided: "It gets tough now. Are you ready to die horribly?"

"I've arranged my mind for masochistic pleasure. And sadistic: maybe I can get to watch *you* die horribly."

"Then here we go. Look sharp through your lenses."

Having passed through thinly peopled antechambers, they broke out into the central console hall. Here were people in plethora. Every control console was manned (really *manned*) by one or two technicians; and a large number of midget men in military uniforms patrolled the area peering at visiscreens or earphone-listening to remote commands. On several of the console visiscreens they perceived varying views of Iola: the total planetary land-mass hemisphere with the long long archipelago centered; a southern half-hemisphere, with Gladowr near the top; all of Gladowr, tight in; the seething incandescent vulcanism beneath Glendowr.

In so gigantic a complex, how do you pinpoint the one or two or three consoles on which all depends?

Klaus murmured: "The pictures on that pair of consoles interest me. I mean the one that seems to be a Geek's-eye view of the entire Klarta system seen in wide angle, with what looks like the edge of a black disk on a gray field pushing into the picture at the top, and the adjacent screen which seems to show both Godzha and Iola with all of that black disk beyond them near Godzha."

"I'm focusing on those consoles, Klaus."

"Then you're noticing that in both pictures there's a slight vermilion bulge on the side nearest Iola, and I think it is very slowly growing and sharpening. Those two adjacent operators keep looking at each other's screens and interconsulting, and around them there's a lot of other-people action."

"All right, Klaus. You probably get it that the black-on-gray disk is one of the black holes, probably Four, next to the one you entered, because you can draw a straight line between Four and Iola without hitting any other planet at this

time of this year. The consoles are tempering space color
from black to gray, and the vermilion is an instrumental
representation of invisible gravity; the hole is black. I think
those have to be the key action-consoles. Shall we move in?"

"Luria, what we ought to do first is create a diversion.
Take that console right in front of us with a cross-section of
glowing underground magma beneath Gladowr: that would
make a good diversion, it's far from the central action. How
can we make that console malfunction?"

"The easy way is the quick way: ray it."

Klaus drew his gun and fired at the console body; the console curled, the picture shattered noisily, the shocked but
uninjured operator fell to the floor. All observers and operators instantly spun; the on-foot observers hurried to the damaged console, while the operators nack-nocked their attention
between the damage zone and their own screens.

Now Klaus jerked her arm, and they hurried to room-center, stopping at the pair of interesting consoles. Little chance
to communicate now; their whispering might be overheard.
Behind each console, numerous emerging wires joined into a
single cable which disappeared into the floor. By simply blasting the cables of these two consoles they could abort the attack on Iola, and this they would do as a last resort; but the
obvious damage would be quickly located and repaired,
whereas they needed to delay the showdown for several
weeks while Croyd's task force was being organized and put
into transit. Their purpose was more sophisticated: they intended to *turn the disaster inward upon this Control Center.*

Only, how would they quickly identify the hook-ups on
these elaborate consoles?

Prearrangement did it: they stepped up their acceleration
to a factor of ten, so that each second seemed ten seconds.
Luria knelt behind the consoles inspecting the wires; Klaus
was in front of the consoles, bending over the two operators
who were giving their attention alternately to their visiscreens
and to the back-of-room disturbance. Klaus gripped the operator's chairback; chair and operator went invisible with the
contact but returned to visibility a split-second later; the operator, having experienced a split-second of nothing, rubbed
eyes and frowned. Going behind that console, Klaus whispered to Luria; she nodded, produced from her belt pouch a
hundred-tentacled lambda-meter, and clamped a meter-lead

onto each of the ninety-seven wires leading from the console into the cable. She nodded again at Klaus.

He leaned across the console from behind, rendering console and screen invisible to Godzhalks although perfectly visible to Klaus and Luria above their lenses. From above and behind, successively he pressed the ninety-seven keys at one-second intervals (to him and to Luria, ten-second intervals); each key registered its own type of impulse on Luria's meter which interrupted the cable-circuit so that none of the impulses activated anything except the meter. The Godzha-invisibility of the console was communicating itself back along these wires into the meter and most of the cable.

Confronting *no console*, the operator leaped up, reached out (Klaus avoided his hand), felt the console-bulk (he went momentarily invisible), drew his hand back (he hadn't noticed the intruders), stared. He let out a bellow; his comrade and then others noticed, and soon this invisibility had attracted a throng, counteracting the diversion of the blasted back-of-room console. The word *hueena* sounded prominently in the multiple muttering; the religious tabu was a fortunate deterrence to counter-attack. (Fifty-four keys had been pressed.)

Two technicians now elbowed in and began exploring the situation front and back by feel. Since the console became visible for them whenever they touched it, Klaus gun-butted both of them, dragged them away, and dropped them behind a nearby console; returning then to Luria, who had been holding the console-of-concern to keep it invisible, he relieved her for more wire-checking while he button-pushed and the consternated Godzhalks awaited a report from their invisible technicians.

After the pressing of the ninety-seventh key, Luria noiselessly opened the back of the console, rewired, restored the back, unclamped, and moved to the neighboring console. Total Godzha-clock time, three minutes; for the invisible invaders, it had seemed thirty.

The second console and its operator underwent the same experience, while the first console returned to visibility. By now control-room organization was shattered. Arguments nucleated around the console that was re-visible and the new one that was missing. By now the unconscious technicians had been found; supervisors were beginning to yell orders that sounded coherent. Klaus pressed the ninety-ninth key, and Luria began to rewire, but a counter-attack was closing in; "I need time," Luria hissed; and she pushed a foot against the console to hold its invisibility during some Klaus-diversion while she worked. Klaus ran to another part of the room and fired two shots in opposite directions, killing two overhead lights; ducking the people who were leaving the consoles to run diversely toward one or another of the shattered lights, along with a few cooler souls who headed for the place which might be the shot-source, he returned and bent over Luria.

She closed the second console, stood, wiped her forehead. "That should do it, unless they test and discover. What time is it?"

"Nine fifty-nine. That's H-Hour minus one. We should get going."

"Not yet, but let's get out of *here!*"

Working their way through returning people, they made it into the corridor, cut their self-acceleration back to the five-factor, and peered back into the control room. Luria muttered, "We have to wait and see what happens. After all that commotion, they're sure to inspect; and if they discover the rewiring, we may have to go below and blast cables. How long will it take us to get back to our suits and depart Godzha?"

A leader, probably the top supervisor, was barking orders; operators were returning to their consoles. . . .

"With this fog," estimated Klaus, "at least thirty minutes to get back, suit-up, and get retrieved—which leaves us only about twenty minutes for contingencies. Wait, though—we've interrupted their countdown, that delays H-Hour by a good thirty minutes—"

"Then we have fifty minutes to stay here. It may be enough."

Two new technicians, with the supervisor watching, were examining the first console that Luria had rewired. Presently one of them removed the back and began checking the wiring.

"Oh-oh," Luria murmured. "What time is it?"

"Ten-twenty."

"Leaving us thirty maybe-safe minutes. And they're prowling my work. What do you think, Klaus? Shoot-up the room? Kill that supervisor?"

"Well—I do hate to kill, but we're trying to destroy them

all anyway. And I'm reflecting that blowing cables wouldn't produce enough delay, even if we could find the right ones."

"Then let's massacre all of them right now, it will take time to find and train new personnel for this."

Her hand was going for her gun, but Klaus caught it: "Look! listen!" The supervisor was firing orders; the technicians paused, then shrugged and slowly replaced the back panel. Apparently the supervisor was ordering everybody to resume operations at the point of countdown-interruption.

Klaus whispered: "Thank God he's a nervous bureaucrat, his fear of a demerit for delay seems to have overcome his caution. Luria, I think we may be in."

"Wait a few minutes, Klaus; let's be sure—".

Operations were proceeding; the supervisor, followed by one of the two technicians (the other had slunk out), was proceeding toward his back-of-the-room watch-tower. Just as he reached the stair almost directly in front of the invaders, the technician seized his arm and began arguing furiously, pointing at the rewired consoles. The supervisor listened about half a minute, turned on the technician, angrily jawed him down. (Luria, self-acceleration shut off, was listening; accelerated Klaus heard only slow low roaring like surf in a conch.) The technician shrugged and started away; but as the supervisor mounted the stair, the technician turned and yelled one last warning. Evidently the supervisor rejected it; the defeated technician went out through a side door, the supervisor's legs vanished up the stair.

Luria: "I could barely understand their dialect of Flaric—"

"Get that invisibility back on!"

"It is now, otherwise I couldn't understand you. The technician said it could have been sabotage, the wiring ought to be thoroughly checked. The supervisor said, omitting most of his expletives: 'Balls! get out of here and let's go to work!' "

"Then it's evidently all right. We should get going, I figure it's about H minus fifty."

"If we only need thirty, let's wait still."

"I said at least thirty, without counting contingencies. Why wait?"

"I want to see if something is working. Watch the visi-screens on those two rewired consoles. Pay special attention to the vermilion gravity-bulge."

Eight minutes later, the bulge had elongated into a tornado-like finger pointing directly at Iola across many millions

of cosmic kilometers. Luria let out breath: "Good, it's holding."

"Holding the wrong way, Luria?"

"Holding the right way. Toward Iola for now, so they
won't suspect and cut action. I fixed it to start changing
direction at H-minus-fifteen, it will be too late then to stop
it."

"I'd give a lot to stay and watch it happen. But not our
two lives. Let's move out!"

The fog had thickened to the point of virtually no visibility
through or above their lenses. With care they circled the
bubble-exterior until they came to the position where the
break in the force-field must be; there they peered outward
looking vainly for the field. He whispered, "Hang on to the
back of my belt, I'll move in using my heat sensor."
Watching the small video dial, he inched radially outward
from the building with Luria in belt-contact behind him. A
ghost-field presently emerged on the dial. Cautiously extending his sensored arm far right and then far left, he found a
seeming break on the left, moved to it, scrutinized the dial.
Definitely, the break.

"Here we go," he told her, and moved through.

Luria's foot skidded on a pebble; losing balance, she released his belt and toppled into the force-field; there was a
flash, and an alarm-bell sounded. Klaus wheeled, dragged
Luria away, lifted her, hurried outward to avoid converging
guards whom he couldn't see, luckily didn't run into one,
moved out another ten paces, laid Luria on the ground, bent
to examine her. She was unconscious, possibly alive.

"O God," inwardly he prayed; and then he amended the
prayer: "also, O Goddess. . . ."

Shouldering her body for easier movement, he brought his
compass close to his eyes and moved laterally seeking to locate the point where, coming in, they had first encountered
the guards and the field. He had a memory-feeling of a
forty-eight-pace veer; being now somewhat farther out, he
moved laterally sixty paces watching out for shadow-guards
passing inside him, then used his reverse azimuth to strike
outward. The trick would be to find their space-suits nearly a
kilometer away in dense fog.

After nearly an interminable half-hour of probing onward,
his compass direction frequently distorted by rock outcrops

which had to be flanked, he heard Luria say feebly: "What time is it?"

Overflowing with gratitude to God and the goddess, he drew-up short and queried: "Can you walk?"

"I doubt it, but try me."

Gently he set her down; her legs came unhinged, and he hugged her to him. She gasped: "Better shoulder me again, if you can. I repeat, what time is it?"

"Eleven-seventeen."

"If they make H-Hour at eleven-thirty, that's awful tight."

Carrying her slung in his arms and moving ahead, he reassured her: "The line of rocks that the cave is in must be just ahead, it stretches pretty far left and right, we can't have missed *that*—"

He paused, becoming apprehensively aware of a new and rather stiff gusty breeze in his face, creating wind-chill many tens of degrees below zero Celsius, making itself visible as fog blowing toward and around and past them. Luria got it: "The deflected gravity finger, Klaus—it must be approaching us now, aimed accurately at the control center, it's going to suck us up!"

"Already it's getting the fog." His feet and legs were now visible. "For two or three reasons, I'm hitting dirt!"

Going to his knees, he laid her down on her back. Looking up at him, eyes wide and mouth small, she reported, "Sorry, my friend, it isn't just my legs, my arms are limp too. Leave me like this, you be my eyes."

Lying prone, arm-protecting her, peering forward at ground level, he saw that they were no more than a hundred meters from their cave-mouth. Turning onto his back, hampered by his back-pack accelerator, he gripped Luria's armpits and with his legs crab-thrust both of them forward. It grew increasingly difficult: the wind was fighting them at gale velocity; and with half the distance yet to be closed, they were feeling increasingly insistent tuggings that sometimes lifted legs off the ground. Over wind noise, with her mouth only a head below his ears, she made herself heard: "Leave me here, Klaus, I'm dead anyway, save yourself, see to my tads—" Near exhaustion, he ignored this and heel-pushed forward; but now the ground was unsteady, irregularly trembling and rolling; and there was an audible deep-below rumble. Close to cave-mouth, it was a hurricane wind and a new difficulty, as though their body-weights had been lightened ten-

fold, reducing the friction of his foot-thrust, so that now it
was like back-crabbing unsteady seabottom against unfighta-
bly adverse current. . . .

But he got her inside. "We're in," he told her; and her
eyes, which had been closed, opened wearily while she managed a wan smile for him.

Now it was a problem of working Luria into her space
suit; her paralysis was nearly complete, he even suspected
troubled breathing, he would adjust her air mix to pure oxygen, but first he had to manipulate the body of his limp doll
into the glove-lining of the immovable mass. They were
caught between the mutually neutralizing gravity-pulls of the
black hole and of Godzha, so that he worked in virtual
freefall with every motion threatening to throw him gyrating
out of control in cave-space. Once she muttered: "Forget it, I
love you, I'm dying, save yourself, leave me here—" But he
was determined that she would not die on Godzha; in
Gladowr, Mujis might somehow save her.

He got her in, adjusted her air mix, got her helmet fitted
and sealed just as the hole-gravity began to lift both suits off
the ground. Struggling to his own, he got inside and used an
emergency device to fit and seal his helmet from within. Near
exhaustion, he fought to activate the in-suit instrumentation
for sending a rescue signal to Iola.

The tug from above had pulled them near the roughrock
ceiling.

The tug gradually eased. They sank languidly to the floor.
He could think of no reason for this; the outside wind persist-
ed, screaming across the open-bottle cave mouth in hyper-
resonance that penetrated their rekamatic helmet-hearing to
torture their eardrums with fiendish in-cave amplification.

Look toward the control center! It was the seeming of a
low contralto that penetrated the gothic screaming.

Perversely they swung toward the voice behind them—
Luria with effort could turn her head inside the helmet.
Through their lenses there was nothing; but above the lenses
their hypersensitized vision revealed person-like nebulosity
who insisted *Look!* and pointed past them. They peered out
the cave mouth.

There was no fog, the wind was hideous, the light was
clear day. The control-center bubble was rising up on a
swiftly swelling quivering rock-pimple; the bubble trembled,

great fragments of it fell away . . . and the boil burst in a Kilauea-spume, a lofty yellow-orange lava-geyser . . . whose incandescent heat was now rolling into their cave transforming it into a high-fired kiln baking them at smelting temperatures near the threshold of their suit-resistance. . . .

28. THROUGH A GLASS DARKLY

They were frozen in nonspace: no time, no motion. Above them now, the nude person-seeming had grown somewhat more clear, though still rather indefinite, and the smile on the seeming was beatific. And now the seeming was flanked by two other seemings; on Klaus there was a sense that the main personage and one other were female, while the third was male. . . .

Murmured Luria: "Holy Harmnion!"

The central figure responded: *Apart from the silly honorific, you have my identity wrong. The name on me is Madis Jur; the one to my right is Krandia Gelpo; the one to my left is Helmas Jo, the man she murdered. You two constitute our first assignment on this plane; please help us to do it well.*

Klaus and Luria knew that this converse was coming into their minds directly. Luria mind-gasped: *With you, Madis Jur—a murderer and a man?*

Isn't it quaint? We have to revise our preconceptions, out here. But let me pursue my mission. You can semi-see us because your metabolic acceleration has brought you nearly up to our frequency. . . .

Suggested Klaus: *With a little encouragement from you, we can step up our frequency to a factor of a hundred thousand; somewhere in there, we should be able to see you in clear image.*

Tranquilly said Madis: *That is forbidden as long as you are mortally alive; should you try it, we would vanish. May I now push my purpose?*

Pray do, Luria uttered.

We were sent to judge the success of your mission, to

judge the intent of your mission, and to make appropriate recommendations to those who loosely govern us.

As to the intent of your Godzha mission, it was an act of the highest courage and intelligence; but also it was humane, because you could have destroyed Godzha entirely, but instead you restricted yourselves to the necessary destruction of the control center. You, Klaus, an alien, did it not only for Iola but also for Godzha, hoping ultimately to end the war by peaceful negotiation: all humans, on Iola or on Godzha, female or male, are worthy insofar as they are worthy. You, Luria, did it for Iola and for your tads; it was no less a worthy thing. We immortals honor your intentions.

Mind-silence. Then Klaus, carefully: *Kra Jur, excuse me, but I thought you said you were first to judge the success of our mission. Instead, you have gone directly to our intent which was the second thing. Dare I inquire about our success?*

Mind-silence. Then Madis Jur: *Thank you for forcing me to report what I hate to report. Look behind you at Godzha.*

Solitary in nightspace, the planet Godzha was a fireball. All of it.

Mind-silent agony. Then Luria, semi-stifled: "What is it, Klaus—as if I didn't know?"

But his reply was addressed to Madis Jur, and it was cold, logical, emotionless or rather emotion-suppressed. *It appears that we underestimated either the drag of the gravity-finger or the fury of Godzha vulcanism. Are we to understand that our humane little ploy has blown the crust off the planet?*

Madis: *It is a little bit worse than that. By destroying Godzha, you have reduced the mass of Godzha enough to disturb the intergravity balance of the entire Klarta system. We immortals cannot foresee the future except to the extent that we can logically-intuitively extrapolate from known facts and trends; and you two are quite able to do the same. What is your prediction of the consequences to Iola?*

Luria articulated out of the suffering of Klaus: *A gradually decaying orbit, a slow progressive declination toward our sun. Catastrophic changes of climate, heightened volcanic activity, increasing numbers of violent Iolaquakes. A speed-up of orbital velocity; perhaps with it a speed-up of rotational velocity threatening the stability of every physical thing on Iola including atmosphere and people. A possibility of ultimately falling so far inward that we collide with the planet Zinza, unless first the outer planet Corla should fall so far inward as to collide with Iola . . . O Madis, Madis, what now for my tads?*

Sorrowed Madis: *Klaus, Luria, your intentions and your courage were noble. It is not your fault that the Science Institute, miscalculating the forces involved, approved your mission. Neither is it your fault that the Godzhalks also miscalculated: if you had not turned their gravity-finger back upon Godzha, it would have destroyed Iola and not merely Gladowr; and then it would have been for Godzha to suffer from the intergravitational imbalance, whirling farther and farther away from Klarta toward the black holes and freezing in the process.*

None of this was your fault. But you were the instruments, and Iola will blame you. And you are blaming yourselves.

Low asserted Klaus: *In all our god-stories, the instrument of a god-made-tragedy has believed that he was working for the best while in fact he was working for the worst. Luria must not be blamed, in effect she was my instrument. If there is blame, it is mine. And yet, it is hard for me to believe that you gods or goddesses reached out to bring me all the way from Erth to Iola for the purpose of destroying Godzha quickly and Iola slowly.*

Madis Jur, Luria, and you others: *I do not think that this tragedy was brought about by the immortals. I think instead that we fell into a chance-trap. I say that this tragedy should be taken as a given; and everything depends on what Iola will make of it. There is little help now that I can give; I am an alien whose credit is shot; but there is a very great deal that Luria can do, if she is willing to live and if you give her life. And—and I think now I have said all that I should say, whatever thinking I may be doing.*

Mind-silence. Then Madis Jur: *Luria Threll, what good do you see that Iola can make of this double tragedy—Godzha's, and its own?*

Dying Luria: *In terms of human relations, I think; in terms of the equal dignity and rights of both sexes, together with equality of education and opportunity. The death of Iola will be slow, and a long-deferred fate tends to be ignored by people who live for the moment. Nevertheless, among those who do see long-range truth, the Godzha-Iola tragedy may spur action.*

Unhappily this action could go either way: toward harden-

*ing caste-forms, or toward liberalizing relationships. And it
may be that a useful symbolism could be developed. Godzha
died swiftly, and why? Because Godzha was willing to kill a
planet for supremacy of one sex. Iola was granted time, and
for what? To correct that sort of error. Maybe.*

Her subsidence was weak indeed. Brooding, with Klaus
holding silent but intently involved, and (on still another
plane) St. Cyr intently involved.

Madis Jur: *What could you do, Kra Threll?*

Luria: *If I could laugh, it would be hollow. I was doing
some things—with my tads, but secretly; and in public, but
discreetly. Now I could come out in the open and fight and
lead; except that now my credit is all shot and I may
go on and die.*

Madis: *If you could live, would you stay on Iola and lead?
Or would you go to Erth with Klaus Heller who is sure to be
forced off Iola?*

Mind-silence. Then Luria, shaken: *Is it that sort of choice?*

Madis: *It is that sort of choice. In any event, we are granting you life; but you have to make this choice.*

Luria, soul-torn: *Help me, Klaus!*

His reply was resolute; but because it was mind-to-mind,
she knew and felt the sincere reality of his own self-laceration. *I will try to stay on Iola with you, to die with you if
we must die. But if I am forced to leave Iola without you,
I will keep you high in my heart and live for the time of
union. I love you, Luria. Do your duty as you see it.*

Luria, mind-low: *Then if I live, it has to be on Iola.*

The three specters were fading, but the mind-contralto of
Madis Jur stayed strong and clear until the end:

*This brings us to the last part of our mission: a recom-
mendation to those who loosely govern us.*

*It is not good intentions, but unhappy outcomes of good
intentions, that Hell is paved with. But even when outcomes
are unhappy, the people of good will merit better than Hell.*

*When guilt bears you down, be comforted. We immortals
are not ruled by mortal judgments, although we listen, but
then we judge for ourselves. Worth automatically creates immortality for any woman or man. The worthy men of
Godzha are not lost; the unworthy would have been lost anyway; not as a matter of punishment, but merely because a
disembodied soul without integrity scatters itself into the non.*

We will recommend honor to both of you. Luria, when

*you retire, should your countrymen fail to send you to us
with an apotheosis, we would be sure to confer apotheosis
upon you. And this will be true for you also, Klaus, when
you retire on your own planet.*

*Listen to how it will be for both of you, on our plane. All
challenges enhanced, all physical and mental pleasures more
joyous; all rangings indefinitely widened, limited only by the
limits of your own intelligence and daring. All frustrations
modulated to amusement at self; no woes at all, no bitterness
at all; infinite kindness and loving.*

Part Nine

TERMINUS

Erth, 1-2 August 2495

with reminiscences of

Iola, 2494-95

29. RETURN OF THE WAYFARER

Tuli at her desk felt a mind-voice: *Control your natural shock. friend Tuli—this is Claudine in your brain. Quiet now, good Tuli—quiet—*

Tuli straightened. Claudine, feeling her skin-pallor from within, added: *You don't have to talk, Tuli—just think at me.*

Tule thought: *o god . . . o god . . .*

Think at him or her too, it's never a bad idea; but mainly now, think at me. There's a thing I want you to do for me. Will you?

Claudine felt Tuli's instant reply: *Of course, for you;* and felt also the thought-underlay: *If I'm going nuts, I'd better humor me.*

Bless you, Tuli. Now listen. I want you to get a skimmer and take me to the Cabaret Montreuil. Know where it is?

Chalky Tul mind-stated the address.

As they approached the Montreuil, Claudine instructed: *Don't park in front, go around the block and park. I can't see your outside; are you in uniform?*

No . . .

Very good. Get out of the skimmer, walk back to the main cabaret entrance, go on in, and proceed directly to the back.

When Tuli had done this, jittery in the afternoon cabaret-quiet because she was so conspicuous at this thin time for customers, Claudine directed her through the narrow back corridor, out into the alley, down the alley to the door, down the inward corridor. Stopping Tuli beside Croyd's hidden door, she ordered: *Examine the wall, Tuli. See anything peculiar?*

295

Just that the wall needs replastering.

Why?

That crack there, it's a bad one.

Beautiful, it took me a lot longer to find it. Now listen, Tuli: I am going to direct your actions, I want you to relax and do what I make you do. Can you do that?

Like playing Ouija?

About like that. Okay, here we go.

Unprotesting befuddled Tuli reached out, touched the hidden spring, entered the opening door, activated a down-lift button, shuddered while they dropped. The door slid open; Tuli gasped at the vision of the opulent apartment within. Claudine marched her straight through the salon, back to the little room, into it; then beside her own transparent coffin she poised Tuli and made her look down.

Drawing an inrasping breath, Tuli let it out blurting: "You're there! but you're here! but you're there—"

Claudine gave her no answer, having transferred to her own body in actuality.

Tuli semi-comatose, watched the nude body of her chief. Eyelids fluttered, then opened; labored breathing began; a hand moved convulsively; the mouth opened and closed; there was some feeble general body-motion; Claudine's head slowly turned toward Tuli. Action time! Tuli's fingers began to search for coffin-fastenings—but Claudine managed to rap at her through the transparency and move her head in warning negation.

Croyd appeared beside Tuli who now was past being shocked. He unfastened the coffin-lid, opened the coffin, lifted Claudine to the floor, ordered her to try walking with his support. While he exercised her down his corridor and around his salon, he remonstrated: "You should have given me notice. Luckily I had word immediately from the coffin-monitors, I pulled loose from duty off Wambo—"

Tuli, puppet-following, blinked. This Croyd had appeared within minutes of the Claudine-reanimation; yet Wambo was ten light-years away.

Soon Croyd could release Claudine; and she walked under her own power, stretching arms and legs, deep-breathing, presently trying a couple of conservative pirouettes. She announced then: "I want, for a change, an Erth-drink."

"Scotch?"

"Too much like kromoweel. Try Tequila, that's purely local. Tuli?"

"Beer," specified the lieutenant. For her, it was daring.

He poured and brought while Claudine dressed. They sat and sipped silently; now and again, Tuli closed eyes and shook her head. Said Croyd then: "Want to report now?"

"Mission accomplished," thoughtfully and hesitantly responded Inspector St. Cyr—adding, "I think."

"Some loose ends yet?"

"Only one that I can't tie logically, and it's logically untiable.'"

"And?"

"For now, Croyd, just tell me one thing. Why didn't you send that rescue squadron to Iola?"

He stared, then slowly responded: "For now, Claudine, I won't ask you how you know this. The reason was, that after the destruction of Godzha, Iola reneged. We offered to send them the squadron nevertheless, to take people off dying Iola and resettle them elsewhere; again, negative. It appears that they regarded their tragedy as a visitation upon them by their Immortals in retribution for their mistreatment of males; they asked that in their dying time they be left alone to work out their own sort of reform. Consequently there was no way for us to act. We did send a frigate of observers, and they were well treated on Iola; but eventually they had to withdraw to save themselves, and they were not allowed to bring any Iolans out with them. It was a curiously Erth-oriental demise of a planet.

"Well, before your departure, you kept asking me what finally happened to Iola. Probably now I could give you nothing that you have not already surmised—nothing but elaborative details."

"Right, Croyd. Surmised—and witnessed."

"*Witnessed!* But how—"

"Well, almost witnessed, before I bugged out."

"But you came back with Klaus, and he departed in December '94, and the end for Iola didn't come until May of this year . . . Eh, I see what you must have done. Then you disobeyed my orders which you had accepted. In the words of Peter Pan and Captain Hook—bad form, Inspector."

"Chief, it would have been impossible to follow your orders. You told me not to stay on Iola later than last January, but in fact it was already July when I *got* there."

A slow smile spread on the face of Croyd; Claudine, mouth small, ducked her head. He told her: "I have composed your epitaph. 'St. Cyr, First of the Interime Lawyers.' "

Soberly she looked up, and he too sobered. She said: "We shouldn't joke about this. Yes I disobeyed your orders, I *had* to follow it out; and very particularly I had to pursue that Luria after Klaus and Kyria were gone.

"Croyd—favor to ask: say no if impossible. Could I maybe stay here with you tonight? To eat, to sleep maybe, but not for love?"

He pondered, gazing at her. He said, "Regretfully, no."

"Impossible?"

"Unwise. Tonight, you really want to be alone."

"I do?"

"You have an inquiry to summarize. For that, you alone are your own best committee. After the case is closed, let's one of us look the other up."

Thought. Then: "Yes, let's—"

Arising without dizziness, Claudine turned on Tuli. "This is top-secret, Lieutenant: all that has happened today between you and me and Croyd—and this place."

Tuli fretted: "I have a problem. I don't want to remember all this. But I never forget anything."

Croyd, already standing, pulled Tuli to her feet. "We'll fix your problem."

On the street, around the corner from the cabaret entrance: "Enter, girls," he invited, holding the passenger door of the skimmer for Claudine. Closing the door after her, he leaned in the window and whispered: "For the small disobedience, absolvo te. Later, I hope." He lightly kissed her ear-tip.

Then he whipped around the skimmer to close the driver door on Tuli who had zombied thereto and worked her length in. He bent to the window: "Both of you please listen. Claudine returned directly to her apartment from the far place where she was, and she phoned Tuli who went there to pick her up and take her to headquarters. Tuli, that's what you're going to do now. And you haven't seen my place or me. Got it?"

"But I still know about your place and you and the other stuff—"

"You won't. 'Bye till next time." He walked away.

Tuli automation-drove to Claudine's apartment building and parked in front of it. Claudine descended, entered the building, came out again, went to the skimmer's driver door, bent to the open window: "Hi, good Tuli. Thanks, but I changed my mind, I'll report to Wong tomorrow. You can take off, honey."

Frowning, Tuli remarked: "I seem to have forgotten something—"

"What?"

"I forget. So it probably wasn't important anyway."

Tuli drove away.

Before we look in on Claudine's night alone, a preview of her meeting next morning with Wong seems expedient.

Sitting gravely across the desk from Galactic Detective Superintendent Wong, she handed him a thin sealed envelope. "There's my report, Wong—in full. Read it carefully, because I prefer not to answer questions."

Orientally inscrutable were his eyes; occidentally inscrutable was her return gaze. He slit open the envelope. The report began:

> The following constitutes the full report terminating my investigation of the deaths of Dr. Klaus Heller, Miss Kyria Heller, and Dr. C. D. Murchison.

After a terse two-pages of development eliminating Erthnatural hypotheses, the report wound itself up:

> Through a reliable source at the highest level, this investigator has learned the following pertinent extraplanetary facts. (1) Both Dr. Heller and Dr. Murchison were physically on the planet Vassili IV during late November and early December 2494 GTC. (2) The so-called Kyria Heller was not actually the sister of Klaus, but instead was a native of Vassili IV brought to Erth by Dr. Heller. (3) On Vassili IV, it was customary to honor outstanding persons, after their retirement by killing them with two convergent rayguns which inflicted 75° chest wounds similar to those which killed the two Hellers; while death was executed upon capital criminals by two convergent rayguns which inflicted 50° chest wounds similar to that which killed Dr. Murchison. (4) Vassili IV had a religious technique for conferring invisibility by physical means. (5)

In May of this year 2495, the planet Vassili IV was destroyed by collision with the planet Vassili V, and there could not have been any survivors.

Through Captain Arroya of Houston Police, it is learned that among several fingerprints on the firing button of the ray weapon which was in the possession of Dr. Voelker and which killed Dr. Murchison, the print of the middle finger of Dr. Murchison's right hand was the most recent by several hours.

Conclusions.—That Klaus and Kyra Heller were killed as a ritual honor by invisible and unfindable beings related to Vassili IV. That Dr. Murchison, remorsefully despondent for some shame incurred on Vassili IV, happened to learn about Dr. Voelker's experimental 50° raygun; he used Dr. Voelker as an innocent tool, and he killed himself in this mode which would symbolize guilt on Vassili IV. (The confessions by Dr. Voelker may be discounted if psychiatrists confirm this investigator's impression that he is or was paranoid psychotic.)

Recommendations.—That Ms. Wilson, Dr. Voelker, and Dr. Murchison be dropped as suspects in the Heller deaths. That Houston authorities consider the suggestion and evidence of a Murchison suicide. Finally, that the cases of the Klaus and Kyria Heller deaths be closed without preferring any charges, on grounds of irrefutable inscrutability.

C. St. Cyr

Wong read the report twice, folded and enveloped it, laid down the envelope, interlaced fingers, inspected Claudine. "Welcome home, St. Cyr."

"Acknowledged, good Wong."

"And you won't talk beyond this report?"

"Only in court, and there isn't enough to take the cases to court."

"What if I should put somebody else on these deaths—like for instance Captain Venuto?"

"Not Venuto. It's a lost cause, and she doesn't deserve that—she needs kick-ups, not set-backs. But somebody more experienced from another department—rots o' ruck."

"I see."

"Yes."

"You don't know *anybody* who might give us a lead?"

"Not any *body,* no sir."

"What does *that* mean?"

"I said I wouldn't talk further."

"Make an exception, do."

She said low: "The Hellers were killed in July. I said in the report that I thought they were killed by persons connected with Vassili IV. But I also said that Vassili IV had been destroyed two months earlier, with no survivors.

"I think the Hellers were honored with death by people already dead at the time. And I may have known the loving-and-beloved instigator, already dead at the time. And I think both Hellers welcomed this; and that last May, when Klaus Heller learned that Vassili IV had been destroyed, he retired in order to receive this."

"They welcomed holes in their chests?"

"Those chest-holes, Wong, were kisses of love."

Silenced. Then Wong, softly: "Oboy."

"And one more thing. When I departed in July, I was forty-six. I am now fifty-six."

Gruffly declared Wong: "I'd have said thirty-six. Get out of here, my naughty love."

The Voice: *Well done, Inspector. All of us are grateful. Out.*

30. DÉNOUEMENT FOR IOLA

The preceding late afternoon and night for Claudine alone had been an intricately absorbing process of meditation, thought-arrangement, reverie. After contacting Captain Arroya by phone and learning about the Murchison fingerprint, she knew where that part of her report would go; and this freed her to concentrate on the perplexing problem of her major report about the Heller deaths. And this in turn led her into prolonged selective musing on the days which had followed the foray on Godzha, and on one later final day.

What characters! Klaus Heller: keen, audacious, mature, resourceful, kind, always honest with himself. Duke Murchison: intensively intellectual but a foreign-language moron and a chronic misunderstander of people; a scholar of high repute, whose brittle forebrain sought to crust-contain a lava of emotionality; honest with others, dishonest with himself; impulsively pretending toward goals, then emotionally blowing their attainment; achieving at terminus a guilt-symbolic suicide. (Would he have killed himself if Claudine had accepted him?) Kyria Lladyr, a stereotype well-adjusted young woman of her society, a gentle lovable sex-prude, having the forgiveness and guts to help rescue Duke who had run away from her when she was in trouble. Luria Threll: a tough liberated world-woman with the sort of logical-intuitive mind that Claudine most admired, yet appealing for a man like Klaus, and drawn by a man like Klaus; courageous to a cool extreme; countering social prejudice by persistently culturing-up her male tads; idealistically loving to the point that she painfully traded her Klaus-love to stay on a world under death-sentence, fighting for a principle and guarding her tads into and through death.

Claudine was drawn into a scanning of specific memories. . . .

Most of it was speed-review. The return of Klaus and Luria from the Godzha-foray, guardedly celebrated by the Science Institute staff who knew the extent of the planetary destruction and already felt forebodings. (The invasion fleet never arrived on Iola; presumably the holocaust had recalled them to fiery nothingness by activating fail-safes.) Luria's miraculous-joyous return to her tads—who of course saw nothing special about it. Luria's concern with preparing the defense of Duke—a defense which she was now relating directly to the principle of equal human rights. The arraignment, and Duke bound over for trial, and Duke unemotionally learning that his punishment if found guilty would be execution by two rayguns at a fifty-degree angle.

Over the trial of Duke (no jury), Claudine's thoughts lingered, mainly because of Luria who proved to be a courtroom Portia. Luria was faultlessly effective in cross-examination of prosecution witnesses: the four arresting officers; the two surviving male witnesses from Warren Matae; the jail physician who swore that she had found no evidence of psychosis in Duke. Then, after a low-key defense opening statement, she orchestrated her defense witnesses. Klaus established their mission and Duke's part in it; showed that Duke would have accompanied Klaus to Godzha had Duke not been prevented by imprisonment "for legitimate self-defense against a personal outrage" (prosecution objected and was sustained, but the judge had heard); about the attitudes and laws of Erth relative to rape and to killing in self-defense.

Doctors Mujis, Vlotny, and Myrna testified to the apparent character and intelligence of the accused. Mujis introduced into evidence a sworn affidavit by the World Council Chairman accepting the ambassadorial credentials of Dr. Duke along with Dr. Heller, and stating that evidently Dr. Duke had planned to accompany Dr. Heller on the rescue mission to Godzha. Mujis also testified concerning the treatment of Kyria for the Iola-frequent malady of amniotic rupture in season.

Daringly Luria now put Kyria on the stand. With reluctant courage, Kyria told how she had been attracted to Duke, how her season had abruptly fallen upon her while she was with him, how she had urged him to help her, how she had ruptured while copulating with him. Prosecution wanted to know whether he had been violent with her; with dignity she responded: "Not at all. Duke was more gentle than any male I have known."

And now Luria took the very long chance; after obtaining court permission for Klaus to translate, she placed Duke on the stand to relate in his own words the events of 27 and 28 November. This he did with lethargic economy, relating his hideous guilt when he thought he had ruined Kyria, his flight into the nocturnal streets, his feeling of male relief when invited by Jinni and Kandis to the hospitality of Warren Matae, his shock and horror when he discovered that he had been homosexually solicited, his vaguely remembered berserk when they tried to gang-rape him. He foggily recalled attacking violently at least two of the men. "No, I did not know that I was killing anybody. Well, yes, under the circumstances, I would have done the same even if I had known that I was killing them." Why? "On Erth, a man or woman has the legal right to resist rape violently and to kill in self-defense if necessary." This, translated, drew gasps from the spectators, and Luria heard the word "Barbarians!"; but she pulled it from the fire by demanding: "Dr. Duke—*why* is it legal to kill in self-defense?"

Here was Duke's proud answer. "On Erth, our highest value is our god or goddess or ideal; and after that, our highest values are the honor and integrity of every person; and after those, our highest value is the preservation of human life. The men of Warren Matae threw away their own honor and integrity in order to attack my honor and integrity, and I rightfully defended mine. In doing so, I did not know that I was risking a death penalty; but if I had known it, I would nevertheless have acted the same, because my honor and integrity are to me higher values than the preservation of my own life."

After that, prosecution could not cross.

Luria's final witness was Dr. Kruhat, Chief of Neuropsychiatry in the general hospital directed by Dr. Mujis. Kruhat expressed judgment that Dr. Duke could be thrown into acute emotional stress by certain types of events, particularly sexual events, which outraged his sense of what was right; and systematically she led the court along the shock-road which had led to the culminating crimes. She summarized: "I judge that Dr. Duke is not and was not psychotic, that he knows and knew the difference between right and wrong—but here I mean, right and wrong in terms of his own acculturation on another planet. And it does appear to me that he acted in a way which he considered right and which his culture would consider right. Under great cumulative stress, he may have over-reacted; but he did so repulsing an attack which he and his culture considered deeply wrong."

Defense rested.

Prosecution's closing statement was conventional: a recital of the letter of the law, a denial that the law provided for extenuating circumstances, a reminder that the case must be judged on existing law. It had been proved that the accused had committed the slayings charged, and the accused had admitted this. No contrary evidence had been offered. Even the psychiatrist had provided no more than a descriptive deepening which was irrelevant to the fact of the crime. Admitting that Dr. Duke had been apparently a voluntary ambassador from a friendly power, and had allegedly been ready to perform a heroic service which in fact he did not perform. it remained that the laws of Flaria were impartial, permitting no special cases, and any breach of this time-honored custom might seriously undermine law in Flaria. Earnestly the prosecutor urged a finding of guilty as charged, and a sentence of death.

Duke sat impassive.

In her closing plea, Luria extended herself in a comminglement of intellectual precision and restrained passion.

She began: "I recommend to Your Honor that this case be considered and judged in a manner that is both individual and general." Here, Klaus straightened in his seat. Luria expanded: "Your Honor well appreciates that the laws of Flaria, to which the prosecution has rightfully attached so much value, are founded on our constitution, but are subsequently modulated and given meaning by judicial decisions; and that these decisions, in turn, grow out of new and unforeseen events which *insist* on a need for modulation. Just so, in science, laws of the cosmos are proposed, tested, accepted, and pursued until some unforseen event shows the laws inadequate to cover all relevant cases, whereupon science generates new and more generally adequate laws."

Having then moved item-by-item through the various qualitative points brought out in the trial, she came to her court-unsettling close:

"Your Honor, I would be the first to agree that the laws of Flaria as presently set forth do not allow for these extenuating circumstances. But I would point to an irony. This honored ambassador who defended himself against a shameful gang-rape is in jeopardy of his life, *under the present laws of Flaria;* whereas those who survive among his attackers are in jeopardy only of being declared misdemeanants, *under the present laws of Flaria.* Your Honor, this is more than an irony, it is a serious anomaly, it is a grave contradiction in principle. The case of Dr. Duke therefore becomes a test case of the pertinent body of law, and any decision is subject to appeal to the World Council by one side or the other.

"On this showing, grounds for acquittal of Dr. Duke seem evident. Simplifying legal expression, the grounds are these: that in any case where an adversary *male or female* attempts forcible assault on the physical person of a victim *female or male,* forcible resistance by the intended victim is no crime even when it causes the death of one or more attackers.

"Your Honor, here is the recommendation of the defense. Let this court realistically modulate existing law by defining these grounds. Then, on these grounds, let this court find the accused, Dr. Duke, not guilty as charged."

So had Luria raised the case from a simple murder trial to a broad creative generalization of the law. But she had done this on her own, without consulting Klaus or Kyria or even her death-jeopardized client Duke. This was the unhappy burden of her silence during most of the Luria-Klaus-Kyria drinking and spare eating in a discreet booth at a select small restaurant.

Luria knew, of course, that this generalization met her ideals and her client's needs at the same time. Why had she been returned alive to Iola, if not to press for an equalization of human rights on Iola during the brief remaining span of Iola's life? On the other hand, there was no other way under Klarta whereby she had any chance of getting a reprieve for Duke, and even this high try could lose. Nevertheless, she had not consulted her client; and it was in guilt that she wallowed.

Over post-dinner liqueurs, she came out with it.

Klaus consulted his liqueur. "The course you took was right, my friend. Any other course would have failed totally. This may fail, but not totally, because it is a seed sown. But I did wonder during the trial whether you had discussed this course with Duke. And I suspect that Duke recognized it also, and wondered in kind."

"Klaus—if I had proposed this course to Duke, how would he have instructed me as his attorney?"

"Of course you mean that if he had disapproved the generalization of his case, ethically you could not have attempted it. You may have underestimated your client. At any rate, he is the only one who can answer your question. I want to go see him this evening; shall we three go together?"

Luria agreed. Kyria, however, understandably pleaded fatigue and was excused.

They found Duke in a state of trembling. Luria went to him and clasped his wrists: "Brace up, my friend, have faith that it will all work out." Klaus, as always, translated.

Unsmiling, Duke told her, "I'm not in a state of fear, Luria. I'm in a state of self-laceration."

"That's my condition too, Duke. Please let me confess first."

"You mean, you're worried because you generalized my case instead of merely pleading my innocence?"

"No, because my way was the only way that had a chance to work. But I chew myself because I didn't get your permission first. In the process of trying to save you, I used you."

"That's what I thought you were doing. That's great with me, I whole-heartedly approve."

She stared at him, paled, covered her face, wept. She was brought into self-control by Duke's hand reassuringly clutching her shoulder.

He told her steadily, "Listen to the quick story of my own breast-beating. They honor me as an ambassador, but I'm not even supposed to be here, I'm supposed to be out there in our ship, only I just couldn't stay out of that black hole adventure, so I followed Klaus in, and here I am. Being here, I wanted to help Klaus, and I could have helped him on the Godzha sortie, but I blew that in panic about Kyria. So I blew it twice; and by killing those guys instead of just clubbing them down, I blew it a third time. So what good am I here, Luria? What am I but a self-imposed burden here? So

all that being the case with me, the one thing I want above
all else is to be useful in *some* way; this I want even more
than I want Kyria. If I can serve as a test-case to improve the
laws and undermine the sexual discrimination here, that is
my small contribution, my partial redemption. If I die of it,
what the hell: I'd a lot rather die with inward honor than live
with inward shame."

It was emotionally most difficult for Klaus to translate.
When he got it all out, there was a long interbreeding silence.

Then Heller sent Luria out of the cell: he was about to say
a thing that Luria as an officer of the court wouldn't want to
hear. He whispered to Duke: "Believe me, my friend, you
have been useful here, far more useful than you would have
been aboard ship. And believe another thing. Even if you are
found guilty and sentenced to death—*you will not die!*"

Duke stood before the bench with Luria at 0900 on 3 December, with Klaus and Kyria present as spectators, and sto-
ically heard the court's findings. The judge had found him
guilty as charged on grounds of existing law, but was cogni-
zant of the defense recommendation for a retroactive liberalizing of law to permit slaying in self-defense under proved
conditions of unprovoked personal assault. The defendant
was sentenced to death by the usual method on 10 December,
provided, that passage of a new retroactive law prior to 10
December by the World Council would call for a revised
finding.

Luria and Klaus achieved a hearing by the Council that
same afternoon; and she argued eloquently the case for such
a new retroactive law applicable to females and males alike.
She added that if action could not be taken immediately, at
least Duke's execution should be stayed until the proposed
law could be acted upon.

They were temporarily excused; nearly two hours later,
they were readmitted. Kra Alui considered them with an expression of melancholy weariness; and when she spoke, her
voice had undertones of profound sadness:

"Kra Threll, Krazia Heller, before we address the matter
of Krazia Duke, there is another matter that is overdue for
addressing. This Council had wished to meet with you and
honor you on your successful prosecution of the Godzha
foray; but we were delayed when Krazia Vlotny drew our attention to some unhappy consequences."

Luria and Klaus gazed at her without expression. They knew what was coming; they were about to learn worse.

Alui nodded to Vlotny—who said concisely: "As a result of your foray, Godzha blew off a very great deal of mass. Consequently the finger of gravity dislodged Godzha from its established planetary orbit, pulling it into a spiral outward toward the black holes. This of course is swiftly weakening the Godzha pull upon our immediate neighbor Corla, so that Corla's orbit is rapidly decaying. Our calculations are not yet firm, but it is our preliminary guess that during the second season from now, that is, between one hundred fifty and one hundred eighty days from now, during our annual perturbation toward Black Hole Two, either Corla will fall into Iola, or Corla will pass so near us that its gravity will precipitate crust-exploding vulcanism everywhere on our planet. In short, Iola will experience what Godzha has just experienced."

The jaws of Klaus were hard-knotted; Luria was biting blood out of a lip.

With solicitude, Vlotny added: "However, two aspects of the matter may offer some sort of comfort to our heroic guests. One is, that had they not acted as they did, the gravity-finger would have done the same thing to Iola. Godzha had underestimated its power. The other is, that we at the Science Institute, erroneously imagining that Godzha knew exactly what it was doing, had no way to anticipate and warn that the redirected gravity finger would destroy more than the control center on Godzha." She folded hands and sat back in deep trouble.

After long silence, Alui: "As of now, these facts are known only by Doctors Vlotny and Myrna, by this Council, and by yourselves. You are rigidly enjoined against mentioning the matter to anyone else. When eventually it must come out, we will use our own methods of preparing the people—and I confess that those methods have not yet occurred to us.

"When you two first returned from Godzha, it was our intent to honor both of you publicly by conferring upon you the privilege of apotheosis. But this would now be inadvisable, because then eventually the public would blame you for our tragedy and would blame us for honoring you for it. We of this Council know you were not to blame, and privately we accord you the highest imaginable honor; but apotheosis, apart from the impossibility of conferring it in public, would now be an empty privilege to grant, since it is evident that neither of you will be retiring before Iola ceases to exist.

"Now, as to Dr. Duke. Once again we are caught in a vise.

"Kra Threll, we compliment you on your superb pleading at the trial and before this Council. It hits us at a time when we are vulnerable to the notion of improving human rights, particularly with respect to males. A number of us are seeing our fate and its cause as a judgment upon us by the Immortals: we oppressed males, we ended by killing a male planet, and so its death is killing us. We respond well to the idea that our final weeks of life should be dedicated to atonement. That is one jaw of our vise.

"The other jaw is, that when the general public learns about our coming death, the necessary disorder would only be augmented if major social change were in progress. Our males and our females have known just this state of affairs for aeons, and most of them do not even question it. Conceive their acute soul-torment if they were already in upheaval when the news of our final end would come out.

"We have therefore sought a way to release Dr. Duke without explicitly recognizing your human rights thesis, without revision of existing pertinent law. Kra Threll, I see how your face is changing, I know that this defeats your aim, and perhaps it defeats ours also, but at least it is a small gesture in the direction of atonement.

"Pardoning Dr. Duke is out of the question, the public would never accept it. But we found another way. In addition to transcripts of the arraignment and trial, we have read your statement to Inspector Vaxo at the time of Dr. Duke's arrest. And we were intrigued by your mention of a principle of diplomatic immunity, although you omitted pursuing this principle.

"Accordingly, we are resolved to frame a law granting diplomatic immunity in the presence of extenuating circumstances, and to make such a law effective as of the arrival date of Dr. Heller and Dr. Duke. I will stay the execution of Dr. Duke, and free him from imprisonment under the supervision of Dr. Heller, until such time as the law can be framed and passed so that a new finding can be made by the court.

"In return, Dr. Heller, we place upon you the following enjoinments. First, you are to contact your chief, Croyd, and

inform him that we rescind our request for intervention. We
do not want his squadron—not even for rescue, since only a
few of us could be removed, and this would be contrary to
our planetary ethos. Second: as soon as Dr. Duke is freed,
you and he are to depart Iola. You will appreciate the interweaving reasons for this command.

"Dr. Heller, Kra Threll, this Council blesses both of you. *I*
bless both of you. May the goddesses expedite and smooth
all your journeys."

Having been pre-advised, Duke and Luria, with Klaus
present, stood before the judge next morning and heard the
World Council decision. It did not please Duke, and he made
a statement which Klaus reluctantly translated:

"Your Honor, I am one who believes that the principle of
extenuating circumstances is one that should apply to *all* humans regardless of sex or diplomatic status. I am one who re-
jects the principle of diplomatic immunity, and therefore I do
not wish to be protected by that principle. I hereby reject the
stay of execution. Unless a law of broader application is earlier passed by the Council, I demand that I be executed on 10
December as sentenced by this court."

Luria, clutching Duke's arm, urged him to suspend the demand until she had talked with him privately. Shaking her
off, he stood proud before the shocked judge.

The judge then said, angry to the point of pallor, leaning
across the bench toward the accused: "You have placed me
in an impossible position which can only be resolved by the
Council. In my opinion, your refusal applies also to your release. You are dismissed to your place of confinement."

Afterward, in his cell, Luria pressed: "Duke, look: I have
obtained *some* liberalization from the Council, along with
some recognition of the broader principle—but your bull-
headedness is going to blow *all* of it!"

Head high, Duke retorted, "Now listen, Luria. I suspect
that your world has little experience of martyrdom. I know
what you want, and I support it with all my soul; and if I
support it also with my life, you will have a martyr as a soul
for your movement. Klaus, I hope you'll remember that I did
some good on this God-damned planet! I love both of you—
but get out."

Kyria, back on hospital duty, learned about this in a phone call from Luria. Shocked, she put Luria on hold, obtained a reluctant release from Mujis, and told Luria to meet her with Klaus in half an hour at a mutually known coffee house on the west side.

She found them somberly sipping something like espresso. "Let's walk," she half-commanded. Together the three went out and strolled aimlessly, Klaus between the women. There was no talk, there was bitter three-way thinking.

Out of backstreets, they emerged at the western waterfront at approximately the place where the Warren Matae punks had picked up Duke. Seen from above, this area was a snaggle-toothed array of piers, some empty, some harboring a congeries of ships; seen from the quai-street, it was a series of broad-doored warehouse-ends, the doors topped by firm-name signs some of which were length-of-the-world romantic to the women. One gate was open, the one which Duke had nocturnally penetrated; they negotiated this gate and the empty pier (a couple of female guards or stevedores neglected them), strolled out to pier-end, stared at landless horizon; presently sat as Duke had sat, kicking heels against rotting pier-boards, staring at birds resembling gulls and pelicans some of whom transiently perched while some squatted on ripple-tickled spiles.

Klaus exploded: "Damn this mess of obscenities!"

Kyria puckered, about to cry. Luria tonelessly inquired: "As if I didn't know, what obscenities?"

Agonized Heller strained his face at the sky and tried to formulate the mess. "Duke shouldn't be here, only he is. But being here, Duke should be a hero, only he blew that too, so now he's a convicted felon. Luria defends him on a human-rights generalization and wins a nod from the World Council: they find a technicality for releasing him, but he refuses in order to make a martyr of himself, blowing it again. I sympathize with his chronic human weaknesses, but also I have contempt for those weaknesses; and because he yields to them, finally I have to feel contempt for him, and that I hate."

Said Kyria: "Perhaps I wanted to fly in the face of our biohistory by loving a man in a sexual connotation. Luckily, they have jerked my glands, I won't even be looking at a man in a sexual connotation again." She turned her face to *this* man: "But you I do love as my brother, Klaus, and that is something new on the face of Iola."

He pressed her hand; they frowned at water.

Luria said low: "*I* love a man in a sexual connotation."

He told her: "And I love you, in all the ways there are."

Luria savored that. And then her mood changed: "Klaus, what in *hell* do we do about this Duke?"

"Luria," he declared, "it's out of your hands now."

The women stared at him. Faintly hurt, Luria demanded: "You are discharging me as his attorney?"

He hugged her shoulders. "With unqualified praise and gratitude and love, I am doing just that. And don't ask me why, because as an officer of the court you won't want to know."

Kyria was vaguely forming an unthinkable hypothesis. For Luria, it was horribly full-formed. "Now listen to reason, my Klaus. Maybe you didn't know that anyone who helps a prisoner escape inherits the prisoner's guilt and sentence for himself!"

"I know it now, Luria. Since I have to leave you anyway, what does it matter?" He achieved a whimsical smile: "So soon I subtract twenty-five degrees from my unawarded death-wound."

Kyria asserted, "You can't do it alone, my brother Klaus. I will help you. No, Luria. Now listen. Klaus feels obligation to rescue his comrade, and this motive I strongly endorse."

Klaus and Kyria brought it off that night, wearing the accelerator packs for invisibility and using a little raygun on the cell-door lock. Duke objected. Klaus had to slug him.

So now Klaus and Duke were about to depart Iola and return to Erth. And according to Croyd's orders and warnings, the Claudine-soul must stay in contact with the Klaus-brain, must therefore return with Klaus. And that would terminate her ongoing experience of a planet according itself extreme unction.

In the observatory, staff installed somnambulatory Duke into one of the gargantuan suits, sealed-on the helmet, used overhead lifts to move Duke into the transmission cage. Myrna touched a control; Duke vanished.

Watching, Klaus hugged Luria and Kyria; they hugged him.

Word came from the ship: "Dr. Duke has been received, seemingly intact, but he appears dazed; possible trauma en route?"

"I doubt it," Klaus responded; "he was sedated here, by rather a primitive method. How are his metabolics?"

"Check in progress; wait . . . All right, he seems normal taking your sedation into account. Are you transmitting more bodies?"

Klaus looked at Luria and Kyria. Letting go of him, the sisters embraced. Kyria protested, just intelligibly: "Even so, I don't want to leave our Iola—"

Luria gripped her shoulders. "You've just sprung a murderer. So now you are his proxy along with Klaus, and he has refused stay of execution. So he would have been shot, so you would be shot. Do you want to die with a fifty-degree chest-hole, my sister?"

Kyria clung trembling. But at length she hard-bit her upper lip, and labored-out a small smile at her sister. She straightened and faced Klaus. "On your Erth, in your household, I will be your companion-sister; and when you want to be with someone else, I will feel no trouble. Is it good or not, my brother?"

"It is very good, Kyria."

In pain, she swung to Luria. "I swear I am not stealing him—"

"I know, dear, dear Kyria. I love both of you."

After hesitancy, Kyria turned her face up to the face of Klaus. "Let's go, my brother."

They big-suited her, lift-caged her, transmitted her.

Ship's response, a bit surprised: "A lady has been received, in good condition. Will you follow, Dr. Heller?"

Klaus had Luria by the upper arms. "You are the one I want with me."

"I want to go with you, my Klaus. You know why I have to stay."

"Then I will stay too."

Her eyes were wet, her wide smile trembled. "Take care of Kyria, my love. And I wouldn't like you nearly so much with a fifty-degree chest hole."

All at once it seemed to the watchers that they were trying to crush each other.

They thrust each other away and stood gazing, quivering.

She said steadily: "You and I are going to be together. All

challenges enhanced, all physical and mental pleasures more joyous; all rangings indefinitely widened, limited only by the limits of our own intelligence and daring. All frustrations modulated to amusement at self; no woes at all, no bitterness at all; infinite kindness and loving.

"Believe, my Klaus! Believe!"

31. ANOTHER KIND OF APOTHEOSIS

The Manhattan morning was wee. Claudine, meditation suspended, went to her dictotranscriber; she knew how her report was going to go. She activated the machine . . . then touched the idle key . . .

Klaus had donned an ordinary space-suit, and then had turned to Luria for a final handclasp and kiss. At that instant, it came into Claudine how she could play it.

As Luria, heartbroken, she watched Klaus go.

As Luria, then, she set about her various tasks on dying Iola.

Until the predicted time when Corla drew near. Long before then, Claudine had established contact with the brains of Herder Maxus and several other adult males in Luria's contingent, with two results: she found that they were indeed potentially equal to female brains on Iola or anywhere else, and she was enabled to collate brain-viewpoints for the effect of separated objectivity.

Vivid flash-memory image of Luria and Herder Maxus and Landis Garder and eight other adult men trying to shepherd and calm their terrified tads while sky-filling Corla glared down and the ground violently shook and in every direction volcanic flares lit the night. Just above the noise, yet low enough so that the tads had to strain attentively to listen, Luria was talking to them, saying words meaningful to those who could partly understand and calming to those too young for understanding:

"Children, look at the very bright moon just above us: that is Corla, she is a world like our world, she is getting ready to kiss us and bring us into beauty. And look all around us,

316

there: see all the bright lights? those are new mountains of
fire rising up from the sea to celebrate the coming of Corla.
Oh my children, be easy, be courageous men, face Corla,
look her in the face: she is kissing us with fire, and afterward
our lives will be joyous—"

Fire erupted half a kilometer away. Compelled yet bitterly
ashamed of herself, Claudine seized upon the brain of Luria
and, just before that brain fire-died, uptimed out of there
. . . to the final passionate embrace of Klaus and Luria in
the observatory, transferring to the Klaus-brain, experiencing
subjectively his soul-torn self-suiting, then standing erect and
seeing and hearing Luria:

"You and I are going to be together. All challenges enhanced . . . Believe, my Klaus! Believe!"

Recommended for Star Warriors!

The Dorsai Novels of Gordon R. Dickson

☐	DORSAI!	(#UE1342—$1.75)
☐	SOLDIER, ASK NOT	(#UE1339—$1.75)
☐	TACTICS OF MISTAKE	(#UW1279—$1.50)
☐	NECROMANCER	(#UE1353—$1.75)

The Commodore Grimes Novels of A. Bertram Chandler

☐	THE BIG BLACK MARK	(#UW1355—$1.50)
☐	THE WAY BACK	(#UW1352—$1.50)
☐	STAR COURIER	(#UY1292—$1.25)
☐	TO KEEP THE SHIP	(#UE1385—$1.75)

The Dumarest of Terra Novels of E. C. Tubb

☐	JACK OF SWORDS	(#UY1239—$1.25)
☐	SPECTRUM OF A FORGOTTEN SUN	(#UY1265—$1.25)
☐	HAVEN OF DARKNESS	(#UY1299—$1.25)
☐	PRISON OF NIGHT	(#UW1364—$1.50)
☐	INCIDENT ON ATH	(#UW1389—$1.50)
☐	THE QUILLIAN SECTOR	(#UW1426—$1.50)

The Daedalus Novels of Brian M. Stableford

☐	THE FLORIANS	(#UY1255—$1.25)
☐	CRITICAL THRESHOLD	(#UY1282—$1.25)
☐	WILDEBLOOD'S EMPIRE	(#UW1331—$1.50)
☐	THE CITY OF THE SUN	(#UW1377—$1.50)
☐	BALANCE OF POWER	(#UE1437—$1.75)

To order these titles,

please use coupon on the

last page of this book.

GREAT NOVELS OF HEROIC ADVENTURES ON EXOTIC WORLDS

To order these titles,
please use coupon on the
last page of this book.

DAW BOOKS

If you *really* want to read the best . . .